SOCIAL STRUCTURES IN
MOLIERE'S THEATER

LES
OEVVRES DE
Mr.
MOLIERE
TOME I.

F.C.   fe.

SOCIAL STRUCTURES IN
MOLIERE'S
THEATER

BY JAMES F. GAINES

OHIO STATE UNIVERSITY PRESS
COLUMBUS

Portions of chapter four, under the title "Usurpation, Dominance, and Social Closure in
L'Ecole des femmes," were published originally in *Papers on French Seventeenth Century Literature*, vol. 9, no. 17 (1982), pp. 607–26. Reprinted by permission.

Portions of chapter five, under the title "*Ménage* versus Salon in *Les Femmes savantes*,"
appeared originally in *L'Esprit Créateur*, vol. 21, no. 3 (1981), pp. 51–59. Reprinted by permission.

Library of Congress Cataloging in Publication Data

Gaines, James F.
    Social structures in Molière's theater.

    Bibliography: p.
    Includes index.
    1. Molière, 1622–1673 — Political and social views. 2. Social history in literature. 3.
Literature and society — France. 4. France — Social life and customs — 17th–18th centuries. I. Title. II. Title: Molière's theater.
PQ1864.P6G34   1984   842'.4   83–27342
ISBN 0-8142-0358-2

C O N T E N T S

ILLUSTRATIONS

Frontispiece: Molière as valet and ridiculous marquis. Originally served as frontispiece to volume one of the 1666 Paris edition of Molière's *Oeuvres*. Reproduced by permission of the Houghton Library, Harvard University.

ACKNOWLEDGMENTS

This study, which grew out of my doctoral dissertation on "Social Structures in Molière's Major Plays," presented at the University of Pennsylvania, owes its primary inspiration to my adviser and mentor, Jean V. Alter, whose pioneering work on social criticism of early modern literature has always been an example worthy of emulation. I also owe special thanks to Gerald Prince and Joan DeJean, who have provided ongoing advice and encouragement, and to Ralph Albanese, Jr., and Harold Knutson, whose generous and thoughtful comments helped shape the final manuscript.

A stipend from the National Endowment for the Humanities allowed me to complete important research work that contributed to this book, and a research grant from Southeastern Louisiana University provided help in preparing the manuscript. Among the institutions that gave me access to their collections and assistance with my work, I would like to thank the British Library, the Bibliothèque Nationale, the Bibliothèque de l'Arsenal, the Bibliothèque Sainte-Geneviève, and the libraries of Harvard University, Louisiana State University, Northwestern University, the University of Pennsylvania, Southeastern Louisiana University, Williams College, and Yale University.

I am grateful to Claudia Duczer, Bobbie Threeton, and Glenda Wellington for their careful preparation of the typescript. Nancy K. Hymel, my research assistant, also provided invaluable assistance.

Portions of chapters four and five appeared originally in *Papers on French Seventeenth Century Literature* and *L'Esprit Créateur* under the titles "Usurpation, Dominance, and Social Closure in *L'Ecole des femmes*," and "*Ménage* versus Salon in

Les Femmes savantes." These passages are included here with the kind permission of the journals.

Above all, I owe thanks to my wife, Josephine Roberts, without whose steadfast love, support, loyalty, and collaboration this project could never have been brought to fruition.

SOCIAL STRUCTURES IN
MOLIERE'S
THEATER

INTRODUCTION

The purpose of this book is to provide, by means of a sociocritical study, a deeper insight into the theatrical works of Jean-Baptiste Poquelin (1622–1673), better known by his stage name Molière, the great Parisian dramatist who is credited with perfecting the comedy of manners and character. Two decades ago such an undertaking might have called for a lengthy *apologia* justifying the sociological branch of literary criticism and outlining its benefits, but during that span of time, there has been such an explosion of interest in this area that neither its legitimacy nor its utility can be seriously questioned any longer. Refinement of critical techniques has led to a profusion of research methods, from the empirical and quantitative work of Roger Escarpit and his associates at the University of Bordeaux to the ideological approach practiced at the University of Birmingham. During this period of critical proliferation, there has been much controversy, particularly in the wake of Lucien Goldmann's genetic structuralism, over how literary forms relate to the social forms of the early modern period and which structures best lend themselves to literary analysis. A work of such modest proportions as this cannot pretend to solve all these thorny questions or to offer anything more than a close study of one outstanding author in the context of his lifetime. My method involves two basic steps: first, an identification of the status levels of the characters through reference to an index of social indicators, and, second, a comparison of their behavior patterns with the norms of the groups to which they belong. These norms are reconstructed as nearly as possible on the basis of historical evidence and seventeenth-century social theory. The discussion of Molière's major plays is then organized around four polar structures that coincide with important social concerns of Louis XIV's subjects: exemplary nobility and unworthiness, social closure and usurpation, bourgeois reciprocity and imbalance, and finally, socioeconomic integrity and parasitism.

The decision to write on Molière, whom legions of critics through the ages have treated in so many ways, comes not at all from disrespect for previous scholarship but rather from high personal admiration and from a feeling that he is great enough to deserve the tribute of each generation. He is, after all, an ideal subject for sociocriticism, having traveled the far-flung provinces as actor, director, and writer before returning to his native Paris. Along the way he performed for an audience of unusual diversity and learned to cultivate an acute sensitivity to human relationships. As his Parisian career developed, he was able to capture the imagination of the cosmopolitan public in the capital by enriching the stock characters of traditional farce and intrigue comedy with a far more penetrating perspective on social behavior.

Before proceeding to the inventory of social indicators, it may be useful to review a few important historical definitions and previous critical attitudes. Molière lived under the ancien régime, that unbroken line of French monarchical rule that stretched from the eighth century to the Revolution of 1789; furthermore, his life-span fell in the subdivision usually referred to nowadays as the early modern age, since it marked a transition from the medieval culture, which with its feudal-manorial system had largely disappeared by the late fifteenth century, to the subsequent phase of industrial culture. The rather complex social hierarchy that prevailed in France during this time is termed by historians the *société d'états*, or society of estates.

Today, thanks to the efforts of such scholars as Roland Mousnier, Pierre Goubert, Robert Mandrou, and Pierre Deyon, critics
once again have at their disposal a reliable description of the
environment in which Molière composed his masterpieces.[1]

The *société d'états* supplanted the medieval system of the
société d'ordres, which had divided the population into the
three orders of the clergy, the nobility, and the common people,
or *roturiers*. The first of these categories continued to exist as a
separate formal entity in the seventeenth century, but social
historians have pointed out that its economic activity and chain
of command had fallen almost completely under the domination of prominent noble and bourgeois families and thus were
subsumed into the other groups. As for the nobles, knighthood
no longer existed as an independent military force; and the
descendants of the knights, the *noblesse d'épée*, had to share
their privileges with the *noblesse de robe* or *noblesse de fonctions*, relative newcomers who had been ennobled by the king
in recognition of service in the courts or royal administration.
The latter had access to a formal mechanism for making their
nobility just as hereditary as that of the *épée*, by paying fees to
the crown and occupying an ennobling office for three generations. The new *anoblis* often surpassed in wealth and influence
a large segment of the gentry that lived in rural semi-poverty,
being too poor to afford a stay at court and thus receiving the
pejorative designation of *hobereaux*.

The common people had also changed drastically in composition since the Middle Ages. By Molière's time there remained
only a handful of serfs, most of the peasants having achieved a
measure of theoretical autonomy as tenant farmers, or *tenanciers*. Yet the standard of living in the countryside had for the
most part declined in the seventeenth century, and the peasants
were often obliged to tread the fine line between misery and
extinction. The medieval flood of farmers to the towns had been

reduced to a mere trickle, as the bourgeois artisans and merchants organized ever stricter guilds to conserve their trade advantages. Often the only point of entry for a peasant in the town was in the lowest levels of urban life, as a servant, apprentice, or laborer. The bourgeois, those who exercised municipal rights, had formed a hierarchy of their own, each livelihood or *métier* having its own rung on the ladder, with artisans below merchants and merchants below royal officers, or *officiers*. The latter group, which included magistrates of the sovereign courts and *parlements*, was paralleled by another body of "bourgeois living nobly"—that is, those who had retired from active commerce to live off income from investments in anticipation of furthering their families' social ascension through advantageous marriages or the acquisition of offices.

Unlike the society of orders, the society of estates featured a limited social mobility. All opportunities for advancement depended on possession of considerable sums of money. To reach the coveted rank of *maître* in a guild or *corporation*, a workman had to spend what to him was a small fortune on a showy *chef d'oeuvre*, as well as on fees and on a banquet for the whole organization. Few passed this hurdle who were not already relatives of *maîtres*. The next great divide was the distinction between artisans and merchants; as soon as a lucky man passed this point, he hastened to designate himself in contracts as *marchand drapier*, *marchand épicier*, and so on. Acquisition of office was the apogee of bourgeois life and also the most significant road leading into the upper reaches of the nobility. The ideal plan was to purchase one that brought instant hereditary nobility, such as the post of *secrétaire du roi*. Failing that, a social climber could search for a lesser position that would entail personal nobility or at least exemption from the *taille*, a tax that was the distinctive onus of the common folk. Money alone was not enough to fulfill such a program of betterment, for the changes required several generations, with great attention to marriages that would consolidate capital in dowries, match daughters with superior families that could be powerful allies, and produce heirs capable of carrying on the ascent through the hierarchy.

A formidable apparatus of social closure stood in opposition to anyone who tried to rise in society without meeting the slow, expensive conditions of social mobility. Almost all positions of power were in some way privileges granted by the monarch and protected by his law. Despite this, there seems to have been no shortage of usurpers. They ranged from those who invented officer ancestors to accelerate the formula *patro et avo consulibus* (the three-generation requirement for hereditary nobility), to those who tried to avoid paying taxes or institutional fees like the *franc-fief* and the *paulette*, to those who faked possession of noble lands. There were undoubtedly more than a few who spent their money to acquire the superficial trappings of aristocracy—houses, clothes, carriages, swords—in hopes that they might rapidly gain the acceptance of public opinion.

Additional controls on social status were provided by the conventions of *dérogeance* and *déchéance*, which prohibited some forms of behavior to privileged groups, on penalty of official loss of standing. The nobility was the group most directly affected by these restrictions covering all commercial and financial activity, as well as various infamous crimes. However, some of the provisions also applied to officers and bourgeois living nobly, on the principle that candidates for honorable *conditions* must demonstrate noble behavior before being admitted to the uppermost ranks.

With the main categories and the mechanisms of mobility and closure thus defined, we may examine the traditions of criticism that have shaped, and in some cases distorted, early social assessments of Molière's comedies.

In an environment preoccupied with social status and ambition, Molière himself claimed the role of a jocular corrector of behavioral abuses. He expresses this axiom of *castigat ridendo mores* in the *Premier Placet présenté au roi sur la comédie de Tartuffe*: "Le devoir de la comédie étant de corriger les hommes en les divertissant, j'ai cru que, dans l'emploi où je me trouve, je n'avais rien de mieux à faire que d'attaquer par des ridicules les vices de mon siècle."[2] The expression of this critique in terms of moral reform rather than social change is typical of Louis XIV's France, where political challenges to the hierarchy by commoners were generally punished by imprisonment, exile to the galleys of Marseille, or even public execution. Molière, who was born the son of a furnisher to the king's household, had already been jailed for debts in his youth and could allow himself only a limited amount of audacity.[3]

Despite Molière's efforts at diplomacy and prudence, he became involved in personal quarrels almost from the moment he brought his wandering troupe of players back to Paris in 1658. These disputes quickly took on social overtones. Donneau de Visé accused him of satirizing certain *personnes de qualité*, and one suspects that the allusion in *L'Ecole des femmes* to a Monsieur de l'Isle, a noble surname usurped by Thomas Corneille, may have had much to do with this charge.[4] Boulanger de Challusset repeated Donneau's claim in 1670 and further implied that Molière sought to please common groundlings rather than noble theatre-goers—although anyone who could afford the minimum admission of 15 *sols* was hardly destitute![5] Pierre Roullé, among the most vitriolic detractors of the dramatist, called Molière an immoral monster, "un démon vêtu de chair," and an enemy of all society.[6] This double association of Molière with *roturiers* and heretics was to have interesting repercussions as time went on.

Opponents of the theatre eagerly seized upon the view of a

libertine Molière in order to further their puritanical ends. Echoing Roullé and the converted prince de Conti, the preacher Bourdaloue denounced him from the pulpit, claiming that he confused the public by blending virtue with vice in his comedies.[7] Bossuet, bishop of Meaux, joined in this attack after Molière's untimely death on stage; he maliciously hinted that the comedian had been struck down in divine retribution.[8] Such viewpoints did not die out with the end of the Classical Era, but continued to be expounded in the eighteenth and nineteenth centuries by men such as the converted Italian comic Luigi Riccoboni and the overly zealous critic Louis Veuillot.[9]

Even those astute contemporaries who sought to achieve an objective, aesthetic criticism of Molière's work were profoundly influenced by the allegations of his enemies. Boileau and Fénelon, in their concern for the purity of literature, renewed the myth that Molière had been somehow contaminated by his popularity.[10] Consequently, his language was sometimes too vulgar for their tastes, despite the fact that the speech of his characters, no matter how realistic, was far more refined than that of competitors such as Raymond Poisson.

Molière's friends and admirers were quick to claim that he had indeed succeeded as a social reformer. His fellow actor Brécourt, Charles Perrault, and even the burlesque poet D'Assouci were among those to sing his praises.[11] Donneau de Visé, antagonist turned ally, lauded Molière as a philosopher as well as a dramatist—testimony that was to be seconded by La Grange and Vivot in their preface to the 1682 edition of his collected works.[12] As the word *philosophe* changed to take on increasingly political overtones during the eighteenth century, Molière was assimilated into a current of protest against the recently perceived injustices of the ancien régime. His legend grew, for Fontenelle, Bayle, and a legion of minor authors portrayed him in an increasingly glorious light, but the most decisive step in the radicalization of Molière was the completion of his first major biography by Grimarest.[13] The latter, a nearly unknown man of letters, compiled a multitude of anecdotes demonstrating Molière's humanitarianism and exaggerating his ties to the freethinking school of Gassendi.

Throughout the Age of Enlightenment, the prevailing attitude of the *philosophes* toward Molière was one of high regard for his artistic achievements and solidarity with what they imagined to be his ideological hostility to the aristocracy. Voltaire, eager to claim the author of *Tartuffe* as a distinguished precursor, wrote his own biography of the dramatist, retouching Grimarest to emphasize his compatibility with the goals of reform—beliefs that were generally shared by the Encyclopédistes Diderot and Marmontel and by other literary authorities, including Chamfort.[14]

One great exception was, of course, Jean-Jacques Rousseau. In the *Lettre à D'Alembert sur les spectacles*, he accused Molière of conspiring against the "honnête homme" Alceste, hero of *Le Misanthrope*.[15] To put an essentially good man in a ridiculous position was, he contended, to make the theater a vehicle for social evil. The attack was motivated by polemical concerns, for D'Alembert had, in his article on Geneva for the *Encyclopédie*, suggested that the only virtuous institution lacking in Rousseau's homeland was a theater. By jumping to the defense of the theocracy, Rousseau hoped to effect a timely reconciliation. His lack of comic sensibility (that capacity of even the most virtuous men to laugh at themselves) led Jean-Jacques to several interesting contradictions, such as the hypothesis that the author and his characters have separate intentions for their society. Yet, many in the Revolutionary generation looked to Rousseau as a beacon of truth, and his impact is manifest in Fabre d'Eglantine's *Le Philinte de Molière* (a "sequel" that crowns Alceste's outspoken virtue while castigating his friend's complacency toward aristocratic abuse), as well as in the heavily revised versions of Molière that appeared after 1793.[16]

If the partisans of the Revolution regarded Molière as a tool of the oppressors, a curious reversal took place once the Bourbons were restored to the throne of France, for *Tartuffe* was hailed in turn as a denunciation of ultraconservatism and an important statement on the rights of the individual. A new generation of writers, including Sainte-Beuve, Hugo, Musset, and Michelet, helped form a different image of Molière, that of the brooding, melancholic philosopher who was incapable of fulfilling his visions of reform.[17] Obviously, the Romantics had begun to project onto Molière and his theater the anxieties and social dramas of their own period, a process that was facilitated by a growing ignorance of pre-Revolutionary conditions and by the disappearance of much of Molière's dramatic production — particularly the farces, court ballets, and early comedies — from the repertoire and consciousness of the age.

At the same time that the nineteenth-century literary public was losing track of much of Molière's work, a great interest arose in his private life. Initiated by the research of the police official, Beffara, and carried on by Soulié and by the entire team of the review *Le Moliériste*, this movement was to result eventually in a clearer picture of the dramatist, his family, and his environment. Equally important to the reconstitution of Molière's social context was the publication by Paul Lacroix and Georges Monval of most of the polemical literature that attacked or supported him during the stormy moments of his career and after his death.[18]

Academic critics, however, did not always greet the work of the Moliéristes with enthusiasm. On the contrary, the latter were sometimes regarded as fanatics chasing lost documents or as amateurish *bon vivants*. To Ferdinand Brunetière and Emile Faguet, who reflect the school of positivism and the moralistic atmosphere of the Catholic Revival, Molière incarnated *le bon sens bourgeois*—a materialistic mediocrity that was denounced as immoral and anti-Christian by Veuillot and defended, albeit weakly, by Charles Jeannel and others.[19] It must be noted that this concept of Molière as a spokesman for bourgeois ideology came into being at a time when the bourgeoisie was profoundly different from what it had been in his own day. Neither Brunetière and Faguet nor Molière's defenders take into account the disunity of Louis XIV's common subjects, the ambiguous *petit officier* status of Molière's family, or the patronage of the court.

The twentieth century has brought a proliferation of critical responses to Molière's theater. Gustave Lanson helped renew interest in the farce element in his plays, Maurice Pellisson restored the status of his *comédies-ballets* and palace entertainments, and the great biographical and critical syntheses of Gustave Michaut and Antoine Adam swept away the influence of dubious anecdotes while calling attention more and more to the plays themselves as the final word on the dramatist's views and ideology.[20] At the same time French historians, led by the members of the *Annales* school, were laying a new foundation for socioeconomic history through the quantitative study of records and documents pertaining to every level of pre-Revolutionary society. These scrupulous documentary methods were eventually applied to the dramatist himself by such researchers as Jurgens, Maxfield-Miller, and Mongrédien.[21]

The traditional interpretation of Molière as bourgeois spokesman is still propounded by John Cairncross, and Rousseau's view of a Molière with aristocratic sympathies has been renewed with greater objectivity and care by Paul Bénichou; but perhaps the most influential trend to emerge since World War II is based on the hypothesis that Molière was a strictly disinterested man of the theater whose preoccupations with the forms of the stage left no room for social comment, a position strongly represented by W. G. Moore and René Bray.[22] Even though its dismissal of a social component in Molière's work is rather peremptory, the latter standpoint has made some important contributions to the understanding of his comedies, for it stresses the relevance of the entire canon and reminds us that Molière's mode of expression was eminently theatrical and indirect. The man of the stage used a many-voiced form of discourse where speeches can only be analyzed in relation to other speeches, rather than as direct expressions of authorial intent. Indeed, the theatrical Molière complements, rather than negates, the social Molière; for early modern communities were intensely ceremonial in character, and the formalities of mask, mime, speech, and gesture are ultimately affiliated with the realities of collective life. The work of Moore, Bray, and their followers makes possible an enhanced social criticism that seeks to uncover the unity of dramatic evolution and behavioral analysis. This has been the object in recent years of research by Myrna Zwillenberg, Karolyn Waterson, and especially Ralph Albanese.[23] The methodology of this book provides for a scrutiny of the entire theatrical production of Molière, with added emphasis on the problem of identity, and on the diverse forms of relationship between the individual and the social body. With this goal in mind, I have attempted to maintain as much as possible of the representational context of the social elements in Molière's masterpieces, while at the same time relying on an ongoing comparison between internal portrayal of manners and external codes of behavior.

1. Roland Mousnier, *La Vénalité des offices sous Henri IV et Louis XIII*; *Fureurs paysannes: les paysans dans les révoltes du XVIIe siècle (France, Russie, Chine)*; *Les Hiérarchies sociales de 1450 à nos jours*; *Les Institutions de la France sous la monarchie*

absolue; and *La Stratification sociale à Paris aux XVIIe et XVIIIe siècles: l'échantillon de 1634, 1635, 1636*. Pierre Goubert, *Beauvais et le Beauvaisis de 1600 à 1730*; and *L'Ancien Régime*. Robert Mandrou, *Introduction à la France moderne 1500–1640*; *Classes et luttes de classe en France au début du XVIIe siècle*; and *Louis XIV en son temps 1661–1715*. Pierre Deyon, *Amiens capitale provinciale*.

2. Molière, *Oeuvres complètes*, ed. Georges Couton, 1:889. This edition will be used for all subsequent references to Molière's plays. Additional references to supplementary writings or to Couton's critical material in this edition will be designated *OC* Couton.

3. The best account of Molière's life based on documentary evidence is Madeleine Jurgens and Elizabeth Maxfield-Miller, *Cent ans de recherches sur Molière*. For information on his imprisonment, see pp. 104–7.

4. Jean Donneau de Visé, *Nouvelles Nouvelles, 3e partie* (1663), in *OC* Couton, 1:1018–19. The persons alluded to by Donneau may have been in the same situation as the younger Corneille. See *L'Ecole des femmes*, 1.1. 175–82.

5. Boulanger himself notes that many bourgeois returned five or six times, paying 30 *sols* (a worker's weekly salary) each time to see a "hit" like *L'Amour médecin*. See his *Elomire hypocondre ou les médecins vengés* (1670), in *OC* Couton, 2:1241.

6. Pierre Roullé, *Le Roi glorieux de ce monde* (1664), in *OC* Couton, 1:1143.

7. Armand de Bourbon, prince de Conti, *Traité de la comédie et des spectacles selon la tradition de l'église*, pp. 23–24. Barbier d'Aucour, sieur de Rochemont, *Observations sur une comédie de Molière institulé Le Festin de Pierre* (1665), in *OC* Couton, 2:1199–1208, Adrien Baillet, *Jugements des savants sur les principaux ouvrages*, 9:110–26; Louis Bourdaloue, "Sermon sur l'hypocrisie," in *Sermons choisis*, pp. 81–97.

8. Jacques-Bénigne Bossuet, "Maximes et réflexions sur la comédie," in *L'Eglise et le théâtre*, pp. 172, 184–87.

9. Luigi Riccoboni, *De la réformation du théâtre*, pp. 14–16, 62, 312. The contrast is vivid between this work of repentance and Riccoboni's earlier *Observations sur la comédie et sur le génie de Molière*; Louis Veuillot, *Molière et Bourdaloue*.

10. Nicolas Boileau, "L'Art poétique," in *Oeuvres complètes*, p. 104. Boileau's supercilious attitude contradicts his highly laudatory "Satire II: A Molière," written ten years earlier (ca. 1663), in *Oeuvres complètes*, pp. 15–16. François de Salignac de la Mothe Fénelon, "Lettre à M. Dacier, secrétaire perpétuel de l'Académie Française, sur les occupations de l'Académie," in *Oeuvres complètes*, 6:637–38.

11. Guillaume Marcoureau de Brécourt, *L'Ombre de Molière* (1673). Charles Couppeau d'Assouci, "L'Ombre de Molière et son épitaphe," (1673). Charles Perrault, *Les Hommes illustres qui ont paru en France pendant ce siècle*, pp. 79–80.

12. Jean Donneau de Visé, *Oraison funèbre de Molière* (1673). Charles Varlet de La Grange and Vivot, "Préface" (1682), in *OC* Couton, 1:996–1002.

13. Bernard Le Bouvier de Fontenelle, "Dialogue de Paracelse et de Molière," in *Oeuvres*, 1:177–83. Pierre Bayle, *Dictionnaire historique et critique*, 12:363. Among

minor works one must note the anonymous *Molière le critique et Mercure aux prises avec les philosophes*, an unusual tract in which a philosophical Molière debates points of theology with Bayle, Jean Le Clerc, and others. J. L. de Grimarest, *La Vie de M. de Molière*, (see especially pp. 101, 112).

14. Voltaire, *Oeuvres complètes*, 23 (Mélanges 2): "Vie de Molière," 89–106; 33 (Correspondance 1): "Lettre n. 343, A un premier commis," 354; 14 (*Le Siècle de Louis XIV*): 105; and 21 (Romans): 279, where the sensible protagonist of *L'Ingénu* prefers *Le Tartuffe* to all other comedies. Denis Diderot, *Oeuvres complètes*, 3:191, 414, 433, and *Le Neveu de Rameau*, pp. 59–61. M. Delon notes, in "Lectures de Molière au XVIIIᵉ siècle," that Laclos and Sade, like the fictional nephew, distort Molière in order to rationalize amoral behavior. Jean-Francois Marmontel, "Comédie," in *Encyclopédie ou dictionnaire raisonné des sciences, des arts et des métiers*. N. S. R. de Chamfort, *Eloge de Molière*, in *Oeuvres complètes*.

15. Jean-Jacques Rousseau, *Lettre à M. D'Alembert sur les spectacles*, pp. 45–60.

16. Philippe Fabre d'Eglantine, *Le Philinte de Molière*.

17. Charles-Augustin Sainte-Beuve, "Molière," in *Les Grands Ecrivains français*. Victor Hugo lists "Molière en pleurs" as one of "Les Mages," in *Les Contemplations*, p. 412. Alfred de Musset admires Molière's "mâle gaieté, si triste et si profonde" in "Une soirée perdu," *Poésies complètes*, pp. 389–91. Jules Michelet, *Louis XIV et la révocation de l'édit de Nantes*, pp. 66–70, 83–84, 111–14. On post-Revolutionary bourgeois formulations of Molière, see Ralph Albanese, "The Molière Myth in Nineteenth Century France," in *Pre-text / Text / Context: Essays on Nineteenth Century French Literature*. For a general perspective on the critical reception of Molière, consult Jean Collinet, *Lectures de Molière*, and Laurence Romero, *Molière: Traditions in Criticism, 1900–1970*.

18. Louis Beffara, *Dissertation sur J. B. Poquelin-Molière*. Eudore Soulié, *Recherches sur Molière et sur sa famille*. Paul Lacroix and George Monval, eds., *Collection moliéresque* and *Nouvelle Collection moliéresque*.

19. Ferdinand Brunetière, "Les Dernières Recherches sur la vie de Molière," in *Etudes critiques*, p. 149; "La Philosophie de Molière," *Etudes critiques*, 4ᵉ série, pp. 149, 217–18; "La Langue de Molière," *Etudes critiques*, 7ᵉ série, pp. 85–133; and "Molière," in *Histoire de la littérature française classique (1515–1830)*, 2:382–454. Emile Faguet, *En lisant Molière*, pp. 2–3, 92, 128, 149. Louis Veuillot, *Molière et Bourdaloue*. Charles Jeannel, *La Morale de Molière*. Alphonse Leveaux echoes Jeannel in *L'Enseignement moral dans les comédies de Molière*; and Gustave Larroumet declares Molière bourgeois by definition in *La Comédie de Molière: l'auteur et le milieu*, p. 53.

20. Gustave Lanson, "Molière et la farce," reprinted in *Molière: A Collection of Critical Essays*, ed. Jacques Guicharnaud (Englewood Cliffs, N.J.: Prentice-Hall, 1964), pp. 20–28. Maurice Pellisson, *Les Comédies-ballets de Molière*. Gustave Michaut, *La Jeunesse de Molière*, *Les Débuts de Molière*, and *Les Luttes de Molière*. Antoine Adam, "Molière," in *L'Apogée du siècle*, vol. 3 of *L'Histoire de la littérature française au XVIIᵉ siècle*.

21. Madeleine Jurgens and Elizabeth Maxfield-Miller, *Cent ans de recherches*. Georges Mongrédien, *La Vie privée de Molière*, and *Recueil de textes et de documents du XVIIe siècle relatifs à Molière*. Also see the numerous articles by these writers listed in the bibliography.

22. John Cairncross, *Molière bourgeois et libertin*. Paul Bénichou, *Morales du Grand Siècle*. W. G. Moore, *Molière: A New Criticism*. René Bray, *Molière, homme de théâtre*.

23. Ralph Albanese, *Le Dynamisme de la peur chez Molière: une analyse socioculturelle de Dom Juan, Tartuffe, et L'Ecole des femmes*. Karolyn Waterson, *Molière et l'autorité*. Myrna Zwillenberg, "Arnolphe, Fate's Fool" and "Dramatic Justice in Tartuffe."

Arnolphe and Agnès in bourgeois attire, receiving laurel crowns from the comic muse. Frontispiece to volume two of the 1666 Paris edition of the *Oeuvres* published by J. Guignard fils and his associates. Reproduced by permission of the Houghton Library, Harvard University.

CHAPTER ONE

SOCIAL INDICATORS IN
SEVENTEENTH-CENTURY FRANCE

Clues to social status were of paramount importance to Molière's audience, for the spectators had no program or critical apparatus to acquaint them rapidly with the essential facts about dramatic characters. Although the seasoned spectator was familiar with the actors of the major troupes and their usual roles, Molière's plays demanded special attention. As an actor, Molière was capable of portraying any *condition* from servant to nobleman and even the single figure of Sganarelle appeared sometimes as a valet and other times as a bourgeois. The treatment of broad and varied social subjects called for a quick exposition of group affiliations through both the verbal and physical aspects of the comedy. In general, Molière's use of such clues is subtly effective, for he manages to communicate social identities in numerous indirect ways, without interrupting the flow of the dialogue by plodding, stereotypical descriptions or heavy-handed introductions.[1]

Seven of the most salient groups of social indicators in Molière's theater are money, offices, clothing, servants, houses and land, transportation, and language. Lest these factors be dismissed as merely picturesque, superficial effects, it should be remembered that the ability to notice outward appearances and to distinguish between them was vital to Europeans in the seventeenth century, when each social body had its place in a hierarchy of possessions, uniforms, and behavior. The success of a courtship or a seduction, an *anoblissement* or a usurpation, often depended on the existence of conspicuous indicators, which were thought to be the outward manifestations of an individual's essential virtue or *caractère*. La Bruyère's parallel of Giton and Phédon, the quintessential rich man and pauper, illustrates the ideal union of appearance and identity, as well as the aristocratic uneasiness over the domination of money in all forms of success.[2] Externals, whether they reflected conditions of birth, financial strength, or simply aspirations, established the basic conditions for interpersonal contact at court, in the marketplace, in the village, or in the theater. The seven categories of indicators to be examined are those that recur most frequently in Molière's work, and, though they are not all-inclusive, they do permit reference to a significant cross-section of early modern society.

MONEY

In order to evaluate the sums of money mentioned in Molière's comedies, it is necessary to understand the rather complex monetary system of the ancien régime. Louis XIV's coinage carried no direct numerical value; its worth was fixed by the government in relationship to an arbitrary scale. Thus, there were two separate economic systems: the coins themselves, or units of exchange, and the theoretical units of account.

The basic unit of account in the seventeenth century was the *livre tournois*.[3] The "franc," taken from the name of a sixteenth-century coin debased in the monetary reform of 1641, was an unofficial unit of account synonymous with the *livre*. The *livre tournois* contained twenty *sous* or *sols*, each of which contained twelve *deniers*, a scale of values similar to the former English pounds, shillings, and pence.

The principal French coins of the reign of Louis XIV were the silver *écu*, worth three livres, and the gold *louis*, worth ten. There were also half and double louis, and some rarer multiples of four louis and above. In addition, there had been a gold *écu*, worth approximately five livres, which had been officially replaced by the silver écu in 1641, but some of these coins continued to circulate as late as 1653. The existence of the gold écu has led some editors to make disturbing errors in evaluation,[4] but we must emphasize that it was already a rather rare coin by the time Molière returned to Paris, and that when his characters said "écu," his audience certainly would have understood the common silver coin worth three livres. There also existed various coins of copper and alloy in multiples of sous and deniers, such as the *liard* (3 d.), the *double* (2 d.), the *blanc* (5 d.), and the "pièce tapée" (1 s. 3 d.), but their value was so questionable that they were often not accepted in trade.[5]

Besides the French coins, certain foreign coins came to be assimilated into the French economic system. Such was the case of the Spanish double *escudo*, popularly known as the "pistole," a coin of very high quality first minted by Charles V in 1537, tacitly accepted into the French system by Henri III forty years later, and fixed at a value of ten livres in 1652. The pistole circulated widely in France, particularly after the marriage of Louis XIV to Maria Theresa in 1660.

To add to this confusion, the coins tended to fluctuate in value according to supply and demand, despite governmental efforts at regulation. When Harpagon figures the interest on twenty pistoles at the *denier douze* to be 18 livres, 6 sols, and 8 deniers, (one for twelve, or about 8%) he shows us that the current value of the pistole was eleven, rather than ten, livres (*L'Avare*, 1. 4). Other illegal practices, such as counterfeiting and coin-trimming, forced the public to be constantly on guard against bad coins. Scoffing royal authority, merchants and servants alike resorted to weighing coins on a scale (*trébuchet*) to assure themselves of their value. Even Alain, the blockheaded swain in *L'Ecole des femmes*, complains that Horace has given him two old écus "qui n'étaient pas de poids" (3. 1. 670).

Money held a different place in the life of each social group.

Peasants dealt largely through a barter system, making payments in kind and saving their coins for tax payment. Only a small minority of them could amass, through several generations, a modest herd of livestock, worth perhaps 2,000 or 3,000 livres, and so become a *laboureur*. The urban worker earned between forty sols and ten livres per month, enough to provide lodging, bread, and vegetables for himself and perhaps for a small family, provided that a grain shortage did not send staple prices skyrocketing.[6]

Only at the income level of the artisan and the merchant does one begin to see the possibility of considerable sums of money, usually in the context of dowries and land transactions. Marriage contracts, postmortem inventories, and other documents reveal a surprising lack of liquidity in bourgois fortunes, for cash is rare and is often replaced by notes, offices, *rentes* (which represent about $1/12$ of the capital invested), and goods. In seventeenth-century Paris, most bourgeois dowries were under 5,000 livres, with many under 1,000 livres, even in the relatively prosperous neighborhood of the Marais, where the most frequent figures hover between 2,000 and 8,000 livres.[7] Dowries of 10,000 livres and above seem to have been reserved mainly for the strata of officers, lawyers, and the wealthier merchants.[8] It is worth noting that Molière's maternal grandmother, Marie Asselin, was married with the modest *dot* of 4,000 livres.[9] Above the level of 10,000 livres, fortunes tended to escalate rapidly. For example, the *parlementaire* Bullion, whose parents married with 22,000 livres, eventually commanded a fortune of 8,000,000 livres.[10] In fact, fortunes above 100,000 livres usually coincided with the ascension from the common order into the nobility, as was the case for Louis XIV's *secrétaires d'état*, who were worth 800,000 to 900,000 livres.[11]

Money is thus a rather remarkable social indicator in Molière's comedy, for it specifies, whenever mentioned, a minimal level for a character in the social hierarchy. In the case of dowries, the sum may even permit a narrowing of possible identities to two or three distinct groups. Other indicators may then contribute to a clearer parallel between a given character and a *condition* in the social order.

OFFICES

The multitude of offices available to buyers in Molière's time included such relatively insignificant charges as his father's post of royal upholsterer, minor places in the forest and road administrations, or provincial notary bureaus. The rather large proportion of bourgeois who scurried to pay a few thousand livres for such offices (1,000 officers out of 22,000 townsmen in Dijon) tended to settle, if no royal appointments were available, for even the most diminutive ones in princely service, even "piqueur au vol pour corneilles!"[12] Meager honors were often matched by meager remuneration, which suggests that the main attractiveness in offices was their status as a foothold in the ascending hierarchy of "dignities" that led eventually to tax exemption and nobility.

Above the minor offices just mentioned were the lower levels of the provincial magistrature and financial administration, costing between 10,000 and 20,000 livres.[13] These posts, including *élu*, *bailli*, and *receveur-général*, were typical of a somewhat dull, endogamous layer of society that sometimes opened the way for continued aspiration. The more important offices in the provincial sovereign courts, such as *président à mortier*, were worth upward of 60,000 livres, compared with nearly half a million livres in the capital. In the parlements, the post of *conseiller* cost at least 45,000 livres, whereas less prestigious (but more accessible) places in the *cour des monnaies* and *grand conseil* began at 30,000 livres.[14] High offices such as these were naturally rewarded with the dignities and privileges of the *noblesse de robe*.

Office-holding generally signified substantial fortunes and

social mobility, a combination of circumstances that led to a particular set of social values. For the families associated with the sovereign courts, it meant an emphasis on lineage at least as important as that encountered in the ranks of the *noblesse d'épée*. A royal edict in 1600 had set forth the rule whereby the third generation to possess an office acquired not only the personal nobility of the officer himself but also a full hereditary and perpetual dignity.[15] Because the office itself was irrefutable proof that could stand the test of any challenge or inquest, it stayed in the family as long as nine generations.[16] This led to a high degree of endogamy and clannishness among officers, whose fortunes usually alienated them from the penniless *hobereau*, as well as from the "vile" artisan.

The officer group was neither as placid nor as secure as their enviable privileges may suggest. In reality there were many rifts between different corps of officers, such as the prolonged dispute between the *trésoriers de France* and the *élus*, on the one hand, and the magistrates of the *cours des aides* and *chambres des comptes*, on the other. The struggle resulted in the victory of the latter party in the matter of authority over financial administration.[17] Bickering between the sovereign courts and the royal governors and *intendants* eventually prompted Louis XIV to effect dictatorially a reduction of the courts' powers. This coincided with the king's intention to separate power and privilege, dispensing one or the other when it suited his purposes. He seized upon every opportunity to abolish "independent" offices, such as the municipal government of Marseille.[18]

The ideological effects of the officer corps in seventeenth-century France were all-pervasive. Jan De Vries has given a name to the mentality of this slow economy, dominated by nepotism and patronage, which immobilized the most important accumulations of capital through the purchase of offices—he calls it *empleomania*.[19] Its influence extended over all the urban groups, from artisans to judges, as well as rural entrepreneurs, and impinged on the *noblesse de robe* and the *noblesse d'épée*, for even aristocrats were concerned with offices of a type. The old nobility did not need to worry about acquiring status, but rather about preserving it. Military service was the only activity sanctioned for them and the only proof they could muster for the *recherches de noblesse*, but most of the desirable commands in the army and navy were just as subject to venality as the sovereign courts! In 1653 the duc de Noailles was obliged to borrow 500,000 livres to purchase a post as *capitaine-lieutenant des chevau-légers.*[20] As money became a deciding factor in the military, many a prepubescent boy became the titular captain of a ship or commander of a unit in the field. Unless he was very lucky, the scion of a warrior family had to pay for his position, just as the son of a merchant would. It is no wonder, then, that Molière associated many of his important characters with the anxieties and privileges of the officer groups.

CLOTHING

Seventeenth-century society insisted upon observance of certain conventions in dress, for it was important to recognize immediately and by sight the status of those in one's environment in order to render or demand the proper honors. Failure to do so could result in a sound caning from a superior, interrupted economic or class cooperation among equals, or a loss of face before inferiors.

One of the most distinctive garments was the robe, worn by most of the clergy and by the legal and medical professions. Clerical robes ranged from the simple black *soutane* of the village priest to the splended fur-lined and embroidered costumes in fine red cloth worn by a cardinal. Much of the clergy also wore the familiar rounded hat with a wide brim. The medical robe was an outgrowth of university attire, the traditional black gown.[21] As for the men of law, they were divided into those of the long robe and those of the short. The latter were subordinate officers such as *huissiers* and *sergents*. Among the wearers of the long robe, the costume ranged from the relatively simple black cloth for a young lawyer to expensive satin and velvet, sometimes in bright colors and trimmed or embroidered, for royal attorneys, high judges, and *parlementaires*.[22]

Masculine attire for the bourgeoisie consisted of a white shirt, or *chemise*, a pair of knee breeches called the *haut-de-chausses*, cotton hose, the vest-like *pourpoint*, a collar, or *rabat* (of lace if the wearer was wealthy), a hat, a mantle, and buckle shoes.[23] At the beginning of Molière's career, this outfit would lack pockets (hence, the necessity of a purse hung from the belt) or buttons (fasteners, laces, and pins were used), but by 1700 these items had become the key to fashion. On the other hand, ribbons, which were an indispensible part of the earlier costume (to cover the fasteners), had almost disappeared from masculine apparel, even for nobles, by the turn of the century.

As bourgeois fashions were soberly evolving, the court nobility, led by such eminent dandies as Cinq-Mars, Montauron, the duc de Candale, Lauzun, Vardes, Villeroy, de Guiche, and Lenglée, outdid each other to launch ever newer and more outrageous styles.[24] The *pourpoint*, which in the early part of the century reached the waist, shrank during the 1660s into a small *brassière* with puffy sleeves. The *chemise* became vast and was allowed to protrude in great folds over the stomach, making the distinctive *jabot*. From the neck, a cascade of lace descended toward the navel. The *haut-de-chausses* might be quite voluminous, as in the so-called *rhingrave* style. Over his silk stocking, the aristocratic peacock might place hoops of lace (*canons*); his high-heeled shoes might be made even more awkward by a profusion of ribbons. The largest clusters of ribbons, called the *petite oie* or *affûtiaux*, could reach ridiculous extremes. The truly smitten fop would top this all off with a long blond wig and a hat adorned with a cluster of expensive plumes.

Foppish attire coincides with usurpation of rank in many "nobles," especially the marquis, to create a particularly troublesome ambiguity. Of course, a legitimate marquis could attract ridicule by dressing immoderately. In addition, however, there seems to have been an unusually large number of upstart bourgeois who laid claim to this title, so much so that the term *faux marquis* became a synonym for usurper. It is often difficult to tell whether one of these gaudy aristocrats is a fool or a fraud, or both. Perhaps Molière is suggesting that there is not much difference between the two. In any case, Brossette, informed by a highly reliable source, reports that Molière modeled his ridiculous marquis figures on the usurpers: "M. Despréaux m'a dit que les *faux marquis* de la cour étaient enragés contre Molière parce qu'il les jouait et qu'il mettait leurs mots aussi bien que leurs manières dans ses comédies."[25] If we are to believe this testimony by Boileau, the fool and the upstart do indeed go hand in hand in Molière's plays.

In distinguishing between prescribed bourgeois and noble attire, fabric and color were just as important as style. The middle and upper bourgeoisie generally wore black broadcloth or other dark-colored fabrics, with a *chemise* of fine linen. Nobles preferred as much silk, satin, and velvet as possible. They chose lively colors, and some were veritable walking sunbursts. In addition, their costumes were often decorated with a profusion of lace, feathers, and fancy embroidery of gold or silver thread or imitations.

The engravings by Brissart and Sauvé in the 1682 edition of Molière's works show that, nine years after the playwright's death, fashions had already made considerable progress toward a more reasonable and modest standard. Serge and *droguet* were rapidly replacing silk and satin in the outer garments. Both court and town adopted the *justaucorps*, a kind of ancestor to the frock coat, which almost completely covered the other clothes and became the focus of design; a minor change in the angle of a pocket or the location of a buttonhole would send ripples through the fashion-conscious world. Already in 1672 Mme de Sévigné's son-in-law, Grignan, was paying between 800 and 1,000 livres for a *justaucorps*.[26]

People of the lower classes, men as well as women, wore whatever they could afford, which generally was a somewhat coarse gray linen called *grisette*. Slightly more elegant was the *toile de Troyes*, which appealed to the *petites bourgeoises*. The poorer laborers, such as water-carriers, could not afford a *rabat*. Often the *haut-de-chausses* was replaced by a loose culotte and the hose by rough leggings. Footwear was simple, for the wooden *sabot* was still very much in use among the people. Men wore various types of floppy hats, ancestors of the Revolution's Phrygian cap, and women favored bonnets. Old, baggy *pourpoints* and slightly-used brimmed hats were available at the used clothing shop, or *friperie*.[27]

Lackeys and valets were frequently better off than the working poor, for they might be provided with their master's livery. They might receive smocks or other work clothes, or even some castoffs from their employer's own wardrobe. The beret was the common headwear for servants, although special domestics such as cooks and coachmen might have different hats: one thinks of Maître Jacques in *L'Avare* (3. 1), who had a different hat for each of his jobs. Sometimes the costumes of the valets in Molière's comedies were influenced by the stylized stage costumes of the *commedia dell' arte*; this is the case, for instance, with Sbrigani of *Monsieur de Pourceaugnac* (1. 3), who wears a "Neapolitan" suit.

Molière's characters occasionally wear obsolete items of clothing. The most noteworthy example is Sganarelle's "fraise," a kind of ruff dating back to the reign of Henri IV. Sganarelle's association with this collar makes him appear to be a relic left behind by the rush of other bourgeois toward powerful offices and a noble lifestyle.

As for women's clothes, there was less variation in terms of style. Dresses were long and necklines low for all classes of society. A *fichu*, or kerchief, could cover the neck and bosom in case of cold weather or pruderie. Several petticoats were worn under the dress. Materials and workmanship were even more important than in men's clothing. For the rich there were damask, various types of velvet, and satin. Economy-minded wives might content themselves with *camelot de Hollande* (silk and wool) or *ferrandine* (silk and cotton). With fancy stitching and perhaps a few pearls as well, the price of a dress could easily exceed 300 livres. Jewelry ranged from the jade hairpins of the middle bourgeoisie to gold and diamonds for the wealthy. Rich women dispensed with bonnets in order to preserve their expensive and towering coiffures, but only those of the rank of duchess or higher had to trouble themselves with more than three yards of train on their dresses.[28]

The extent to which seventeenth-century French society was obsessed with clothing as a mark of rank is shown in the king's repeated attempts to promulgate and enforce sumptuary laws. Louis's informal influence on fashions was tremendous: it was he who launched the billowing wigs that forced men to shave their heads until the turn of the century, and they rushed to trim off their moustaches as well, when he shaved his in 1680. In this as in all other matters, Louis strove for absolute control, which proved elusive. He intervened in 1691 to suppress cloth-covered buttons and tried eleven times to ban all "étoffes d'or et d'argent et . . . broderies, piqures, chamarrures, guipures, passements, etc."[29] Establishing an elite uniform, the famous "justaucorps bleu," he allotted sixty of them to the most prestigious people in the country. He even intervened, in vain, in the field of women's hair styles, ordering ladies to abandon their two- or three-foot-high creations. No wonder that everyone in France was constantly scrutinizing what everyone else was wearing!

SERVANTS

The domestic staff required by the aristocratic or upper bourgeois household could be very numerous, and its management was consequently a complex problem. An eminent contemporary guidebook to domestic management, Audiger's *La Maison réglée*, informs us that the proper gentleman required no fewer than thirty-seven servants, of which five were servants to other servants![30] Wages would amount to more than 4,000 livres per year, room and board to 9,000 or more livres. A *président* in the Bordeaux parlement, for example, could make do with a minimal staff of a cook, a coachman, a valet, two lackeys, and several maids.

The basic manservant was the *laquais*, or footman, a utility worker whose tasks could include serving table, running errands, cleaning, tending the fire, and acting as receptionist. At dinner one man was required for each guest just to serve his wine, for drink and glasses were kept on a sideboard rather than on the table. These lackeys were often peasants who had left the land because of the chronic famine during Louis's reign, and many went by the name of provinces, hence, the profusion of Bourguignons, Picards, and Champagnes. Even in the best houses, they could not expect to collect much more than 100 livres per year in wages, and the average must have been far lower, with frequent lapses in payment. It is true that the *laquais* were fed and sometimes clothed, but we can understand their avidity for gratuities from any source.

The valet enjoyed a better position than the *laquais*. His main duties consisted of dressing his master and looking after his personal effects. He might be called upon to serve as cupbearer or to do all sorts of odd jobs. Although he was more closely supervised than the *laquais*, and just as expendable, his salary was generally two or three times higher, 200 livres or more. In addition, he might expect to receive a fairly substantial bequest, should he survive his master: Boileau gave his valet 6,000 livres.

Maids, or *servantes*, were the female counterparts of the *laquais*. A *servante*'s tasks, which were as tiring as a man's, included such unglorified work as emptying chamber pots and scrubbing floors. The one field with which she had nothing to do, at least in the larger houses, was the preparation and serving of food. For her efforts she received a meager compensation of some 25 livres per year.

These low-ranking servants were completely at the mercy of their masters and mistresses. Any infraction or misbehavior could result in a beating with fists or sticks, although, fortunately, it was considered ignoble to draw sword against a mere servant. Although there are examples of "upstart" servants going unpunished, there are also incidents of servants being crippled or even killed.[31] On the conventionalized stage, these kickings, poundings, and canings were sublimated into the *bastonnade*, a ritualized beating that involved the traditional slapstick. This instrument was made of sticks fastened together to produce a loud clack at the least impact.

There were other members of the domestic staff who belonged to an ambiguous category somewhat above that of the preceding servants, but who would still have been considered by the master as "mes gens." Apart from apprentices and journeymen in the trades, these included the wet nurse and the *suivante* among the women, and the cook, *maître d'hôtel*, tutor, and *intendant* among the men.

Wet nurses were required for all children of the aristocracy and of the *haute bourgeoisie*, for it was definitely unfashionable for women of those classes to nurse their own offspring. The nurse could be hired from a Parisian agency or selected from among trusty servant women. Pay was better than that of a maid, 24–33 livres per year. The nurse could expect relatively good food and light work, for the health of the child depended on hers. Her own infant would become the *soeur* or *frère de lait* of the young aristocrat, which traditionally entitled the child to some form of preferential treatment.

The term *suivante* is used to designate a type of woman servant who served a single mistress and whose duties, like the valet's, included dressing and grooming this person. As a result, the *suivante* had a certain status that protected her from the corporal punishment inflicted upon lesser servants. The latter were usually of peasant origin, but the suivante might well be a *petite bourgeoise*, perhaps a widow. The *suivante* would be expected to possess, if not some education, at least a talent for matters of fashion and etiquette, for she must not embarrass her mistress before her friends. She would usually profit from her proximity to the mistress in sharing her more comfortable living conditions and, perhaps, more elegant clothes.

The cook, or *cuisinier*, was a sort of semiprofessional in seventeenth-century France. Although not a member of a corporation, like a pastry cook, he had to possess all kinds of diversified skills, for he might have to judge meat "on the hoof" and to dress entire animals. Consequently, he enjoyed a certain respect and a salary of about 300 livres, which surpassed that of many artisans.

The authority of the cook ceased at the threshold of the kitchen, where the *maître d'hôtel* took over. Like the cook, the *maître d'hôtel* would be addressed as "Maître" or "Monsieur" by the other servants. His salary of 500 livres was equal to that of eight or ten *laquais*. Often he would be in charge of the entire domestic staff and most of the household stores. Besides supervising work, he would greet visitors and orchestrate the serving of elaborate meals.

If a man of means had a male child, he would generally provide him with a private tutor. (Girls were usually sent to convent schools.)[32] Since the three main requirements for the tutor were that he be unmarried, poor, and more or less learned, it is not surprising that most were penniless members of the clergy. From the time the boy ceased wearing infants' skirts to the time he entered a *collège*, the tutor woke him, instructed him in manners, ate with him, taught him a little reading and writing (Latin, naturally), and put him to bed.

An *intendant* would have been employed only by an extremely wealthy bourgeois or aristocrat. His job would be to manage not just one but several households, and his presence would indicate the existence of large real estate holdings. Such a man would have to have a solid background in mathematics, a rather rare thing in the seventeenth century, and at least a rudimentary knowledge of farming, agricultural tenant leases, and the collection of land taxes and duties. The fact that such men were beginning to be seen more and more frequently in bourgeois households corresponds to the growing power of the upper bourgeoisie and their desire to consolidate both status and investment income in land holdings.

All of these different servants and workers appear in Molière's plays and can be used as clues to the status of the householder. Moreover, the relations between the master and the servant tell us much about whether the head of the household is behaving in a manner consistent with his social status.

HOUSES AND LAND

By 1684 Paris was estimated to have 23,372 houses, to accommodate a population of about a half million. If we consider, then, as a rough average, that there were twenty people per house, we are not surprised to find foreign visitors reacting with surprise to the crowded conditions: "'Tis also most certain, that for a quantity of ground possessed by the common people, this city is much more populous than any part of London; here are from four to five and to ten *ménages*, or distinct families in many houses."[33]

Who owned these twenty-three thousand homes? No servant, peddler, or laborer, no worker below the rank of *maître* in a corporation could hope to own one. A small artisan's house in provincial Troyes cost between 600 and 1,200 livres, and Paris property was much more expensive! For example, Molière lent his father, Jean Poquelin, 10,000 livres to rebuild his modest home under the pillars of Les Halles, and this does not include the cost of the land.[34] Unless he made a fantastic marriage or came into a miraculously large inheritance, no ordinary worker could expect to acquire a house.

The sumptuous *hôtels* of the aristrocracy were certainly the most prominent feature in the urban landscape, but this does not mean that the nobility dominated the housing market. In fact, some large *hôtels* were kept solvent by renting the ground floor space to merchants. Certainly the average nobleman, arriving in Paris from the country in search of royal appointments or personal amusement, could hardly afford to buy an entire building. Even the relatives of so illustrious a person as Mme de Maintenon were forced to rent. She recommended that her brother, D'Aubigné, spend no more than 1,000 livres on housing; but then, she was notoriously tightfisted and D'Aubigné's household relatively small. Molière himself, who did not have to make much of a show of luxury, spent between 550 and 1,300 livres each year to rent apartments of up to ten rooms with kitchen, cellars, attics, and, in the case of the higher figure, stable space.[35] Suffice it to say that many a noble must have rented rooms costing more than 1,000 livres per year.

The majority of urban real estate seems to have been in the hands of the middle and upper levels of the bourgeoisie, men at or above the station of Jean Poquelin. Jean-Baptiste himself lived in houses owned by a royal physician, a royal apothecary, a royal secretary of finance, and a tailor to the queen. The possession of a house in Paris implied a capital investment of tens of thousands of livres.

Rural lands, with few exceptions, were subject to the seigneurial system. A *seigneurie* consisted of two parts: the demesne (manorial residence and fields belonging directly to the *seigneur*) and the *censives* or *tenures*.[36] Peasants living in the latter (*censitaires* or *tenanciers*) "owned" the land in the sense that they enjoyed hereditary usufruct of it (*domaine utile*), but they still owed fees to the seigneur (*domaine éminent*). These included the manorial dues (*cens*), payments for all milling, wine-pressing, and bread-baking (*banalités*), a tax on all exchange of property (*droit de mutation*) and a kind of manorial tithe on the produce of grain fields (*champart*), which amounted to from $1/9$ to $1/3$ of the crop. The *seigneur* held monopolies on hunting, fishing, use of waterways, and dovecotes. In addition, he often disputed the peasants' ancient right to collect wood in the forests and graze livestock on the meadows without charge. Since it was the *seigneur* who, through a corps of legal officials, administered civil law in the *seigneurie*, the peasants seldom had a chance to win disputes with the overlord. Such arguments were manifold, but only in the Midi did the peasants succeed in gaining a more or less equal footing, achieving parity in the courts and often converting the complicated and onerous dues into a single annual payment.

Not all the peasants were *tenanciers*. Many held no land in their name and wandered from farm to tenant farm or worked as day laborers, sleeping in a stable or ruined building, or perhaps in a cottage loaned by the *seigneur*. Some peasants, like the *mainmortables* of Burgundy, were virtual slaves. Resident *tenanciers* could be reduced to wanderers by taxes, debts, a few bad harvests, an illness in the family, or a military campaign in the area. Moreover, they were not free to dispose of their own land; all transfers of title other than hereditary had to be approved by the *seigneur*, who could exercise his universal option, the *retrait*, thus substituting himself for the buyer.

By far the most lucrative part of the *seigneurie* was the demesne, which usually contained one or more farms owned entirely by the *seigneur* himself. The products raised on these lands could be harvested and sold before those of the *tenanciers*. The *seigneur* might exploit these farms himself, often using the indebted *tenanciers* as a labor force. On the other hand, the *seigneur* was increasingly an absentee and resorted to tenant farming on his domaine lands.

Known as *fermage* or *métayage*, tenant farming was widespread under the ancien régime. The true *métayer* received half of the advance costs from the *seigneur* and, in turn, repaid half of the crop to him, but this could vary under the different local types of *fermage*. Obviously, this arrangement offered a ridiculously high percentage of profit to the overlord, but it had its problems, too. It was common for *métayers* to break their contracts and flee in bad years, perhaps after eating the seed grain and a few of the *seigneur*'s animals to keep from starving.[37] The *seigneur* himself might lack the tools, seed, or livestock necessary for *métayage*. Thus, in order to provide for a more stable income (though at a lower rate of profit), the *seigneur* might enter into an agreement with an agricultural contractor or *laboureur*.

Laboureurs formed the upper stratum of the peasant world, for as more and more *seigneurs* became absentees and as smaller farmers became increasingly impoverished, they came to enjoy a virtual monopoly on draught animals, plows, farm equipment, and seed; these vital materials were not only used on their contract farms but also rented to poorer peasants. In return the *laboureur* took cash, crops, labor, or even parcels of land in lieu of debts, which were inevitable in the famine-ridden countryside. Many *laboureurs* thus became large-scale entrepreneurs, stockpiling agricultural materials, involving themselves in money-lending and the commerce of grain, and sometimes owning properties themselves. Becoming the general manager of a *seigneurie* (*receveur*) was often a crucial step in the acquisition of power and opportunities for advancement. By purchasing a tax official's office and gaining exemption from the *taille*, a person from a *laboureur* family could enter the comfortable and upwardly mobile world of the bourgeoisie.

While the most successful peasants sought to join the mobile urban world, the most prosperous city-dwellers were consolidating their economic and social gains by procuring land, in almost any quantity imaginable. Even an actress like Madeleine Béjart could afford a small farm.[38] Many bourgeois became landowners by a mechanism called *rente constituée*: a bourgeois would lend a sum of money to a noble, but this would be disguised as the sale of an annual rent on the noble's lands, which, in case of nonpayment of the rent, became the property of the creditor. Officers, legal men, notaries, craftsmen, even members of the clergy commonly engaged in this practice.[39]

A burgher's purchases were not limited to the *censives*, for he could buy fiefs within the demesne, provided he paid the king a duty called the *franc-fief*. This tax amounted to $1/20$ of the land's production, with another $1/20$ for each change of ownership. The advantages of these acquisitions were not merely economic; they could provide a veritable "back door" into the nobility. If a family was unable to acquire nobility directly by purchasing letters or high offices, they might assume nobility gradually by purchasing a fief, procuring a minor but *taille*-exempt office (since absence from the tax rolls was used as a way of verifying nobility), changing their name, and eventually paying the king's agents a fee to certify their noble standing.

TRANSPORTATION

Modes of transportation are often reliable indicators of social status. It is important to remember, in the first place, that most people in Molière's France did not travel long distances: they grew up, married, worked, and died within the scope of a small community, whether urban or rural. For this majority, walking was the only way to travel. The average farmer or shopkeeper did not have a saddle horse, and the title *chevalier* remained a descriptive term, inasmuch as horsemanship was still largely a noble prerogative. Pierre Deyon mentions that the great merchants of Amiens, who were compelled to make commercial voyages to neighboring provinces, did use saddle horses, but had no carriages.[40] For a winegrower a mule and a cart were marks of distinction, and a *laboureur*'s teams and wagons made him a man to be reckoned with in the farm country.

For the bourgeois who possessed sufficient means and was unwilling or unable to use his feet, many types of conveyances were available. The foremost of these was the sedan chair, or *chaise à porteurs*, which was fairly economical and carried people of such diverse rank as the actor Louis Béjart (who had a leg injury)[41] and the more old-fashioned members of court society. Charles Perrault owned a sedan chair valued at only 50 livres, as opposed to 550 livres for his small carriage.[42] Thus, almost any merchant with a couple of strong lackeys could probably afford a chair. Even if this modest investment was too much, he could always hire a chair borne by professional carriers. A cheaper and less appealing vehicle was to be found in the *vinaigrette*, a sort of Parisian rickshaw.

The most sophisticated and expensive way to travel was by the carriage, which underwent rapid technological evolution in the course of the century. French and English coachmakers led the world in their increasingly refined craft, fitting their creations with rear suspension and pivoting front axles, for greater comfort and maneuverability. Soon steel springs and glass windows were added; the body of the carriage was elegantly shaped and adorned with rich fabrics, painted decorations, and metal ornaments.[43] The carriage became an indispensable part of a gallant aristocrat's possessions, since it was necessary for the carrousels, excursions, and ritualized parades that took place in the Cours la Reine and other fashionable gathering-places. The king's fondness for the vehicle did much to encourage this wave of fashion. Elaborate forms of coaching etiquette and rules on ornamentation became so complex as to vex even princes of the blood. To ride in the king's coaches, one had to prove one's noble ancestry back to the fourteenth century. As La Bruyère noted, carriages were so exclusive that ladies would immediately become excited when one stopped at their door, for it meant the visit of a high aristocrat or a distinguished magistrate.[44]

It is not surprising that increasing expenses caused carriages to remain a luxury item: in 1658, when Molière returned to the Parisian stage, there were only about 300 of them in the city.[45] Most carriages needed four to six horses, with the exception of the lighter *cabriolet*, which took only two. Besides the large quantities of fodder consumed by these animals, there was the necessity of hiring a coachman at about 400 livres a year, plus room and board; a lady's *écuyer* might cost even more because of his more extensive duties. Additional money had to be spent on a stable and storage rooms for feed and tack, and for the rental of a large house with porte cochère, as well as for incidental expenses like shoeing. In all, Audiger estimates the median expenses for a nobleman's stable and carriages to be over 10,000 livres per year.[46]

Rental carriages catered to city dwellers who needed a vehicle only for limited lengths of time, and could be rented yearly for about 2,400 livres. The Englishman Lister notes that they were numerous enough to make business difficult for hired cabs.[47] The first omnibuses, the *carosses à cinq sous*, were fashionable for a while, especially after the king took several rides in them, but at that price they proved uneconomical. More successful were the stage coaches linking Paris to the provinces; these vehicles were too crude and uncomfortable to be used by ceremonious noblemen, but they provided an essential service by facilitating long-distance travel for people of the middle social ranks.

LANGUAGE

In Molière's day, linguistic indicators offered much vital information to the theater-going public. Because of limited mobility and poor communications, local dialects flourished everywhere in France, a fact that allowed the average man to be geographically identified by his speech. Molière took advantage of Parisians' delight with geolinguistic mimicry in such plays as *Monsieur de Pourceaugnac*, where he introduced characters who masqueraded as Picards and Gascons, complete with their provincial patois.

An equally important dimension is sociolinguistics, for it was likewise possible to differentiate between many social levels on the basis of a person's language. Peasants, townspeople, and aristocrats had particular vocabularies suited to their needs and livelihoods. This fragmentation was superimposed on the jigsaw puzzle of regional dialects: stevedores on the Paris waterfront, lawyers in the Palais, and courtiers in the Louvre all had their own idioms, thriving within a few hundred yards of each other. Part of the reason for this may be the strong professional ties of urban guilds and *métiers*, which protected manufacturing and trade secrets with a formidable armor of shibboleths and obscure cant. The most prominent jargons in Molière's theater are those of the "liberal professions" — doctors, lawyers, and scholars. These groups were set apart by their uniforms and by their association with the taboo areas of death, courts, and schools, which were shrouded in the mysteries of Latin. This fact suggests that Molière may have been tapping an unseen but powerful reservoir of primitive, superstitious resentment in his culture.

Obviously, it would be impossible to reproduce, in the narrow confines of this study, a comprehensive guide to sociolinguistics in Molière's France. Seventeenth-century dictionaries, especially Furetière's, and reference works, such as Livet's lexicon and Francis Bar's study on the burlesque genre, furnish a wealth of information on this topic.[48] For our purposes, it must suffice to call attention to specific instances of linguistic identification in the context of individual plays.

Mention must be made here, however, of one aspect of language that affects almost every play — the use of titles and forms of address to signal status. Curiously enough, these forms of address are least revealing among the nobility, for the ubiquitous appellatives, Monsieur and Madame, were used everywhere in aristocratic surroundings. After all, there existed a parity of quality for all those born into the hereditary nobility, regardless of whatever fiefs they might possess. A vicomte, a marquis, and a landless chevalier were entitled to equal respect. This becomes clear when one considers that in the same family three sons might have very different titles but identical birth.

There were a few significant exceptions to the homogeneity of the nobility, with respect to title. Certain of them, such as baron, had fallen into disuse and disregard, mainly through the whims of fashion and the prejudice against *hobereaux*.[49] Other titles (for instances, écuyer and marquis) were frequently usurped by commoners. The term *gentilhomme* was reserved for a person of the highest degree of nobility and thus withheld from *anoblis* and their sons. De facto authority was conferred upon dukes by their vast wealth and power (they had the prerogative of being addressed as Monseigneur) and upon the *maréchaux de France* by virtue of their service to their king as delegates in civil and military crises.

It is among the socially mobile bourgeoisie that one finds a true obsession with title. *Bourgeois de Paris* was in itself not only a description but also a legal distinction that conferred advantages in taxation and other areas, especially in the ownership of farmland in the Parisian Basin. Merchants were almost always explicit in their claim to this title, so prestigious that some officers and recently ennobled individuals continued to use it.[50] Marcel Couturier, in his socioeconomic study of Châteaudun, traces the evolution of the term *bourgeois* through the seventeenth century, from its beginnings as a designation of those who participate in municipal government, to a stage where it meant someone free of manual labor, often the owner of a *seigneurie*, until it eventually implied status as a *rentier*, a possessor of ennobling office, or someone retired from commerce and "living nobly."[51]

The bourgeois also laid claim to other titles in order to distinguish themselves as landowners or officeholders. Meyer notes the inclination of the leading families of Rennes to intermarry and to call each other "sire" or "noble homme," and Frondeville finds that almost all of the *conseillers* in Normandy designate themselves as "sieur" (*seigneur*) of a certain country estate, displaying coats of arms to support their noble ambitions.[52] Furthermore, Roland Mousnier discovered that bourgeois who were usurping the title of *écuyer* often called each other "sieur" in an attempt to sway public opinion.[53] The same people might try to abandon their family name: first they would append the name of a property, transforming Corneille into Corneille de l'Isle, then eventually dropping the former in order to leave a noble-sounding name beginning with the *particule*.

Yet, there were also methods of reminding a bourgeois of his low birth. The title Monsieur, usually used alone to address an aristocrat, when coupled with the family name of a *roturier*, implies not only identification of his "vile" origin, but also a personal degradation.[54] It is as though the luster of the polite form of address emphasizes the unworthiness of the commoner's lineage and his failure to achieve social acceptance.

Having discussed the most common types of status indicators present in Molière's comedies, we will turn to a practical analysis of their appearance in the texts. It will prove most useful, in dealing with such a variety of works, to begin with the simplest uses of indicators and to proceed to the more complex questions. Thus, before approaching the major plays, which portray profound challenges to the basic norms of ancien régime society, attention will be given to an unjustly neglected area: the collection of early works, short farces, and plays with foreign settings, which complete the corpus of Molière's theater and on which the dramatist spent much of his career.

1. To appreciate the quality of Molière's exposition, one need only compare the smooth unfolding of his comedies to the turgid beginnings of plays by such contemporaries as Poisson and Chevalier. On the comic unity of the multiple Sganarelle characters, see Jean-Michel Pelous, "Les Métamorphoses de Sganarelle: la permanence d'un type comique."

2. Jean de la Bruyère, *Caractères*, pp. 202–5.

3. René Sedillot and Franz Pick, *All the Monies of the World*, pp. 307–11; H. Hoffman, *Les Monnaies royales en France depuis Hugues Capet jusqu'à Louis XVI*, pp. 168–91; A. Blanchet and A. Dieudonné, *Manuel de numismatique française*, 2:99, 350–62.

4. An example of an error in calculation is to be found in Léon Lejealle's edition of *L'Avare* in the Nouveaux Classiques Larousse series (Paris: Larousse, 1965). On page 32 Lejealle confuses "dix mille écus en or" (1. 4) with "dix mille écus d'or" and thus inflates a sum of about 30,000 livres to 100,000.

5. The anxiety over the instability of the lesser currency is evident in the riots in the Rouergue in 1643 caused by a reduction of the value of the "double" to one denier. See

Monique Degarne, "Etudes sur les soulèvements provinciaux en France avant la Fronde: la révolte du Rouergue en 1643."

6. Louis Gueneau, *Les Conditions de la vie à Nevers (denrées, logements, salaires) à la fin de l'Ancien Régime*, pp. 93–98. See also Georges Mongrédien, *La Vie quotidienne sous Louis XIV*, p. 134. For a broad perspective of the development of money in the theater, see Leo Forkey, *The Role of Money in French Comedy during the Reign of Louis XIV.*

7. Jean-Pierre Labatut, "Situation sociale du quartier du Marais pendant la Fronde parlementaire (1648–1649)."

8. Roland Mousnier, *Paris au XVIIᵉ siècle*, pp. 237–69; Pierre Deyon, *Amiens*, pp. 122–25, 258–60.

9. Wilma Deierkauf-Holsboer, "La Famille de la mère de Molière."

10. Jean-Pierre Labatut, "Aspects de la fortune de Bullion."

11. François Bluche, "L'Origine sociale des secrétaires d'état de Louis XIV."

12. Gaston Roupnel, *La Ville et la campagne au XVIIᵉ siècle*, pp. 124–28; V. L. Tapié, "Less Officiers seigneuriaux dans la société provinciale du XVIIᵉ siècle."

13. Pierre Goubert, "Les Officiers royaux des Présidiaux, Baillages, et Elections dans la société française au XVIIᵉ siècle"; M. Foisil, "Les Biens d'un receveur-général des finances à Paris."

14. Parlement offices are treated most thoroughly in Roland Mousnier's *La Vénalité des offices* and François Bluche's *Les Magistrats au Parlement de Paris au XVIIIᵉ siècle (1715–1771)*, although these works bracket the lifetime of Molière. For more information on the prices of these positions, see Franklin Ford, *Robe and Sword: The Regrouping of the French Aristocracy after Louis XIV*, p. 147, and J. B. Voisin de la Noiraye, *Mémoire sur la généralité de Rouen (1665)*, pp. 80–85. On the other sovereign courts, consult François Bluche, *Les Magistrats de la cour des monnaies de Paris au XVIIIᵉ siècle (1715–1790)* and *Les Magistrats du Grand Conseil au XVIIIᵉ siècle (1690–1791)*, pp. 14–27 and 22–40 respectively.

15. Mousnier, *La Vénalité des offices*, p. 539.

16. Roland Mousnier, *Etat et société en France au XVIIᵉ et XVIIIᵉ siècles*, vol. I, *Le Gouvernement du pays*, p. 24.

17. Roland Mousnier, "Recherches sur les syndicats d'officiers pendant la Fronde: Trésoriers généraux de France et élus dans la révolution."

18. Charles Carrière, *Négociants marseillais au XVIIIᵉ siècle*, 1:213.

19. Jan DeVries, *The Economy of Europe in an Age of Crisis, 1600–1750*, p. 18.

20. M. L. Fracard, *Philippe de Montaut-Bénac, duc de Noailles et Maréchal de France (1619–1684)*, p. 52.

21. For an illustration of a somewhat ornate medical gown trimmed with fur, see Max Barsis, *The Common Man through the Ages*, p. 93.

22. Charles Sorel's hero, Francion, discovers the unfortunate consequences of his failure to recognize and respect these robes when he is beaten by a *greffier*. See the *Histoire comique de Francion*, in *Romanciers du XVIIe siècle*, p. 216.

23. Useful works on seventeenth-century clothing include: Camille Piton, *Le Costume civil en France du XVIIe au XIXe siècle*; Georges G. Toudouze, *Le Costume français*; and for neckwear, Doriece Colle, *Collars, Stocks, Cravats: 1655–1900*. Mongrédien, *La Vie quotidienne sous Louis XIV*, contains a good presentation of men's clothing on pages 67–83. A very useful text on fashions in the decades prior to Louis XIV's reign is Louise Godard de Donville, *Signification de la mode sous Louis XIII*.

24. Interesting illustrations are found in Jurg Stockar, *Kultur und Kleidung der Barockzeit*, pp. 36–102.

25. *Correspondence entre Boileau-Despréaux et Brossette*, pp. 565–66.

26. Mongrédien, *La Vie quotidienne sous Louis XIV*, p. 80.

27. See for instance the illustrations provided by John Laurence Carr in *Life in France under Louis XIV*, pp. 119–44.

28. Mongrédien, *La Vie quotidienne sous Louis XIV*, pp. 70–77.

29. Ibid., p. 67. Regarding the women's hairstyles attacked by the king, see Carr, *Life in France*, p. 62.

30. Audiger, *La Maison réglée et l'art de diriger la maison*, pp. 12–14. For the situation of the Bordeaux *président* mentioned below, see Ford, *Robe and Sword*, p. 157. Mongrédien's *La Vie quotidienne sous Louis XIV* presents useful information on servants' conditions on pages 56–60, 95, 209, and 222. In the light of such factual information on servants, it is curious to note that they have been analyzed mainly as stock comic figures in Marcel Gutwirth, "Le Comique du serviteur chez Molière"; L. Leon Bernard, "Molière and the Historian of French Society"; and in Jean Emelina's study, *Les Valets et les servantes dans le théâtre de Molière*. Emelina's more recent work, *Les Valets et les servantes dans le théâtre comique en France de 1610 à 1700*, gives greater weight to the social significance of this group, as do Millie Gerard Davis, "Masters and Servants in the Plays of Molière," in *Molière: Stage and Study; Essays in Honour of W. G. Moore*, ed. W. D. Howarth and Merlin Thomas, and J. Van Eerde, "The Historicity of the Valet Role in French Comedy during the Reign of Louis XIV."

31. Carr, *Life in France*, p. 48.

32. Ibid., p. 59.

33. Martin D. Lister, *A Voyage to Paris in the Year 1698*, p. 6. Conditions in the capital are discussed in Mousnier, *Paris*, pp. 18–32. François Lebrun mentions about 4,000 houses for 30,000 inhabitants to Angers in his *Histoire d'Angers*; and Charles Carrière estimates 9,000 houses for a population of 75,000 in Marseille in *Négociants marseillais*, 1:198, which shows that the provincial centers were also crowded.

34. Madeleine Jurgens and Elizabeth Maxfield-Miller, *Cent ans de recherches sur Molière*, pp. 170–71, 431, and 438.

35. Ibid., pp. 136–39.

36. For an excellent discussion of land tenure under the French monarchy, see Pierre Goubert, *L'Ancien Régime*, 1: 73–96. Also useful are Jean Imbert, *Histoire économique (des origines à 1789)*, pp. 315–19, and René Baehrel, *Une Croissance: la Basse Provence rurale (fin du XVIe siècle–1789)*, pp. 379–400.

37. Goubert, *L'Ancien Régime*, 1:71, 108, and Henri Drouot, *Mayenne et la Bourgogne: étude sur la Ligue (1587–1596)*, 1:37.

38. Jurgens and Maxfield-Miller, *Cent ans*, pp. 174 and 650.

39. Goubert, *L'Ancien Régime*, 1:110 and 129.

40. Deyon, *Amiens*, p. 294.

41. Jurgens and Maxfield-Miller, *Cent ans*, p. 188.

42. Jacques Barchilon, "Charles Perrault à travers les documents du minutier central des Archives Nationales—l'inventaire de ses meubles en 1672."

43. See Laszlo Tarr, *The History of the Carriage*, pp. 221–22, and Jacques Damase, *Carriages*, pp. 30–42.

44. La Bruyère, *Caractères*, ed. R. Garapon, p. 216.

45. Tarr, *The History of the Carriage*, p. 236.

46. Audiger, *La Maison réglée*, p. 9.

47. Lister, *A Voyage to Paris*, p. 13.

48. Antoine Furetière, *Dictionnaire universel*; Charles L. Livet, *Lexique de la langue de Molière comparée à celle des écrivains de son temps*; Francis Bar, *Le Genre burlesque en France au XVIIe siècle*.

49. Denis Godefroy, *Abbrégé des trois états du clergé, de la noblesse et du tiers état*, 2:47–48. See also pages 70 and 75 regarding the use of the terms *gentilhomme*, *seigneur*, and *sieur*, as discussed below.

50. Marc Venard, *Bourgeois et paysans au XVIIe siècle*, p. 31, and Mousnier, *Paris*, p. 251.

51. Marcel Couturier, *Recherches sur les structures sociales de Châteaudun 1525–1789*, pp. 215–23, and also Deyon, *Amiens*, p. 309.

52. Jean Meyer, *Histoire de Rennes*, p. 173, and Odette et Henri de Frondeville, *Les Conseillers au parlement de Normandie de 1641 à 1715*, vol. 4.

53. Mousnier, *La Vénalité des offices*, p. 537.

54. Charles Sorel, "Les Lois de la galanterie," p. 212.

Exotic costuming in the Italian plays: the Brissart and Sauvé engraving of *Le Sicilien*, showing Hali's oriental clothing. Originally appeared in the 1682 Paris edition, republished in 1697. Reproduced by permission of the Houghton Library, Harvard University.

CHAPTER TWO

FUNDAMENTAL SOCIAL STRUCTURES IN MOLIERE'S THEATER

Before he created the series of intricate comedies of manners beginning with *L'Ecole des femmes*, Molière had already experimented with status indicators and explored simple hierarchical structures in his farces and in two full-length intrigue comedies, *L'Etourdi* and *Dépit amoureux*. His subsequent perfection of fully-developed networks of interaction in masterpieces from *Le Tartuffe* to *Le Malade imaginaire* did not prevent him from continuing to write a variety of short comedies, *comédie-ballets*, mythological plays, and pastorals, in which the use of social indicators remains limited and the organization relatively uncomplicated. A preliminary understanding of these simple structures is essential to the study of their elaborate counterparts.[1]

Since all of Molière's works are set either in France or in three Mediterranean lands, they can be easily grouped according to the societies they depict. Though largely fictive, the non-French societies nevertheless reflect an existing set of mental values assigned to a geographic area. Moreover, plays with common settings exhibit quantitative and qualitative similarities in status indicators and tend to share predominant *conditions* and interpersonal concerns. A single exception to this pattern is *Dom Juan*, which supposedly unfolds in Sicily but contains numerous contradictory elements that are obviously French; its highly detailed relationships, focused on the problematics of examplarity and unworthiness, call attention to the gulf between it and other plays set beyond the boundaries of French civilization.

The three distinctly different Mediterranean settings include southern Italy for *Les Fourberies de Scapin*, *Le Sicilien*, and *L'Etourdi*; classical Greece for *Psyché*, *Les Amants magnifiques*, *La Princesse d'Elide*, *Amphitryon*, and *Mélicerte*; Spain for *Dom Garcie de Navarre*.[2] We will turn our attention first to the works set in Italy, a land that was for Molière a perpetual fountain of influence and from which he received plots like Beltrame's *L'Inavvertito*, stage techniques of the *comédie italienne*, and two brilliant (albeit temporary) collaborators, the stage designer Vigarani and the operatic composer Lulli.

THE ITALIAN PLAYS

The foreign setting in Molière's Italian plays serves to establish an atmosphere of exoticism, where the group boundaries of seventeenth-century France cease to apply. Sometimes this is expressed in extravagant costumes, as is illustrated in the Brissart and Sauvé engraving of *Le Sicilien*, where Hali, Adraste's zany Levantine valet, is shown wearing a strange costume topped with a conical hat.[3] Hali refers to himself as an "esclave" in his first speech (scene 1), and the presence of slavery introduces an entirely new register of class relations. Isidore is described as "une esclave que l'on a affranchie, et dont on veut faire sa femme" (scene 6), but who is still in the power of Dom Pèdre. Four more slaves appear in the eighth scene to perform the Turkish serenade. Finally, there is Climène, the comely slave-girl who, by posing as Adraste's veiled bride and then changing clothes with Isidore, helps the lovers to succeed in their ultimate ruse.

As for the masters, their status as exotic "cavaliers" sometimes fails to correspond to any familiar condition in the French hierarchy. The rank of the young lover, Adraste, is not in question, for he is repeatedly described as a "gentilhomme français" (scene 10). Yet, Dom Pèdre, Isidore's former owner, is an ambiguous case. His title seems to suggest that he is a nobleman, but Adraste addresses him as "Seigneur" rather than as "Monsieur." Dom Pèdre appears to have a great number of servants, since, to chase away some serenaders, he calls: "Francisque, Dominique, Simon, Martin, Pierre, Thomas, Georges, Charles, Barthélemy" (scene 4). He also has a veritable arsenal of weapons. However, when Hali, disguised as Dom Gilles d'Avalos, asks whether it is better to fight a duel with his enemy or to have him assassinated, Dom Pèdre responds immediately, "Assassiner, c'est le plus court chemin" (scene 12), which puts his honor in question. In fact, the status of Italian nobility poses a major problem; there was no clear line of demarcation between aristocrat and bourgeois in Italy, where the merchant-prince was a long-established tradition. Thus, we cannot accuse Dom Pèdre of committing a breach of nobility either in his disdain for the duello or in his appeal to a senator to set the law on Adraste (scenes 18–19).

In *Les Fourberies de Scapin*, which is set in Naples, we once again find a strong exotic element, centered around the character of Zerbinette, a Gypsy slave-girl (3. 3). Scapin himself takes advantage of the exotic atmosphere to spin his tale of the Turkish galley that carries off Géronte's son (2. 7). This valet does not consider himself a professional servant, but a "fourbe" who has already had trouble with the law (1. 2). His boldness contrasts sharply with the poltroonery of Sylvestre, who resembles the traditional slave and Hali[4] and always has before him the vision of "un nuage de coups de bâton qui crèvera sur mes épaules" (1. 1).

Another similarity between *Le Sicilien* and *Les Fourberies* is the ambiguous status of the leading families. Argante and Géronte appear to be bourgeois: they have gone off together on "un voyage qui regarde certain commerce où leurs intérêts sont mêlés" (1. 2). Both carry substantial sums of money: Argante has 200 pistoles (2,000 livres) in his purse (2. 6), and Géronte has just received 500 écus in gold (1,500 livres [2. 7]). Both reveal a typical bourgeois attitude of reverence toward the law: the former insists on suing a swashbuckling *bretteur* (2. 5), and the latter wants to send the police across the high seas to bring back his "kidnapped" son (2. 7). The famous sack scene ridicules Géronte's faith in a business agreement: he suffers two beatings although he has hired Scapin to protect him in exchange for some old clothes (3. 2). Yet, the sword carried by Géronte's son, Léandre (1. 3), would be strictly a noble prerogative in the French hierarchy.

The same exotic elements abound in *L'Etourdi*, a comedy dominated by the schemes of Mascarille. Time and again the wily valet demonstrates his ability to dupe powerful merchants, only to see his efforts wasted by his dim-witted master, Lélie: emperor of scoundrels, he is doomed to serve a dunce. Set in the colorful port of Messina, this play has its slave-girl, Célie (1. 3. 91), who is loved by Lélie and his rival Léandre, as well as by the Egyptian mercenary, Andrès (5. 2. 1709–38).

The role of money is more developed than in the other Italian plays, and the large sums mentioned give some indication of the socioeconomic affiliations of the leading families.[5] Trufaldin, alias Zanobio Ruberti, is a merchant who deals in slaves as collateral, and Anselme has loaned out as much as 2,000 francs (1. 2. 95 and 1. 5. 213–14). Lélie's father, Pandolphe, would seem to belong to the same category of merchants, for he possesses a large number of promissory and credit notes, which Lélie briefly "inherits" when he claims his father has died (2. 2. 524). Yet, like the other Italian families, Pandolphe's shows some noble characteristics and his son wears a sword (3. 6. 1208). The fact that the slave girl must be bought, rather than simply seduced, necessitates much manipulation of money. Lélie's wily valet, Mascarille, tries to steal Anselme's purse while regaling him with stories of how a certain lady loves him (1. 5. 235–36). Anselme recovers his money by duping Lélie with the lie that some of the coins given him were counterfeit (2. 5. 639–49). Mascarille later intends to neutralize the threat of Andrés's carrying off Célie by bribing corrupt police officials to detain the "Egyptian" a while (4. 7. 1669–74). Both foreign money (*ducats*) and French currency (écus, francs) are mentioned, a technique that mixes the exotic with the familiar in the economic domain.

A similar social tension is found in the beginning of these three Italian plays: the young man wishes to marry below his station with a slave-girl (misalliance) and employs all sorts of ruses to overcome the twin obstacles of raising the purchase price and overcoming parental censure. In *L'Etourdi* and *Les Fourberies de Scapin* this "blondin" is the son of merchant aristocrats, and in *Le Sicilien* he is a foreign nobleman. In the former two plays, the wily valet dominates his master, whereas in the latter the master's boldness and delicacy contrast with his servant's cowardice. The practice of a man marrying a woman from an inferior social group (*hypergamie des femmes*, as Mousnier calls it)[6] was not uncommon in seventeenth-century France, provided the girl brought with her a sufficient dowry. In these plays, on the other hand, we seem to find an example of extreme and perhaps unacceptable hypergamy, since the women are all penniless slaves. Sometimes this state of slavery allows Molière to subject the heroine to both the authority of a father and the desires of a potential husband, the two roles being combined in Dom Pèdre. *Le Sicilien* is also an example of how social ambiguity can permit the satire of bourgeois vices (avarice) and aristocratic shortcomings (breach of honor) in the same character.

But the theme of hypergamy is not sustained in the dénouements of these plays. Adraste cuts short his conflict with Dom Pèdre by obtaining approval to marry Isidore through the ruse of disguise. The social disarmament of Dom Pèdre is manifested in the last scene of the play, where the senator (symbol of the laws of society) refuses to interest himself in Dom Pèdre's complaints. In *Les Fourberies de Scapin* and *L'Etourdi*, hypergamy is obviated when, in the recognition scenes, the slave girls are elevated into the merchant aristocracy, thus making the weddings perfectly proper. At any rate, the quest of the sons for money to marry their chosen brides is not very different from the problem of young men in the French plays, who try to pry *dots* and *douaires* away from tightfisted fathers. The social parallels exist, but the structures of these Mediterranean plays remain undeveloped. Ambiguity of social affiliations, use of money as a plot accessory rather than as a full-fledged device of classification, and the short-circuiting of potential social conflicts by ruse and chance typify the romanesque atmosphere of the Italian plays.

THE GREEK PLAYS

The Greek plays present an entirely different social orientation. The bourgeois element is entirely absent and the servant class is reduced to a single major character, usually a clown-servant characterized by ineptitude and cowardice. Indeed, since money and intrigue disappear in these plays, so does the scheming valet of the Italian plays. The atmosphere of the Greek pieces is refined and pastoral; they have been purged of most of the physical activity and concrete, colloquial speech associated with the *roturiers*.

Without going into detail over the genesis of the Greek plays, we must note that, except perhaps for *Amphitryon*, all were written expressly for the court. The haste with which Molière composed most of them is shown by the fact that several are unfinished: he completed only two acts of *Mélicerte*, one act plus a few scenes of *Psyché*, and rendered but one full act of *La Princesse d'Elide* into verse. The extent of this interested patronage is shown by the fact that Molière gives Louis XIV credit for "inventing" the plot of *Les Amants magnifiques*.[7]

Considering the noble audience for which the Greek plays were intended, one is not surprised that the majority of the characters belong to the high nobility. Amphitryon and Alcmène are aristocrats; Jupiter and Mercury are immortals. At the court of Elis, we find princes from the houses of Messina, Pylos, and Ithaca. The "amants magnifiques," Iphicrate and Timoclès, are visiting princes who are wooing the Princess of Thessaly, and Sostrate is a general in the armies of that state. Psyché's father is a king, and her two earthly suitors, Cléomène and Agénor, are princes — not to speak of her other admirer, the god of love. Even the young Thessalian shepherds of *Mélicerte* have elements of nobility, for we know that Mopse and Lycarsis are not the real parents of Mélicerte and Myrtil. The favorite pastimes of these illustrious figures are hunting, warfare, pastoral entertainments, and solemn festivals, like the Pythian Games.[8]

The thematics of love, particularly a refined and somewhat precious variation on the "dépit amoureux," assume primary importance in the Greek plays. Alcmène's dialogues with Jupiter and with her spouse, Myrtil's meeting with Mélicerte, Amour's pursuit of Psyché, Eriphile's conversations with Sostrate, and Euryale's verbal sparring with the Princesse d'Elide all belong to this category. The aristocratic characters are extremely concerned with preserving their honor and reputation, fulfilling their duties, and otherwise retaining their "noble" traits in the face of the surrender that Love demands. This exchange is typical of such confrontations:

Mélicerte

Ah! Myrtil, prenez garde à ce qu'ici vous faites:
N'allez point présenter un espoir à mon coeur,
Qu'il recevrait peut-être avec trop de douceur,
Et qui, tombant après comme un éclair qui passe,
Me rendrait plus cruel le coup de ma disgrâce.

Myrtil

Quoi? faut-il des serments appeler le secours,
Lorsque l'on vous promet de vous aimer toujours?

[*Mélicerte*, 2. 3. 452–58]

With a few significant exceptions, the vocabulary of these plays is purged of any words that might be associated with the "gross" world of the common people. The key terms are honor, courage, duty, merit, homage, and esteem. The following passage from a monologue, spoken by the Princesse d'Elide as she reflects on reluctance to fall in love, will serve as an illustration:

De quelle émotion inconnue sens-je mon coeur atteint, et quelle inquiétude secrète est venue troubler tout d'un coup la tranquillité de mon âme? Ne serait-ce point aussi ce qu'on vient de me dire! et, sans en rien savoir, n'aimerais-je point ce jeune prince? Ah! si cela était, je serais personne à me désespérer; mais il est impossible que cela soit, et je vois bien que je ne puis pas l'aimer. Quoi? je serais capable de cette lâcheté! J'ai vu toute la terre à mes pieds avec la plus grande insensibilité du monde; les respects, les hommages et les soumissions n'ont jamais pu toucher mon âme, et la fierté et le dédain en auraient triomphé! J'ai méprisé tous ceux qui m'ont aimée, et j'aimerais le seul qui me méprise! [*La Princesse d'Elide*, 4. 6]

Social conflict does not play an important role in the ideal courts of the Greek plays: commoners like Moron are only tolerated at the pleasure of the aristocrats. The nobles strive to outdo each other in appearing more purely aristocratic, honorable, and refined. One might object that Sostrate, the general in *Les Amants magnifiques*, is not precisely the equal of his rivals, Iphicrate and Timoclès, who are princes. It is not, however, a conflict of groups, but at best a dispute of rank within the same group. An important social precept held that, despite different degrees of power attached to different fiefs, all nobles were of equally honorable birth. Thus, all three men are addressed with identical respect by their inferiors and enjoy the same honors from fellow princes. Clitidas makes this explicit when he tells Sostrate:

> Vous savez que votre présence ne gâte jamais rien, et que vous n'êtes point de trop, en quelque lieu que vous soyez. Votre visage est bien venu partout, et il n'a garde d'être de ces visages disgrâciés qui ne sont jamais bien reçus des regards souverains. Vous êtes également bien auprès des deux princesses; et la mère et la fille vous font assez connaître l'estime qu'elles font de vous. [1. 1]

In addition, Sostrate is universally known as a man of valor, who has conquered Brennus and the Gauls. This disproportionate merit contrasts with the rather scurrilous behavior of the two princes (4. 3) who attempt to dupe the young princess by bribing an astrologer to arrange a convenient miracle in favor of their causes. If this conduct falls short of *dérogeance de noblesse*, it nevertheless tends to diminish their status, for their behavior does not conform rigorously to the code of honor. The gap is further reduced when Sostrate bravely saves Aristione from a wild boar (5. 1). Yet, the most important factor in legitimizing Sostrate's marriage to Eriphile is the presence of a higher authority, for the princess and her mother naïvely believe that Venus has decreed Eriphile should marry the man who saves her life. The code of absolutism that prevailed in the France of Louis XIV implied that any matter might be decided by appeal to a transcendent power, which was epitomized by the divine king, the ultimate commander who might elevate the children of his mistress or his ministers or disgrace Fouquet or Catinat. Thus, as we shall see again in *Tartuffe* and in *Dom Juan*, the *deus ex machina* had a special relevance to Molière's audience.

The noble society of the Greek plays is not only homogeneous; it is stifling and narrow-minded—a perfect example of social closure in action. Comic opportunities do not flourish in such an environment. Realizing this, Molière sought to use special generic terms to classify these special works. *La Princesse d'Elide* is called a "comédie galante," *Mélicerte* is a "comédie pastorale héroïque," *Psyché* a "tragi-comédie." Nevertheless, this author who had no difficulty creating *galant* roles for his troupe could not bring himself to play a noncomic role. In each play he portrayed a clown-valet, the only representative of the nonaristocratic world: Moron, Clitidas, Lycarsis, Sosie, Zéphyre.[9] Far from initiating class conflicts, these clown-valets are obsequious and faithful. Like Zéphyre, they admire authority and love to follow and to be protected: "En tout vous êtes un grand maître: / C'est ici que je le connois" (*Psyché*, 3. 1. 946–47).

The valet-clowns are in a unique social position. Since there is no intrigue of the type one finds in the Italian plays, no exchange of money, no possibility for a wily servant to assert his superiority to a foolish master, the mainstay of traditional comic potential is missing. Perhaps the only source left to Molière is to exploit the stereotypical cowardice of the servant.[10] Not only does he welcome the protection of the nobles, but he is also afraid to fend for himself. Consider Clitidas's conduct when a boar attacks Aristione:

> Le sanglier, mal moriginé, s'est impertinemment détourné contre nous; nous étions là deux ou trois misérables qui avons pâli de frayeur; chacun gagnait son arbre, et la Princesse sans défense

demeurait exposée à la furie de la bête, lorsque Sostrate a paru, comme si les Dieux l'eussent envoyé. [*Les Amants magnifiques*, 5. 1]

Moron, the fool in *La Princesse d'Elide*, reveals his poltroon's spirit in the first lines he speaks: "Au secours! sauvez-moi de la bête cruelle." (1. 2. 162) He reveals that he has dropped his arms and fled, leaving a woman to fight the boar that was chasing him. Later, when he addresses a menacing bear as he would a duke, he explicitly connects his cowardice to his conception of his own inferiority:

Ah! Monsieur l'ours, je suis votre serviteur de tout mon coeur. De grâce, épargnez-moi. Je vous assure que je ne vaux rien du tout à manger, je n'ai que la peau et les os, et je vois de certaines gens là-bas qui seraient bien mieux votre affaire. . . . Monseigneur, tout doux, s'il vous plaît. . . . Ah! Monseigneur, que Votre Altesse est jolie et bien faite! [Deuxième Intermède, scene 2]

The noblity of the court, watching the Greek plays, could only be pleased to see the contrast between the fright of the *roturiers* and the quintessential courage of their own estate. By dividing personality characteristics into two distinct groups and giving the nobility only the positive ones, Molière drew upon a social model that flattered the vanity of his prospective audience.

The remaining foreign play, *Dom Garcie de Navarre*, has always been considered a curious anomaly. The only outstanding failure among Molière's works, it is also one of the few plays where Molière himself played the role of a noble. Indeed, all the characters in *Dom Garcie de Navarre* belong to the aristocracy. Even the confidants, Dom Alvar and Dom Lope, possess noble titles. The play lacks even the limited *roturier* presence (and the humor) that the valet-clown furnishes in the Greek plays.

Dom Garcie is an ambiguous character, always treading the

thin line between pathos and bathos. Molière does not seem to
have intended for the jealous prince to be totally ridiculous,
since he enjoys the esteem of the wise and courtly Done Elvire
(1. 1. 11–15). Yet, this fickle character changes his mood much
too quickly after seeing two apparently incriminating letters
(1. 3. 331–32 and 2. 4. 476–515), after finding his beloved
with Dom Sylve (3. 3. 996–69), and after observing her in the
arms of a "man," who is really Done Ignès in disguise (4. 7.
1238–41). Such conduct can only lead us to lower our opinion of
the prince and to ask ourselves exactly what it is that Elvire finds
in him to admire. His alternate outbursts of temper and beg-
ging for forgiveness conflict certainly with the spirit, if not the
letter, of the code of noble behavior.

Dom Garcie is juxtaposed to two other unworthy noblemen:
the usurping tyrant Mauregat, who had brutally imprisoned
Done Elvire, and Dom Lope, who chooses to play the role of evil
parasite to Dom Garcie because of unrequited love for Elise,
Elvire's confidante. Mauregat stands at one end of the spectrum, for he commits the supreme crime of self-pride by acts of
lèse-majesté against the royal family. On the contrary, Dom
Lope has such a low opinion of his own *gloire* that he devotes his
life to bad service of his liege lord, as he deliberately thwarts
Dom Garcie's courtship of the princess and exacerbates his self-
destructive tendencies.

Despite his generous offer of military aid to his beloved
Elvire, Dom Garcie shares some aspects with the negative exem-
pla of both Mauregat and Dom Lope. His passion for Elvire
resembles Mauregat's usurpation in that it is based on an imperative of power that fails to consider the rights of others.[11] In lines
that will be echoed in *Le Misanthrope* (4. 3. 1422–32), he
reveals this egotistical recklessness:

> Oui, tout mon coeur voudrait montrer aux yeux de tous
> Qu'il ne regarde en vous autre chose que vous;

Et cent fois, si je puis le dire sans offense,
Ses voeux se sont armés contre votre naissance;
Leur chaleur indiscrète a d'un destin plus bas
Souhaité le partage à vos divins appas,
Afin que de ce coeur le noble sacrifice
Pût du Ciel envers vous réparer l'injustice,
Et votre sort tenir des mains de mon amour
Tout ce qu'il doit au sang dont vous tenez le jour.

[1. 3. 217–26]

No wonder the princess remarks, "Prince, de vos soupçons la tyrannie est grande" (1. 3. 283). Dom Garcie is similar to Dom Lope in his willingness to assume the worst about others and about himself — a gnawing distrust that fuels his jealousy and impels him to form suicidal thoughts. Vacillating wildly between the extreme self-pride of Mauregat and the cynicism and abjection of Dom Lope, Dom Garcie reveals a schizophrenic pattern of behavior that violates the aristocratic ideals of honor and self-respect.

There has been much debate about the failure of this play. Antoine Adam lists several possibilities: "Il est fort possible que le goût du public ait été blessé surtout par le jeu médiocre d'une troupe mieux faite pour jouer la farce que pour faire valoir les romanesques beautés d'une tragédie galante. . . . On peut imaginer également que Molière déplut parce que les Parisiens avaient pris l'habitude de l'applaudir en Mascarille ou en Sganarelle, et ne le reconnaissaient plus en prince chimérique."[12] There may be another, equally fundamental reason for the setback. The comic element in the predominantly aristocratic Greek plays resided in the discrepancy of class traits favorable to the nobility; the social closure was complete but group interaction and, to a limited extent, interdependence was upheld, for the ridiculous and cowardly servant was admitted as a contrapunctal factor to enhance the virtues of the well-born. In *Dom*

Garcie de Navarre, on the other hand, *hidalgo* society is totally closed off. Dom Garcie's character "infects" the nobility with vices that were reserved for the servants of the ideal Greek world. His jealous flaws, both petty and serious, challenge the essential superiority of his class; but they cannot be erased, for he is a prince and, in all other aspects, a virtuous one!

THE FRENCH PLAYS: THE BOURGEOISIE

In many of the French plays, Molière announces the setting at the very beginning of the text. We learn that *Sganarelle*, *L'Ecole des maris*, *L'Amour médicin*, and *Monsieur de Pourceaugnac* take place in Paris, *L'Impromptu de Versailles* in the "salle de comédie" of the palace, and *La Comtesse d'Escarbagnas* in Angoulême. These indications are supported by numerous textual allusions. In some of the other plays, we must rely entirely on allusions to furnish the setting. At the beginning of *Les Fâcheux*, Eraste recounts his afternoon with a ridiculous marquis, including an invitation to take a ride in the Cours la Reine, one of Paris's most famous meeting places: "Allons au Cours faire voir ma galèche" (scene 1, 76). *La Jalousie du Barbouillé* contains a reference to two villages near Paris: "Qu'il vienne de Villejuif ou d'Aubervilliers, je ne m'en soucie guère" (scene 2). In *Les Précieuses ridicules*, Mascarille tells the porters of his sedan chair to return to take him to the Louvre (scene 7). The fact that *Le Mariage forcé* is set in France is confirmed during Sganarelle's conversation with the philosopher Pancrace (scene 4). Elise, the wise lady of *La Critique de l'Ecole des femmes*, speaks of the Louvre and the place Maubert (scene 1). The "cautère royal," a type of iron used to brand French criminals, is mentioned by Sganarelle in *Le Médecin volant* (scene 14). Jacqueline, the voluptuous nursemaid who attracts Sganarelle in *Le Médecin malgré lui*, speaks in her native dialect of "toutes les rentes de la Biauce" (2. 1). The only play which seems to have no clear indication of the setting is *Dépit amoureux*, which is very similar to an Italian play, *L'Etourdi*, but which we shall treat with the French works, as it offers some pertinent similarities.

The shorter French plays contain, on the whole, many more indicators of status than do the foreign plays. The sums of money, styles of dress, and other details serve not solely as pretexts for the intrigue but also to establish rather precise social identities for many of the characters. However, conflict between groups, which seems at first glance to play an important role in these plays, is in fact almost completely absent. This applies to both types of French plays: the bourgeois group (*La Jalousie du Barbouillé, Le Médecin volant, Dépit amoureux, Les Précieuses ridicules, Sganarelle, L'Ecole des maris, Le Mariage forcé, L'Amour médecin, Le Médecin malgré lui*, and *Monsieur de Pourceaugnac*) and the aristocratic group (*Les Fâcheux, La Critique de l'Ecole des femmes, L'Impromptu de Versailles*, and *La Comtesse d'Escarbagnas*).

To demonstrate the prevailing social closure in the former group, let us consider *Les Précieuses ridicules*. In the first scene, Molière establishes the social identity of two suitors, La Grange and Du Croisy, who address each other with the upwardly mobile bourgeois title "Seigneur,"and are rejected by the pair of *précieuses*. Commoners do not please these affected girls, who, like Mascarille, are guilty of trying to "faire l'homme de condition" (scene 1). They dismiss proposals of marriage as "marchand" (scene 4), but their own efforts to transform themselves into aristocrats by means of cosmetics are doomed to failure. Indeed, the ridiculous profusion of *mouches* they wear in the Brissart and Sauvé engraving clearly labels them as counterfeits.[13] The bourgeois status of La Grange and Du Croisy is confirmed when Gorgibus, described in the *dramatis personae* as a bourgeois, addresses them simply as "vous" (scene 2). He later explains that "je connais leurs familles et leurs biens" (scene 4), and the latter element would not be necessary, we presume, if they were nobles. As for old Gorgibus himself, his speech suggests that he is a businessman or merchant, for he repeatedly refers to the courtship as "affaires" (scenes 2, 16). Critizing the way his daughter and niece use expensive cosmetics, he declares that "quatre valets vivraient tous les jours des pieds de mouton qu'elles emploient" (scene 3), a strictly economic evaluation. His language is that of the people, for he calls the girls "pendardes" and uses such quaint expressions as "se graisser le museau," "balivernes," and "se mettre dans de beaux draps blancs" (scenes 4, 16). Gorgibus is literate and rich enough to have paid for an education for Cathos and Magdelon, with the result that they have been spoiled by the elevated notions of courtly novels such as *Le Grand Cyrus* and *Clélie*.

Clothing plays the central role in the social aspirations of all the "counterfeit" characters. The *précieuses* scorn La Grange and Du Croisy because they do not meet the superficial standard of foppishness that they associate with nobility:

> Venir en visite amoureuse avec une jambe toute unie, un chapeau désarmé de plumes, une tête irrégulière en cheveux, et un habit qui souffre une indigence de rubans! . . . Mon Dieu, quels amants sont-ce là! Quelle frugalité d'adjustement. . . . J'ai remarqué encore que leurs rabats ne sont pas de la bonne faiseuse, et qu'il s'en faut plus d'un grand demi-pied que leurs hauts-de-chausses ne soient assez larges. [Scene 4]

The proper costume according to Cathos would thus be large *canons*, a hat with many plumes, a large wig, lots of ribbons, a large *rabat*, and a *rhingrave*. This is exactly the way Mascarille is dressed when he appears disguised as the marquis, as shown in the Brissart and Sauvé engraving and as described in the text. This exaggerated attire contrasts with the more sober clothing of such gentlemen as Dom Garcie, Adraste of *Le Sicilien*, and Valère of *L'Avare*.[14] It stresses the fact that Mascarille does not show the discretely elegant taste of a true aristocrat, and immediately casts doubt on his so-called nobility. *Les Précieuses ridicules* was, in fact, one of a long series of plays by Molière and his contemporaries that lambasted those whom the eminent social theorist Charles Loyseau called "nos modernes port-épées qui n'ayans point de seigneurie dont ils puissent prendre le nom, ajoutent seulement un de ou du devant celui de leurs pères."[15] Mascarille's vulgar behavior is announced by the manner of his entrance: he makes the porters carry his sedan-chair into the salon of Gorgibus's house (scene 7)! For a marquis to appear in a rented chair is bad enough, but to argue over the fare with the porters and then to back down when threatened with a beating constitutes an appalling breach of propriety. To compound their unworthiness, Mascarille and Jodelet show that they have no knowledge of the essence of nobility, military skill; Jodelet ingenuously recounts, "La première fois que nous nous vîmes, il commandait un régiment de cavalerie sur les galères de Malte" (scene 11). Rather than a commander, Mascarille is more like the convict rowers who propelled those sleek vessels, which were, of course, incapable of carrying horses! Yet, these would-be generals are actually subject to a master's commands, an irony that is underscored when Mascarille, after calling out the names of nine imaginary lackeys, observes, "Je ne pense pas qu'il y ait gentilhomme en France plus mal servi que moi" (scene 11). Under orders from their masters, the valets undertake an imposture so outrageous that they would never have seriously attempted it in a discerning environment. More than anyone else, they are stunned by the success of their deception and by the fact that the giddy girls have even less understanding of *conditions* than they do.

By stressing the fictitious nature of aspiration to nobility on the part of the valets and the *précieuses*, the author makes it clear that there is no group conflict in the play. The only tension is between commoners who acknowledge their station and those who harbor wild notions of belonging to another social level. It is true that the criticism of false nobles applies by extension to those who are masquerading as nobles in the real world, but one must observe that the punishment here comes from within the bourgeois class itself, as the suitors strip and beat their valets, thus humiliating the snobbish women who had accepted the fakes as nobles.

A variation on the same theme of unreasonable aspirations by commoners is found in *Monsieur de Pourceaugnac*. In this case the false noble is a Limousin, and his disguise is not just a joke but a way of life. Like Mascarille, Pourceaugnac calls attention to his extravagant clothes from the beginning of the action:

> MONSIEUR DE POURCEAUGNAC: Pour moi, j'ai voulu me mettre à la mode de la cour pour la campagne.
> SBRIGANI: Ma foi! cela vous va mieux qu'à tous nos courtisans.
> MONSIEUR DE POURCEAUGNAC: C'est ce que m'a dit mon tailleur: l'habit est propre et riche, et il fera du bruit ici. [1. 3]

This costume is described in the inventory made after Molière's death as "un haut-de-chausses de damas rouge, garni de dentelle, un justaucorps de velours bleu garni d'or faux, un ceinturon à frange, un chapeau gris orné d'une plume verte."[16] The clash of red, blue, gray, and green naturally illustrates the sarcasm of Sbrigani's comment on the clothes. The Brissart and Sauvé engraving, which shows Pourceaugnac pursued by the apothecaries, faithfully renders the excessive amount of lace.[17] this gaudy outfit, with its trim of false gold, contrary to sumptuary laws, clearly associates the Limousin with ridiculous marquis and social usurpers. The illicit background of Pourceaugnac is reinforced by the fact that Limoges was a place of exile for prominent criminals, such as Fouquet's wife.[18]

Nérine gives us an important indication of the wealth of this suitor when she notes that he has three or four thousand écus (9,000–12,000 livres) *more* than Eraste (1. 1). Eraste himself later quotes a figure of four to five thousand, which would push the difference in wealth alone to around 15,000 livres. We may estimate on the basis of these figures that Pourceaugnac's fortune could easily exceed 30,000 livres, placing him above the level of all but the richest tradesmen.

We are also given an idea of the total wealth of Oronte, the father of the bride. The "Flemish merchant" (Sbrigani in disguise) characterizes him as being "riche beaucoup grandement" (2. 3). In addition, Oronte agrees, in the last scene of the play, to *raise* Julie's dowry by 10,000 écus (30,000 livres). Although this falls short of the half-million livres that the richest burgher might leave his daughter, it still places him in the middle to upper reaches of the class.[19]

In the third scene of the play, Pourceaugnac introduces himself as "gentilhomme limousin"; but he qualifies this by adding that he has studied law, which a born gentleman would scarcely do, for it would constitute a derogation of nobility. Thus, he is possibly an *anobli*, but it remains for us to determine his exact status. It seems unlikely that he could have been ennobled directly by holding office, for the Limoges area had no sovereign courts.[20] He may have bought letters of nobility or he may simply be usurping the title and dress and pretending to own a *seigneurie*. His family contains other lawyers and officers: a consul, an assessor and an *élu* (1. 3). Through these offices the family would already have acquired the much-sought-after exemption from the *taille*, which would place them in the same

tax category as the real aristocracy. Sbrigani voices the opinion
that the legal background and the pretended *noblesse d'épée*
are incompatible:

MONSIEUR DE POURCEAUGNAC: . . . Quand il y aurait information, ajournement, décret, et jugement obtenu par surprise, défaut
et contumace, j'ai la voie de conflit de juridiction, pour temporiser,
et venir aux moyens de nullité qui seront dans les procédures.

SBRIGANI: Voilà en parler dans tous les termes, et l'on voit bien,
Monsieur, que vous êtes du métier.

MONSIEUR DE POURCEAUGNAC: Moi, point du tout: je suis gentilhomme.

SBRIGANI: Il faut bien, pour parler ainsi, que vous ayez étudié la
pratique.

MONSIEUR DE POURCEAUGNAC: Point, ce n'est que le sens commun qui me fait juger que je serai toujours reçu à mes faits justifi-
catifs, et qu'on ne me saurait condamner sur une simple accusation,
sans un récolement et confrontation avec mes parties.

SBRIGANI: En voilà du plus fin encore.

MONSIEUR DE POURCEAUGNAC: Ces mots-là viennent sans que je
les sache.

SBRIGANI: Il me semble que le sens commun d'un gentilhomme
peut bien aller à concevoir ce qui est du droit et de l'ordre de la
justice, mais non pas à savoir les vrais termes de la chicane. [2. 10]

Other unworthy acts serve to indicate that Pourceaugnac does
not behave as a noble truly should. He allows himself to be
struck by a gentleman of Périgueux without responding (1. 4).
Furthermore, he comes all the way to Paris in a common stage
coach (1. 1). The author returns to the question of *dérogeance*
posed by Monsieur de Pourceaugnac's legal training and makes
explicit the upstart's concern with proofs of nobility. After
being told by consulting attorneys that "la polygamie est un cas
pendable" (2. 11), he moans: "Ce n'est pas tant la peur de la
mort qui me fait fuir, que de ce qu'il est fâcheux à un gen-

tilhomme d'être pendu, et qu'une preuve comme celle-là ferait tort à nos titres de noblesse" (3. 2). Treatises on nobility do in fact support the Limousin's fears: certain infamous penalties could entail *dérogeance*.[21]

In *Monsieur de Pourceaugnac*, it is once again the bourgeois who take it upon themselves to put the false noble back in his place. To this end, they employ professional rogues like Nérine and Sbrigani, who have spent their entire lives in fraud and illicit activities (1. 2).[22] They also engage all the resources of their own order to undo the Limousin: the doctors and apothecaries who are promised 560 livres if they "cure" the visitor, the *exempt* and his men who fleece him of the 200 livres in his purse, the *suisses*, the merchant who destroys his credit with Oronte, and the lawyers who give him false counsel. This connivance has led such eminent critics as Jules Brody to remark that Molière seems immoral in the play, a perception that is transcended by Pourceaugnac's usurpation and by the homogamous imperative at work in the text.[23]

La Jalousie du Barbouillé is, in contrast, a brief farce, but Molière gives enough information on the background of the characters for us to include it among the bourgeois plays. Le Barbouillé, although a home-owner and family man (scene 8), squanders his money at the cabaret while his wife indulges in social frivolities (scene 1). In business-like fashion, he offers a philosopher good money in exchange for advice on his marital problems. Yet, his scholarly neighbor spurns the money in a long tirade:

Sache, mon ami, que quand tu me donnerais une bonne bourse pleine de pistoles, et que cette bourse serait dans une riche boîte, cette boîte dans un étui précieux, cet étui dans un coffret admirable . . . que je me soucierais aussi peu de ton argent et de toi que de cela. [Scene 2]

The conflict between the imbibing husband and the pleasure-seeking wife, resulting in the burlesque "lock-out" scene, remains on a bourgeois level, although Molière will transform the situation in *George Dandin* to reflect the incompatibility of *hobereaux* and *laboureurs*.

Le Médecin volant, another farce, contains several indicators of bourgeois status. Gorgibus, the father of Lucile, is rich enough to have a valet, Gros-René, and a fine house with a garden and a nearby summer house (scene 1). Valère, his child's secret suitor, also has a valet, Sganarelle, and is willing to pay 100 livres for him to impersonate a doctor (scene 2). When Gorgibus offers Sganarelle more money in order to cure his daughter, the valet tacitly accepts it (scene 8). The fact that Gorgibus has a lawyer for a friend suggests further that he is an important man in the community, and he finally agrees to take Valère as a son-in-law in view of his family's money and prestige (scene 16).

Wealth is relegated to a secondary role in *Dépit amoureux*, where inconclusive indicators recall the merchant-prince world of Italian plays and also give a glimpse of peasant life. The three main families in the plot (those of Albert, Ascagne, and Polidore) all seem to have a certain amount of riches and power. Both young men, Valère and Eraste, have valets, and even Ascagne has a follower in the person of Frosine. Dorothée takes on the Ascagne disguise in order to retain control over an inheritance that otherwise would have been lost (2. 1. 359–62). Both Lucile and Valère also stand to inherit fortunes, for their fathers are powerful men whose wealth can cause problems for their enemies, as we learn in the scene where they reach a marriage settlement through misunderstanding, only to fall out again when each knows the whole truth (3. 4. 832–33). A humorous sidelight is provided in the love affair of Gros-René and

Marinette, who at one point return each other's meager gifts during a lovers' spat:

> Marinette
> Voilà ton demi-cent d'épingles de Paris,
> Que tu me donnas hier avec tant de fanfare.
> Gros-René
> Tiens encor ton couteau; la pièce est riche et rare:
> Il te coûta six blancs lorsque tu m'en fis don.
> [4. 4. 1427–31]

Molière could not have found a funnier way of showing that the love of the young commoners is based on economic reciprocity and homogamy, whether the economic register be 30 sous or 30,000 livres.

Yet, the most prominent character of the shorter French plays, the bourgeois Sganarelle, is always as opposed to this reciprocity as one can be. Molière certainly seems to have discovered a whole new social dimension when he conceived of this character, who reappears in different forms in five plays: *Sganarelle*, *L'Ecole des maris*, *Le Mariage forcé*, *L'Amour médecin*, and *Le Médecin malgré lui*. Each time he is shown in a different context. In *Sganarelle*, he is a husband who fears that his wife may be unfaithful; in *L'Ecole des maris*, a guardian who has designs on his ward; and in *L'Amour médecin*, the father of a marriageable girl who is trying to arrange the best possible match. In *Le Médecin malgré lui*, he appears as a worthless *père de famille* and a drunkard, who is put in the unique position of being able to flirt with buxom Jacqueline and to escape from shrewish Martine, if only for a while; *Le Mariage forcé*, on the other hand, portrays him as an aging bachelor who stumbles into an expensive and humiliating union, a ready-made cuckold.

Economically, Sganarelle's status varies considerably from play to play. He is presented in *Sganarelle* as a bourgeois, but probably not a rich one, since his wife treasures Lélie's locket as something beyond their means (1. 6. 150).[24] The fact that he appears in the twenty-first scene wearing an old suit of armor may provide a clue. The strange apparel, which Sganarelle calls "un habillement / Que j'ai pris pour la pluie" (scene 21, 519–20), connects him with one of the municipal guards formed by the guilds since medieval times (and through the Wars of Religion) to protect French cities in time of strife. In this case, Sganarelle would belong to one of the artisanal *métiers*.[25] His language confirms this, since he uses many collo-quialisms ("voilà vraiment un beau venez-y-voir," scene 6, 200), threatens to break his wife's neck, and insults her with names like "Madame la carogne."[26]

In *L'Ecole des maris*, Sganarelle and his brother Ariste are comfortably rich bourgeois, for the latter mentions that he has 12,000 livres in rent at his disposal, just for the dowry of his ward, Léonor (1. 2. 201). Nevertheless, Sganarelle wants his wife to dress and live *à la petite bourgeoise*:

> Que d'une serge honnête elle ait son vêtement,
> Et ne porte le noir qu'aux bons jours seulement,
> Qu'enfermée au logis, en personne bien sage,
> Elle s'applique toute aux choses du ménage,
> A recoudre mon linge aux heures de loisir.
>
> [1. 2. 117–21]

Ariste gives his fiancée servants and money to spend for clothes (1. 2. 112 and 193), but Sganarelle does not have a single servant in his house (1. 4. 342)! This avarice is all the more astonishing because Sganarelle owns land in the country: he talks of sending young Isabelle back to "revoir nos choux et nos dindons" (1. 2. 262).

Le Mariage forcé once again portrays Sganarelle as a man of substantial bourgeois standing, who has a house and servants, as well as extensive financial enterprises (scene 1). The fact that he has lived in Rome, England, and Holland suggests that he may be involved in international commerce or banking. Géronimo informs us that he can afford to buy jewelry, a luxury item (scene 3). Sganarelle himself says he possesses neither carriage nor chaise and uses this as evidence of his fitness.

L'Amour médecin shows Sganarelle on equal terms with his prosperous neighbors, Josse and Guillaume, who represent two powerful corporations, the goldsmiths and the *tapissiers*. Their solicitations in the first scene prove that Sganarelle can afford their expensive wares. (Molière himself owned tapestries valued at over 900 livres.)[27] Sganarelle also offers to buy his daughter a dress and a cabinet from the fair, and to pay for clavichord lessons (1. 2). However, he reveals that his reluctance to let her marry stems in part from his unwillingness to provide dowry money:

> A-t-on jamais rien vu de plus tyrannique que cette coutume où l'on veut assujettir les pères? rien de plus impertinent et de plus ridicule que d'amasser du bien avec de grands travaux, et élever une fille avec beaucoup de soin et de tendresse, pour se dépouiller de l'un et de l'autre entre les mains d'un homme qui ne nous touche en rien? [1. 5]

Unable to accept the positive and necessary changes in his family, Sganarelle fails to see their advantages—further prolongation of his lineage and enhanced strength in the community through the marriage alliance. When it finally comes to marrying off the girl, Sganarelle gives her 20,000 écus (60,000 livres), thinking at the moment it is a sham ceremony (3. 7).

The riches of Sganarelle are considerably reduced, however, in *Le Médecin malgré lui*, where his occupation as woodcutter is not even a real *métier*. Such a humble business is all the more puzzling, since he has some education. Yet, he is a drunkard who has sold all his wife's furniture (he must have made a rather extraordinary marriage!) down to the bed they slept on (1. 1).

The distinctive mark of the bourgeois Sganarelle is his peculiar costume, which always contains anachronistic elements. The indispensible item is the *fraise*, an archaic piece of neckwear. The odd yellow and green costume he wears in *Le Médecin malgré lui* (doubtless something he would have collected at the *friperie*) leads Lucas to exclaim, in his rustic dialect: "Un habit jaune et vart! C'est donc le médecin des paroquets?" (1. 4). In order to justify to Ariste the somewhat old-fashioned clothes he favors, the protagonist mocks the new-fangled fashions of the foppish marquis in *L'Ecole des maris*:

> Ne voudriez-vous point, dis-je, sur ces matières,
> De vos jeunes muguets m'inspirer les manières?
> M'obliger à porter de ces petits chapeaux
> Qui laissent éventer leurs débiles cerveaux,
> Et de ces blonds cheveux, de qui la vaste enflure
> Des visages humains offusque la figure?
> De ces petits pourpoints sous les bras se perdant,
> Et de ces grands collets jusqu'au nombril pendants?
> De ces manches qu'à table on voit tâter les sauces,
> Et de ces cotillons appelés hauts-de-chausses?
> De ces souliers mignons, de rubans revêtus,
> Qui vous font ressembler à des pigeons pattus?
> Et de ces grands canons, où, comme en des entraves,
> On met tous les matins ses deux jambes esclaves,

Et par qui nous voyons ces Messieurs les galants
Marcher écarquillés ainsi que des volants?

[1. 1. 23–38][28]

Does Sganarelle's obsolete costume associate him with some past ideology, in conflict with current bourgeois ideas? If so, it would be difficult to determine exactly what he speaks for. What is certain is that his clothes reveal two essential aspects of his character: a reluctance to spend accumulated wealth and a streak of stubborn, extreme nonconformity. His attack on the fashions of court marquis, while quite accurate, does nothing to explain why Sganarelle himself cannot dress like a reasonable member of his own bourgeois group.

Sganarelle's presence focuses the public's attention on the definition of acceptable bourgeois behavior. Molière takes care to set the problem in relief by underscoring the diversity of function and wealth within the class as a whole. Sganarelle must often deal with men who, though they are also *roturiers*, seem to have more money and power than he does; such is the case with Gorgibus and Géronte, the fathers in *Sganarelle* and *Le Médecin malgré lui*, and with Valère, the young suitor who outwits Sganarelle in *L'Ecole des maris*. In the latter play, there even appear to be some socioprofessional differences between Sganarelle and his brother Ariste. Molière was certainly familiar with the intricacies of family business alliances, since, as Elizabeth Maxfield-Miller has shown, his mother's family comprised people involved in the trade of books, wine, gold, and bonnets, as well as shoemakers, barber-surgeons, doctors, writers, and officers.[29] All the Sganarelle plays portray a double consciousness of definition of roles within the family and within the bourgeois world.

As a bourgeois, Sganarelle is particularly sensitive to the powerful mediating role played by the legal and liberal professions.

When, under duress, he usurps the status of a doctor in *Le Médecin malgré lui*, he exploits the opportunity to enrich himself not only at the expense of Géronte but also at the expense of poor peasants, Perrin and Thibaut, who give him their savings of two écus in payment for a useless remedy (3. 2). In *L'Amour médecin* Sganarelle becomes the victim of the same profession. Tomès, Des Fonandrès, Macroton, and Bahys force Sganarelle to pay them in advance, and then give him only contradictory, worthless advice: "Il vaut mieux mourir selon les règles que de réchapper contre les règles" (2. 5). Sganarelle then squanders thirty sous on a bottle of worthless *orviétan*. Disguised as a doctor and surrounded by an aura of medical secrecy, Clitandre is able to visit his beloved Lucinde ("Un médecin a cent choses à demander qu'il n'est pas honnête qu'un homme entende" [3. 6]) and to trick him into permitting Lucinde's marriage. Ironically, Sganarelle insists on signing the marriage contract before a notary, thus sealing his fate through the most respected of bourgeois institutions.[30]

Nowhere is the institutional framework of justice more important than in *L'Ecole des maris*. As the legal *tuteur* of Isabelle, Sganarelle is bound by obligations so solemn that the eminent jurist Domat used the *tutelle* as a prime example of "involuntary engagement:" "Celui qui est appelé à une tutelle est obligé, indépendamment de volonté, à tenir lieu de père à l'orphelin qu'on met sous sa charge."[31] Nevertheless, Sganarelle tries to circumvent the spirit and letter of the law by denying his ward access to her fortune or to the pleasures of life and by plotting to marry her himself, which smacks of incest, given his paternal duties. His contempt for the concerns of his lineage is apparent in his treatment of his brother, Ariste, whose honor, he says, is not worth twenty écus (3. 2). The same cynical distrust is extended to the police commissioner and the notary, representatives of bourgeois norms whom he suspects of being susceptible to bribes, and tells, "Ne vous laissez pas graisser la patte, au moins" (3. 4). The duplicity of this attitude is evident to everyone except Sganarelle, who actually expects the officials to sanction the marriage he thinks he has forced between Ariste's ward, Léonor, and Isabelle's suitor, Valère. In fact, they serve as witnesses to Sganarelle's consent for Isabelle to marry Valère, as the tutor falls victim to his own machinations. Justice thus serves ironically to ensure the triumph of bourgeois conduct, as manifested in the reasonable marriages of Ariste with Léonor and of Valère with Isabelle (reasonable, because they are the result of mutual choice based on a clear appreciation of values, rather than simply on force or deception).

In many respects *Le Mariage forcé* furnishes a study in counterpoint to *L'Ecole des maris*, for although the latter builds toward a marriage involving the good faith of both partners, the former culminates in just the opposite. That Sganarelle is acting in selfish bad faith is shown in his first speech, when he bids his servants to accept immediately any incoming funds, but to delay indefinitely paying any bills that should arrive (1. 1). He goes on to explain to Géronimo that his desire to marry stems not from the willingness to assume conjugal and paternal responsibilities but from the pleasure he will receive from the presence of a mate and offspring. His in-laws likewise betray their falsehood as soon as they appear on stage. Alcantor is referred to as "seigneur," the same title shared by Sganarelle and Géronimo, yet his son "se mêle de porter l'épée" and his daughter wears a dress with a long train. These two aspects, the prerogatives of a chevalier and a duchess, reveal that Alcantor's children are usurping a higher station than that to which they are entitled. After consulting Géronimo, fortune-tellers, and a magician, and after hearing Dorimène's description of how she intends to live with him, Sganarelle attempts to withdraw from the commitment he had made to the Alcantor clan; but having chosen to ally himself with would-be nobles and having refused the challenge or *cartel* offered him by Alcidas, he is beaten into submission. This display of violence, even though perpetrated by a false noble, denotes Sganarelle's acceptance of the role of victim, which is further underlined in the final ballet entries that depict a *charivari* and his bride's flirtations.

The spirit of the shorter French bourgeois plays, particularly those that feature Sganarelle, is thus one of experimentation with the relationships between nonconformist characters and the behavioral norms of their group. It is when Sganarelle tries to defy or manipulate the most solemn codes, such as those dealing with marriage or other legal obligations, that he is portrayed in the most pathetic and ignorant manner. His lesser frauds, such as the medical trickery in *Le Médecin malgré lui*, appear to go unpunished, partly because they are not completely of his doing and partly because his victims are no worse off than they would have been if they were dealing with "legitimate" doctors. On a small scale, Sganarelle's non-reciprocity and bad faith in such plays as *L'Ecole des maris* and *Le Mariage forcé* prefigures more detailed analyses of the type found in *L'Ecole des femmes* and *George Dandin*.

THE FRENCH PLAYS: THE ARISTOCRACY

In contrast to the intrabourgeois orientation of the preceding plays, Molière's four remaining short works reveal a predominantly aristocratic milieu. Whether this society is close to the court, as in *Les Fâcheux*, *La Critique de l'Ecole des femmes* and *L'Impromptu de Versailles*, or situated in a provincial city, as in *La Comtesse d'Escarbagnas*, it contains two types of nobles: those who embody all the positive traits of the class (honor, elegance, wit, discretion, good judgment) and those who by their foolishness cast a bad light upon the order, but who are nevertheless tolerated in aristocratic circles — at least, temporarily.

Eraste, the protagonist of *Les Fâcheux*, belongs to the former group. In recounting his afternoon with the fop, he reveals that he is a marquis, but he does not demonstrate the attributes of the ridiculous (visibly fake) marquis of *Les Précieuses ridicules*; the Brissart and Sauvé engraving shows a man in aristocratic dress, with a certain amount of lace but no flaring *canons* and no *petite oie*.[32] He has a valet, La Montagne, has served fourteen years in the army (1. 6. 275), and is a member of the Court (3. 2. 650). As for his beloved Orphise and her uncle Damis, we are told very little about them — too little to confirm absolutely their nobility. However, all that we do know points to that conclusion. Orphise has a carriage and appears in the last scene carrying a silver torch (1. 5. 246). Eraste wins her in a typically noble way, by defending her uncle with his sword, thus manifesting aristocratic courage (3. 5. 791).

All the other characters in the play, the *fâcheux*, demonstrate unworthy or absurd behavior; they form a real panorama of all that was unsavory at the French court. Lysandre, the musician, Alcandre, the duelist, Dorante, the hunter, and Filinte, the protector, all are fellow nobles who employ the familiar pronoun *tu* when addressing Eraste. In contrast, Caritidès and Ormin are commoners who follow the court, *occasionaires*, trying to sell their schemes or to obtain pensions or appointments.[33] It is interesting that Molière chose to enter into the rather delicate matter of the *donneur d'avis* at court, for many of the aristocrats there made a living from the graft involved in these affairs. Molière's Eraste discreetly dismisses the two offers made to him.

The same division of traits is evident from the beginning of *La Critique de l'Ecole des femmes*. Elise is witty and judicial and, like the chevalier Dorante, supports Molière's cause, but

Uranie, whose house is "le refuge ordinaire de tous les fainéants de la cour" (scene 1), sides with the affected Climène, the poet Lysidas and the ridiculous marquis. The latter immediately places himself in the same category as the imposter Mascarille, when he barges into the salon and roughs up the lackey, Galopin, in a most undignified fashion (scene 4).

Molière continues to juxtapose exemplary noblemen with ridiculous marquis in *L'Impromptu de Versailles*. As in so many other cases, he casts doubt on the status of the fops, played by himself and La Grange, though he never explicitly designates them as upstarts. Here, the unworthy behavior begins with a wager on which of the marquis served as the model for the one in the *Critique*. Apparently unable to appreciate the character's undesirable qualities, each claims credit for him and bets 1,000 livres, although between them they can raise only a tenth of the sum in cash (scene 3)! Inasmuch as these marquis overstep the new aristocratic codes of fine but modest dress and elegant but lucid speech, they present a vivid contrast with the Chevalier. Their infractions extend also into matters of taste, for they take it upon themselves to correct the abuses of Molière. When the Chevalier begins to defend the dramatist, the fops can only reply by chiding him for not wearing *canons* (scene 4). (In fact, the Brissart and Sauvé engraving shows Molière clad in an outrageous costume.)[34] The debate is interrupted by Madeleine Béjart's inquiry on the way Molière handled his polemic battle with Boursault (scene 5).

The final noble play, *La Comtesse d'Escarbagnas*, represents, in a sense, Molière's last word on the problem of the ridiculous aristocrat. In the character of this provincial countess, whom he contrasts to the exemplary nobles like Julie and to the ambitious officer Tibaudier, Molière puts many of the unworthy traits already observed in the marquis. She proves to be a distorter of speech who can neither communicate with her servants nor control them, a miser who buys tallow candles instead of waxen *cierges*, and an insensitive ingrate who had made her own *soeur de lait* a mistreated charwoman (1. 2). If her servants rebel against her, it is exactly what she deserves, since Audiger places responsibilty for this relationship squarely on the master: "les bons maîtres font les bons valets."[35] Rather than being welcomed and acknowledged by the Parisian nobility, she has been obliged to stay at public inns like the Hôtel de Mouhy. As proofs of her late husband's nobility, she can only cite such dubious marks as his hounds, his country house, and the fact that he "prenait la qualité de comte dans tous les contrats qu'il passait" (1. 2), which implies that he might well have been a simple businessman.

As Julie, a real noble, observes, the countess violates custom by entertaining the proposals of two *roturiers*, Harpin the tax-collector and Tibaudier the attorney. At least she is conscious enough of the laws of *préséance* to insist that Tibaudier take a folding chair instead of an armchair (1. 5). Yet, Charles Chappuzeau, a contemporary social theorist, expressed a common sentiment of the day when he discouraged any remarriage by widows with children, lest a divided family be created.[36] The countess lacks culture, never having heard of the Latin poet, Martial, nor knowing any Latin at all (1. 5 and 8). We eventually learn that she has already sent letters to Harpin assuring him of their impending marriage and asking for money (1. 8). The letter that arrives in the last scene, informing the Vicomte and Julie that their aristocratic families have finally terminated their feud, allows Molière to end the play with a double humiliation for the countess: on the one hand, she is made a *cocue avant la lettre*, and on the other, she is forced to wed the commoner Tibaudier out of spite, thus providing a rare example of female hypogamy that forever compromises her already doubtful status as a member of the second estate.

The variety of models, both in the overseas plays and in the French ones, suggests that a major feature of Molière's ideology is social polyvalence, a quality that he shares with theorists of the société d'états such as Bacquet, Loyseau, and Chappuzeau. From the nearly complete closure of the idealized Greek plays, where noble behavior is set in bold relief against that of *vilains*, through the vague affiliations of merchant princes and slaves in the Italian plays, to the relatively realistic group portraits of French bourgeois and aristocrats, the playwright offers a panorama of values that neither overlap nor infringe upon one another. Sostrate's magnanimous courage triumphs in one play, Scapin's knavish opportunism in another, Ariste's sense of good faith and reciprocity in a third, the Chevalier's *honnêteté* in a fourth. By refusing to construct his plays according to a single rigid behavioral standard, Molière tacitly accepts and reinforces the notion that the underlying principle of interpersonal relations must be difference. Values diverge, even contradict one another, and assume greater importance through specificity and distinction rather than through universality. The cement of legality, embodied in a sovereign monarch and a transcendant God, was necessary to hold the elements of this system in position. Since both king and church were banned from the stage by *bienséances* and could appear only in the form of proxies like Jupiter in *Amphitryon* or the Exempt in *Tartuffe*, cohesion was provided most frequently by a secular type of sovereign good that entails the happiness of the greatest number of characters. Achieved at the expense of alienated individuals such as Pourceaugnac, Sganarelle, and Le Barbouillé, this consensus often takes the shape of *fiançailles* or marriage contracts formalizing the acceptance of fulfillment and exchange. In Molière's theater, human diversification is prescribed, mediated, and reconciled by Law, which channels the procreative drives into relationships that bear the seal of sociality and are accompanied by symbolic mutual donations of commercial wealth. This interdependence of Law and differentiation is basic to the very concept of ideology, for as Françoise Gaillard has shown, the primordial Commandment, whether Mosaic code or incest taboo, served to define the subject (even before it set his limitations) and immediately inserted him into a legitimate order of temporal and spiritual exchange.[37]

To a large extent, the abundance of social indicators in the plays shows the direction of development not only for Molière's major comedies but for the comedy of manners as a genre. The greater the number and significance of the indicators, the greater the opportunity to evaluate a character's actions and ideas in relation to others of his station. When social indicators are sparingly used, as in the Italian and Greek plays, comedy must depend on other factors, such as intrigue or the banter of a single witty clown, and runs the risk of confusion with the pastoral, the heroic drama, or other genres.

In the shorter French plays, where the frequency of social status indicators is greatest, Molière shows a growing preoccupation with the problems of unworthy nobles and unworthy bourgeois. The former, represented by several of the *fâcheux*, the ridiculous marquis of *La Critique de l'Ecole des femmes* and *L'Impromptu de Versailles*, the comtesse d'Escarbagnas, and Pourceaugnac, threaten the existence of a system of valid social values and must be judged and dealt with by the peers or by others. The latter are represented by the bourgeois Sganarelle, who poses a different kind of danger. Although he does not claim the power or prerogatives of nobility, Sganarelle is a nuisance to the continued well-being of his own group because he will not adhere to its standards of reciprocity in such important matters as marriage, and—what is worse—he tries to prevent others from doing so. These sketches of misbehavior, combined with the tensions present in the foreign plays, provide the basic material from which Molière created his major comedies, rich in detail and elaborate in social structure. The dramatist thus developed the simple discrepancies between status indicator and personal behavior toward their logical artistic conclusions.

1. Among the plays to be considered in this chapter are two, *Amphitryon* and *Les Fourberies de Scapin*, which are admittedly equal in comic achievement to such major works as *L'Avare* and *Les Femmes savantes*, but which owe this stature chiefly to dramaturgical elements rather than to social features. By virtue of their fairly simple detail of identity and their type of orientation, they may best be treated along with other plays set in Greece and Italy. Two other especially significant and complex three-act plays set in France, *George Dandin* and *Le Malade imaginaire*, deserve more lengthy analyses in later chapters devoted to their prominent structures of social closure and socioeconomic integrity. The allegorical implications of *Amphitryon* have been examined in Paul Römer, *Molieres Amphitryon und sein gesellschaftlicher Hintergrund*, and Ralph Albanese, "Une sociocritique du mythe royal sous Louis XIV: *Tartuffe* et *Amphitryon*."

2. *La Pastorale comique* seems to take place in Greece, but our knowledge of this fragmentary play is so slight that we cannot attempt to reconstruct its social framework.

3. Molière, *Oeuvres*, ed. Ch. La Grange and Vivot, 3:277. This edition of collected, but not complete, works will be henceforth cited as *OC* La Grange.

4. See especially *Le Sicilien*, sc. 5.

5. Judd Hubert, "From Corneille to Molière: The Metaphor of Value," in *French and English Drama of the Seventeenth Century*, discusses how the attitudes of Molière's characters are frequently reflected in terms dealing with money.

6. Mousnier, *Fureurs paysannes*, p. 17.

7. Louis's influence is explicitly stated in the *avant-propos* of the *Divertissement royale* program description, *OC* Couton, 2:645.

8. Hunting is featured in *La Princesse d'Elide*, 1. 2, and in the first two *intermèdes*, as well as in *Les Amants magnifiques*, 5. 1. The five *intermèdes* of the latter play emphasize the importance of pastoral, as does *Mélicerte*, 2. 3, where Myrtil presents the heroine with a sparrow he has captured. The Pythian games are represented in the final *intermède* of *Les Amants magnifiques*. The chariot race held between acts 2 and 3 of *La Princesse d'Elide* also provides a symbolic test of noble quality for aristocrats in that play.

9. The role of the clown-valet, which is enhanced by his rhetorical use of the burlesque *récit*, has been studied in my article "The Burlesque *Récit* in Molière's Greek plays."

10. Lycarsis, the character played by Molière in the unfinished *Mélicerte*, manifests

the "baseness" of his condition mainly through coarse speech, which is liberally sprin-
kled with oaths and insults.

11. See Judd Hubert, *Molière and the Comedy of Intellect*, pp. 36–37.

12. Adam, "Molière," p. 271.

13. *OC* La Grange, 1:225.

14. *OC* La Grange, 3:227 and 4:94 respectively.

15. Charles Loyseau, *Traité des ordres et simples dignités*, p. 138. Another theorist,
Denis Godefroy, notes the frequency of usurpation of the rank of marquis in *Abbrégé
des trois états du clergé, de la noblesse, et du tiers état*, pt. 2, p. 32.

16. Jurgens and Maxfield-Miller, *Cent ans*, p. 567.

17. *OC* La Grange, 5. 128.

18. Charles Cassé, "Limoges et Quimper, terres d'exil au XVIIᶜ siècle."

19. Mongrédien, *La Vie quotidienne*, p. 146.

20. Ford, *Robe and Sword*, pp. 31–41, gives a list of the sovereign courts in France
during the ancien régime.

21. H. Jougla de Morenas, *Noblesse 38*, p. 73, notes that infamous crimes "faisaient
perdre au noble et à sa descendance son état."

22. Sbrigani was probably as much a knave on the prison galleys as he was in the
streets of Paris. Charles G. M. de la Roncière relates in his *Histoire de la Marine
Française*, pp. 605–6, that the Spanish admiral called the commander of the miserable
French galleys the "general de la comedia!"

23. Jules Brody, "Esthétique et société chez Molière," in *Dramaturgie et société au
XVIᶜ et XVIIᶜ siècles*, ed. Jean Jacquot.

24. A jeweled portrait locket valued at 1,500 livres is described in Hippolyte Roy, *La
Vie, la mode et le costume au XVIIᶜ siècle: époque Louis XIII*.

25. Roland Mousnier numbers the armed workers at 46,000 in *Paris*, pp. 194, 244.

26. A. Lottin notes that such coarse insults were common grounds for divorce in the
ecclesiastical courts of Cambrai, in "Vie et mort du couple — difficultés conjugales et
divorce dans le Nord de la France aux XVIIᶜ et XVIIIᶜ siècles."

27. Jurgens and Maxfield-Miller, *Cent ans*, pp. 562–63.

28. These lines, which echo the seventeenth-century minor genre of the *pasquil*, or
fashion satire, give additional evidence that Molière was willing to transform ironically
the everyday forms of discourse in his society. For examples of the *pasquil*, see Godard
de Donville, pp. 251–60.

29. Elizabeth Maxfield-Miller, "La Famille de la mère de Molière."

30. Molière's use of notaries, like that of his contemporary dramatists, was a mainly
symbolic convention, necessitated in part by the prohibition against portraying the
religious aspects of marriage on stage. According to Jean-Paul Poisson, the vast majority

of notarial acts concern credit and property transfer, rather than marriage; see his "Introduction à l'étude du rôle socioéconomique du notariat à la fin du XVIIe siècle."

31. Jean Domat, *Les Lois civiles dans leur ordre naturel*, 2: vi and 147–61. Domat's views are corroborated by Gabriel Argou in *Institution au droit français*, 1:49–69.

32. *OC* La Grange, 2:84.

33. Molière's portrayal of the *occasionnaires*, though fanciful, translates a true political phenomenon into the language of comedy; their presence at court was both evident and aggressive, as Ernest Lavisse related in his *Histoire de France*, 7:381–82. The *fâcheux* with a plan to transform all of France into seaports reflects, no doubt, the numerous schemes for building canals, as noted in Jean Meuvret, *Etudes d'histoire économique*, pp. 23–24.

34. *OC* La Grange, 7:87.

35. Audiger, *La Maison réglée*, p. xiii.

36. Charles Chappuzeau, *Le Devoir général de l'homme en toutes conditions*, pp. 30–36.

37. Françoise Gaillard, "Au nom de la Loi: Lacan, Althusser et l'idéologie," in *Sociocritique*, ed. Claude Duchet.

CHAPTER THREE

EXEMPLARY NOBILITY AND UNWORTHINESS

Between the spring of 1665 and the late autumn of 1666, Molière completed and staged two great plays that explore the innermost structures of the nobility, *Dom Juan* and *Le Misanthrope*. In discussing the social framework of these comedies, it is imperative to avoid the many pitfalls of anachronistic prejudices. Lucien Goldmann, for instance, presents an orthodox Marxist viewpoint when he characterizes the ancien régime nobility as idle and divorced from the means of production; yet, such statements presuppose a dichotomy of material and idea, as well as an equation of industrial expansion with progress — concepts alien to the perceptions of seventeenth-century Frenchmen.[1] Louis XIV's nobles enjoyed power, respect, and material benefits that induced many bourgeois to abandon lucrative careers and to risk fortunes to join their ranks. Far from considering itself to be a mechanism of production, where positions must be justified by economic output, this social order took the image of preserver of an age-old status quo, the alternative to which was sporadic anarchy. The officer corps of the nation's army, as well as some entire specialized units, maintained a predominantly noble character, even though more and more commanders, especially in the engineers, were of relatively recent nobility. Louis XIV himself did much to revive the military mystique of the second order when he led several successsful campaigns in his youth. The *noblesse* did face problems of

identity, values, and organization caused by the growing numbers of *anoblis*, the deepening schism between the court nobility and the impoverished gentry, and the tendency of the king
to draw upon the civilian officers for much aid and advice.
Nevertheless, the obsolescence of the nobility was the last thing
on anyone's mind at the time, and the works of Sorel, La
Bruyère, and others are replete with examples of commoners
scrambling to buy, or to usurp, noble status. It may be stated as
an axiom that Molière's audience was conscious of the aristocrat's dominant and enviable position at the top of the active
secular hierarchy.

Any attempt to depict the collective mentality of the *noblesse*
as reflected in the discourse of the mid-century comedy of manners must take into account the temporal factors that contributed to the differentiation of behavior at that moment in history. Noblemen of the grand siècle were not simply turned loose
on the world, armed with ill-gotten wealth, libido, and *lettres
de cachet*, as were some of their counterparts in eighteenth-
century novels. Aristocratic status carried an important concomitant obligation to shun unworthiness in its many forms. Treatises on nobility were in general agreement that noble behavior
had to be exemplary, and that it was incumbent upon the individual to pass on an "unsullied" name to his descendants, in
recognition of his own duty to the lineage. Nobles were not
compelled to demonstrate brilliance, to amass fortunes, or to
achieve anything at all extraordinary. However, they were
expected to sacrifice even their lives if collective or personal
honor should demand it. In this codified existence, many of the
most unworthy acts came under the heading of *dérogeance* or
déchéance, that is, behavior that causes the loss, temporary or
permanent, individual or familial, of noble status. It should be
pointed out that neither seventeenth-century social theorists nor
more modern ones are in complete agreement as to the defini-

tion and extent of loss of nobility—a state of confusion to which
the legal heterogeneity of monarchial France did much to contribute. Most authorities do concur that crimes of treason and
lèse-majesté caused a loss of status that supplemented whatever
corporal penalties were imposed.[2] Some go on to include a variety of other "infamous" crimes, such as counterfeiting, larceny,
and even bankruptcy![3] Explicit proof of Molière's interest in the
question is supplied by *Monsieur de Pourceaugnac*, where the
protagonist worries that if he is hanged for bigamy, an infamous
crime, his entire family might lose its claim to nobility (3. 2).
The majority of theorists agree that commerce or manufacturing, especially on the retail level, constituted *dérogeance*,
although there were old exceptions for glass-making and more
recent ones for certain types of maritime commerce.[4] The province of Brittany was particularly permissive in that it allowed for
a sort of dormancy of nobility during commercial activity, after
which the individual could resume his noble status and behavior
simultaneously. Beyond the more obvious unworthiness of
crimes and commerce, certain theorists extend the range of
derogatory behavior to a much broader area, which is variously
classified as nominal *dérogeance* or as *la mort civile*.[5] In fact,
during Louis XIV's reign, any aristocrat or officer who failed to
"vivre noblement"—to obey the codes of honor, dress, speech,
decorum, and so on—could not expect to receive full respect
and might even arouse suspicion as to the validity of his claim to
nobility.[6]

In Molière's lifetime two events served to make both *noblesse*
and *roturiers* more sensitive than ever to the precariousness of
social privilege. The first of these was the inauguration of a
large-scale program of *recherches de noblesse*, or, more omi-
nously, *réformations*.[7] To review the status of all the noble families of the realm, the king established commissions, consisting
largely of civil officers, to inquire into their backgrounds—a

process that went on intermittently through most of Molière's creative period. Although some aristocrats applauded this scheme (at least publicly) as a means of purging the order of usurpers and *anoblis*, the government ministers acted from the more pragmatic motivation of returning a large number of exempt individuals to the rolls of the *taille* tax. To many families, the process was undoubtedly humiliating, since it involved justifying their cherished preeminence before supposedly inferior magistrates, in terms of the judges' own legalistic jargon and documentary expertise. It could also be costly, for official certification and unofficial extortion were sometimes inevitable. In the end, some "false nobles" were ferreted out, but powerful upstarts like Colbert could cause even patently imaginary genealogies to be accepted through their political influence.

The second unsettling event for the nobility was a mass prosecution in the Auvergne carried out by a special royally appointed court. Charged with ending the lawlessness and brigandage which plagued that province, these *Grands Jours* took their ruthless toll and resulted in some well-publicized hangings. Once again, the fate of aristocrats lay in the hands of socially inferior judges. Like the *réformations*, the *Grand Jours d'Auvergne* were full of troubling implications for the *noblesse*: they called attention to the existence of significant numbers of unworthies among their ranks and to the fact that these unworthies would be held accountable for their actions by an all-powerful king. What so many nobles had come to accept as eternal honors and privileges in the social hierarchy were in fact revealed to be very vulnerable.[8]

Despite the fact that Dom Juan Tenorio is perhaps the most outstanding negative exemplum for noble behavior in French classical literature and despite his appearance on the Paris stage in February 1665, when both the events in Auvergne and the *recherches de noblesse* were nearing a crucial peak, Molière's

Dom Juan ou le Festin de Pierre has seldom received attention as a comedy of hierarchical irresponsibility. The eponym, played by Molière's urbane young leading man, La Grange, is a knight of the highest station who violates the codes of social relationship in every imaginable way. He has abandoned his wife, Elvire, before the play begins, and repudiates her again to her face in acts one and four and indirectly in act five, just as he has previously done with countless other women. Her brothers, Carlos and Alonse, bent on restoring their family's injured honor, dutifully pursue Dom Juan and manage to catch up with him in the third act, only to be obliged by ironic circumstances to grant him a temporary reprieve. He has killed a fellow aristocrat sometime in the past, and when he blasphemes in the dead man's tomb, a statue comes to life and also begins to close in on him. In the course of the first three acts, Dom Juan tries to kidnap a young bride, escapes from a shipwreck, tricks two country lasses with false proposals, flees incognito from the peasant village, gets lost in the woods, takes part in one sword fight, narrowly avoids another, and unexpectedly encounters the supernatural. Throughout this fast-paced baroque journey, he endures the constant prattle of his valet, Sganarelle, who neurotically but convincingly combines the archetypal roles of the good and evil parasites ito a single erosive, disorderly character, played by Molière himself.

The broad outlines of this legend had been in place since the early part of the century, when the Spaniard Tirso de Molina originated the figurè of Dom Juan in his *Burlador de Sevilla*. Parisian audiences were quite familiar with the story, since several versions in French and Italian had been presented to them on stage and in print during the decade preceding Molière's play. Conscious of these limitations, Molière strove to offer the public a revival of the lucrative atheist-blasted-by-heaven tradition, while at the same time fulfilling his desire to construct a thought-provoking comedy on the lines of contemporary society.

The author had the misfortune to succeed a bit too well, to make Dom Juan so glib, so realistic that the legend was propelled to new heights; and the character—a wretched villain in Tirso's play, a clever scoundrel in his own—was eventually dubbed by Enlightenment men of letters an anticlerical hero, a philosopher, an engaging man of the world, and became a libertine demigod of love in Mozart's opera *Don Giovanni*. Post-Revolutionary generations have scoured the text for every shred of philosophical content, and though Dom Juan's statements are no more than shreds of philosophy, critics were spurred on by the play's controversial aspects: its emergence so soon after the suppression of the first *Tartuffe*, the presence of false devotion and sacrilege, the abrupt reediting and mysterious disappearance of *Dom Juan* from the troupe's repertory. All these details lead to speculation over undocumented struggles with the shadowy, archconservative Compagnie du Saint Sacrement and possible links with Molière's rumored libertine literary activity, the translation of Lucretius reported by Grimarest.[9] In fact, critics of this work diverge widely in their interpretations, and it even has been suggested by the staunchest partisans of a resplendent, libertine Dom Juan, those who seek to localize in him the myth of Promethean revolt, that attempts to restore the character's social context are bourgeois plots aimed at destroying his universality.[10]

Unfortunately, those who admire a glorious libertine image of Dom Juan are prone to repeat what Rousseau did to Alceste, that is, to endow the character with a personality other than that which the author created. Objectivity is very necessary in order to comprehend *Dom Juan*'s often overlooked significance as a study in *déchéance*. After all, Molière's Dom Juan is remarkably tight-lipped for a philosopher. His utterances on the nature of the universe are limited to some undeveloped taunts at the heavens, a simple mathematical equation, and an injunction on the need to disregard (not avoid) social commitments, so as to be ready to indulge in any opportunity for pleasure that presents itself. His interest in truth and knowledge, other than carnal, is definitely limited, and one does well to remember that when Sganarelle says, "il vit . . . en pourceau d'Epicure" (1. 1), he illustrates his master's brutal degradation and lack of orderly thought.

Dom Juan explains all there is to his "philosophy" when he states, "Je crois que deux et deux sont quatre, Sganarelle, et que quatre et quatre sont huit" (3. 1). The statement is shallowly plagiarized from an anecdote about the dying prince Maurice de Nassau recounted by Guez de Balzac and Tallemant des Réaux; a contemporary critic noted that it served merely to identify the character as an atheist too fashionable and sybaritical to waste much time in the rigorous search for truth.[11] Sganarelle, who believes in spooks, mocks the mathematical credo, which is too fragmentary and superficial to be associated with the schools of leading philosophers such as Gassendi or Descartes. Above all, Molière's slick, fatuous Dom Juan, having mastered the arts of appearance, is an opportunist who is willing to sacrifice his fellow humans' lives and dignity in order to indulge his appetites. Sganarelle labels him truly as "un grand seigneur méchant homme" (1. 1) and "l'épouseur du genre humain" (2. 4). Religion and philosophy, like gallantry, are simply garments this dandy tries on or discards as his whims evolve, for he can mouth the dictums of Lucretius and those of François de Sales with equal ease.

Molière significantly chooses to place major emphasis, in terms of stage time and strategic juxtaposition, on the relationship of Dom Juan and Sganarelle as master and servant. Forming the only basic social attachment that Dom Juan can accept for long, they are together almost constantly. One of the only exceptions is the opening scene of the play, the famous and mysterious "tobacco scene," but even here Sganarelle is not really separated from his master. That the valet has taken on the trappings of luxury as a result of his proximity to Dom Juan is evident from his attitude toward snuff, the use of which he associates with courtly behavior:

> C'est la passion des honnêtes gens, et qui vit sans tabac n'est pas digne de vivre. Non seulement il réjouit et purge les cerveaux humains, mais encore il instruit les âmes à la vertu, et l'on apprend avec lui à devenir honnête homme. [1. 1]

Sganarelle has also managed to acquire other benefits, such as better than average clothes, for we learn in act two that his attire has made a great impression on Pierrot: "Ceux qui le servont sont des Monsieux eux-mesme" (2. 1). Moreover, beyond these superficial objects, Sganarelle has acquired a vision of society that is just as careless and stilted as that of his master, for his appreciation of tobacco is based on the idea that reciprocal giving and taking of the weed is the very basis of aristocracy: "Ne voyez-vous pas bien, dès qu'on en prend, de quelle manière obligeante on en use avec tout le monde, et comme on est ravi d'en donner à droite et à gauche, partout où l'on se trouve?" (1. 1). This parody of a popular if minor literary topic of the 1660s serves to illustrate Sganarelle's confusion and corruption.[12] Although in the ensuing dialogue with Gusman Sganarelle puts aside his affected language and derides his master's depraved behavior, he justifies his own continued service by claiming, "La crainte en moi fait l'office du zèle" (1. 1). Like Dom Juan, the valet refuses responsibility for his actions and tells Gusman that if news of their conversation reaches the master's ears, he will accuse Gusman of lying. As Patrice Kerbrat's sensitive portrayal of the role in the 1979 Comédie-Française production showed, Sganarelle, alternately ambitious and servile, helpful and cowardly, superstitious and materialistic, has a great emotional and social stake in Dom Juan's affairs.

If Sganarelle's attitudes demonstrate internal conflicts, so do Dom Juan's, for the aristocrat vacillates in his relationship with his servant from unseemly fraternization to excessive intimidation and violent threats. Early in the play, Dom Juan lets down all barriers of expression between himself and his valet: "Je te donne la liberté de parler et de me dire tes sentiments" (1. 2). But when Sganarelle stumbles onto the forbidden topic of divine retribution, even in the indirect form of a "story," Dom Juan is quick to anger; "Hola maître sot, vous savez que je vous ai dit que je n'aime pas les faiseurs de remontrances" (1. 2). When, in a later scene, Dom Juan strikes Sganarelle by mistake instead of Pierrot, he does not seem to regret it and snickers, "Te voilà payé de ta charité" (2. 3). He threatens Sganarelle with even more severe punishment if the valet continues to try to change his ways:

> Ecoute. Si tu m'importunes davantage de tes sottes moralités, si tu me dis encore le moindre mot là-dessus, je vais appeler quelqu'un, demander un nerf de boeuf, te faire tenir par trois ou quatre, et te rouer de mille coups. M'entends-tu bien? [4. 1]

In alternating between excessive familiarity and excessive brutality, Dom Juan both slackens the laws of separation of *états* and overemphasizes power, rather than respect, to maintain his authority.

The bizarre nature of this master-servant pair becomes most clear at the moment when Dom Juan proposes to exchange clothes with Sganarelle in order to escape his pursuers. Such an expedient certainly verges on *dérogeance* through violation of the sumptuary codes that were reinforced during the reign of Louis XIV: to change into the garments of an underling, particularly when avoiding a confrontation where honor was at stake, was to deny one's class. Sganarelle's negative response to the plan is an interesting instance of cowardice, for he forsakes the chance to live nobly if it means the risk of life and limb, and admits no more responsibility for his master than the master does for him:

> DOM JUAN: . . . Bien heureux est le valet qui peut avoir la gloire de mourir pour son maître.
> SGANARELLE: Je vous remercie d'un tel honneur. O Ciel, puisqu'il s'agit de mort, fais-moi la grâce de n'être point pris pour un autre! [2. 5]

Dom Juan's notion of a noble sacrifice is rather amusing, for he seems to ignore the fact that it is the aristocrat, rather than the valet, who should scorn death. Even the naïve Sganarelle realizes that in dying one should always attempt to establish one's identity, if not one's honor.

The self-centered distortion by Dom Juan of the master-servant relationship is accompanied by a general devaluation of all family bonds, the most important and most obvious of which is the one between husband and wife. Sganarelle in the first scene of the play reveals to Gusman the perverted nature of Dom Juan's views on marriage:

> Tu me dis qu'il a épousé ta maîtresse: crois qu'il aurait plus fait pour contenter sa passion, et qu'avec elle il aurait encore épousé toi, son chien et son chat. Un mariage ne lui coûte rien à contracter; il ne se sert point d'autres pièges pour attraper les belles, et c'est un épouseur à toutes mains. Dame, damoiselle, bourgeoise, paysanne, il ne trouve rien de trop chaud ni de trop froid pour lui; et si je te disais le nom de toutes celles qu'il a épousées en divers lieux, ce serait un chapitre à durer jusques au soir. [1. 1]

Literature offers many examples of the *amant volage*, but Molière's Dom Juan is a unique case of a *mari volage*, a sort of professional bridegroom who has no objection to marriage in name, but only to its lasting obligations. For the protagonist, the greater the number of marriages, the greater the amount of sexual enjoyment. Such a concept is obviously foreign to ancien régime mores, which saw marriage as a solemn mutual duty.

It is essential to understand that the French nobleman of Molière's time did not necessarily expect to make a marriage that was founded on passion. Although married life could bring joys, it was first a duty, involving the cooperation of the bride, the groom, and both families. The latter supplied the young couple with their *condition* and with an honorable name, and the couple in turn provided for the continuity of the lineage.[13] The gentleman and the lady enjoyed an equal status guaranteed by family and peers. If romantic love was not a part of this respectful social bond, *tant pis*! Other liaisons were socially and even religiously condoned, provided the aristocrat assumed the proper role toward the beloved. The best-known practitioner of this code was the king himself, who took a series of semiofficial mistresses and carefully raised his bastard children as princes.

Dom Juan continually perverts the existing norms of sexual and marital conduct. As a suitor, he is far from a model of gallantry: his idea of a good courtship is one that proceeds apace. Perhaps his long, tedious wooing of Elvire left him with a distaste for the more time-consuming amatory customs, for his approach to women with marital or religious obstacles is to resort to immediate violence. Before the play begins, he has already kidnapped Elvire from a convent, then married her to legitimize his lust. Yet, even this constituted rape in the seventeenth century and was punishable by hanging; according to the gruesome adage in Loysel's *Institutes coutumières*, "Il n'y a si bon mariage qu'une corde ne rompt."[14] Later, when he finds himself attracted to a woman formally engaged, he decides to try full-scale piracy in order to force his affections on her: "Toutes choses sont préparées pour satisfaire mon amour, et j'ai une petite barque et des gens, avec quoi fort facilement je prétends enlever la belle" (1. 3). Violence can be convenient, for it is the shortest distance between two points.

Dom Juan's violent acts had many precedents in contemporary society, as the records of the Grands Jours d'Auvergne amply demonstrate. Another *grand seigneur méchant homme*, Gilbert de Trintry, shot dead a peasant who was sleeping in the field, cut off another's hand, and also, the judges note, killed the guinea fowl belonging to a third! Guillaume de Beaufort-Canillac assassinated a fellow noble in a rigged pistol duel. His evil kinsman, Jacques-Timoléon, marquis de Canillac, employed a private army of scalawags with names like "Brise-tout" and "Sans Fiance" to terrorize his neighbors. His son and namesake rustled cattle, held captives for ransom, killed fellow noblemen, and had pregnant women mauled by his followers. Another Canillac, Charles, hunted a curate in a field with a gang of friends and riddled his corpse with bullets; still another, Gabriel, was executed for ambushing a gentleman. Defying law and order, the Combalibeuf family murdered a finance officer, the Bastides beat a *huissier* nearly to death, and the sire de Veyrac pillaged a notary's house. The marquis du Palais and his gang of thugs attacked a group of peace officers, killing three and capturing the rest. Louis de Mascon attacked an enemy's elderly mother with a pitchfork. Guy de Leans, sieur des Héraux, tortured two innocent workman. The *grand prévôt* de Bourbonnais made two valets fight a duel to the death and had the victor strangled. The baron de Sénégas imprisoned an enemy in a small, damp box for several months until his clothes decayed and his skin was covered with white mold. Gaspard d'Espinchal sexually mutilated his page and was suspected of infanticide. The list goes on, and the offenses are not limited to the Auvergne but spread across the land.[15] The audience could not help but identify Dom Juan with this class of real degenerates, who resembled Molière's protagonist in that they could be charming one minute and bloody the next.

Molière reinforces Dom Juan's criminality by giving his play the dramatic tensions of a cops-and-robbers tale in a way that differs from previous French versions of the story. For three acts the protagonist and his stooge light-heartedly plot *enlèvements*, seductions, and blasphemies, evading family and justice-doers alike, and taunting the heavens along the way. Dom Juan slips free of his responsibilities toward his wife with ease. Accustomed to aristocratic parity and to treatment befitting her station, Elvire is more insulted than heartbroken when she learns that he has jilted her permanently: "C'est une lâcheté que de se faire expliquer trop sa honte; et, sur de tels sujets, un noble coeur, au premier mot, doit prendre son parti" (1. 3). Neither natural phenomena, such as the storm that takes place before act two, nor the vengeance of Elvire's brothers seem capable of stopping the irrepressible scoundrel, and it almost appears that his dream of becoming the Alexander the Great of erotic pleasure might be within his grasp. Feeling bold and intelligent as a result of the doctor's gown he wears in act three, Sganarelle undertakes to correct his master's cynicism, but his optimistic exploration of man's powers literally falls flat on its face. The failure of Sganarelle's mock-Cartesian proof of existence through spinning prefigures the ultimate collapse of Dom Juan's intellectual opportunism, which might well have as its axiom *delecto, ergo sum*. Servant and master both would qualify as examples of what Pascal called *demi-habiles*. Indeed, pleasure keeps eluding Dom Juan through a series of frustrating mishaps: his pirate ship is blown off course, the arrival of a posse prevents him from enjoying the conquest of two simple-minded farm girls, a miserable beggar stubbornly refuses his gold, and finally the very stone of a victim's statue comes to life to check his mockery of the supernatural.

Sensing something out of place, the criminal retires to his lair, where he continues to rail at the warnings brought by his purveyor, his repentant wife, and his disgusted father. He turns the discourse of cordiality against them and sneers as they depart, crestfallen, without having swayed him an inch. Nevertheless, heralded by a ghostly apparition, the statue penetrates his hideout and issues a challenge for a final showdown. To escape the weapons that heaven has promised to turn against him, Dom Juan attempts the ultimate trickery in act five by feigning to become devout, but to no avail; for although he continues to manipulate mortal opponents like his father, his servant, and Dom Carlos, the unearthly vindicator seeks him out and destroys him.

Molière's brilliant restructuring of the traditional Dom Juan drama, familiar to French audiences through the versions by Dorimon, Villiers, and the Comédie Italienne, tightens the focus on the manhunt for the antihierarchical criminal. Much of the protagonist's most shocking behavior, including his abduction of Elvire and the commandeur's murder, are placed before the beginning of the play and recounted by characters like Gusman and Sganarelle. A series of powerfully symbolic scenes are concentrated in act four after the fast-moving pursuit, at the moment of reprieve when the aristocrat is trying to enjoy his feast. Before confronting the protagonist with his stony nemesis, Molière created innovative interviews with the slow-witted bill collector Monsieur Dimanche, Elvire, and the ghostly apparition. All three scenes stress the fleeting nature of happiness and the inevitability of a final accounting for one's deeds. In addition, Molière relocated to this sequence Dom Juan's conversation with his father Dom Louis (in all earlier versions it had taken place in act one or two), thus avoiding a preemptive condemnation and strengthening the paternal figure—a strategic move suggested to him perhaps by Corneille's *Le Menteur*,

which his troupe often performed. Even Sganarelle contributes
to the thematic grasp for pleasure by voraciously devouring mor-
sels from the feast, only to choke when his master sadistically
interrupts or orders the plates changed. It is true that Dom Juan
momentarily routs his correctors with ridiculous sallies, but the
inherent foibles of human justice only underscore, as Pascal
pointed out, the necessity of divine punishment.

It is left to Dom Louis as symbol of the family and its system
of obligations to condemn explicitly his son's "amas d'actions
indignes . . . cette suite continuelle de méchantes affairs, qui
nous réduisent, à toutes heures, à lasser les bontés du Souverain" (4. 4). This character is no irritable old codger, but a
devoted *paterfamilias* who has used every bit of his influence at
court to extract pardons for his peccant son. His memorable
speech is designed to warn Dom Juan of impending danger and
to appeal to him with rational arguments for familial duty and
for a return to the *race* from which he has alienated himself:

> Et qu'avez-vous fait dans le monde pour être gentilhomme?
> Croyez-vous qu'il suffise d'en porter le nom et les armes, et que ce
> nous soit une gloire d'être sorti d'un sang noble lorsque nous vivons
> en infâmes? Non, non, la naissance n'est rien où la vertu n'est pas.
> Aussi nous n'avons part à la gloire de nos ancêtres qu'autant que
> nous nous efforçons de leur ressembler; et cet éclat de leurs actions
> qu'ils répandent sur nous nous impose un *engagement* de leur faire
> le même honneur, de suivre les pas qu'ils nous tracent, et de *ne
> point dégénérer* de leurs vertus, si nous voulons être estimés leurs
> véritables descendants. [4. 4, italics added]

This *apologia* for exemplary noble behavior rings like an echo of
social works such as those of Loysel, Domat, Chappuzeau, and
especially of the Portuguese treatise *La Noblesse civile et chrestienne* ("Puisqu'il est donc manifeste que la Noblesse a sa naissance et sa mort, ceux la veritablement meritent d'estre eslevés

jusques au Ciel, qui ont acquis ce lustre glorieux à leurs familles, comme les autres meritent d'estre hays de tous les hommes, qui ont terny ce lustre par les taches des vices") and La Mothe Le Vayer's *De la noblesse* ("La vertu sert de fondement à la vraie Noblesse . . . une noblesse nue et sans merite est un O en chiffre, mais si elle sert de base aux belles actions elle en augmente le prix").[16] Dom Louis's blistering accusations are directly borne out by the conceited young man, who first impertinently suggests that his father take a seat and then calls sardonically after him as he leaves: "Eh! mourez le plus tôt que vous pourrez, c'est le mieux que vous puissiez faire. Il faut que chacun ait son tour, et j'enrage de voir des pères qui vivent autant que leurs fils" (4. 5). Because Dom Juan insults the lineage that binds him to his *condition*, he deserves to be stricken from the rolls of the nobility. His wish that Dom Louis should die quickly cheapens him by reducing him to the level of an ordinary spendthrift, impatient to squander the family savings as he has already squandered its reputation.

The utter contempt of the "grand seigneur méchant homme" for the system of relationships in the *société d'états* may also give a new meaning to the famous "deux et deux sont quatre," which is generally interpreted as a statement of libertine materialism. Together with Dom Juan's inability to distinguish between unlike elements (Sganarelle stated that he would marry servant, dog, and cat as well as lady), this simplistic arithmetic betrays a social atomism inimical to the estate system. The statement "Two and two makes four" implies that all units are alike, that only quantitative calculations matter and that qualitative differences do not exist. Consequently, Dom Juan makes no difference between *paysanne*, *bourgeoise*, and *aristocrate*; they are the same to him, and each conquest gives him a new occasion to gloat. This formula also explains why Dom Juan's activities jeopardize not only the nobility but also the entire pluralistic social structure.

The challenge posed to the French hierarchy as a whole is articulated at each separate level, from the impoverished peasant village to the loftiest circles of the nobility, including *en passant* the mercantile bourgeoisie. Most of the second act is devoted to Dom Juan's adventures among the rustics, after his pirate enterprise is thwarted by bad weather. He enters this environment as a debtor, for he has been saved from the sea by Lucas and Pierrot: " . . . Tout gros Monsieur qu'il est, il seroit par ma fique nayé si je n'aviomme esté là. . . . Ô Parquenne, sans nous, il en avoit pour sa maine de féves" (2. 1). Soaked to the skin, Dom Juan has been obliged to strip naked, which allows Pierrot to give a description of the nobleman's clothing; the picture that unfolds is not that of the average discreet noble but that of the foppish marquis who stood out even at the court of Louis XIV:

> Quien, Charlotte, ils avont des cheveux qui ne tenont point à leu teste, et ils boutont ça après tout comme un gros bonnet de filace. Ils ant des chemises qui ant des manches où j'entrerions tout brandis toy et moy. En glieu d'haut de chausse, ils portont un garderobe aussi large que d'icy à Pasque, en glieu de pourpoint, de petites brassières, qui ne leu venont pas usqu'au brichet, et en glieu de rabas un grand mouchoir de cou à reziau aveuc quatre grosses houpes de linge qui leu pendont sur l'estomaque. Ils avont itou d'autres petits rabats au bout des bras, et de grands entonnois de passement aux jambes, et parmy tout ça tant de rubans, tant de rubans, que c'est une vraye piquié. [2. 1][17]

The wig, the *rhingrave* and *jabot*, the *canons*, the *affûtiaux* are all marks of the ridiculous marquis, and one need only compare Pierrot's description with those given by Cathos in *Les Précieuses ridicules* or by Sganarelle in *L'Ecole des maris*. It follows that Dom Juan is decidedly out of his element in the village, for he hardly resembles the local *seigneur* with whom the peasants might be familiar: he might just as well have landed from another planet as from the world of the *courtisans*.

In contrast to the aristocrat, the farmers are presented in the social context of their own micro-economy and village customs. Pierrot relates the wager he made with Lucas as to the nature of the creatures writhing in the sea: "quatre pièces tapées, et cinq sols en doubles" (2. 1). These obsolete and devalued coins were seldom used in urban commerce, for their worth was too infinitesimal to guarantee. Their survival in this village shows to what extent the economy of rural areas could be retarded. In this system, barter often replaced the concept of abstract worth. It is in terms of barter that Pierrot explains his love for Charlotte: "Je tachete, sans reproche, des rubans à tous les Marciers qui passont, je me romps le cou à taller dénicher des marles, je fais joüer pour toy les Vielleux quand ça vient ta feste" (2. 1). Moreover, Pierrot insists that Charlotte give him something tangible in return, namely, an occasional push, shove, or smack! In a similar incidence of barter, Charlotte tries to assuage Pierrot's hurt feelings with the economic benefits of the dairy trade at her future château: "Va, va, Piarrot, ne te mets point en peine: si je sis Madame, je te ferai gagner queuque chose, et tu apporteras du beurre et du fromage cheux nous" (2. 3). Over this order preside the elderly women of the countryside, who were frequently recognized as *chefs du feu* by the village assemblies, matriarchs like Pierrot's mother, Simonette, and Charlotte's aunt, to whom the jilted boy goes to complain over his broken engagement.[18]

Dom Juan, arriving in the village in a state of obligation, wastes no time in disrupting the local equilibrium, without ever settling his own debt. No sooner does he lay eyes on Charlotte than he begins to shower her with the most out-of-place compliments and to propose marriage—his usual shortcut to seduction:

DOM JUAN: Sganarelle, regarde un peu ses mains.
CHARLOTTE: Fi! Monsieur, elles sont noires comme je ne sais quoi.

DOM JUAN: Ha! que dites-vous là? Elles sont les plus belles du monde. [2. 2]

This courtship bears a striking resemblance to that of Don Quixote and the drab Aldonza, with which Molière was probably familiar, since he performed from 1659 to 1661 Guérin de Bouscal's *Sancho Pansa*.[19] Certainly the two cases are equally grotesque. This is no impecunious count marrying a banker's daughter to replenish the family's treasures; it is a rank manipulation of the girl's wildest hypergamous fantasies.[20] The fact that Dom Juan mass-produces such deception is revealed when Mathurine announces she has accepted the same proposal. The rake's attempts to use double-talk to confuse the two prospective brides succeed more because of the girls' curiosity and village rivalry than because of his unctuous charm.

Instead of giving Pierrot a reward, as rural barter and noble *largesse* would have it, the ungrateful aristocrat becomes a rival for the fiancée of the man who saved his life. The bewildered peasant takes flight after being pushed and struck several times, but not before he points out the brutality of Dom Juan's character: "Testiguenne! parce qu'ous estes Monsieu, ous viendrez caresser nos femmes à notre barbe? Allez-v's-en caresser les vôtres" (2 3). Dom Juan's interlude in the village, which is cut short by the approach of Elvire's brothers, disturbs interpersonal relations at all levels: between the betrothed young people, between rival lasses, between whole family units, and between the peasants and the *seigneur*.

A second confrontation with the lower classes takes place in the famous "scène du Pauvre." Once again, Dom Juan begins by making an obligation that he never fulfills. A penurious hermit tells him the way to town, but Dom Juan will give him no gratuity; in fact, he begins to insult him. The pauper explains his situation in terms of a simple economic exchange, money for prayers, which recalls the tangible micro-economy of barter in the peasant village.

> DOM JUAN: Quelle est ton occupation parmi les arbres?
> LE PAUVRE: De prier le Ciel tout le jour pour la prospérité des gens de bien qui me donnent quelque chose. [3. 2]

Dom Juan tries to subvert this structure by offering to pay the pauper a louis d'or on condition that he blaspheme, to which the latter protests that he would rather starve. The exchange is no longer equal, for in gaining his deserved recompense, the hermit would be losing both his pride and his perceived spiritual good standing. Eventually Dom Juan bids him take the coin "pour l'amour de l'humanité," but it is well to remember here that this ostentatious generosity is actually no more than the pauper had earned.[21] For many decades there was confusion over this point, since the edulcorated 1682 edition of the play by La Grange and Vivot had canceled the lines in which Dom Juan tempted the hermit, thus making it seem the nobleman was being magnanimous. Since we now have the complete text of the play, there is no need to persist in this misunderstanding. The treatment given this scene in the 1979 Comédie-Française production, directed by Jean-Luc Boutté, is worth mentioning here, for the *seigneur's* grand gesture was greeted by a long moment of icy silence from the hooded figure, who then turned and left *without* accepting the coin, a bold interpretation that accentuates a turning point in the play, the first time that one of Dom Juan's cynical gambits fails utterly.

The relationship between the wayward aristocrat and the befuddled local merchant, Monsieur Dimanche, has many elements similar to the peasant courtships. Dom Juan's outlandish compliments extend to the merchant's complexion, to his wife, children, and even "votre petit chien Brusquet" (4. 3). He breaks the laws of *préséance* not only by seating his socially inferior creditor, but by seating him in the highest style, in an armchair. He lowers himself to shake hands with the man and even offers to escort him home personally, as a vassal would for his liege lord. Instead of paying his debt or at least bearing his financial burdens with some dignity, Dom Juan undermines the business relationship between the noble debtor and the bourgeois creditor, as outlined in Jacques Savary's commercial manual, *Le Parfait Négociant*, and in Domat's fourth general rule of law; "Ne faire tort à personne, et rendre à chacun ce qui lui appartient."[22]

In dealing with his fellow noblemen, Dom Juan shows himself to be every bit as unworthy and pernicious as he is toward the peasantry and the bourgeoisie. He succeeds in evading his aristocratic responsibilities toward Dom Louis and Elvire through a combination of insult, neglect, and deceit. It is only necessary to contrast him with Elvire's brother Dom Carlos, a figure of similar age, birth, and potential, in order to measure the distance between exemplary and derogatory conduct. The first meeting between the two men, in which Dom Juan rescues Dom Carlos from a group of bandits, poses some fundamental questions about the place of strength and courage among the gamut of noble attributes. Dom Juan explains his intercession by saying, "La partie est trop inégale, et je ne dois souffrir cette lâcheté" (3. 2). Can this phrase, which follows immediately the *scène du pauvre*, indicate that Dom Juan, shamed by the pauper's righteous resolution, is moved by an attack of conscience to try to substitute a display of valor for the generosity he had failed to show, to replace one sort of magnanimity with another? Certainly his plot of piracy in act one proved that he is no stranger to violent and reckless ventures. Above all, it is the bold but capricious response of a man of action, who is interested mainly in the mathematical aspect of the contest and who would just as gladly have come to the aid of one robber pursued by three gentlemen.

As if to remind Dom Juan of his own misdeeds, Dom Carlos explains to him that he and his brother have been obliged to search the woods "pour une de ces fâcheuses affaires qui réduisent les gentilshommes à se sacrifier, eux et leur famille, à la sévérité de leur honneur" (3. 3). Elvire's brother is surely no ruffian, for he proceeds to say that he regrets the necessity for the code of the *point d'honneur* and wishes there were a more civil way of resolving such questions, a speech that must have pleased the partisans of the king's policy against dueling.[23] Unlike Dom Juan, Dom Carlos recognizes his debt to a man who saved his life and does not wish to fight with him over the crimes Elvire has suffered: "Ce me serait une trop sensible douleur que vous fussiez de la partie" (3. 3). Even after Dom Alonse reveals the identity of the disguised kinsman, Carlos refuses to exact revenge without first repaying the life-debt:

> . . . La reconnaissance de l'obligation n'efface point en moi le ressentiment de l'injure; mais souffrez que je lui rende ici ce qu'il m'a prêté, que je m'acquitte sur-le-champ de la vie que je lui dois, par un délai de notre vengeance, et lui laisse la liberté de jouir, durant quelques jours, du fruit de son bienfait. [3. 4][24]

He goes so far as to throw himself between Alonse's sword and its target and to suggest that they resolve the matter by negotiation rather than by force, a rational alternative that Dom Juan rejects out of hand.

When Dom Juan and Dom Carlos meet again in the third scene of the last act, the former has assumed another disguise, this time that of a *dévot*, or religious zealot. The courteous brother-in-law once again invites him to take part in a reasonable settlement, but Dom Juan gives the incredible response that heaven has instructed him to remain chaste and to repudiate his wife. He evidently hopes to escape from his responsibilities as a nobleman and a husband by attaching his fate to the codes of the first estate rather than the second, a perversion of the system of group differentiation that makes him more of a social danger than his simple fugue ever did. Carlos, who knows well that piety does not excuse divorce and desertion, is not fooled by this feint and finally resolves to meet Dom Juan in combat, later and in a more appropriate place. In doing so, he accepts his *condition* and its duties, even though it means very possible death at the hands of a skilled swordsman like Dom Juan. The protagonist, however, continues to the very end to deny his proper station by monstrously combining the habit of a saint with the weapon of a murderer.

Why then does not Dom Carlos, as exemplary noble, have the task of meting out justice to the social transgressor? It is only because there is another character who represents values that take precedence even over the *point d'honneur* and the noble codes of family loyalty—the commandeur's statue. Significantly, this figure embodies ultimate civil and religious authority and thus blends clerical piety with knightly valor, fusing physical and metaphysical might. The title of "commandeur" generally designated an officer in one of the military-monastic organizations, such as the Knights of Malta. In the first Dom Juan play, Tirso de Molina's *El Burlador de Sevilla*, he belongs to the Order of Calatrava. Molière's stately champion of "le ciel" and avenger of villainous abuses bears particular comparison with the king of France, who was both the first noble of the land and the head of the Gallican church. Louis XIV was especially proud of his duties as defender of the faith, "Rex Christianissimus" and scourge of heretics. Furthermore, the mobile statue's magic is of the same type as the magic that the French monarch claimed to possess, as a heavenly healer who could cure scrofula.[25] The commandeur's sartorial and architectural trappings serve to reinforce his affiliation with royalty. Dom Juan himself notes "son habit d'empereur romain" (3. 5). The splendid mausoleum that opens to reveal its interior reminds one of the king's ostentatious building projects and of the magnificent *pompes funèbres* of the court. Gazing at the tomb, Sganarelle exclaims, "Ah! que cela est beau! Les belles statues! le beau marbre! les beaux piliers! Ah! que cela est beau!" (3. 5). Like the king, an officer of the military orders could claim direct service not only to the state but to God himself.

If, in killing the commandeur, Dom Juan has murdered an analogue to the king, he has committed the most heinous crime of the seventeenth century, the most awful form of *lèse-majesté*. Molière's countrymen had not forgotten the assassin of Henri IV and his horrible demise, nor had Louis XIV dismissed his brushes with danger during the Fronde. In the figurative world of the theater, serious sociopolitical crimes were often tantamount to sacrilege, and the systems of punishment easily overlapped. In *Tartuffe* the king's police apprehend a counterfeit *dévot*, and in *Dom Juan* supernatural forces seize the master criminal. Can the latter heavenly intervention be attributed to the doctrine of *noblesse oblige*? In any case, enemies of secular order and disturbers of the spiritual peace require a suitably spectacular end.

An understanding of the social significance of the commandeur helps to set the entire structure of the comedy in perspective. Dom Juan's first encounter with the statue, at the end of the pivotal third act, concludes a sequence of disquieting events for the protagonist. First shamed by the pauper, then forced to oppose the admirable Dom Carlos, of whom he says, "Il est assez honnête homme . . . j'ai regret d'avoir démêlé avec lui" (3. 5), Dom Juan makes fun of the statue, ordering Sganarelle to invite it to dinner, and subsequently doing so himself. He has systematically disbelieved in the existence of supreme civil and supernatural power (which were, to the seventeenth-century mode of thinking, two aspects of a single immanent phenomenon) and is shocked by the proof of the animated statue. By the beginning of the next act, he has relegated the incident to the status of an optical illusion, "une bagatelle." Yet, the second meeting with the commandeur's statue, coming at the end of a series of "reminders" from M. Dimanche, Elvire, and Dom Louis, presents an undeniable challenge to the rake's bravado, for the statue says to him, "Je vous invite à venir demain souper avec moi. En aurez-vous le courage?" (9. 8). Like an aristocratic criminal on parole, Dom Juan promises to appear for the reckoning. When the statue finally arrests him, it is almost anticlimactic, for the unrepentant murderer has no alternative to an execution by "special effects," as leaping flames envelop him. The three meetings with the commandeur parallel the stages of civil justice: the trial (with presentation of evidence), the sentencing, and the punishment itself. Like the *exempt* in the denouement of *Tartuffe*, the commandeur is a proxy for the divine and earthly aspects of royal power, a knight from Heaven who reestablishes law and the noble order.

Le Misanthrope, produced about eighteen months after *Dom Juan* in 1666, differs radically in some respects from the earlier aristocratic play. *Dom Juan*, written in prose and embellished with the complicated spectacle of "machines," strains at the confines of the unities and features the actor Molière in an unusual role ancillary to the protagonist; an instant success, it was abruptly stricken from the repertory. On the other hand, *Le Misanthrope* contains some of Molière's most polished verse, adheres to classical conventions, and restores Molière the actor to the center of attention. Although its debut met mediocre success, it soon came to be recognized as a masterpiece. On a behavioral level, the misanthrope, Alceste, contrasts with his fellow nobleman, young Dom Juan. The latter boasts of his merit but behaves in a consistently demeaning manner, whereas the former is superficially modest about his contributions to society but actually quite haughty toward his equals. Thus, *Dom Juan* and *Le Misanthrope* represent opposite ends of a spectrum of misbehavior that, by indicating the extremes of abuse, makes straight and clear the path of exemplary nobility.[26]

Alceste's social affinities are evident from the beginning of the play. The courtier Oronte recognizes his standing by declaring, "Mon coeur au mérite aime à rendre justice, / Et je brûle qu'un noeud d'amitié nous unisse" (1. 2. 257–58). Arsinoé acknowledges him as "un homme . . . de mérite et d'honneur" (5. 4. 1714). Moreover, Alceste chooses to associate himself closely with a particular notion of *honneur* that goes to the very heart of his problems of alienation and malfunction: "Je veux qu'on soit sincère, et qu'en homme d'honneur / On ne lâche aucun mot qui ne parte du coeur" (1. 1. 35–36). Unlike Dom Juan, who sought to collapse society to a single social level, Alceste places great emphasis on the necessity for hierarchies in all relationships, and he chides his extroverted friend Philinte:

> Sur quelque préférence une estime se fonde,
> Et c'est n'estimer rien qu'estimer tout le monde.
> Puisque vous y donnez, dans des vices du temps,
> Morbleu! vous n'êtes pas pour être de mes gens.
> [1. 1. 57–60]

Behind the insistence on hierarchical distinctions is a desire for social eminence, a wish that others should place him above the average members of the courtly society he frequents. For the misanthrope, any equality or solidarity, even with those of his native stratum, is incompatible with his need for individual dignity: "Je veux qu'on me distingue; et pour le trancher net, / L'ami du genre humain n'est point du tout mon fait" (1. 1. 63–64). Such self-importance recalls the values of older generations of nobility, when the notion of personal *gloire* demanded total attention.[27]

That Alceste's concept of nobility based on inflated *honneur* is out of touch with the ideas of his contemporaries is evident in his conversations with Philinte, who represents a prevalent standard of *honnêteté*. This faithful friend believes that even the petty social ceremonies should be observed, just as petty debts must still be paid: "Lorsqu'un homme vous vient embrasser avec joie, / Il faut bien le payer de la même monnoie" (1. 1. 37–38). Alceste condemns this line of thought in the spirit of the superannuated nobility, calling it a "lâche méthode."[28] Yet Philinte's principles are in complete accord with the codes of behavior of Louis XIV's court, as expressed by the theoretician of the *honnête homme*, the chevalier de Méré, who referred to the models of the New Nobility as "esprits doux . . . coeurs tendres" and observed, "Ils n'ont guère pour but que d'apporter la joie partout, et leur plus grand soin ne tend qu'à mériter de l'estime, et qu'à se faire aimer."[29] Méré goes on to note that the ideal *honnête homme* should, unlike Alceste, deliberately avoid matters of morality. In terms so perfect that Méré could find none better, Philinte explicitly describes the new standards to Alceste and reproaches his friend's attachment to obsolete values:

> La parfaite raison fuit toute extrémité,
> Et veut que l'on soit sage avec sobriété.
> Cette grande roideur des vertus des vieux âges
> Heurte trop notre siècle et les communs usages.
> [1. 1. 151–54]

If Alceste's misbehavior places strain on friendship, it makes love all but impossible. From this paradox of the *atrabilaire amoureux*, the misanthrope in love, the play derives most of its comic force. Although *Le Misanthrope* sprang from the ill-fated *Dom Garcie de Navarre*, the central figure of Alceste is far superior to the jealous prince of the earlier play, for his difficulties are caused by internal contradictions rather than by outpourings of passion and the memorable confrontation scenes with his beloved are organized around misunderstandings of character rather than of appearances. Alceste's love, Célimène, is an independent and coquettish widow whose wily maneuvers add much depth to the problems of this strange noble courtship. As Alceste tries unsuccessfully to present his proposal — or, more appropriately, ultimatum — to Célimène, he has opportunities to criticize her entertainment of other men (" . . . Votre humeur, Madame, / Ouvre au premier venu trop d'accès dans votre âme" [2. 1. 457–58]), her gossiping ("Vous avez des plaisirs que je ne puis souffrir" [2. 4. 692]), her duplicity ("Ah! que ce coeur est double et sait bien l'art de feindre!" [4. 3. 1322]). It is no wonder that she complains of Alceste's gallantry-in-reverse:

> . . . La méthode en est toute nouvelle,
> Car vous aimez les gens pour leur faire querelle;
> Ce n'est qu'en mots fâcheux qu'éclate votre ardeur,
> Et l'on n'a vu jamais un amour si grondeur.
> [2. 1. 525–28]

More than mere ineptitude, his treatment of Célimène is based on a profound distortion of noble values, for as he eventually explains, he wishes to establish a marriage in which she would be utterly subjugated: "Je voudrais . . . / Que vous n'eussiez ni rang, ni naissance, ni bien" (4. 3. 1425–28). This urge to destroy Célimène's *condition*, like so many elements of Alceste's conduct, is diametrically opposed to the code of *honnêteté* promulgated by the New Nobility, which insists on the social eminence of the aristocratic lady.

Alceste has been dubbed by Ralph Albanese an "héros de la rupture," a mock tragic figure who wishes to rail against his fellow humans' vices and feels entitled to do so because of his deliberate and systematic defiance of social norms; but as Judd Hubert observes, "Hélas, Alceste partage la futilité et même les défauts de la société qu'il condamne."[30] Even before the misanthrope has a chance to speak with his ill-chosen lady (shared scorn for others does not a marriage make), Molière provides a clear example of the character's weakness in the second scene of the comedy, where the pompous poetaster Oronte asks for an opinion on one of his sonnets. To his credit, Alceste attempts to avoid this chore; but after he reluctantly agrees to hear the poem—a trivial but typical product of mid-century gallantry, bubbling with facile sentimentality—he ruthlessly dissects and dismembers it, stubbornly refusing to play the game of literary criticism by any but his private rules. When he offers to give an example of good verse, one expects him to produce some artistic gem that would put Malherbe, Maynard, and Saint-Amand to shame; but alas, all he quotes is a cheerful, fashionable ditty from the previous generation. "Si le Roi m'avait donné Paris" is elevated in Alceste's system of value only because it belongs to yesterday's fashion rather than today's. A potent critic of external shortcomings, Alceste proves La Rochefoucauld's maxim that others' faults are much easier to find than one's own. When it comes time to enter Célimène's salon in act two, Alceste finds that his masterful debunking of Philinte's maudlin embraces does nothing to help him avoid ridicule himself, for his gruff comments soon have the laughers united against him. As in *L'Ecole des femmes*, where Arnolphe browbeats his friend Chrysalde at the opening curtain but cannot get his moronic servants to open the door for him in the next scene, the dramatic structure of *Le Misanthrope* serves to undermine the putative hero's pretensions; for Alceste falls from the confident intellectual debate of the first moments into the complicated emotional world of later scenes, where his ideas fail to fit the shapes of reality. In contrast to Molière's exemplary noble figures, such as Dom Carlos, Elvire, Dom Louis, and Philinte, who accept to a great degree the absurd reversals that result from mankind's imperfect passionate nature, perfectionists like Alceste and Dom Juan are especially vulnerable when ironic fate stands against them.

Le Misanthrope recalls *Les Fâcheux* by virtue of its dramatic structure of deferral, for the desired interview between a gentleman and his lady is put off by a series of interruptions: first Oronte's, then in the second act the arrival of Acaste and Clitandre, followed by the intrusion of Arsinoé—not to mention a succession of importunate messengers from the courts. Acaste and Clitandre stand out as a pair of preening courtiers who have nothing better to do than drop names, sneer at their acquaintances, and wager on which is more dear to Célimène. Along with their hostess, they constitute the heart of the acidulous clique that delights in the protracted discussion of Parisian fools, including the extravagant Cléonte, the boring Damon, the secretive Timante, the affected Géralde, shallow Bélise, conceited Adraste, and others whose only fault it is to be hospitable or refined. Yet, the unity of the salon is illusory, for as the third act begins, Acaste and Clitandre give a perfect animated illustration of the narcissism that La Rochefoucauld's *Maximes* explored in the abstract ("On peut, par tout pays, être content de soi" [3. 1. 804]), jostling for the prestige of amorous recognition while scrupulously avoiding any true emotional commitment or any hint of failure. The impression of disunity is strengthened by the ensuing contest between rival females, as the coquette turned false prude, Arsinoé, misguidedly attempts to match wits and tongues with Célimène. The tone turns bitter when Célimène succeeds in discrediting her antagonist's vanishing sex appeal, leading Arsinoé to suggest ever so politely that Célimène is a whore by maintaining:

Qu'on n'acquiert point leurs coeurs sans de grandes avances
Qu'aucun pour nos beaux yeux n'est notre soupirant,
Et qu'il faut acheter tous les soins qu'on nous rend.

[3. 4. 1014–16]

The *dévote* woos Alceste with promises of power and consolation, but she only receives a measure of attention from him by appealing to his obsession with Célimène's infidelity.

Molière shows, however, that third parties are not the real *fâcheux* in this drama, for the misanthrope and his coquette furnish more than ample obstacles to conjugal cooperation. He tries to corner her throughout act two, but she dodges him and laughs in his face: "Vous vous moquez, je pense," to which he can only splutter, "Non; mais vous choisirez; c'est trop de patience" (2. 4. 564–65). When he finally catches up with her again, she cleverly slips away, leaving him in the clutches of lecherous Arsinoé. Alceste then hampers his cause by flying into a jealous rage at the incomplete evidence of a fragmentary love letter of Célimène's that Arsinoé has intercepted and shown to him. Like Dom Garcie de Navarre, he looks all the more pathetic when his fury turns to groveling, as Célimène applies her crafty policy of denial and derision: "Allez, vous êtes fou, dans vos transports jaloux, / Et ne méritez pas l'amour qu'on a pour vous" (4. 3. 1391–92). In fact, Molière uses double-edged irony, for Célimène *is* guilty and Alceste *does* deserve the love he gets from her—that is to say, very little. Though intellectually justified in denouncing fawning embraces and idle gossip, Alceste reveals at the crucial instant that he is even more prone to be tricked by superficial considerations (and to trick himself) than any other character.

Besides the misanthrope's personal embroilments with Philinte, Célimène, and other nobles, he runs afoul of some of the prominent mechanisms of the ancien régime, especially the courts of law. Molière hints that Alceste's haughtiness derives at least in part from the unfortunate progress of a lawsuit, for the protagonist cites as an example of the "universal" success of unworthy villains the impending victory of his opponent, a mere *pied plat* (one who does not wear high-heeled noble footwear, hence, a commoner). Alceste is so enraged by this fraudulent suit that he refuses to visit the judges in order to dispense the customary bribes necessary to win the case. The ineptitude of the Old Nobility in confronting the legal world had already been depicted by many seventeenth-century writers: one thinks, for instance, of Charles Sorel's *Francion*, in which the protagonist's father, Monsieur de la Porte, nearly reduces his family to misery through his clumsy handling of a suit.[31] Alceste's incident goes much farther, for he is aware of the established channels of bribery and refuses to use them, thus deliberately botching the affair through self-deception.

The misanthrope manifests his rejection of the normal enforcers of the social order in a more serious way when he attracts the attention of the tribunal of the Maréchaussée and then balks at following their decisions. The Court of the Marshals of France was a direct delegate of the power of the throne, charged since 1651 with arbitrating all questions involving the *point d'honneur*, among other duties. Unlike the civilian law courts, the Maréchaussée was presided over by noblemen close to the royal family, the most distinguished representatives of the second estate.[32] After arguing with Oronte about the sonnet's merit, Alceste receives the warning from Philinte that he has gained a dangerous antagonist: "Vous voilà sur les bras une fâcheuse affaire" (1. 3. 440). The appearance of the marshals' guard elicits little respect from Alceste, who boasts, on the contrary, that only the king himself can sway him:

> Hors qu'un commandement exprès du roi me vienne
> De trouver bons les vers dont on se met en peine,

Je soutiendrai toujours, morbleu! qu'ils sont mauvais,
Et qu'un homme est pendable après les avoir faits.

[2. 6. 769–72]

The adjective *pendable*, applicable only to commoners, conveys
Alceste's judgment that there is something ignoble about the
frothy little poem and that its author is too unworthy for truly
aristocratic thought. As in the opening scene, the protagonist
rejects equality with his hierarchical peers. At the beginning of
the next act, we learn from Philinte's report to Eliante on the
proceedings of the tribunal that the misanthrope steadfastly
refused to change his position, enabling the marshals to arrange
only a partial reconciliation. This important incident serves to
underscore Alceste's anachronism and his defiance of the
authority on which the *société d'états* was founded. Domat, for
instance, lists submission to authority as the second general rule
of law; Loyseau states that, regardless of the equality of all
gentlemen, comparison of a subject to his king is "odieuse,
insolente, et comme blasphamatoire"; and La Mothe Le Vayer
concurs that "un homme ne saurait être plus ridicule que de
vouloir prendre de l'avantage du côté de sa généalogie . . .
chacun se doit accommoder doucement à sa condition."[33] The
Maréchaussée incarnated the manners and mores of Louis XIV's
court, the prevalence of reasonable self-effacement over inflexi-
ble violence and the claims of *gloire*. The persistence of selfish-
ness in spite of the authoritarian mechanisms recalls the spirit of
the Old Nobility that had challenged royal power during the
Fronde, and Alceste's righteous appeal to "Mon bon droit"
(1. 1. 187) echoes the cry of many a rebellious subject.

Although Alceste's refractory behavior before civil and noble
courts suggests that he wants to play the role of a prince, all
evidence points to the conclusion that he is not illustrious and
that his *mérite* is not based on material power. He stands to lose

20,000 livres in his suit with the *pied plat*, but this sum is not really impressive for a noble fortune. His lone servant, the valet Du Bois, is an illiterate, uncouth lout with whom he interacts in a laughable manner unbefitting a *grand seigneur*.[34] Unlike Arsinoé, he does not seem to possess a carriage. Illustrations of the misanthrope's clothing show a modest gentleman's outfit consisting of *justaucorps*, baggy *haut-de-chausses*, lace cuffs, tasteful shoulder ribbons, wig, and hat, but he differs from Philinte in that his hat has no plumes and he carries no sword.[35] His language, throughout the comedy unmistakably aristocratic in its clarity and precision, stands out in relief to that of Du Bois, whose expressions such as "déloger sans trompette . . . plier bagage . . . pis que démon . . . le diable d'enfer n'y verrait goutte" (4. 4) represent the idiom of the common folk. Yet, interjections like "morbleu" and "sangbleu" crop up again and again, recalling the antiquated oaths of past generations. Far from being a remarkable personality, Alceste seems to be in most details a mediocre noble who is not in a position to look down on his fellow *chevaliers*.

In fact, the other nobles of the play, apart from Philinte and his feminine counterpart Eliante, are hardly models of exemplary conduct. Count Oronte, vain and quarrelsome, is a powerful figure at court who boasts to Alceste, "Je crois qu'un ami chaud, et de ma qualité, / N'est pas assurément pour être rejeté" (1. 2. 259–60). The prudish Arsinoé is rich and equally influential, for she promises the protagonist, "On peut pour vous servir remuer des machines, / Qui vous feront à tout un chemin assez doux" (3. 5. 1078–80). Nevertheless, Oronte's presumptuousness and Arsinoé's backbiting and mistreatment of servants are qualities not to be found in the truly *honnête* person, and their standing among the nobility is based purely on power. As for Acaste and Clitandre, the so-called marquis, their status is ambiguous. When they appear at Célimène's, they are given the same chairs as the other nobles gathered there, a sign of equality according to the codes of *préséance*. Clitandre wastes no time boasting of his presence at the king's *lever*. Alceste concedes the acceptance of Acaste and Clitandre in the palace circles when he calls them "mes bons amis de cour" (2. 4. 651). Yet, the misanthrope debunks Clitandre's ridiculous foppery: his blond wig, large *canons*, flowing *rhingrave* and superabundance of ribbons, the long fingernails he displays as a sign of leisure. Célimène also stresses the laughable nature of the pair when she refers to them as "ces grands brailleurs" (2. 2. 548) and calls Clitandre in a letter "le petit marquis . . . de ces mérites qui n'ont que la cape et l'épée" (5. 4). Acaste mentions that he has arrived in a *chaise à porteurs* rather than a carriage and speaks of love in terms that smack of the bourgeoisie: "Aimer à crédit et faire tous les frais" and "Il faut qu'à frais communs se fassent les avances" (3. 1. 816, 822). Another suggestion of less than noble standing is the fact that Célimène is using Clitandre to further her lawsuit—an enterprise where a *gentilhomme* would presumably be of little help but where the scion of a robe family would be useful. Finally, the lack of *honnêteté* among Oronte, Arsinoé, Acaste, and Clitandre is revealed conclusively when all four turn maliciously on Célimène in the last act of the play and seek to exploit her weakened position.

The uniqueness of Philinte and Eliante as exemplary figures lies not only in their ability to avoid attacking others through vicious gossip or inconsiderate moralizing, but also in their collaboration as lovers and friends. Like Méré's ideal *honnête personne*, both are good listeners; but when they speak, their language is invariably clear and elegant, as when they resolve to wed at the end of the comedy.[36] Eliante rejects Alceste's second-hand wooing by engaging herself to his friend: "Ma main de se donner n'est pas embarrassée; / Et voilà votre ami, sans trop m'inquiéter, / Qui, si je l'en priais, la pourrait accepter" (5. 4.

1796–98), to which Philinte responds, "Ah! cet honneur Madame, est toute mon envie. / Et j'y sacrifierais et mon sang et ma vie" (5. 4. 1799–1800). This exchange expresses the kind of sincerity to which Alceste aspires but which is absent in his sparring with Célimène. That yearning for merit that the lovers admired in the misanthrope, which Eliante was willing to reward at one time by her hand in marriage (and to which Philinte would gladly have sacrificed his own happiness), is eventually realized in the exemplary couple. Even after the debacle of the fifth act, where Célimène is disgraced and Alceste ruined, Philinte and Eliante adhere to their friends, for their attachment is founded on the concern for the common good rather than on self-interest, a devotion to the *souverain bien* that contemporary thought placed above *amour propre* and self-gratification.[37]

The conclusion of *Le Misanthrope* entails the accomplishment of several inevitable events that had been delayed by the accidental comings and goings of the four previous acts, the most dramatic of which is the public exposure of Célimène's mendacious coquetry. Indications of the difficulty of keeping secret the widow's motives occur as early as the beginning of the second act, where she confronts Alceste's growing curiosity. Opportunities for disclosure multiply with the confidences of the marquis in act three and with Alceste's reading in act four of a telltale letter intercepted by Arsinoé. Célimène's misdeeds consist not so much in ill will toward any of her suitors as in a lack of aristocratic honesty in her own activities. She is a character of pure *amour propre*, claiming to do nothing to excite her admirers ("Des amants que je fais me rendez-vous coupable? / Puis-je empêcher les gens de me trouver aimable?" [2. 1. 461–62]) and promising to Alceste "Le bonheur de savoir que vous êtes aimé" (2. 1, 503), as she has done to all the other gentlemen. Her strategy is an aggressive program of mockery and accusation that preys on the lack of self-assurance in others, thus diverting attention from her own shortcomings. Even as Alceste offers her a last alternative to disgrace in the form of sharing his lonely provincial retreat, she tries to take advantage of him through a mock compromise that would commit her to be his wife in name only: "Si le don de ma main peut contenter vos voeux, / Je pourrai me résoudre à serrer de tels noeuds" (5. 4. 1777–78). To the very end, she twists and evades with every word, in violation of the convention that a noble's promise must be an inviolable bond.

As for Alceste, he has resolved from the outset to allow the *pied plat* to win the contested lawsuit and to leave Célimène's salon, with or without a bride, as soon as he presents his ultimatum. It seems momentarily that the events of the dénouement will afford him the occasion to marry, not with Célimène the social butterfly, but with a woman reduced to a state of misery, dependent on him in every way. He may finally fulfill his wish: "que j'eusse la joie et *la gloire*, en ce jour, / De vous voir tenir tout des mains de mon amour" (4. 3. 1431–32; emphasis added). The chance to become more than a noble husband, to become a monarch with his mate as an adoring subject and his *désert* as his realm, appeals greatly to this man who dreams of a world devoted to his glorification. When Célimène refuses to accompany him, Alceste vows to reject all human society, which he judges to be in a state of *déchéance* from his personal standards: "Je vais sortir d'un gouffre où triomphent les vices, / Et chercher sur la terre un endroit écarté / Où d'être homme d'honneur on ait la liberté" (5. 4. 1804–6). The *désert* thus signifies not only a natural landscape but also a sociopathic space empty of people. Blinded by the impulsion to flee and by his own mock-tragic rhetoric, Alceste fails to notice that society is by no means permeated by vice—in reality, justice and truth are at hand in the chastisement of Célimène and the enlightenment of her suitors, and the brightest virtues are to be celebrated by the marriage of the *honnête* couple, Philinte and Eliante. In the midst of their joy, the betrothed aristocrats do not forget their dedication to a *souverain bien* or to their deluded misanthrope, who must still be rescued from the wilderness of his imaginary honor.[38]

It is customary to emphasize that the dénouement of *Le Misanthrope* is problematical, and, indeed, too many productions of the play become mired in sadness when they reach the fifth act. There is a tendency to treat the empty stage at the conclusion as a tomb for the lonely crowd that had filled Célimène's salon with its giggles. Nevertheless, one must ask oneself whether such gloom is absolutely necessary or justifiable. Although the typical seventeenth-century comedy concludes with a joyous assembly prepared to witness a marriage contract, a more ironic ending was not unusual, particularly when one or both of the partners in the potential couple proved unsuitable for wedlock, as in Desmarets de Saint-Sorlin's *Les Visionnaires* and in Molière's own farce *Les Précieuses ridicules*. Alceste's brusque departure follows the archetypal pattern of *pharmakos* exclusion represented in earlier Molière comedies such as *L'Ecole des femmes*. Furthermore, Célimène's banishment is equally logical, since by degrading sentimental love, as Dom Juan had done with marital commitment, she reveals herself to be a manipulating parasite akin in many ways to Tartuffe and Trissotin. Ludicrous but hardly sad, Acaste, Clitandre, Oronte, and Arsinoé flutter away from Célimène's salon toward other centers of self–aggrandizement, well paid for their time and troubles by the delicious tales of scandal that will gain them entry to the choicest circles of gossip. They will continue to show off their ribbons, to write occasional sonnets, and to parade their sanctimoniousness, thus satisfying the audience's appetite for cyclical verisimilitude: *plus ça change, plus c'est la même chose.*

Moreover, it bears repeating that the setting of the play is a salon rather than a *ménage*, a space by nature ephemeral because of its association with unmarried or unreproductive women and with the rise and fall of courtiers, the favorite motif of the age. As incontrovertible evidence in the form of letters and *procès verbaux* attests to the group's fundamental lack of cohesion, the space empties; but not without a last theatrical flourish from Alceste, who makes the most of his exit by hamming up his righteous anger before his indulgent friends. The famous parting smile that Madeleine Renaud gave to her Célimène, and that has since become an institution, offers hope that she will reappear in a forthcoming sequel. Alceste's melancholy rural utopia and Célimène's circus of scorn may be as impossible as they are undesirable, but there exists a more practical alternative in the form of the new *honnête* relationships that will spring up *chez* Philinte.

Having completed in *Dom Juan* a telescopic panorama of criminal unworthiness, and in *Le Misanthrope* a microscopic dissection of civil misbehavior, Molière did not devote another full-length comedy to the structure of exemplary aristocracy. The single subsequent play to put on stage any appreciable number of nobles is *La Comtesse d'Escarbagnas*, a brief sketch of the salon of a provincial lady whose utterly burlesque antics convey a strong suggestion of usurpation. Molière himself did not act in the production, nor did he provide a truly positive example of group codes, since the "normal" couple, Julie and her suitor the vicomte, are little more than sarcastic spectators. The reason why the author abandoned a social structure that had furnished the basis for two consecutive masterpieces is unclear. One may speculate that the reception of the plays, suppression on the one hand and disappointing receipts on the other, dissuaded him from further explorations into the foundations of the second estate, but such timidity would be incompatible with the struggling personality that battled for years against incredible odds and constant danger of persecution in order freely to present *Tartuffe*. It is much more probable that Molière was satisfied to have analyzed the significant dimensions of the structure in two contexts that complement each other in every way. He had seized upon this social tension at the precise moment when it was at the forefront of public attention because of political developments. In the same years, if the critic Charles Boudhors is correct, the chevalier de Méré was hard at work on an explicit theoretical formulation of the concept of *honnêteté*.[39]

Whatever the attitudes of Jean-Baptiste Poquelin in private life, the playwright Molière seems generally to have accepted *in toto* the validity of the social codes applied to the *noblesse*. He raises no questions about the modification of the standards of behavior, nor about the category of nobility itself. His only reservation about the legitimacy of aristocratic status concerns the claims of individuals to the order, and this was a commonplace of seventeenth-century social writings. Abuses committed by the unworthy characters are clearly portrayed as transgressions of the behavioral codes, and hence there is no mention of the complaint aired a century later by Beaumarchais, that aristocrats are permitted by the system to perpetrate certain types of wrongs. As for the exemplary characters, Philinte, Eliante, Dom Carlos, Elvire, and Dom Louis, they are neither centers of attention nor sources of laughter. Their function is to provide depth of vision and the prospect of comic delight, whereas willing and unwilling clowns, particularly Sganarelle and Alceste, provoke bursts of ironic glee. The brilliance of exemplary nobility on the comic stage, unlike the radiance of *gloire* in such tragic heroes as Horace and Polyeucte, deliberately avoids overwhelming the other elements of the play and takes its place in the *chiaroscuro* of a human tableau, in juxtaposition to the darkness of depravity and confusion.

Class struggle is absent in *Dom Juan* and *Le Misanthrope*. Indeed, recent historical research seems to have laid to rest the contention of some Marxist historians that seventeenth-century France was seething with revolutionary turmoil; careful work has revealed that the sporadic uprisings and *jacqueries* of the age were initiated by diverse causes and attracted support from a broad spectrum of social groups.[40] The closest thing in the plays to a dispute between *conditions* is Pierrot's indignant admonition to Dom Juan that he should woo women of the court and leave peasant girls alone. Yet even this feeble cry is hardly unique to the peasantry, since it would have been seconded by the distinguished Dom Louis, nor is it shared by "the masses," since Charlotte and Mathurine are both very willing to marry a courtier. The origin of any activity that can be called "antiaristocratic" is to be found in an aberration within the estate itself, in a dissonance between an individual and his *milieu*. Far from demonstrating revolutionary, class-conscious traits, this type of misbehavior invariably is associated with a lack of solidarity and with a desire to enlarge limitlessly upon what the misguided "grand seigneur méchant homme" and "atrabilaire amoureux" consider to be their personal privileges.

It is significant that Molière does not choose to highlight any subdivisions of nobility in the context of this structure of exemplary nobility and unworthiness: the ruptures between robe and sword, *gentilhomme* and *anobli*, courtiers and poor gentry, are never specifically mentioned. The only hint that any character in these plays is less than a full-fledged *chevalier* involves a few inconclusive details of possible bourgeois associations for Acaste and Clitandre. The consciousness of an internal hierarchy of distinctions does not intrude into the homogeneous atmosphere of Dom Juan's *parentèle* and Célimène's clique. One must observe that, of all possible causes of unworthiness, Molière depicts only those that violate the most intrinsic rules and avoids commercial *dérogeance* completely. The reason for this is two-fold: on the level of verisimilitude, it would be ridiculous for Dom Juan Tenorio or Alceste to take up shopkeeping; on the historical and structural level, commercial *dérogeance* was prob-ably rather rare. There was no collective movement of noblemen anxious to involve themselves in business activities under the ancien régime; quite to the contrary, the tendency of merchants to retire and to immobilize their capital in *rentes foncières* in order to "live nobly" was a massive cause of economic stagna-tion. By concentrating on unworthiness linked to crime and civil misconduct, Molière was proving his timeliness and realism.

Both in *Le Festin de Pierre* and in *Le Misanthrope*, unworthi-ness is eventually punished by the expulsion of the *pharmakos* through a process of rational analysis.[41] Each time the unworthy one is given ample explanations of the codes and frequent warn-ings, even from such reluctant antagonists as Dom Carlos and Célimène. Neither Dom Juan nor Alceste is manipulated in any way by deterministic forces. The chance to reintegrate themsel-ves into society is reiterated and rejected to the bitter end. Comic judgment in Molière's plays is a rigorous but fair proce-dure that arrives at the exclusion of the misbehaver only as a last resort. Molière's *Dom Juan* is unique in that it does not rely on the well-known dramatic tradition of the "athée foudroyé," which doomed the man from the ouset, but instead articulates a logical hierarchy of crime and punishment with which the rake insistently contends. If Alceste faces a mitigated exclusion by self-imposed exile, it is because he has freely chosen a punish-ment more severe than that which society would have given him. Such a fate is appropriate and, with Philinte's intercession, may be only temporary; for Alceste is harmless except to him-self, and his distortion of actual aristocratic values stems more from inflation than from denial.

Thus, Molière's exemplary aristocrats are well-rounded, idealized versions of the New Nobility promulgated by the court of Louis XIV: respectful of authority, scrupulously moderate, conscious of the *souverain bien*. Although they do not flaunt their superiority, they continually take part in the relentless comparison of the individual to the standards of what he should be; they never for a moment concede or justify the unreformed misbehavior of their fellow noblemen. The unworthy, who place their confidence in an immutable order of privilege and who do nothing to merit their dignity, are winnowed out by the moment-to-moment testing process of civil life. Action is for Molière's nobles the ultimate proof of status.

1. Lucien Goldmann, *Sciences humaines et philosophie*, p. 114.

2. Mousnier, *La Vénalité des offices*, p. 538; Ford, *Robe and Sword*, p. 25; Loyseau, *Traité des ordres*, 1:59–60. The latter also specifies: "L'ordre de chevalerie se perd par l'infamie pour ce que toute tache y est formellement contraire," (1:54).

3. Gilles-André de La Roque de la Lontière, *Traité de la noblesse*, pp. 459–69.

4. Gaston Zeller, "Une notion de caractère historico-social: la dérogeance"; Jougla de Morenas, *Noblesse 38*, p. 73.

5. François Bluche, *La Vie quotidienne de la noblesse française au XVIIIᵉ siècle*, p. 39; Argou, *Institution au droit français*, 1:17–19; Antoine Loysel, *Institutes coutumières*, 2:219.

6. J. H. Shennan, *Government and Society in France, 1461–1661*, pp. 25–28; Goubert, *L'Ancien Régime*, 1:133–38.

7. Robert Mandrou uses the term "feudal reaction" to describe a tightening of social closure in the seventeenth century that encompassed the verification of noble titles; see *Classes et luttes de classes*, p. 82. Pierre-Adolphe Cheruel, in *Dictionnaire historique des institutions, des moeurs et des costumes de la France*, 1:267–68 and 2:861, notes the success of the *réformations*, as does Louis de la Roque, in *Armorial de la noblesse de Languedoc*, 1:xxxii–xliv, who observes that many people attempting to live nobly were fined and obliged to declare themselves non-noble.

8. For the social reverberations of the *Grands Jours* and the *recherches de noblesse*, see Robin Briggs, *Early Modern France 1560–1715*, pp. 63–64; and Jean Meyer, *La Noblesse bretonne au XVIIIᵉ siècle*, 1:29–61.

9. Adam, "Molière," pp. 329–30; Cairncross, *Molière bourgeois et libertin*, pp. 21–38; Jacques Guicharnaud, in *Molière, une aventure théâtrale*, pp. 177–343, presents

an interesting analysis of Dom Juan's expressions in the light of the philosophy of nature.

10. Roland Barthes, "Le Silence de Dom Juan." Besides Barthes and Cairncross, some of those to present arguments in favor of a "positive" Dom Juan are: James Doolittle, "The Humanity of Molière's *Dom Juan*"; André Villiers, "Dom Juan Revisited," in *Molière, A Collection of Critical Essays*, pp. 79–89; Jean-Marie Teyssier, *Réflexions sur le Dom Juan de Molière*, pp. 15–20; and Micheline Sauvage, *Le Cas Dom Juan*, pp. 153–57. Janine Krauss, in *Le Dom Juan de Molière: une libération*, concurs with the idea that the play is a libertine document, but stops short of admiration for the protagonist (pp. 111–31). Among the most eloquent analyses of a criminal, ridiculous Dom Juan are: W. G. Moore, "*Dom Juan* Reconsidered"; H. Gaston Hall, "A Comic *Dom Juan*," in *Molière, A Collection of Critical Essays*, pp. 103–10; Edouard Guitton, "Molière juriste dans *Dom Juan*"; Jean Dubu, "Dom Juan et la notion de l'honnêteté chez Molière"; Jacques Morel, "Le comique de Molière a-t-il un sens?"; and Francis Lawrence, "Dom Juan and the Manifest God: Molière's Antitragic Hero." Jules Brody's engaging essay "*Don Juan* and *Le Misanthrope*, or the Esthetics of Individualism in Molière" offers a tempting compromise to the problem by asserting that the protagonist is morally wrong but esthetically right (just the reverse of Alceste); however, this argument depends to a great extent on the dissociation of vice and error and on the premise that a character is wrong if he is wronged—points that remain to be proved. Jacques Guicharnaud puts his finger on the source of Dom Juan's much vaunted liberty: "Dom Juan étant totalement aveuglé par la satisfaction sensuelle et amorale de son être . . . piétine les codes du monde qu'il traverse, et ne s'apercevrait pas des dégâts qu'il commet si on ne les lui signalait pas. C'est là sa liberté: celle de l'homme à idée fixe qui pénètre dans des propriétés interdites parce qu'il ne voit pas les pancartes; si on les lui montre, l'idée fixe est trop possessive pour qu'il les prenne au sérieux" (*Molière, une aventure théâtrale*, p. 199).

11. On the anecdote, see *OC* Couton, 2:1310. The criticism comes from the *Lettre sur les observations d'une comédie du sieur Molière intitulée Le Festin de Pierre*, *OC* Couton, 2:1222.

12. Baillard, *Discours du tabac*, summarizes several contemporary opinions on tobacco and agrees, on p. 64, that tobacco makes the head "plus flexible à toutes les actions de l'esprit, soit qu'il juge, soit qu'il imagine."

13. On marriage conventions, see Donald Hunt, *Parents and Children in History*, pp. 57–67; Henri de Campion, *Mémoires*, p. 231; and, regarding the sadistic implications of Dom Juan's own marriages, Guicharnaud, *Molière, une aventure théâtrale*, pp. 209–22.

14. Loysel, *Institutes coutumières*, 1:162. See also on elopement as rape J. Gaudemet, "Législation canonique et attitudes séculières à l'égard du lien matrimonial au XVIIe siècle." François Lebrun, *Les Hommes et la mort en Anjou aux XVIIe et XVIIIe siècles*, pp. 419–22, observes that noble crimes and armed attacks were not rare in the French countryside during this period. See also Guitton, "Molière juriste."

15. All details on the Grands Jours come from Arlette Lebigre, *Les Grands Jours d'Auvergne: désordres et répression au XVIIe siècle*, pp. 97–120. Other instances of crimes by nobles, based on Chancellor Séguier's correspondence, are to be found in Ralph Albanese's "Historical and Literary Perceptions on 17th Century French Criminality."

16. Loysel, *Institutes coutumières*, 1:50 ("Nul ne nait chevalier"), and 2:203 ("Le fait juge l'homme"); Domat, *Les Lois civiles*, p. v; Chappuzeau, *Le Devoir général*, pp. 82–88; Godefroy, *Abbrégé des trois états*, 2:1 ("La vertu est donc la principale cause de la noblesse, et la noblesse un effet de la vertu"); *La Noblesse civile et chrestienne*, trans. H. Estienne, p. 98; and François La Mothe Le Vayer, *De la noblesse*, in *Oeuvres*, 2:191–200, which goes on to state, "Si un noble est sans vertu, ses défauts paraissent au double et son infamie croît autant à proportion de son rang que de son vice." Annie Ubersfeld's article "Dom Juan et le noble vieillard" tends to present Dom Louis as an avatar of reactionary repression, but she significantly omits to discuss the father's indulgent, sentimental side, which appears especially in act five. For a detailed discussion of similarities between this scene and the admonition sequence in Corneille's *Le Menteur*, as well as other intertextual elements, see my article, "*Le Menteur* and *Dom Juan*: A Case of Theatrical and Literary Adaptation."

17. Also see illustration, *OC* La Grange, 7:128.

18. Jean Jacquart, *La Crise rurale en l'Ile-de-France 1550–1670*, p. 558. Pierre de Saint-Jacob notes that as the peasant/seigneur division deepened, the village assemblies would meet clandestinely in the graveyards after mass (*Documents relatifs à la communauté villageoise en Bourgogne*, p. xiv).

19. Bray, *Molière, homme de théâtre*, pp. 110–15. Raymond Lebègue, in "La Bipolarité des personnages de Molière," suggests that Quixote and Sancho exercised a considerable influence on the entire Molière canon.

20. Leo Weinstein underscores the fact that Molière's Dom Juan is not really a very successful seducer or a model of gallantry (*The Metamorphoses of Dom Juan*, p. 29).

21. See Jacques Morel, "A propos de la scène du pauvre dans *Dom Juan*," which analyzes this scene from the point of view of charity and stresses the traditional exchange of money for spiritual well-being.

22. Jacques Savary, *Le Parfait Négociant*, pp. 314–19, and Domat, *Les Lois civiles*, vii and 77. Molière heightens the effect of Dom Juan's *dérogeance* by making Sganarelle chase Monsieur Dimanche away with mock-aristocratic brutality in the following scene.

23. Carlos's situation is not so much an impossible dilemma as the conflict between emotion and moral values which ancien régime ethics continually pose; see Guicharnaud, *Molière, une aventure théâtrale*, p. 264. For evidence that persistent duelling still gave rise to such debates in Molière's time, see François Billacois, "Le Parlement de Paris et les duels au XVIIe siècle," in *Crimes et criminalité en France sous l'Ancien Régime*.

24. Michel Pruner, "La Notion de dette dans le *Dom Juan* de Molière," undertakes a thorough study of the contractual relationships in the play and notes that Dom Carlos is

just one of several characters who contrast with the infractions of Dom Juan. Joseph Pineau, "Dom Juan 'mauvais élève'," refers to the character as an "anti-noble qui contesterait ouvertement toutes les valeurs de sa propre classe" (p. 567).

25. See Marc Bloch, *Les Rois thaumaturges*.

26. Among those studies that echo Rousseau in praise of Alceste are M. Magendie, "Le véritable sens du Misanthrope," in *Mélanges de philologie et d'histoire littéraire offerts à Edmond Hughet*; and René Jasinski, *Molière et Le Misanthrope*. Gustave Michaut, *Les Luttes de Molière* p. 227ff.; P. J. Yarrow, "A Reconsideration of Molière," and Gérard Defaux, "Alceste et les rieurs," agree that Alceste is fundamentally ridiculous, but the latter two stress a perceived shift to seriousness at the end of the play. An excellent and lucid summary of critical opinions on Alceste is Francis Lawrence, "Our Alceste or Molière's?"

27. Jasinski makes a notable attempt to identify the sentiments toward mankind expressed by Alceste with those found in La Mothe Le Vayer's *Prose chagrine*; see *Molière et le Misanthrope*, pp. 258-75.

28. The nature of the relationship between Alceste and Philinte has been viewed in many ways; two of the alternatives are W. D. Howarth, "Alceste, ou l'honnête homme imaginaire," whose ideas on Philinte as an example of *honnête* behavior to the unworthy Alceste we have followed rather closely; and L. Hippeau, *Essai sur la morale de La Rochefoucauld*, pp. 174-94, which interprets Alceste as a stoic battling unsuccessfully against the epicurean Philinte. Another essential point in the discussion of the social dynamics of the play is made by Robert Horville, "La Cohérence des dénouements de *Tartuffe*, de *Dom Juan*, et du *Misanthrope*," who states that Alceste constantly stressed person-to-person relationships to the detriment of the entire social fabric.

29. Antoine Gombaud, chevalier de Méré, "De la vraie honnêteté," in *Oeuvres complètes*, ed. Charles Boudhors (Paris: F. Roches, 1930), 3:71.

30. Ralph Albanese, "Théâtre et anomie: le cas du *Misanthrope*"; Judd Hubert, "Molière et les deux styles burlesques." A good treatment of Alceste's place in Molière's satire of the idea/ideal is found in Carlo François, *La Notion de l'absurde dans la littérature française du XVIIe siècle*, pp. 101-11.

31. Sorel, *Francion*, pp. 156-60.

32. Regarding the important functions of the *Maréchaussée*, see Voltaire, *Le Siècle de Louis XIV*, in *Oeuvres complètes*, 14: 507-11; Cheruel, *Dictionnaire historique*, 2:733-34; and Meyer, *La Noblesse bretonne*, pp. 1137-39. The peacekeeping power of this body was associated with the legal principle expressed by Loysel in *Institutes coutumières*, 2:167:"Il ne se donne ni trêve ni paix entre les sujets du roi, mais on les met en assurance et sauve-garde."

33. Domat, *Les Lois civiles*, p. vii, Loyseau, *Traité des ordres*, p. 66; La Mothe Le Vayer, *De la noblesse*, pp. 197-98. On Alceste's marginality in this respect, see Albanese, "Théâtre et anomie."

34. On the conventions of treating servants, see Chappuzeau, *Le Devoir général*, pp. 103–4.

35. *OC* La Grange, 3:117. An earlier illustration of the play shows basically similar attire, except for the *justaucorps*; see Roger W. Herzel, "The Decor of Molière's Stage: The Testimony of Brissart and Chauveau."

36. Méré, "De la vraie honnêteté," pp. 76–77. A fine discussion of Philinte and Eliante is provided by Marie-Odile Sweetser, "Structure et signification du *Misanthrope*."

37. Domat, *Les Lois civiles*, p. viii.

38. Quentin Hope, in "Society in *Le Misanthrope*" correctly insists on the importance of this ending, as opposed to the abbreviated one used by Arnavon in order to augment the "noble pathos" of the play.

39. Méré, "De la vraie honnêteté," p. 190.

40. For important corrections to the major revolutionary thesis, Boris Porschnev's *Les Soulèvements populaires en France au XVIIe siècle*, see Roland Mousnier, "Recherches sur les soulèvements populaires avant la Fronde," and Hubert Méthivier, *L'Ancien Régime*, pp. 75–78.

41. For a broader perspective on the expulsion of the antisocial *pharmakos*, see Ralph Albanese, "Quelques héros criminels chez Molière."

GEORGE DANDIN

George Dandin, dressed as a gaudy upstart, kneeling before the Sotenville family. Note the father's medieval helmet. Brissart and Sauvé engraving for the 1682 Paris edition, republished in 1697. Reproduced by permission of the Houghton Library, Harvard University.

CHAPTER FOUR

SOCIAL CLOSURE AND USURPATION

The attraction exerted by noble status and privilege caused the French aristocracy to be concerned not only with maintaining the internal cohesion of their group through emphasis on nonderogation, but also with forestalling a possible displacement or dilution of their power by the rapid influx of bourgeois into their estate. Many hereditary nobles of both the *épée* and *robe* categories felt threatened by totally "unqualified" usurpers and by recent beneficiaries of the *noblesse de fonctions*, whose vertical mobility was guaranteed by law. Mousnier, Deyon, and others have pointed out that during the seventeenth century more and more restrictions were placed on mobility, as a reaction against change of status reduced access by the third estate to aristocratic positions.[1] The percentage of *anoblis* in the noble population dropped from about 51 percent in 1500 to about 10 percent at the close of the grand siècle.[2] Although the entries to the upper strata were never entirely shut off to those who could place at the disposal of the crown large sums of money, the mechanism of closure became increasingly efficient.

Under the reign of Louis XIV, social closure became centralized and institutionalized. A main factor in this evolution was the role of the *recherches de noblesse*, which insisted upon explicit documentary proof of noble status. This in turn implied almost complete reliance on recognition of status by the formal organisms of the state. Families that otherwise might have felt content to claim nobility on the basis of a vague history of participation in military campaigns, service to a princely house, or gradual assumption of a noble life-style now were forced to consolidate their claim with letters of nobility, offices, exemptions, or fief ownership that could be provided only by the king's delegates.

The same process of restricting mobility operated on the lower levels of society and fulfilled an important preemptive function by limiting vertical movement into the bourgeoisie proper. Louis XIV's policy of establishing *corporations* and *maîtrises* for nearly all skilled professional and artisanal activities made it difficult for any but members of the masters' families to rise through commerce or industry. Expensive corporate rites of passage minimized the possibility of competition from newcomers. The gap between the masters of the trades and the nascent proletariat of journeymen, apprentices, day laborers, and servants insulated the privileged groups from any massive upsurge of *nouveaux riches*.

The imperative of social ascension nevertheless continued to exert pressure on the groups occupying lower places in the hierarchy of power. Lapeyre's study of the Ruiz merchant dynasty in Nantes shows that after only two generations of commercial activity in France, this family was fully involved in the search for nobility.[3] There is abundant evidence that the appeal of tax-exempt status in the nobility drove commoners from almost every corner of the nation to try to usurp aristocratic privileges, thus avoiding the time-consuming path of office-holding and the exorbitant expenses of title purchase.[4] Despite the risks of usurpation and the dogged investigations of the *recherches de noblesse*, Ernest Lavisse concludes that false nobles were a common phenomenon in the *société d'états*.[5] After all, the average bourgeois could hardly wield the financial and political power that permitted Colbert's family to achieve a spectacular ascent in rank through service to the crown. Denied the means of speedy and legitimate betterment, the ambitious *roturier* often had no recourse except to use what wealth he possessed to acquire some of the superficial attributes of superiority, in the hope that society would accept him on the basis of his clothes, his lands, his life style, or some other aspect of outward recognition. The usurper thus can be seen as one who manipulates the normative *paraître* that rules his environment in order to assign himself a new identity, or *être*—a process that seeks to subvert the social order without changing it in any but a single individual detail.

In the work of Molière, usurpation first appears in *Les Précieuses ridicules*, where both the "false" *précieuses*, Cathos and Magdelon, and the masquerading valets, Mascarille and Jodelet, play at being members of the aristocracy. The critique of usurpation is attentuated in the play because the girls owe a good part of their failure to their provincialism, which is a geographic rather than a social issue. Their understanding of noble behavior is based on the impressions given by idealized novels, rather than on acute observations of Parisian hierarchical customs. As for the valets, they undertake to pass for nobles only because they have been encouraged and cajoled by their masters, Du Croisy and La Grange. Other than dressing in foppish costumes and engaging in what they believe to be aristocratic conversation, they make no serious attempts to claim the privileges of the upper groups. It is clear from the outset that Mascarille and Jodelet are performing strictly within the limitations set for them by the masters. Since neither the girls nor their ridiculous suitors can entertain any hopes of making the larger world accept their travesty, they are all "false" usurpers, harmless because their potential for disrupting the social order through illicit mobility is totally devalued.

In 1662 Molière's first fully developed five-act comedy, *L'Ecole des femmes*, provided a far more detailed picture of usurpation than had appeared in his previous farces. The action of the drama catches the protagonist, Arnolphe, in the midst of

a subtle plot to alter radically his identity as a prosperous bourgeois in an unnamed French city. On the one hand, he has
already dared to appropriate a noble name, Monsieur de la
Souche, and on the other, he is on the point of marrying his
own ward, Agnès, a peasant girl whom he deliberately has
raised to be a model of ignorance. At first glance, it might seem
that Arnolphe's passage from bourgeois to noble, described
largely in the liminary discussion with his fellow townsman,
Chrysalde, is almost a *fait accompli* and is detached from his
"courtship" of Agnès. Yet, in fact, there is a double bond
between the phenomena. Arnolphe's plans for Agnès emanate
from his desire to avoid being accused of usurping a high position, to have a wife who cannot reproach him his humble beginnings or embarrass him by claiming an equal footing in the
family. It seems necessary that Arnolphe marry the woman of
his choice (one might almost say, of his creation) in order that
his ambitious projects may reach fruition: the possibility of
assuming supremacy in the social hierarchy hinges on his ability
to establish first of all an unchallenged domination within the
family unit. The fundamental paradox of his position is that the
very strengths of his double identity become weaknesses once an
alternative destiny for Agnès is proposed. Horace, his rival, is
not only young and relatively powerless, but he is subject to the
commands of a father who is among Arnolphe's best friends and
who has other plans for the boy's future that preclude his marrying the poverty-stricken ward. It would seem that nothing
would be easier than to remove Horace from the scene once and
for all. Yet, in doing so, Arnolphe would have to admit publicly
his double identity and to bring unwanted critical attention to
his highly irregular plans for advancement.

Arnolphe's wealth is acknowledged by all his fellow citizens,
even though they may hold him in less respect than he believes.
Horace has heard that he is: "Riche, à ce qu'on m'a dit, mais des
plus sensés, non; / Et l'on m'en a parlé comme d'un ridicule"

(1. 4. 330–31). The fact that he carries in his purse 100 pistoles, more than 1,000 livres, indicates that he is a man accustomed to handling very large sums of money. In addition, he owns land in the country, for he has just returned from an eleven day visit to his *métairie* (1. 4. 253–56). It was not unusual for the bourgeoisie of provincial towns to monopolize the prime agricultural lands in their vicinity and to make extended trips to the farms during the planting and harvesting seasons in order to supervise the workers and to make sure that not a penny of profit escaped them; Couturier mentions that this was the practice around Châteaudun, and Drouot notes the same for Mayenne and Burgundy.[6] Venard adds that in the area of Avrainville the burghers had made such an institution of these visits that their farms contained comfortable houses with carriage facilities.[7]

It is from his sense of property ownership that Arnolphe has progressed to the stage of usurpation. Chrysalde mocks the vanity of this erstwhile transformation, as well as the lack of imagination reflected in the unfieflike name of la Souche:

> Qui diable vous a fait aussi vous aviser,
> A quarante et deux ans, de vous débaptiser,
> Et d'un vieux tronc pourri de votre métairie
> Vous faire dans le monde un nom de seigneurie?
>
> [1. 1. 169–73]

These comments imply that Arnolphe's activities are both unusual and illegal, for he has skipped several steps in the legitimate process of upward mobility by failing to acquire a noble fief (even a *seigneurie* was no grounds for a claim of nobility) and by avoiding the payment of the *franc-fief*, which would authorize a commoner like himself to possess such land. Avarice is probably at the root of this plan, for to purchase a fief and pay the fee to the king would be a costly undertaking.

Molière supplies other indicators that would confirm the

audience's impression that Arnolphe is a wealthy but tightfisted bourgeois and an eminent person in his community. He owns two houses in the town, one for his sequestered ward and the other for himself. The latter is frequented at all hours of the day by all sorts of people: "Ma demeure / A cent sortes de monde est ouverte à toute heure" (1. 1. 143–44). Such a busy house might be the home of a prosperous merchant or, even more likely in view of the social cross-section represented by the visitors, that of an *officier*, a magistrate, or a tax collector. The greed of the latter two professions was already legendary in Molière's day. This type of man could be expected to wear the traditional bourgeois suit, shoes, and hat pictured in the well-known engraving by Chauveau that served as frontispiece to the play.[8] The same illustration shows lace ornaments adorning the suit, a testimony to Arnolphe's desire to enhance his standing in the town. Yet, just as the protagonist has not completely freed himself from the costume of the bourgeoisie, he employs clumsy servants who have only recently left their farms and hence lack the bearing and the cunning of domestics in a distinguished house.

Somehow Arnolphe has already managed to gain the connivance of the townspeople in his project of usurpation. Chrysalde shows him considerable respect and vows to use his assumed name: "Je prendrai le soin d'accoutumer ma bouche / A ne plus vous nommer que Monsieur de la Souche" (1. 1. 191–92). Dominating the town, Arnolphe seeks to consolidate his authority both by entering the superior class and at the same time by setting himself up, as Alceste longs to do, as an unquestionable patriarch within his own household. His words recall the Misanthrope's longing for an abject wife:

> Je me vois riche assez pour pouvoir, que je crois,
> Choisir une moitié qui tienne tout de moi

Et de qui la soumise et pleine dépendance
N'ait à me reprocher aucun bien ni naissance.

[1. 1. 125–28]

The will to dominate, objectify, and exploit other creatures, which such critics as Bernard Magné and Ralph Albanese have discerned in Arnolphe, is paradoxically an important ingredient in the ridiculous dissonance of his character.[9] At first it may seem that these plans for a hypogamous marriage to a peasant girl are incongruous with the upward pretensions of a social climber. On close examination, however, we find in Arnolphe's double scheme a careful, if twisted, method that makes him qualify as one of Molière's most interesting pseudo-intellectual dupes. His frenzied efforts to establish aristocratic status in the town are not as uncommon as they may seem, for Gustave Roupnel and Pierre Goubert have discovered similar efforts in real life by the Taisand family of Dijon and the Foy family of Beauvais.[10] What Arnolphe has fixed as his goal is to avoid the interference of a wife in his usurpation schemes—a difficulty that will later befall both George Dandin and Monsieur Jourdain. A would-be noble could be betrayed by the inappropriate views and manners of a thoroughly bourgeois wife or by the contumely of an over-proud aristocratic one. By taking a wife from the bottom of the social order, Arnolphe hopes to enhance his loftiness and to re-create in the home the same upstart hegemony that he seeks to establish over his fellow-citizens.

This project also explains his abiding fear of cuckoldry, which is far more here than a mere farcical theme. Having eliminated the possibility of being dwarfed by his wife's social stature and also having blackmailed the local husbands into compliance, Arnolphe is conscious of only one remaining danger: his spouse may put the horns on him, thus shattering his precarious respect and proving his lack of honor or worthiness. It is revealing that

Arnolphe refers to his personal attempts to avoid cuckoldry as a "noble dessein" (4. 7. 1196). The danger is paramount, since Arnolphe always congratulates himself as being better than other unfortunate city-dwellers:

> . . . Est-il au monde une autre ville aussi
> Où l'on ait des maris si patients qu'ici?
> Est-ce qu'on n'en voit pas, de toutes les espèces,
> Qui sont accommodés chez eux de toutes pièces?
> L'un amasse du bien, dont sa femme fait part
> A ceux qui prennent soit de le faire cornard;
> L'autre, un peu plus heureux, mais non pas moins
>   infâme,
> Voit faire tous les jours des présents à sa femme
> . . . .
> Enfin ce sont partout des sujets de satire;
> Et comme spectateur ne puis-je pas en rire?
>
> [1. 1. 21–28, 43–44]

Arnolphe hints that Chrysalde may be a cuckold, too, and boasts to young Horace, "C'est un plaisir *de prince*; et des tours que je vois / Je me donne souvent la comédie à moi" (1. 4. 297–98). No sooner does Arnolphe hear that Horace has embarked upon an amorous intrigue than he sets out to record it in his annals of municipal dishonor: "Bon! voici de nouveau quelque conte gaillard; / Et ce sera de quoi mettre sur mes tablettes" (1. 4. 306–7). Of course, Chrysalde, who accepts infidelity as a social fact and sometimes even a pleasant arrangement, does not share his friend's extremist views. But since Arnolphe defines his own honor not in positive terms but according to the dishonor, lowliness, and misfortune of those who surround him, one incidence of cuckoldry will be enough to destroy his chimerical ambitions of power and prestige as a noble.

Part of the comic delight of *L'Ecole des femmes* is the gap between the demands of social living and Arnolphe's image of them, for despite his far-reaching plans, it is clear to the audience that Arnolphe is not capable of living an exemplary life or behaving like an aristocrat. In the second scene of the play, when he tries to reassert his mastery over the doltish servants, Alain and Georgette, he is locked out, delayed, insulted (when Alain obstinately refuses to doff his hat), and even slapped (1. 2. 218). After he has found out that the domestics accepted money from Horace to conceal his visits, he literally goes wild, and Alain comments: "Quelque chien enragé l'a mordu, je m'assure" (2. 2. 392). Even Arnolphe admits he has lost the self-control so essential to a noble. Anger transforms him into an atavistic savage: "Ouf! Je ne puis parler, tant je suis prévenu: / Je suffoque, et voudrais me pouvoir mettre nu" (2. 2. 393–94). Moreover, this odd example of regressive behavior is by no means atypical, for later on (4. 6), we learn that he has thrown a tantrum in Agnès's bedroom, smashed china, and even kicked the dog!

Instead of accenting his superiority, Arnolphe is forced as the action develops to draw closer and closer to the rustic servants. Before sending them out to ambush Horace, he calls them "mes fidèles, mes bons, mes vrais amis" (4. 4. 1093). The ambush is hardly an honorable aristocratic combat, and Arnolphe augments his unworthiness by letting Alain and Georgette push him about for practice. In the light of this awkward and ineffective relationship with the servants, one has trouble imagining how some dramatic interpreters, such as Roussillon, were able to maintain that Arnolphe is a Hitlerian manipulator worthy of melodrama.[11]

Arnolphe's difficulty with the domestics is nothing compared with the problems of dealing with the ingenuously rebellious Agnès. Her anodyne prattle in the beginning of the play about kittens, insects, and nightgowns is merely the superficial appearance of simplemindedness. Her *récit* in the second act reveals that she has already begun to form with Horace a relationship that springs from politeness and is maintained by generosity:

> Toujours comme cela je me serais tenue,
> Ne voulant point céder, et recevoir l'ennui
> Qu'il me pût estimer moins civile que lui
> . . . .
> Et pouvais-je, après tout, avoir la conscience
> De le laisser mourir faute d'une assistance?
>
> [2. 5. 500–502, 539–40]

When the time comes for communication, Agnès masters the sophisticated language of love with surprising ease and natural inclination.[12]

With the famous concluding line of the second act, "Je suis maître, je parle: allez, obéissez," taken from Corneille's *Sertorius*, Arnolphe tries to regain control by ordering Agnès to forget her instincts and obey the command to marry him.[13] The usurper is trying to assert himself like the chivalric hero of some tragedy, little knowing that he will have tragedy enough when the play ends. He also calls himself "un sage directeur" and notes that he has elevated his ward from the "vil état de pauvre villageoise" to be his mate. This pattern of overevaluation of the self, as Ralph Albanese calls it, runs contrary to the prevailing ideas of homogamous, contractual marriage, free of constraint.[14] Marriages that featured a wide discrepancy in age were condemned explicitly by the decisions of the church and the folk custom of the *charivari*, implicitly by such legal codes as Domat's tenth general rule: "Tous les engagements qui blessent les loix et les bonnes moeurs sont illicites."[15]

Strangely enough, Arnolphe admits that he has refused other, more normal offers of marriage, and describes himself as "un homme qui fuyait tous ces engagements, / Et dont à vingt partis, fort capables de plaire, / Le coeur a refusé l'honneur qu'il vous veut faire" (3. 2. 686–88). He declines these opportunities in order to wed someone according to his private rules ("ma mode") and to construct his own version of society in which he will be the lord and Agnès his thrall:

> Du côté de la barbe est la toute-puissance.
> Bien qu'on soit deux moitiés de la société,
> Ces deux moitiés pourtant n'ont point d'égalité:
> L'une est moitié suprême, et l'autre subalterne.
>
> [3. 2. 700–703]

This man, who has tried to procure for himself princely pleasures at the expense of others, likens himself to generals and pontiffs, to everything short of king. The *Maximes* that he makes his ward recite are inimical to the form of equal marriage that was customary among the nobility he hopes to join; they leave the woman no alternatives to ugliness, illiteracy, solitude, and subordination. Once again, Arnolphe's twisted ambitions do not match the conduct of the class to which he aspires. Yet he believes he has convinced Agnès of his dominance and boasts: "Comme un morceau de cire entre mes mains elle est" (3. 3. 810).

Arnolphe's illicit ambitions have not reckoned with the force of love, which, according to Horace, really does have the power to make people behave in ways far above their apparent abilities or conditions:

> Il le faut avouer, l'amour est un grand maître:
> Ce qu'on ne fut jamais il nous enseigne à l'être;
> Et souvent de nos moeurs l'absolu changement

> Devient, par ses leçons, l'ouvrage d'un moment;
> De la nature, en nous, il force les obstacles,
> Et ses effets soudains ont de l'air des miracles.
>
> [3. 4. 900–905]

In fact, the miracle has occurred in Agnès, for, throwing off the abject role Arnolphe has given her, she manifests an almost aristocratic generosity by giving herself symbolically in her letter to Horace, an act that represents the final conquest of free speech.[16]

From this point on, resistance is hopeless; Arnolphe is fighting in vain against all the social rules of the world in which he lives. The best he can hope for is a stalemate. This point is driven home by the appearance of the notary in the fourth act. The scene is not simply professional satire, for the notary represents the laws and customs of the society. He carefully elaborates the different forms of successful marriages and all the acts of generosity the prospective husband may perform by dispensing with the dowry and sharing wealth with his wife. Throughout the notary's presentation, Arnolphe is closed within his own sphere, worrying about the endangered reputation of the "superior man," Monsieur de la Souche: "J'ai peur, si je vais faire éclater quelque chose, / Que de cet incident par la ville on ne cause" (4. 2. 1048–49). He finally dismisses the notary with an insult, but the representative of society's laws has the last word, for his observation that Arnolphe already resembles a cuckold ("Je pense qu'il en tient") shows that the tyrant's downfall is imminent.

The arrival of Enrique, the lost parent, provides for a coherent conclusion to the play.[17] The young lovers have already prepared for marriage as much as possible, having only to find a way of signing a contract in order to fulfill their inclinations. Agnès's generosity and her emerging intelligence have raised her above the level of a simpleminded peasant girl, the role Arnolphe has assigned her. Horace has for his part made several sacrifices: spending, borrowing, and even risking death in order to court his beloved, he has proved Arnolphe's prediction that he is as talented at love as at business: "Les gens faits comme vous font plus que les écus, / Et vous êtes de taille à faire des cocus" (1. 4. 301–2). Enrique provides the missing element of paternal protection and approbation, which by its very absence has brooded over the first four acts of the play. This industrious figure, who has enriched himself in the Americas through one of the mercantile ventures so dear to the hearts of Colbert and Louis XIV, serves to legitimize the marriage of the lovers and to remove Agnès from the odious guardianship of Arnolphe, thus breaking the stalemate in favor of the bourgeois marriage codes.

In contrast to the radiant example of Enrique, Arnolphe is unveiled as a thrice illegitimate individual, who has falsely claimed the dignity of father, husband, and noble. It is this triple embarrassment that explains his reaction to the *scène de reconnaissance*, for although he will be reimbursed by the parents of the lovers for the expense incurred in raising Agnès, he is so outraged that he can barely utter "Ouf!" before he leaves the stage.[18] His carefully planned usurpation, meant to substitute for his bourgeois destiny a pseudo-aristocratic authority in the household and in the town, collapses in ruins as soon as it is known that Monsieur de la Souche and Arnolphe are one and the same, and that he is unable to impose his will on Agnès or his vengeance on Horace. Even the relatively uncomplicated transformation of his métairie into a *seigneurie* can no longer be realized, for the city will know that he is a fraud, a fool, and a dupe.

The ultimate irony of Arnolphe's failure is that, despite his efforts to erect mechanisms of closure between himself and the townspeople, whom he despises as bourgeois cuckolds, and between himself and Agnès, whom he seeks to identify with the even less powerful level of peasants and oppressed women, he is finally the victim of legitimate social closure. The key to his ambition was not to take advantage of existing opportunities and to gain the acceptance of his peers but to forge his own rules and to create a caste for himself. It becomes clearer and clearer as Arnolphe's control of domestic affairs breaks down, and as contrary evidence accumulates, that his superiority is an illusion. When self-assured characters arrive to claim their rights, the last lingering remnants are dissipated.

Six years later, in 1668, after having sketched briefly in *Le Mariage forcé* the predicament of an ambitious commoner who chose to marry a woman superior to him in pretention if not in rank, Molière again devoted a major play to the conflict between *arrivistes* and the mechanisms of closure. *George Dandin* features a protagonist who is in many ways the polar opposite of his predecessor Arnolphe. Whereas the latter picks a spouse from what he believes to be the bottommost level of his environment, Dandin boldly weds one of the dominant women of his rural world, for Angélique is a member of the gentry. Agnès and her relatives opposed the ambitions of Arnolphe, but Monsieur and Madame de Sotenville are only too willing to ally themselves to Dandin's money. Arnolphe overanticipates and takes nothing for granted, but Dandin foolishly assumes that his marriage has put him on a par with the Sotenville clan and that they will share his views regarding "honorable" family life. As shown in these and many other possible parallels, Molière seems to have practiced the same tactic of bracketing that he used in portraying nobility and unworthiness; he exposes a phenomenon in depth by focusing on a multitude of its differing aspects.

George Dandin's incompatibility with the *noblesse* is beyond doubt. Although he is described in the list of *acteurs* as a "riche paysan," it is important to specify that his status has more in common with the bourgeoisie than with the "bonne et franche paysannerie" of which he boasts. No ordinary farmer, whether field hand, *censitaire*, or *métayer*, could expect to amass enough wealth to wear the gaudy, silver-trimmed clothes sported by Dandin.[19] Research on seventeenth-century rural society, such as Emile Mireaux's study of the Brie countryside and Jean Jacquart's work on the Hurepoix, has revealed only one group capable of such luxury — the *laboureurs*.[20] Their dominance over all the essential tasks of the agricultural world made them monopolizers of equipment, creditors of the small farmers, managers of absentee interests, suppliers of commodities, and brokers of money, power, and labor in the community. When average farmers collapsed or starved during weather or market crises, the diversity of the *laboureurs'* activities allowed them to continue to flourish and to develop fortunes in the range of 10,000 to 16,000 livres. Jacquart found that a *laboureur* in the Hurepoix named Gaspard Hersant had been able to acquire nobility, but Mireaux mentions that some aspiring members of this stratum, like the office-seeking Bernard family of the Brie, were thrust back into the ranks of the *roturiers* by Louis XIV's commissions of inquest.[21]

Like so many other *coqs de village* who are not content merely to be wealthy and comfortable, Dandin has taken steps to speed his climb up the pyramid of social dignity. Choosing to skip the prescribed steps, which included holding honorable offices, acquiring *seigneuries*, and purchasing letters of nobility, he tries to circumvent the codes of behavior by marrying directly into an aristocratic family. With their help, he has converted one of his parcels of land into a so-called estate and assumed the title of "Monsieur de la Dandinière" (1. 4).[22] Although the name in itself tends to cast aspersions on the origins of its bearer through its rather explicit evocation of the *basse cour*, Molière does not allow us to forget that the equivocal use of titles was one of the most common means of usurpation, particularly if the social climber could gain the connivance of the local notables, as Dandin has done.

It is essential to keep in mind that George Dandin's in-laws, the Sotenvilles, are not great nobles but penniless *hobereaux*. As such, their claims to legitimate dominance over their daughter's lowborn husband are questionable. Some provinces, such as Normandy, attacked the very existence of the poorer gentry by proclaiming that any noble unable to maintain his station in life was automatically guilty of *dérogeance!*[23] Dandin himself tells us that the house of Sotenville was on the brink of financial ruin before the strategic marriage: "Sans moi vos affaires, avec votre permission, étaient fort délabrées, et mon argent a servi à reboucher d'assez bons trous" (1.4).

Although the *hobereaux* enjoyed considerable sympathetic response in seventeenth-century literature (one thinks, for example, of Charles Sorel's *Francion* and of many of La Bruyere's *caractères*), Molière does not endow the Sotenvilles with a single positive feature. The ridiculous, anachronistic attitude of the baron is embodied in the obsolescence of his title and in the ancient helmet in which he appears onstage.[24] Moreover, his speech is punctuated by the rustic oath "Corbleu!" With great sarcastic effect, Molière shows the baron and baroness boasting of ancestors with peasant names like Jacqueline and Mathurine and protesting, a bit too strenuously, that these women refused to become the mistresses of great *seigneurs*. Another ironic joke involves Mme de Sotenville's proud claim that her family of La Prudoterie ennobles by "le ventre," an admission that implies others of her lineage had stooped to marry *roturiers*.[25] Even more ludicrous are the baron's allusions to military prowess. "J'eus l'honneur dans ma jeunesse de me signaler des premiers à l'arrière-ban de Nancy . . . mon père Jean-Gilles de Sotenville eut la gloire d'assister en personne au grand siège de Montauban" (1.5). He might as well have bragged about being on the Maginot Line or at the Battle of Algiers, for the two events he mentions were notable French embarrassments. Ignorant of these shortcomings, M. de Sotenville compounds his errors by offering Viscount Clitandre the pleasure of hunting—not the aristocratic stag but the lowly hare (1. 6)! The baroness fares no better, for she betrays brutality in threatening to strangle her daughter with her bare hands if she has been unfaithful (1. 4). Thus, despite their initial concern for superficial decorum in speech and forms of address, the Sotenvilles reveal themselves to be unworthy of true aristocratic status.

Even had Dandin respected the conventions of social ascension, his marriage to Angélique could hardly be considered a reflection of the usual manners of the *laboureurs*. The general consensus of historians of early modern rural life, including Constant, Goubert, Venard, Couturier, and others, is that *laboureur* society was essentially endogamous, that family solidarity and lineage were as important within this group as within far more privileged segments of the *société d'états*.[26] The same was not true of the *hobereaux*, however, for various forms of misalliance were quite common among the minor provincial nobility.[27] Dandin's choice to marry outside his stratum is more a concession to the practices of those who victimize him than a reflection of any widespread initiative toward mobility by the commoners of seventeenth-century France.

Obviously, Dandin has made a mistake in betting his own advancement on the honor of this discredited family. However, his pretensions go beyond the possession of title, for he also considers it part of his position to avoid the state of cuckoldry. This risky enterprise is rendered absolutely impossible by the personality of his wife, Angélique, who lacks any respect or inclination for her husband or for the exemplary life:

> . . . Je prétends n'être point obligée à me soumettre en esclave à vos volontés; et je veux jouir, s'il vous plaît, de quelque nombre de

beaux jours que m'offre la jeunesse, prendre les douces libertés que
l'âge me permet, voir un peu le beau monde, et goûter le plaisir de
m'ouïr dire des douceurs. Préparez-vous-y, pour votre punition, et
rendez grâces au Ciel de ce que je ne suis pas capable de quelque
chose de pis.[28] [2. 2]

Angélique's frankness in asserting what she regards as her
rights arouses a violent anger in Dandin who rants, "Il me prend
des tentations d'accommoder tout son visage à la compote, et le
mettre en état de ne plaire de sa vie aux diseurs de fleurettes"
(2. 2). Although aristocratic custom condoned the freedom of
the wife, the *roturier*'s attitude could reduce the wife's status to
that of slave or object. It is apparently the latter ideology that
motivates Dandin's ire, and this miserliness in goods and
women opposes itself to the generosity that the noble ideology
prescribes. The fact that Dandin complains publicly about
young Angélique's intrigues is in itself evidence of his lack of
suitability for the title he flaunts, for honorable conduct
required acting with discretion at all times.

Whereas Angélique is "naturally" attracted to the aristocratic
(though far from perfect) qualities of Clitandre, Dandin is in a
sense contaminated by his meetings with the farmhand Lubin.
This swain is staggered by the gold pieces he has earned in the
service of the viscount, for he has grown used to sweating all day
for ten sous (the three louis he receives thus represent about two
months' wages). He shows little deference in speech to Dandin:
the two address each other with the formal "vous," and a parity
is thus established between these characters who come from
opposite ends of the third estate. Lubin's courtship of the beautiful but worldly Claudine is not simply a disparate element;
this relationship underscores the contradictions of the marriage
between Dandin and the heiress of the Sotenvilles. Like Angélique, Claudine is attracted to Clitandre, for she admits, "Je vous
rends service parce que vous le méritez, et que je me sens au

coeur de l'inclination pour vous" (2. 4). Clitandre rewards her
with a gratuity and a kiss, and the two find themselves in each
other's arms again in the second scene of act three. Like Angélique, Claudine seems to know the rules of successful intrigue;
she refuses to give Lubin a kiss because "j'y ai déjà été attrapée."
Lubin resembles Dandin in his lack of politeness when he
retorts, "Adieu, beauté rude ânière" (2. 1). More than providing subplot material or extra comic relief, the parallel between
these two vastly different peasants emphasizes the distance and
tension between Dandin and Angélique.

A great deal of this play is devoted to George's laments and
humiliations, which are found not only in his five monologues,
but in virtually every scene where he appears. His first attempt
to assert himself is thwarted by Clitandre's appeal to the code of
dueling: "Monsieur, vous voyez comme j'ai été faussement
accusé: vous êtes homme qui savez les maximes du point d'honneur, et je vous demande raison de l'affront qui m'a été fait"
(1. 6). Dandin decides in the second act to try to collect more
proof before making another accusation, and thanks to a further
confidence made by Lubin, he believes he nabs Angélique and
the shrewd Clitandre *en flagrant délit*. Nevertheless, the wife
cleverly feigns outrage at the proper moment, and Dandin
winds up receiving the *bastonnade* that was meant for the interloper. These farcical elements become more frequent in the
third act, where Lubin mistakes Angélique and then Dandin for
his beloved Claudine, a burlesque confusion of identity that
rekindles interest in the play's central problem. In a vain
attempt to collect an irrefutable bit of evidence against his
"transgressing" wife, Dandin uses the same locked-door ploy
that Molière had already included in *La Jalousie du Barbouillé*.
Unfortunately for George, his *roturier* cowardice once again
undoes him, for he fears that he might be prosecuted for Angélique's "death" (3. 6). Once again, he must make a painful
excuse dictated by Monsieur de Sotenville. His shame is all the

greater, since he must kneel, thus assuming the final position of submission.

At first glance, it might seem that Dandin's enterprise ends in a tragic fashion, for he reflects, "Lorsqu'on a, comme moi, épousé une méchante femme, le meilleur parti qu'on puisse prendre, c'est de s'aller jeter dans l'eau la tête la première" (3. 8). Yet, it is sometimes forgotten that this play was written as part of the larger scheme of the Grand Divertissement royal de Versailles. Songs and dances framed the play and its separate acts. In fact, Dandin's "suicidal" monologue does not end the entertainment, for the libretto goes on to note: "Enfin un de ses amis lui conseille de noyer dans le vin toutes ses inquiétudes, et part avec lui pour joindre sa troupe, voyant venir toute la foule des bergers amoureux."[29] It is with Bacchic ceremony that *George Dandin* concludes; the ambitious *laboureur* is reunited with his peasant origins and provided with a convenient consolation for his great chagrin. The fumes of wine will make the entire world as dizzy and as formless as his own existence has become.

If *George Dandin* lacks a spokesman for the exemplary life, it is because the issue of *déchéance* is thrust aside by the spectacle of closure gradually isolating a man who thinks he has already broken through the hierarchical barriers. Dandin is locked in a cycle of failure, much like Lélie in *L'Etourdi*; but unlike the latter, he is made to perceive that his dilemma develops ineluctably from the fatal mistake he made in marrying the *hobereau*'s daughter. The flaws of the Sotenvilles are not really out of place in the penurious gentry, and one could hardly expect better behavior from a clan that allied themselves to Dandin's "vile" wealth. In a sense, the play is a global indictment of rural society—that disorderly realm distant from the new and superior polity of Paris and the court. Overambitious *laboureurs* would find few defenders among Molière's spectators, who had not forgotten that it was an upstart member of that group, Antoine Du Roure, who had recently incited a nasty rebellion in the Vivarais.[30] Violent rebels were subject to hanging, but usurpers—unable to compete in the stage world with real nobles or to assert their authoritarian desires—might be humiliated by the natural inclinations of those around them, and forced to withdraw into the limited privileges of their own element.

Despite the fact that *George Dandin* explored a new dimension in the ethics of social mobility, Molière could not have been overly satisfied with the play. It had been patched together in haste for a royal entertainment and later disseminated to a larger audience through publication and production on the Parisian stage. Yet its dialogues between equally flawed and rigid individuals lacked the stature of *L'Ecole des femmes* and the supple wit of most of Molière's theater. Thus, when in 1670 Louis XIV asked the playwright to write another *comédie-ballet* for his hunting excursion at Chambord, the impulse to return to the situation of the *parvenu* began to amalgamate itself to the monarch's stipulation that the play should contain a Turkish ceremony. Was it not possible that the "Turks" could be false and that their ceremony could provide a convenient way to gull some contemporary dupe? A rival comedian, Raymond Poisson, had produced in 1668 at the Hôtel de Bourgogne a brief farce called *Les Faux Moscovites* that featured such a combination.[31] To cover up an abduction plot, Poisson's scoundrels disguise a "crieur de noir à noircir" as a great Russian lord and succeed in bamboozling an innkeeper. The precedent for foreign masquerades existed; it only remained for Molière to blend it with a renewal of his usurpation comedy, raised to a new register of effectiveness.

In Monsieur Jourdain, Molière created a versatile usurper who, unlike Dandin, could interact with a wide spectrum of

social types. We see him as a clumsy patron to teachers and
tradesmen who flatter his craving for *qualité*, as the unfortunate
creditor to a rapacious nobleman, as an aspiring but befuddled
candidate for aristocracy, and finally as a voluntarily redefined
individual—a prisoner of the illusion that Cléonte had spun
around him in order to further the progress of society. In the
course of this evolution, the would-be gentleman is juxtaposed
to characters from each major level, from Nicole, a peasant who
has kept her country ways, to mock royalty in the person of the
Grand Turk's son. This social panorama, reminiscent of *Dom
Juan*, permits a multifaceted evaluation of the phenomenon of
illicit ambition that fulfills the task originally undertaken in
L'Ecole des femmes.

The milieu that serves to introduce Monsieur Jourdain is composed of bourgeois professionals, experts who have mastered
academic disciplines, fine arts, and warfare. These teachers are
not fooled for a second about the extent of Jourdain's attributes
and abilities. They disparage him with epithets such as "notre
homme" and "ce bourgeois ignorant." However, as the music
master explains:

> C'est un homme, à la vérité, dont les lumières sont petites, qui
> parle à tort et à travers de toutes choses, et n'applaudit qu'à contre-
> sens; mais son argent redresse les jugements de son esprit; il a du
> discernement dans sa bourse. [1. 1]

The teachers are simply pursuing their livelihoods, searching for
an introduction to lucrative social circles, and trying to recoup
the losses incurred in serving the penniless Dorante.

Monsieur Jourdain makes his entrance into this businesslike
group dressed in a ridiculous gown and wearing his first pair of
silk stockings. Along with his own garments, he shows off the
livery of his two lackeys. From the outset, Molière makes it clear
that the same Jourdain who itches to be a gentleman has only

very fuzzy concepts of social differentiation. Charles Chappuzeau must have had someone like him in mind when he wrote,
"Beaucoup [de gens] veulent comme des potirons devenir et
paraître riches en une nuit."[32] The verisimilitude of the character
has given rise to much speculation about the identity of his
"model," ranging from the powerful Colbert to homonymous
cloth merchants of Paris and Amiens.[33] Yet Jourdain is so full of
unmitigated extravagance that he surpasses localization.

Only the superficial aspects of nobility are of concern to Monsieur Jourdain, for he cannot grasp that being and seeming are
not the same thing. Naïvely he assumes that others are also
unable to distinguish between counterfeit façades and essential
traits. He takes dancing lessons because he thinks aristocrats do,
and before trying to sing inquires, "Est-ce que les gens de
qualité apprennent aussi la musique?" (1. 2). He explains that
fencing only interests him because "de cette façon donc, un
homme, sans avoir du coeur, est sûr de tuer son homme, et de
n'être point tué" (2. 2). The effect of such cowardice is evident
in his role in the brawl between the teachers: "Oh! battez-vous
tant qu'il vous plaira: je n'y saurais que faire, et je n'irai pas
gâter ma robe pour vous séparer" (2. 3).[34] No wonder the protagonist is bested at fencing by his feeble maid, who is armed
only with a broomstick! Likewise, the humanities only attract
his attention because he wishes to spell correctly the words of a
letter of seduction. The height of Jourdain's exploitation by his
fellow bourgeois is reached when the philosophy teacher goes
further than any of his colleagues and sells the dupe something
he already possesses—the ability to pronounce "o" and "u."

The pathetic image of Jourdain persists into the third act,
where Nicole's fit of laughter at the sight of her master's comical
costume embarrasses him in public. The bourgeois is shown to
be inferior in judgment to his own maid, who does not hesitate
to use her rustic language to call one of the only nobles she

knows "le plus grand malitorne et le plus sot dadais que j'aie jamais vu" (3. 12). Jourdain shows his displeasure at the frank but devoted remarks of his servant by calling her "une pendarde." Yet, this ill humor is not surprising, for he has already underlined his bilious nature by berating his tailor:

> Que la fièvre quartaine puisse serrer bien fort le bourreau de tailleur! Au diable le tailleur! La peste étouffe le tailleur! Si je le tenais maintenant, ce tailleur détestable, ce chien de tailleur-là, ce traitre de tailleur. . . . [2. 4][35]

Of course, Nicole's irreverence for nobility strikes at the root of Jourdain's obsessions, for he had tipped the tailor's apprentices to call him "Mon gentilhomme," "Monseigneur," and even "Votre Grandeur."[36]

The arrival of Mme Jourdain, who makes common cause with Nicole, marks the beginning of explicit condemnation of ambition from within the bourgeois family. She reminds her husband that, instead of squandering his riches to create a carnival atmosphere, he should give serious thought to arranging a suitable spouse for their daughter, "qui est en âge d'être pourvue" (3. 3). She thus responds to what is perhaps the major concern and responsibility of bourgeois parents, family advancement through marriage. The moralist Chappuzeau voices a widespread opinion when he speaks against parents who, like Jourdain, "consument le bien de leurs enfants."[37]

Mme Jourdain has little use for nobility and exlaims to her mate, "Çamon vraiment! il y a fort à gagner à fréquenter vos nobles, et vous avez bien opéré avec ce beau Monsieur le comte dont vous vous êtes embéguiné" (3. 3). When Dorante offers to co-opt her with the gift of a place at the royal entertainments, she retorts sarcastically, "Oui, vraiment, nous avons fort envie de rire, fort envie de rire nous avons" (3. 5). Jourdain's wife seems to represent a conservative, endogamous train of thought, a feeling of identity with their merchant dynasties. French society in the seventeenth century was dominated by small groups of families, such as the twenty that were found by Deyon to control Amiens.[38] To abandon this secure circle of distinguished clans is unthinkable to Mme Jourdain.

If one follows the money in the play, Jourdain's scenario for success becomes clear. Although his wife has accused him of financial carelessness, the bourgeois reveals that he has in fact kept close track of his loans to the count, which he evaluates, "Somme totale, quinze mille huit cents livres" (3. 4). He readily accedes to his debtor's request for another 2,200 francs, and when he hands over the bags of coins, he explicitly states that the motive for these transactions is the seduction of the beautiful marquise Dorimène. This admission lends new ironic meaning to the response he gave his wife when asked what good Dorante can do for them; "Il a pour moi des bontés qu'on ne devinerait jamais . . . des choses dont on serait étonné, si on les savait" (3. 3). This new perspective on illicit ambition goes far beyond the sending of a few *poulets* to a lovely lady, for the expenses involved in acquiring a noble mistress are massive: 18,000 livres to Dorante to serve as go-between, thousands spent on clothes and lessons, a costly diamond, feasts, serenades, and entertainment. Jourdain's road to noble privilege runs through the means of personal relations purchased with his family's patrimony, rather than through the time-sanctioned acquisition of ennobling lands and offices. The illicit nature of this procedure becomes clear when one considers the following fundamental code voiced by Argou: "Lorsqu'une famille n'a pas toujours été noble, elle ne peut le devenir par quelque temps que ce puisse être, si ce n'est par la concession du prince."[39] Jourdain's mistake lies not in his aspiration to join the New Nobility but in his attempt to avoid dealing with the gatekeeper of social mobility—the monarch.

Contrasting with the underhanded schemes of Monsieur Jourdain, the honest and reciprocal affection that Cléonte professes for Lucile is a model of legitimacy. Moreover, the young lovers enjoy a sense of parity that would please Lucile's mother and that makes possible on the dramatic level the wry Moliéresque technique of the *dépit amoureux* (3. 8, 9, 10). In order to wed, the couple must obtain Jourdain's assent, and Cléonte makes a modest but respectable presentation of his case:

> Je suis né de parents, sans doute, qui ont tenu des charges honorables. Je me suis acquis dans les armes l'honneur de six ans de services, et je me trouve assez de bien pour tenir dans le monde un rang assez passable. Mais avec tout cela, je ne veux point me donner un nom où d'autres en ma place croiraient pouvoir prétendre, et je vous dirai franchement que je ne suis point gentilhomme. [3. 12]

The key word in Cléonte's proposal is "charges," since it is generally associated with the *noblesse de fonctions*. It is thus very possible that Cléonte is a titled nobleman, especially considering his previous military service. Although martial valor and a substantial fortune fulfill two of the criteria for nobility, Cléonte is technically correct in saying that he cannot aspire to the status of a *gentilhomme*, which is theoretically reserved for nobles with little or no bourgeois blood in the lineage. The use of "parents" in the speech refers to at least two male predecessors, perhaps a father and grandfather. Parliamentary offices adhered to the formula *patro et avo consulibus*, which made a third-generation officeholder a full-fledged hereditary noble. Although such a man could not compare in standing with great dukes such as Condé or La Rochefoucauld, or even with ancient *hobereau* families, he would be a very acceptable match for the daughter of Monsieur Jourdain.[40]

Cléonte is of course stunned when he hears Monsieur Jourdain's answer to his proposals: "Touchez là, Monsieur: ma fille n'est pas pour vous . . . vous n'êtes point gentilhomme" (3. 12). He goes on to explain that he wishes to marry his daughter to a marquis in order to acquire nobility by association: "J'ai du bien assez pour ma fille, je n'ai besoin que d'honneur." His emphasis on himself at this point underlines the fact that Lucile's marriage has meaning for him only as a means of procuring aristocratic honor. It is left to his wife to stand up for the bourgeois idea of marriage, which stressed a desire for similarity of partners ("un mari qui lui soit propre") and for officeholding ("un honnête homme"). Acutely conscious of the many pitfalls of "les alliances avec plus grand que soi" and of her own identity as the daughter of a cloth merchant from the neighborhood of the Porte Saint-Innocent, she prefers to involve her daughter in a reciprocal alliance with a man "qui m'ait obligation de ma fille." Monsieur Jourdain ignores all his wife's arguments in favor of homogamous kinship and spitefully threatens to arrange an even more disproportionate marriage, to a duke, if she persists. Thus, the stalemate between the ambitious usurper and the forces of social order is complete by the middle of the play.

Documentary evidence on patterns of marriage in seventeenth-century France supports Madame Jourdain point by point and condemns her husband's actions. Jean-Marie Gouesse found that in Normandy not only was homogamy the prevailing rule in upper social groups, but also the marriage of inclination was prospering with the approval of authorities like Saint Jean Eudes.[41] Even premarital lovemaking and extramarital cohabitation were not unknown. Although Monsieur Jourdain intends to compel his daughter to marry a *gentilhomme*, any union by compulsion was frowned upon by most religious and lay theorists, who tended to share the views of Charles Chappuzeau: "Les enfants ne doivent jamais être contraints ni forcés de se marier contre leur volonté."[42] Furthermore, the usurper had implied that he intended to concentrate his wealth on his own whims rather than on a proper bourgeois dowry, thus squandering the funds that his prosperous but unacknowledged *drapier* ancestors had striven to accumulate. The image of Monsieur Jourdain as a crazy flirt gives way to that of a systematic renegade from the codes of his group.

Events reveal, nevertheless, that Jourdain is a failure and a dupe, rather than a successful playboy and social rebel. Dorante, whom the usurper believed to be serving as a pimp in his illicit affair with the marquise Dorimène, has in fact been using Jourdain's money to woo the same woman, following the usual steps of respectable gallantry: declarations of love, serenades, *cadeaux*, presents, and a great deal of patience. Dorimène admits, "Je crois qu'à la fin vous me ferez venir au mariage, dont je me suis tant éloignée" (3. 15).[43] To the wily Dorante, this assiduous courtship represents more than an amorous conquest; its object is much-needed transfusion of power and money. Unlike Jourdain, he is Dorimène's near-equal in all but wealth, and their reciprocal esteem, like that of Cléonte and Lucile, seems to follow group lines.

The usurper's feast in the fourth act furnishes the setting for the count to show off his qualities as a conversationalist and his thorough knowledge of table manners, much to the detriment of the host, for whom Dorimène expresses keen revulsion. The contrast in manners is brought to a head when Madame Jourdain's entrance disrupts the feast. Thinking her husband's schemes to be successful, she mistakenly upbraids the nobles for their complicity:

> Cela est fort vilain à vous, pour un grand seigneur, de prêter la main comme vous faites aux sottises de mon mari. Et vous, Madame, pour une grand dame, cela n'est ni beau ni honnête à vous, de mettre la dissension dans un ménage, et de souffrir que mon mari soit amoureux de vous. [4. 2]

Her outrage as a wronged housewife has driven her to make such extreme statements, for she admits, "Je me moque de leur qualité. . . . Ce sont mes droits que je défends." The aristocrats respond to her attacks within the prescribed behavior for their level; Dorimène calls her an "extravagante," and Dorante tells her, "Prenez de meilleures lunettes." Monsieur Jourdain, however, reacts with a brutality unsuited even to his real status as a bourgeois, ranting, "Je ne sais qui me tient, maudite, que je ne vous fende la tête avec les pièces du repas que vous êtes venue troubler." With the hasty ending of the *cadeau*, all three couples, Cléonte and Lucile, Dorante and Dorimène, Monsieur and Madame Jourdain, are at least temporarily split up, and the prospect of finding a mutually acceptable solution does not seem very bright.

The disguised valet, Covielle, had been planning the Turkish masquerade since the thirteenth scene of act three, having realized at that point that no rational methods stood a chance of swaying the usurper. The ceremony offers a solution to the tension that has been growing between ambition and the forces of closure, for it will permit the others to satisfy Jourdain's outlandish desires while still preserving the equilibrium of society and the marriages of the lovers. It is interesting that the main tactic of the Turkish ceremony is a *surenchère*, an overbidding of Jourdain's original project for usurpation. The bourgeois had already asked Dorante to mention his name to the king, and this desire to associate with royalty seems to become a reality when the possibility arises of marrying Lucile to the son of an oriental monarch, the Grand Turk. Jourdain seizes this opportunity, all the more so because it offers him the personal benefit of becoming an immediate *gentilhomme*, a *mamamouchi*. The masquerade contains elements of superficial nobility, such as titles (*Paladina, nobilé*), a coronet (*turbanta*), and a sword (*schiabbola*); but it also involves distinct unworthiness, since it calls for "Giourdina" to dechristianize himself and to be beaten with sticks, a true "ultima affronta" reserved for commoners.[44]

The conclusion of *Le Bourgeois gentilhomme* is rather fore-shortened, for it is only a matter of making all the characters conscious of the masquerade and of the arrangements that have been made. Dorimène has already consented to marry Dorante in order to save him from further debts incurred through court-ship. Monsieur Jourdain shows the depth of his confusion of social fact and social fiction when he accepts the aristocrats' marriage announcement as a further disguise for his schemes of seduction. On the other hand, neither Madame Jourdain nor Lucile accepts the proposed union with "un carême-prenant" until the mask of deception is lifted. Jourdain is thus totally alone in his illusions at the end of the comedy, and he com-pletes his isolation by breaking any remaining social ties in his last lines: "Je la [Nicole] donne au truchement; et ma femme à qui la voudra" (5. 6).

Monsieur Jourdain's "ultima affronta" reserves for him a fate more benign than that of his predecessors, Arnolphe and George Dandin, who are relegated to celibacy and cuckoldry as a punishment for their illicit ambitions. In all three plays, usur-pation is linked to the possession of a woman, as well as to such visible aspects as clothes, titles, and manners. The three usurp-ers show contempt for social codes by rejecting proper mar-riages, insulting officeholders, short-circuiting the channels of mobility, and belittling their fellow bourgeois. Each time the value-conscious family reorganizes itself and eventually thwarts the usurper by exposing his foolish unworthiness, whether acci-dentally or deliberately, and by casting the misguided transgres-sor into an isolation that he willingly accepts, rather than aban-don his personal notions about the social hierarchy.[45]

Arnolphe, Dandin, and Jourdain are victimized by their own

failure to understand identities and social codes in general. Neither their bourgeois status nor their ambition is to be blamed for their plight, since in each case their particular perversions bring about their most serious problems, while such "normal" bourgeois or *officiers* as exist in the works enjoy the benefits of a reintegrated society. The ultimate test of values is that of the family, for each of the *gentilshommes imaginaires* contradicts his origins and threatens to disrupt collective harmony. The usurpers must ultimately be repelled, be it through illusory "mamamouchization," through the humiliating ritual of seeking pardon from one's superiors, or through the silent, suffocating shame of the man who measured his so-called nobility against the misfortunes of others.

1. Mousnier, *Fureurs paysannes*, pp. 25–26. Deyon, *Amiens*, p. 273.

2. Jean-Marie Constant, "La Mobilité sociale dans une province de gentilshommes et de paysans: la Beauce."

3. Henri Lapeyre, *Une famille de marchands: Les Ruiz*, p. 46.

4. La Roque de la Lontière, *Traité de la noblesse*, pp. 472–74; P. Decharme, *La Ville et les gens de Honfleur au XVIIe siècle* (Paris: Hachette, 1910), pp. 41–42.

5. Lavisse, *Histoire de la France*, 7:373. La Mothe Le Vayer's letter, "De ceux qui ont pris de faux noms," *Oeuvres*, 2:499–503, testifies to the anxiety over usurpation at the time of the *réformations*. James B. Wood found that in Bayeux about ten percent of the nobility were condemned for usurpation, but that a significant number of them were reinstated upon appeal (*The Nobility of the Election of Bayeux, 1463–1666*, p. 35).

6. Couturier, *Recherches sur Châteaudun*, p. 155; Drouot, *Mayenne et la Bourgogne*, pp. 46–47.

7. Venard, *Bourgeois et paysans*, pp. 26–55.

8. Molière, *L'Ecole des femmes*. Chauveau's frontispiece shows Arnolphe pointing to his forehead (3. 2. 677: Là, regardez-moi là durant cet entretien.) This famous scene is also featured in the 1682 *OC* La Grange, 2:140, and in Sylvie Chevalley, *Molière en son temps 1622–1673*, p. 140; Arnolphe's outfit is also visible in the well-known painting of the great farceurs in the Comédie-Française, attributed to Verio.

9. Bernard Magné, "*L'Ecole des femmes* ou la conquête de la parole"; Ralph Albanese, *Le Dynamisme de la peur*, pp. 141–55. Ramon Fernandes points out that this

will to power is at the basis of Arnolphe's ridiculousness in "The Comedy of Will" (*Molière: A Collection of Critical Essays*, pp. 50–53).

10.Roupnel, *La Ville et la campagne*, pp. 127–28; Goubert, *Beauvais et le Beauvaisis*, p. 207. Real-life usurpers frequently obtained the cooperation of neighbors in their schemes; see Wood, *The Nobility of the Election of Bayeux*, p. 38.

11. See Philippe Sénart's theater review in *Nouvelle Revue des Deux Mondes* and Georges Portal, "Arnolphe Hitler."

12. Roger Duchêne, "Molière et la lettre."

13. Serge Doubrovsky, "Arnolphe ou la chute du héros."

14. Ralph Albanese, "Quelques héros criminels chez Molière"; Gaudemet, "Législation canonique," notes that secular jurists stressed the contractual nature of marriage. François Lebrun, *La Vie conjugale sous l'Ancien Régime*, pp. 11–20, explains that, though parental approval was obligatory, constraint was forbidden.

15. On the *charivari*, see Lebrun, *La Vie conjugale*, p. 52; Domat, *Les Lois civiles*, p. vii.

16. Magné, "*L'Ecole des femmes* ou la conquête de la parole," pp. 133–38.

17. Enrique, Orgon, and Chrysalde, the fathers of the couple and their uncle, will constitute the leadership of the new clan, in which Arnolphe will have no foothold of power. Zwillenberg, in "Arnolphe, Fate's Fool," considers the ending to be a retrospective reality that changes the perspective on the protagonist's pseudo-aristocratic struggle against destiny.

18. Couton, like most other editors, sticks to the textual "Oh!" but it is known that "Ouf!" (which connotes the suffocation and expulsion of Arnolphe) was often used on stage. See *OC* Couton, 1:1282. A good discussion of the case for a comic Arnolphe is found in R. Picard, "Molière comique ou tragique? Le cas d'Arnolphe."

19. The inventory of Molière's possessions describes the Dandin costume as "concistant en hault de chausse et manteau de taffetas musque, le collet de mesme, le tout garny de dantelle et de boutons d'argent, la ceinture pareille, le petit purpoinct de satin cramoisy, autre pourpoinct de dessus de diferentes coulleurs et dantelles d'argent" (Maxfield-Miller and Jurgens, *Cent ans*, p. 567).

20. Emile Mireaux, *Une province française au temps du Grand Roi: la Brie*, pp. 97–115, 137–52; Jacquart, *La Crise rurale*, pp. 514–17.

21. Jacquart, *La Crise rurale*, pp. 520–21; Mireaux, *Une province française*, pp. 241–42.

22. This is a case of the same onomastic devaluation that produced Messieurs de la Souche and de Pourceaugnac, as well as such contemporaries as Poisson's Baron de la Crasse. Dandin's tendency to reject facts in favor of his own imaginative aspirations is explored in Ralph Albanese's "Solipsisme et parole dans *George Dandin*."

23. Shennan, *Government and Society*, p. 28.

24. *OC* La Grange, 4:214. Denis Godefroy, in *Abbrégé des trois états*, pp. 47–48,

notes, "La qualité de baron estoit devenuë si commune, qu'il n'y avoit pas un Gentilhomme qui s'en fit honneur. Aujourd'huy elle est entierement bannie de la Cour; et l'on y regarde un Baron comme un homme nouvellement débarqué des terres Australes et inconnües."

25. Loyseau, *Traité des ordres*, p. 56, notes that the custom of matrilineal nobility had fallen into disgrace even in Champagne, its last refuge.

26. Constant, "La Mobilité sociale," p. 20; Goubert, *Beauvais et le Beauvaisis*, p. 170; Venard, *Bourgeois et paysans*, pp. 109–18; Couturier, *Recherches sur Châteaudun*, p. 183.

27. Briggs, *Early Modern France*, p. 63.

28. Angélique has been viewed as a real monster, especially by those who associate her with the contemporary assassins of Nantes and the Affaire des Poisons. See P. d'Estrée, "La Genèse de *George Dandin*."

29. One finds it hard to agree with Joan Crow, "Reflexions on *George Dandin*," in *Molière: Stage and Study*, pp. 3–12, that this ending can be disregarded simply because it was not staged in the Paris production. Marcel Gutwirth points out ("Dandin, ou les égarements de la pastorale") that the ballet sections constitute an essential noble counterpoint to the rest of the plot. See also Helen Purkis, "Les intermèdes musicaux de *George Dandin*," and W. A. Peacock, "The Comic Ending of *George Dandin*," which criticizes the anachronistic elements in recent productions by Rousillon, Planchon, and Han.

30. Yves-Marie Bercé, *Croquants et nu-pieds: les soulèvements paysans en France*, pp. 52–53.

31. Raymond Poisson, *Les Faux Moscovites*.

32. Charles Chappuzeau, *Le Devoir général*, p. 138.

33. Jean Marion, "Molière a-t-il songé à Colbert en composant le personnage de Jourdain?"; Maxfield-Miller, "The Real Monsieur Jourdain of the *Bourgeois gentilhomme*," reveals that a real Jourdain, cloth merchant, lived only a few houses away from the Poquelin family; Deyon found a Jourdain family in Amiens that was *arriviste* and combined title with commerce, in *Amiens*, pp. 301-2.

34. The deep comic potential of this apparently minor scene is explored in René Girard, "Perilous Balance: A Comic Hypothesis." Obviously, one learns early in the play that Jourdain has foibles. In that light, it is hard to understand how a critic can say of the usurper that "intelligence and an ethical sense coexist with his impulse to deny what, after all, is only an accident of birth and fortune" or to claim that "Jourdain is Molière's most sympathetic and accessible character" simply becuase he wants to be one of the Beautiful People! See Nathan Gross, "Values in *Le Bourgeois Gentilhomme*."

35. Jourdain's lapses into such crude speech negate his pretension to elegant language. For a complete study of styles in this play, see R. Garapon, "La Langue et les styles des différents personnages du *Bourgeois gentilhomme*."

36. Bluche, "L'Origine sociale," p. 21, notes that the *secrétaires d'état* did in fact receive the privilege of being addressed as "Monseigneur," thus enjoying titular parity with dukes and doubtlessly causing quite a social stir.

37. Charles Chappuzeau, *Le Devoir général*, pp. 59–68.

38. Deyon, *Amiens*, p. 293.

39. Argou, *Institution au droit*, 1:10.

40. The case of an *officier's* son serving in the army is not a rare exception: Deyon, in *Amiens*, noted that, just as many bourgeois sons left commerce, many magistrates' sons found in the military an attractive guarantee of their nobility (pp. 276, 294); this is corroborated by Ford, *Robe and Sword*, pp. 138–39, and by Jean Chagniot, who notes in "Mobilité sociale et armée (vers 1660–vers 1760)" that many sons of Parisian bourgeois or *anoblis* served in the musketeers or gendarmerie before joining a regiment; André Corvisier, in "Les Généraux de Louis XIV et leur origine sociale," even notes that the beginning of Louis's reign saw the creation of some "généraux de robe!"

41. Jean-Marie Gouesse, "La Formation du couple en Basse-Normandie."

42. Charles Chappuzeau, *Le Devoir général*, p. 20.

43. Despite the generosity implied in this speech and Dorimène's impeccable manners, there was once a trend to malign her. René Talamon's sensible reevaluation, "La Marquise du *Bourgeois gentilhomme*," put an end to this error.

44. J. L. Barrault's circus-like production expertly captured the memorable quality of "mamamouchization," an illusion that dazzles Jourdain and removes him as a social danger. See Ph. Sénart's theater review in *Nouvelle Revue des Deux Mondes* and Barrault's own article, "Le Bourgeois ou la poésie du rire." Richard E. Wood has studied the language of the Turkish ceremony in "The Lingua Franca in Molière's *Le Bourgeois gentilhomme*."

45. On Jourdain's stubborn refusal to abandon his efforts to be *éblouissant*, in the mock-tragic sense, see Robert Nicolich, "Classicism and Baroque in *Le Bourgeois gentilhomme*." Can Jourdain then also function as a reliable representative of social values, as suggested in Odette de Mourges, "*Le Bourgeois gentilhomme* as a Criticism of Civilization," in Howarth and Thomas, eds., *Molière: Stage and Study*, pp. 170–84?

CHAPTER FIVE

BOURGEOIS RECIPROCITY AND IMBALANCE

All social groups must come to grips with problems and tensions within their own boundaries as well as with intergroup confrontations. The survival of the bourgeoisie in seventeenth-century France, torn by bouts of internal strife, depended on a deceptively delicate balance of social engagements and reciprocal gifts, exchanges of children and wealth that were institutionalized in the form of marriages and dowries. No more fitting summary of the ancien régime attitude toward social engagements can be found than that of the great jurist Domat, who wrote, "Dieu ne les forme et n'y met les hommes que pour les lier à l'exercice de l'amour mutuel."[1] We of the twentieth century, who are accustomed to viewing the emerging bourgeoisie through a glass darkened by merchant villains like Dickens's Ebenezer Scrooge and Uriah Heep, Balzac's Baron Nucingen and his accomplice Du Tillet, or Flaubert's Monsieur Lheureux, may too easily forget how essential compromise and reciprocity were to the bourgeois clans during the insecure era before the appearance of organized capitalism and the self-made man. Fernand Braudel's theories about the ancien régime's overriding concern with "material life" and "capital before capitalism" help to put in a proper perspective the force of mutual dependency in the thought of Molière's fellow citizens.[2]

The divine and secular approbation of social relations evoked by Domat found its most perfect expression in the rite of mar-

riage, which provided for a contractual blending of family fortunes in the form of dower and dowry, as well as for the continu-
ation of the lineage through another generation. Ever larger
dowries were, along with land and office investment, consequences of a sluggish economic climate when capital, business
opportunities, and trade were declining in France.[3] The imperative of solidarity through the creation and extension of homogamous (occasionally hypergamous) alliance networks, or *parentèles*, is evident in the major studies of urban life in Dijon,
Beauvais, and Amiens, and in research on groups ranging from
the highly privileged secretaries of state to the humble water-
men of the Seine Basin.[4] It is no wonder that the necessity for
reciprocity is a common concern of writers ranging from the
practical Jacques Savary, who prefaced his ground-breaking treatise on business, *Le Parfait Négociant*, with an explanation that
commerce was necessary and useful because of human interdependence, to theorists like Charles Chappuzeau, who used the
heuristic example of social insects to illustrate human cooperation, and Eustache Le Noble, who stated, "Toutes les fortunes
ne viennent que de l'apui des Amis que l'on se donne dans le
monde."[5]

Of course, it would be unreasonable to expect universal
observation of even a mutually beneficial standard such as the
code of bourgeois reciprocity; the system of exchange contained,
and may even have encouraged, a certain number of
disruptors—individuals who attempted to destroy the balance
of familial alliance for egotistical ends. The phenomenon of
imbalance appears to some degree in many of Molière's plays,
often in combination with other structural failures. For example, the *précieuses ridicules*, Cathos and Magdalon, refuse to
accept bourgeois reciprocity. So do Sganarelle of *L'Ecole des
maris* and Arnolphe of *L'Ecole des femmes*. Yet, it was not until
1668 that a five-act play, *L'Avare*, was devoted particularly to
the struggle between reciprocity and imbalance.

The words spoken by *L'Avare's* protagonist, Harpagon, at the end of a desperate soliloquy on the theft of his buried gold, are most revealing: "Je veux faire pendre tout le monde; et si je ne retrouve mon argent, je me pendrai moi-même après" (4. 7). These utterances express the miser's lonely struggle against a society he can neither understand nor control. They guarantee Harpagon a prominent place in the pantheon of greed, along with such other literary creations as Shakespeare's Shylock and Le Sage's Turcaret. Yet, Molière takes care to show that, unlike Shylock, who extends credit to Venetian merchants, or Turcaret, who farms the king's taxes, Harpagon is not a professional usurer and has no institutional justification for his avarice. Rather than serving the monarch or the business community, he preys upon gullible heirs and seeks to gobble up their patrimonies. Compared to the nonprofessional miser on whom he is based, Euclion in Plautus's *Aulularia*, Harpagon is far more active and dangerous; for Euclion accidentally discovered his gold in a fireplace and passively continued to hide it, but Harpagon seeks to enlarge his treasure by illicit means. From Boisrobert's *La Belle Plaideuse* Molière derived the striking scene of a father arranging to lend at usurious rates to his own child. When angered, Shylock is content to pursue his creditor Antonio in the courts, and Turcaret quells his rage by smashing china; but Harpagon nearly leaps into the audience in his frenzied persecution of those who took his treasure. Molière thus invites the reader to inquire whether his miser's pattern of behavior can be of any benefit to household, family, or state, or whether it threatens, on the other hand, to destabilize the bourgeois world reflected in the play.

Among the numerous status indicators in *L'Avare*, the key to establishing Harpagon's condition as a distinguished burgher is the large sum of money he has hidden in his garden, 10,000 écus, or about 30,000 livres tournois—enough money to buy a political office in the sovereign courts, to establish an attractive dowry, or to pay about one hundred servants' salaries for a year.[6] A messenger who arrives in the third act with further business propositions leads one to suspect that the 30,000 livres may represent only a fraction of Harpagon's cash reserves, which in turn make up, according to Pierre Goubert's research, less than ten percent of most bourgeois fortunes.[7]

As befits his standing, Harpagon has a house, a carriage and team, and numerous servants, including his son's valet La Flèche, Maître Jacques the cook-coachman, the maid Dame Claude, two lackeys named La Merluche and Brindavoine, and most important of all his *intendant* Valère. The services of the latter were required only in a large estate with diverse business interests and farmland, for his duties included dealing with the tenant farmers and signing sharecropping leases, as well as auditing the accounts of the *maître d'hôtel*.[8] The existence of a nearby farm is suggested by the arrival of a *cochon de lait* in act five, an event that the bloodthirsty Harpagon misinterprets, for he believes at first that it is the robber who is to be split open, grilled, broiled, and hung. It was common bourgeois practice to invest heavily in property in the nearby countryside and to stipulate that part of the rent be paid in kind in order to furnish the larder.[9]

These social indicators tend to depict Harpagon as a member of the middle bourgeois stratum, which produced many magistrates and other public officers. The sum of 30,000 livres contained in the strongbox is associated in Furetière's *Roman bourgeois* with the amount of dowry for a woman marrying "un auditeur des comptes, un trésorier de France, ou payeur de rentes." *Officier* or not, Harpagon is identified with the upwardly mobile segment of the bourgeoisie that yearned for nobility. He has clearly risen above the precarious level of the struggling artisan.[10] Even those for whom immediate *anoblissement* was impossible would attempt to "live nobly" from the interest on conventional investments, to avoid any dishonorable activity, and to hope that, with the passage of time, their descendants might, through the accumulation of offices and marriage alliances, elevate themselves to the *état* of nobility.[11]

Molière's audience would expect a man in Harpagon's position to be absorbed with the concerns of his lineage. The son had to be provided with a legal or financial office or with a commission in the army, as well as with a dower for marriage. Even more crucial was the daughter's dowry money, which might well claim the major share of the patrimony. Not only would this sum be the bride's only sure resource in case of need, but the quality of son-in-law it attracted, and his chain of alliances, might also have a decisive effect upon the rise of the family. The signing of the marriage contract would be the occasion for a gathering of the clan, including friends and clients, a practice whose subsequent disappearance heralded the arrival of the modern class system and the nuclear family. The sacrifice of self-indulgent expense in favor of the establishment of future generations was based on the haunting need for a circle of security that Robert Mandrou observes to persist in seventeenth-century bourgeois man, who was only content when "installé dans sa maison, derrière ses remparts, encadré par ses concitoyens."[12]

Having determined as nearly as possible from the status indicators in *L'Avare* the social identity of Harpagon and the normative concerns that Molière's contemporaries would have associated with this level, one must return to the text to appreciate the nature of the miser's transgressions. According to the master plan explained in the first act, Harpagon's son, Cléante, is betrothed to an old widow, his daughter, Elise, to the ancient Anselme, and the miser himself is to wed the young Mariane. The obvious danger in this design is that none of the couples is very likely to produce offspring, thus threatening the survival of the lineage in an age when, as most demographers would agree, nature was given free rein to produce all the births biologically possible.[13] Harpagon has no doubt arranged these sterile unions to protect his hoarded gold from the claims of potential heirs. When the go-between Frosine flatters him by claiming, "Vous mettrez en terre et vos enfants, et les enfants de vos enfants" (2. 5), he characteristically responds, "Tant mieux!"

Relying on what he supposes to be absolute parental authority, Harpagon intends to compel Cléante and Elise to follow his plans, although marriage required the consent of *both* parents and children, and unilateral compulsion was denied legality by jurists: "Droit de puissance paternelle n'a lieu."[14] The miser cannot envision the possibility that two families may both gain through the reciprocal gift of their children and their fortunes, the exchange of their genetic and economic identities. Any provision for the welfare of the youngsters must, in his view, subtract from his personal wealth, if not from his very identity.[15] Thus, he must live by the outlandish credo of refusal, "sans dot" (1. 5), which sounds like a death knell for the future of his family.

It is not surprising that the miser is just as inadequate in the role of suitor as in the role of father. He shows none of the lighthearted generosity that his son demonstrates, and instead of an elegant contract feast, he orders disgusting, inedible dishes: "Il faudra de ces choses qu'on ne mange guère, et qui rassasient d'abord: quelque bon haricot bien gras, avec quelque pâté en pot bien garni de marrons" (3. 1). Whereas most men would seek to regale their lady, he orders the servants to pour the wine sparingly. Rather than to escort her to some gallant entertainment, such as the theater, he offers to take her as far as the fair, which is free. In his overwhelming fear of giving anything away, Harpagon ironically chooses in Mariane a partner who will bring him nothing in return, except an imaginary

12,000 livres annually in spared expenses, enumerated by Frosine, "Cinq mille francs au jeu . . . et quatre mille francs en habits et bijoux . . . et mille écus que nous mettons pour la nourriture" (2. 5). Frosine accurately predicts Harpagon's negative approach to marriage, but this does not help her to pry from him a payment for her services.

Harpagon's relationship with his servants shows that his obsession with hoarding money has discredited him beyond the boundaries of the family unit. Master-servant associations depended to a great extent on decorum and esteem, but as La Flèche says of Harpagon, "Il aime l'argent, plus que réputation, qu'honneur et que vertu" (2. 4). The valet mocks the miser, who, he says, will not even give a person good-day, but only lend it. When the servants show him the holes in their threadbare clothes, he advises them, "Rangez cela adroitement du côté de la muraille, et présentez toujours le devant au monde" (3. 1). It is true that he scarcely takes better care of his own phyical appearance, judging by the obsolete ruff and quaint hat he wears.[16] This fear of the movement of money surpasses thrift and constitutes a wasteful neglect, for Harpagon would rather see his people deteriorate like his decaying carriage and unshod horses than to restore them to a state congruent with his *condition*. The dowries, apprenticeships, and other rewards that many masters bestowed on their servants are unknown to the miser.[17] Instead he subjects the staff to constant humiliations, such as the insults he hurls at La Flèche, "maître juré filou, vrai gibier de potence" (1. 3), and the hilarious close inspection of the valet's pants.[18] Sarcastic Maître Jacques speaks for all the servants when, disappointed that Harpagon pulls a handkerchief from his pocket instead of a reward, he sneers, "Je vous baise les mains" (4. 4). As with his children, Harpagon shirks paternalistic responsibilities toward his servants and crassly exploits them.

Harpagon's patterns of irresponsible misbehavior seem impervious to any lessons of reform; he is certainly one of Molière's most "unreconstructed" characters, to use Robert J. Nelson's terminology.[19] Without some extraordinary measures for survival, his lineage seems doomed to wither and die, for he is in a position to deny his approbation for any normal bourgeois marriage. It is in this light that one must judge the antiauthoritarian reactions of La Flèche, Valère, and Cléante. La Flèche explains that he robs Harpagon not for personal gain, nor to recoup the servants' rightful wages, but as a moral example to combat the miser's perversions: "Il me donnerait, par ses procédés, des tentations de le voler; et je croirais, en le volant, faire une action méritoire" (2. 1). Valère's deception of his master through the disguise that permits him to woo Elise clandestinely is counterbalanced by the suitor's deserving actions. He has earned Elise's love by giving her the precious gift of life when he saved her from drowning. His generosity and her gratitude developed into "cet ardent amour que ni le temps ni les difficultés n'ont rebuté" (1. 1).

The force of natural reciprocity that draws the young people together is thus identified as a sort of bourgeois "cri du sang." Cléante's motives in helping Mariane are typical of this spirit of good will: "Figurez-vous, ma soeur, quelle joie ce peut être que de relever la fortune d'une personne que l'on aime; que de donner adroitement quelques petits secours aux modestes nécessités d'une vertueuse famille" (1. 2). Contrast these sentiments with those of Harpagon, who says of the girl: "Son maintain honnête et sa douceur m'ont gagné l'âme, et je suis résolu de l'épouser, *pourvu que j'y trouve quelque bien*" (1. 4; emphasis added). The miser is quick to reproach his son for indulging in un-bourgeois luxury: "Toutes vos manières me déplaisent fort: vous donnez furieusement dans le marquis" (1. 4). Yet, it is the son who is the true guardian of the family's social identity. When Harpagon is exposed engaging in usury in act two,

Cléante reminds him that such conduct constitutes derogation for anyone claiming to live nobly: "Comment, mon père? c'est vous qui vous portez à ces honteuses actions? . . . Ne rougissez-vous point de déshonorer votre condition par les commerces que vous faites?" (2. 2). This ban rested on the fact that since 1560 *roturiers* holding offices exempt from the *taille* were treated like nobles in matters of derogation and were forbidden even from engaging in commerce; furthermore, all lenders were expressly forbidden to loan to "fils de famille."[20] Indeed, it seems that Harpagon's activities extend far beyond this one incident of derogation, for La Flèche declares that he doesn't recognize any of the furniture mentioned in the promissory note and that it must come from a secret warehouse associated with other loans (2. 4).

In the third act, Clèante's generosity once again confronts Harpagon's avarice, as both seek to woo Mariane. It would seem that Harpagon should have the upper hand, since he enjoys the advantages of money and authority, but he ruins his opportunity to impress the young lady by scrimping on the entertainment and by failing to conceal his coarseness. Speaking of his daughter, he cannot resist the urge to use rustic proverbs: "Vous voyez qu'elle est grande; mais mauvaise herbe croît toujours" (3. 6). Cléante, on the other hand, quickly demonstrates a command of refined conversation when he upstages his father and compliments Mariane:

> Souffrez, Madame . . . que je vous avoue que je n'ai rien vu dans le monde de si charmant que vous; que je ne conçois rien d'égal au bonheur de vous plaire, et que le titre de votre époux est une gloire, une félicité que je préférerais aux destinées des plus grands princes de la terre. [3. 7]

Cléante further emphasizes his own virility and Harpagon's decrepitude by putting the old man's diamond ring on Mariane's finger. In a gesture that demonstrates his willingness to share and his sophistication as a lover, he makes her keep it, insisting, "Il est en de trop belles mains" (3. 7).

On witnessing this, Harpagon erupts in a series of curses.[21] The son, wise and worldly, has stolen the center of attention, proving his mastery of the social ritual of courtship. The more the old man rages, the more Cléante urges Mariane that she must keep the ring. Molière underscores Harpagon's impotence by stressing his inability to share with his betrothed or even to articulate a reasonable response to his son's gallant rivalry. The only recourse he has at the end of the scene is to send his valet to collect the leftovers of the feast, or *cadeau*, that Cléante had secretly arranged for Mariane.

Homogamy is an important influence on the young couples. They are attracted to each other by affinities of sentiment, language, and dignity that prevail despite the concealment of identities at the beginning of the play. Mariane and Valère are actually the children of the Neapolitan Thomas d'Alburcy, whose title "dom" implies that he is a member of the Italian urban aristocracy.[22] Cléante and Elise share this ambiguous condition between merchant life and hereditary *noblesse*, but they are one generation closer to full recognition than their upstart father. Donald Hunt, studying the patterns of family life in early modern France, shows that infractions against homogamous codes more often than not entailed disastrous results.[23] Valère expresses this same idea of marriage as "cette douce conformité qui sans cesse y maintient l'honneur, la tranquillité et la joie"(1. 5).

The miser and his fellow characters differ noticeably in the degree of trust they have in society. Although the young people rebel against Harpagon to the extent that they secretly meet with their lovers, they retain enough confidence in social conventions that they never attack the principle of paternalism or seek to wed without fatherly permission. Both Cléante and

Valère admit to their passions when the truth becomes necessary, the latter declaring, "C'est d'une ardeur toute pure et respectueuse que j'ai brûlé pour elle" (5. 3). It is significant that Harpagon misunderstands this openness, assuming that Valère is a thief, since gold is the only thing the miser considers worthy of devotion. For this sociopath, "de tous les humains l'humain le moins humain" (2. 4), all life becomes the occasion for fear and larceny; he thus fails to appreciate the return of his strongbox by his son. Even his unfortunate borrowers are subjects of suspicion, for when he is tripped up by clumsy La Merluche, he grumbles, "Le traître assurément a reçu de l'argent de mes débiteurs, pour me faire rompre le cou" (3. 9). Harpagon is alienated from both the generous and the needy and lacks faith in all segments of the social network.

The dénouement of *L'Avare* resolves all questions of social disparity by reorganizing a new clan around old Anselme. This paterfamilias might well adopt the motto of Monsieur Orgon in Marivaux's *Le Jeu de l'amour et du hasard*, "Il faut être un peu trop bon pour l'être assez."[24] He withdraws all plans of marriage in favor of his son's future role as family leader. After all, the recovery of his long lost heir removes from his shoulders any responsibility for beginning another family and obviates his motives for marrying Elise. At the same time, his riches replenish Mariane's dowry and eliminate the need for her to choose a husband on the basis of support. For the sake of bourgeois reciprocity, he is obliged to make several petty concessions to Harpagon's avarice, including paying the legal officers and purchasing a wedding suit for the miser, but this is a small price to pay for removing the only obstacle to the double marriage. Valère, his status and fortune restored, may now totally discard his *intendant* disguise and marry Elise. Mariane, freed from poverty, can accept the proposal of Cléante rather than that of his disagreeable father. In a fitting twist of reciprocal irony,

Harpagon's children, who seemed at the beginning of the play to be too well placed in the hierarchy for their loved ones, are finally in a position to benefit greatly from their alliance.

Critics since the eighteenth century have followed the example of Riccoboni in arguing that the ending of *L'Avare* is immoral because it fails to punish adequately either Harpagon or his antagonists, a charge based mainly on the financial crimes of usury and burglary and on the children's disobedience.[25] However, even La Flèche realized that Harpagon's gold was not the central issue of the play when he exclaimed, "Que nous importe que vous en ayez ou que vous n'en ayez pas, si c'est pour nous la même chose!" (1. 3). The morality of fleecing a Shylock or a Turcaret in the name of comic example is at best debatable; the chastisement of Harpagon is never an issue, for sums of wealth are overshadowed by the forms of social solidarity that they are meant to represent. The *scène de reconnaissance* and the advent of Anselme mark the triumph of conscious mutual responsibility over the monomaniacal money interests of the protagonist.[26] Having removed his opposition to the marriages, he can do no further harm and is free of others as others are free of him. As Anselme's new clan leaves the stage to sign the contracts that will solemly bind them together, Harpagon heads for a lonely rendezvous with his *chère cassette*. His isolated and egotistical greed stands in stark opposition to the words of Charles Chappuzeau, who expressed the underlying principle of the codes of reciprocity when he wrote, "Il faut prendre peine pour le mieux, non d'accroître nos richesses, mais de diminuer notre convoitise."[27]

Les Femmes savantes, produced four years later, adds an important dimension to the structure of reciprocity and imbalance, and to the social dynamics of Molière's theatre in general, for it is his only comedy to feature a struggle between two equally developed social units. In earlier plays the dramatist had concentrated his attention on confrontations between an aberrant individual, such as Harpagon or Arnolphe, and a cohesive group of characters representing the values of the seventeenth-century *société d'états*. This form of juxtaposition between a reasonable social body and a mad, even dangerous, nonconformist is as old as Aristophanes, and it provided Molière with an excellent framework for both fully evolved comedies and short entertainments written well into the 1670s, as evidenced by *Le Bourgeois gentilhomme* and *La Comtesse d'Escarbagnas*. Yet by 1672, less than a year before his death, Molière sought to supplement the age-old model with a more evenly matched rivalry. On one side are the remnants of a prosperous bourgeois *ménage*, headed in theory by Chrysale, and including his brother Ariste, his loyal daughter Henriette, her suitor Clitandre, and an old cook named Martine. Opposing them are the members of an upstart intellectual salon founded by Chrysale's imperious wife Philaminte: her daughter Armande, her sister-in-law Bélise, and the obsequious *bel esprit* Trissotin.

The balanced forces of the household and the coterie confront each other in a series of carefully orchestrated and rigorously sustained skirmishes. In fact, the verbal symmetry is nearly perfect, if one takes into account that 50 percent of the lines (889) are delivered by members of the *ménage*, as compared to 49 percent (874) for those of the salon.[28] Soliloquies, which figured so prominently in the roles of Harpagon and Arnolphe, are entirely absent from this play. On one level, the measured discourse of *Les Femmes savantes* reminds the audience of that of a courtroom, for each party is given equal time to present its case and to argue for the survival of the way of life it represents. At stake is not merely the whimsical authority of Chrysale, nor the pleasant companionship of Henriette and Clitandre, but rather the survival of a high bourgeois lineage, of which the *ménage* serves as a single temporal manifestation.

Paradoxically, one cause of the disorder may be the success

and affluence of Chrysale himself. Audiences in 1672 would have quickly recognized him as a comfortable bourgeois by his costume "composé de justeaucorps et hault de chausse de vellours noir et ramage à fonds aurore, la veste de gaze violette et or, garny de boutons, un cordon d'or, jartieres, esguillettes et gands."[29] Moreover, Chrysale's name would recall to seasoned spectators that of an earlier bourgeois character, Chrysalde of *L'Ecole des femmes*. The most revealing indicators of his economic status are that he has invested all his wealth with two colleagues in Lyon, one of the banking capitals of France, and that he has traveled to Rome as a young man. Of course, it is impossible to determine absolutely from such meager evidence whether Chrysale is engaged in commerce, holds an office in the courts or finance administration, or is simply retired, "living nobly." The Lyon investment (somewhat remarkable in that age of prevailing *rente foncière*) and the trip to Rome do hint at the possibility of an *officier* background.[30] What is told about Philaminte's wealth confirms this impression, for she has at stake in a lawsuit 40,000 écus (about 120,000 livres) of her own funds. It may be assumed that this sum represents at least part of her dowry, since that was the only normal source of wealth for a married woman. In Furetière's *Roman bourgeois*, the "Tariffe ou évaluation des partis sortables" matches a dowry of that size with a husband who is "un conseiller au Parlement ou un maître des comptes," a man in whose house servants would provide for every need and idle ladies could afford expensive distractions.[31]

Chrysale's honorary position as *père de famille* makes his presence on stage indispensable and gives him as many speaking scenes as the other major characters. Faced with the problem of portraying a feckless but basically *honnête* person, Molière emphasized the comic irony of the materialist who, having filled his youth with worldly successes and amorous conquests, can only oppose encroaching powerlessness with hazy memories

("Nous étions, ma foi! tous deux de verts galants" [2. 2. 346] and the promise of Henriette's future. His language, a remnant of his former lustiness, is rich in colorful, concrete expressions, such as those he uses to send the meddling Armande back to her mother: "Taisez-vous, péronnelle! / Allez philosopher tout le soûl avec elle, / . . . Qu'elle ne vienne pas m'échauffer les oreilles" (3. 6. 1109–13). It would be wrong to interpret such speeches as vulgar or to brand Chrysale as an extreme anti-intellectual on the basis of his wish to discard all Philaminte's books except an old Plutarch for pressing his collars, for comparison shows that in neither respect is he in conflict with the norms of his group.[32] His well-known motto, "Je vis de bonne soupe, et non de beau langage" (2. 7. 531), is an affirmation of the realistic values of the *ménage* in the face of the salon's aggressive pseudo-idealism.

Henriette summarizes her father well when she tells Clitandre, "Il a reçu du Ciel certaine bonté d'âme, / Qui le soumet d'abord à ce que veut sa femme" (1. 3. 207–8). His failing is one of power, rather than intent, for he repeatedly tries to help the young lovers and reinstates the discharged Martine. It is an overdeveloped sense of compromise that leads to the collapse of his will in the final act, where he seems ready to accept his wife's proposal of a double marriage of Henriette to Trissotin and Armande to Clitandre. He cannot see Philaminte's ruse as anything more than an "accommodement" (5. 3. 1679). Thus, Chrysale lets an unscrupulous opponent take advantage of a propensity for negotiation that would not be out of place in a market or a court of law.

Molière devotes the beginning of *Les Femmes savantes* to an extensive discussion of the phenomenon of marriage in the bourgeois family, first from a theoretical, and then from a practical, view. Armande criticizes her sister's intention to marry and to give up the exalted state of spinsterhood, declaring, "Le beau nom de fille est un titre, ma soeur" (1. 1. 1). In Armande's curious ideology, the unmarried woman enjoys aesthetic and social superiority over the wife, whose household set of priorities she deems "vulgaire . . . sale . . . d'un étage bas" (1. 1. 4, 12, 26). Henriette, on the contrary, describes married life in terms of conventional duties and responsibilities, "un mari, des enfants, un ménage . . . les douceurs d'une innocente vie" (1. 1. 16, 24). Henriette's willingness to assume the responsibilities and risks of marriage, motherhood, and the *ménage* contrasts with her sister's failure to accept even the most harmless preliminary offers of faith and companionship from Clitandre.

It is ironical that, as the debate turns from the general to the particular, Armande reveals that she has deliberately rejected an opportunity to marry Clitandre and adopted a spinsterhood more suited to an *hobereau's* penniless daughter than to a girl from the officer class. In order to appreciate the gravity of Armande's mistake, it is helpful to consider the dilemma faced by many daughters of the poorer nobility. Noblewomen were discouraged from marrying commoners, since the children of such unions would inherit the socially inferior condition of their fathers.[33] In addition, aristocratic girls hoping to find an eligible mate in their class faced stiff competition from bourgeois heiresses with huge dowries, who enjoyed the advantage of female hypergamy. Many aristocratic youths and their families seized the opportunity to renew their finances through alliance with officers or other wealthy bourgeois; for example, the lofty comte d'Evreux married the daughter of the *financier* Crozat.[34] Rather than capitalizing on her status as the daughter of a rich burgher, Armande has allowed her anxiety over staying intact and her penchant for dodging obligations to lead her to a sterile existence in a social unit without a future. Her mother's salon, which seemed to be an environment free of earthly responsibility, entails the cruel and hidden comedy of helpless celibacy.

In contrast to Armande's behavior, Henriette and Clitandre approach marriage in a manner consistent with the norms of their backgrounds. Consoling each other for their misfortunes as *cadette* and spurned suitor, they form a lasting reciprocal bond, the "paroles de futur," which were regarded as a serious form of engagement.[35] Clitandre is justified in saying, "Il n'est rien qui me puisse à mes fers arracher" (1. 2. 150). Moreover, the lovers adhere to custom in seeking the consent of both parents, thus fulfilling the requirements set forth by the eminent jurist Domat: "C'est une suite naturelle de cet ordre divin que le mariage soit précédé et accompagné de l'honnêteté, du choix réciproque des personnes qui s'y engagent, du consentement des parents."[36] This mutual commitment is a fitting conclusion to family attractions that can be traced back to the days when Chrysale and Clitandre's father were youthful companions.

Through her scheme to marry Henriette to Trissotin, Philaminte threatens the survival of the family and denies all social responsibility. Henriette hints that such a couple is unlikely to produce domestic progress or legitimate heirs: "Savez-vous qu'on risque un peu plus qu'on ne pense / A vouloir sur un coeur user de violence?" (5. 1. 1537–38). In reality an impoverished hack writer, Trissotin is likely to dissipate rather than increase the patrimony of the *ménage*, for Vadius reminds him of "ton libraire à l'hôpital réduit" (3. 3. 1024). Furthermore, contemporary legal usage did not recognize any parental right to compel children to marry against their will. As the theorist Gabriel Argou explains, "Dans la coûtume de Paris et dans la plupart des autres, les parents n'ont guère plus de pouvoir sur leurs enfants que les tuteurs sur leurs pupilles."[37] Yet the salon members seek to inflict on Henriette and the other characters their one-sided notions, without any consideration for the *souverain bien* so important to all contemporary moralists.

One of the most crucial elements in the struggle between

salon and *ménage* in *Les Femmes savantes* is the peculiar relationship between Philaminte and Trissotin. Clitandre
denounces this poetaster as "Un benêt dont partout on siffle les
écrits, / Un pédant dont on voit la plume libérale / D'officieux
papiers fournir toute la halle" (1. 3. 234–36); and Vadius eventually points out that he has not only driven his editor to the
poorhouse and drawn the devastating critical fire of Boileau,
but is also plotting to marry Henriette to get at the family
fortune. Yet Philaminte summarily dismisses both indictments
against her "bel esprit," for she appears to be attracted to him by
a combination of bad literary taste and misplaced sexual interest. She responds to nearly every line of his crippled verse with
an undeniable intensity of feeling ("mille doux frissons" [3. 2.
811]). For his part, Trissotin describes the relationship of his
poetic production to his patroness in reproductive (and implicitly erotic) terms: "Hélas! c'est un enfant tout nouveau-né,
Madame. / Son sort assurément a lieu de vous toucher, / Et c'est
dans votre cour, que j'en viens d'accoucher" (3. 1. 720–22).
Philaminte responds by acknowledging Trissotin as the poem's
father, an admirable progenitor![38] There can be little doubt that
the patroness and her creature intend to reign tyranically over
their learned pseudo-society. Having already enlisted the aid of
the more easily confused members of the household, such as
Bélise and Armande, Philaminte will govern her husband with
an iron hand that refuses to compromise: "La contestation est ici
superflue, / Et de tout point chez moi l'affaire est résolue" (2. 8.
635–36). The scribbler of verses is equally unscrupulous in his
efforts to circumvent social codes by marrying Henriette, for he
admits to her, "Pourvu que je vous aie, il n'importe comment"
(5. 1. 1536).[39]

   On the linguistic level, the pointless echoes with which Philaminte, Armande, and Bélise respond to Trissotin's poems are
typical of an attitude that fosters conformity. Vadius and Tris-

sotin treat each other with similar empty praise until a disagreement over a poem sets off a chain reaction of discord between them. The trite, forced, self-serving conversations of the salon barely conceal a hunger for power, made explicit by Armande, which can only be satisfied by the subjugation of the entire Republic of Letters: "Nous serons par nos lois les juges des ouvrages; / Par nos lois, prose et vers, tout nous sera soumis" (3. 2. 922–23).

The scope of the salon's ambitions is truly monumental. On one extreme, Trissotin wishes to supplant the court as the arbiter of literary fortune, a usurpation that verges on *lèse majesté* and draws a sharp rejoinder from Clitandre, who defends the court's ability to discern the common good. On the other hand, much hilarity results from the ladies' efforts to complete their conquest of the *ménage* by making each of the servants submit to their intellectual decrees. Chrysale bemoans the fact that the majority of the staff has already let itself be corrupted, that he has servants but is no longer served, except by the cantankerous cook, Martine, who identifies totally with her *condition*.

Molière uses the character of Martine to illustrate the fundamentally reciprocal nature of the master-servant relationship in the household: although Martine provides her specialized skill for the maintenance of the family, she also depends on it completely for care in her old age and infirmity ("Service d'autrui n'est pas un héritage" [2. 5. 420]). Martine's importance to the *ménage* should not be underestimated, for as the expert Audiger stated, "dans la plupart des maisons de noblesse, gens de robe, partisans et bourgeois, il y a aussi des demoiselles ou filles de chambre qui ont presque tout le gouvernement."[40] Philaminte's clique disregards these responsibilities of work and care in their haste to subordinate the entire society to a single power principle: "La grammaire, qui sait tout régenter jusqu'aux rois, / Et les fait la main haute obéir à ses lois" (2. 6.

465–66). However, Martine takes for granted the customary function of language as an agent of human harmony, which she expresses in the delightfully naïve metaphors of the cock and the hen, and the woman as the book of her man. As for the words themselves, "Qu'ils s'accordent entre eux, ou se gourment, qu'importe?" (2. 6. 503). Unfettered by the conventions of upper-class politeness, Martine can represent the more overtly physical, and even sexual, arguments in favor of the *ménage*. Her expulsion underscores the incompatibility between earthly bourgeois reciprocity and the sterility of the salon as expressed by the *précieuse* aunt Bélise: "Nous en bannissons la substance étendue" (5. 3. 1686).

Bélise has her own bizarre way of distorting social values. Deprived of husband and suitors by unspecified circumstances, she has collapsed all male roles into one category — that of secret admirers. For her the normal progression from eligible bachelor to suitor to husband has been broken, not merely at the uppermost rung, but at every level. The distinction between eligible bachelors and ineligible men has also become so thoroughly confused that Bélise numbers among her "suitors" several married men. As the imaginary object of desire, she convinces herself that she already enjoys the kind of immense power that Philaminte and Armande seek through learning, and that she could easily cause Clitandre to turn his attentions from Henriette. Nevertheless, it is apparent to everyone that Bélise's chimerical notions stem from a deep alienation that, although it is less dangerous than that of the other ladies, is just as blind to personal responsibility.

The solution to the contest between *ménage* and salon must come from a remote, but not completely extrinsic, source — the letters forged by Ariste that announce economic ruin and legal disaster to Chrysale and Philaminte. Far from being considered improper or overly contrived, this *dénouement* was applauded in its day as being both dramatically convincing and aestheti-cally pleasing.[41] Ariste intervenes with his mock crisis only after the normal social conventions, embodied in the notary, have reached an impasse. Faced not only with Bélise's ridiculous request to count the dowry in ancient talents and minas but also with the prospect of two husbands, the notary can only con-clude, "C'est trop pour la coutume" (5. 3. 1624). In simulating a financial crisis, Ariste is simply putting the rival collective entities to the ultimate test, confronting them with the prospect of immediate suffering that could result at any point, either from the plagues and famines of nature or from the wars and injustices of man.

It is significant that Molière wastes no time in removing Tris-sotin from the scene and in convincing Philaminte that this "lâche déserteur" (5. 4. 1766) has misled her. Instead, the play-wright returns again to the theme of reciprocity by examining an unforeseen objection to marriage on the part of Henriette. She had always conceived of her relationship with Clitandre as one that was mutually beneficial, "En satisfaisant à mes voeux les plus doux / J'ai vu que mon hymen ajustait vos affaires" (5. 4. 1742–43). Taken in by Ariste's ruse and thinking that she can offer her generous suitor only a life of want and suffering, Henriette puts the time-honored values of her *milieu* before the gratification of her personal needs, and she only agrees to the wedding once the illusion has been revealed. Such self-control on the part of the bride demonstrates most conclusively that Molière's theatre reflects an ideology in which the decision to marry is a commitment to collective goals rather than an act of self-gratification.

In the end, *ménage* must prevail over salon; for although it is unable to enforce a permanent authoritarian structure, such as the one Philaminte envisions, it is resilient in crises and admira-bly suited to survival. Clitandre's generous example of shared

fortunes and Henriette's forceful insistence on reciprocal benefits in marriage combine to ensure that the next generation will
inherit a patrimony of values as well as of wealth. By contrast,
Trissotin and the learned ladies are so sterile that their only
"children" are misshapen madrigals and so socially deluded that
their alliance crumbles at the first suggestion of poverty. It is
significant that the upholders of the *ménage* never attack the
specific intellectual interests of the clique; Descartes, men in
the moon, and *ruelle* poetry merely served, after all, as pretexts
for the salon's hunger for power. Although it is necessary that
Trissotin and his hopes for marriage with Henriette are van-
quished, there is no reason that the ladies, once they have
abandoned their pretensions as an upstart social unit, cannot
continue to console themselves with philosphy. The *ménage*, its
future assured, can find room even for a trio of bumbling,
peevish bluestockings.

Both *L'Avare* and *Les Femmes savantes* are triumphal plays,
showing a bourgeois order that is healthy and able to respond to
crises. One has only to read a few comedies by such contemporaries as Chevalier or Poisson, who wrote for rival theaters, to
appreciate the delight of a play that provides for the prospect of
prosperous new generations, without recourse to such hack-
neyed devices as drunkenness, mistaken identity, promiscuity,
or elopement. Molière may have been a sharp critic of bourgeois
individuals who challenged the concept of social differentiation
or gradual, conditional mobility, but his treatment of the structure of reciprocity and imbalance shows that he believes in the
bourgeoisie and in its place within the *société des états*. Moreover, his stress on mutual gifts, benefits, concessions, and
attractions evokes an ideology of mercantile exchange that is not
at all out of place under the ministry of Colbert.

Molière's bourgeois families are lineages, not dynasties; there
is no sense that the fortunes or the *conditions* in themselves

predetermine behavior, or even happiness. Quite the contrary, it is human action that is continually called upon to reaffirm values, to amend dissonance, and to shape society. Figures like Harpagon or Bélise are ridiculous because they have refused to play an active role in their dramatic world. They have deliberately transformed themselves, through their egotistical rigidity, into terminal cases of *comédie de caractère* in the midst of an environment that asks only that they mind their manners.

1. Domat, *Les Lois civiles*, p. vi.

2. Fernand Braudel, *Civilisation matérielle et capitalisme, XVᵉ–XVIIIᵉ Siècle*. It is also worthwhile to keep in mind the reservations about Engels's theory of class struggle, which are expressed in Jacques Heers, *Le Clan familiale au Moyen Age*.

3. DeVries, *The Economy of Europe in an Age of Crisis*, pp. 214–15.

4. Roupnel, *La Ville et la campagne*, pp. 124–86; Goubert, *Beauvais*, pp. 305–47; Deyon, *Amiens*, pp. 258–348; Bluche, "L'origine sociale"; Jean-Yves Tirat, "Les Voituriers par eau parisiens au milieu du XVIIᵉ siècle"; Daniel Dessert points out that even the *financiers*, stereotyped as upstarts, were actually the products of a close kinship system in "Le 'laquais-financier' au Grand Siècle: mythe ou réalité?".

5. Savary, *Le Parfait Négociant*, p. 1; Charles Chappuzeau, *Le Devoir général*, pp. 110–11; Eustache Le Noble, *L'Ecole du monde*, p. vi.

6. Bluche, *Les Magistrats au Grand Conseil*, p. 22; Goubert, *Beauvais*, pp. 327, 331.

7. Goubert, *Beauvais*, p. 373.

8. Audiger, *La Maison réglée*, pp. 18–22.

9. Roupnel, *La Ville et la campagne*, pp. 75–80; Goubert, *Beauvais*, pp. 142, 333.

10. Antoine Furetière, *Le Roman bourgeois*, in *Romanciers du XVIIᵉ Siècle*, p. 920. Goubet, in *Beauvais*, mentions the artisan Charles Toupet, a Beauvais weaver who employed twelve workers, but whose wealth consisted only of a few pieces of cloth and 56 *livres*.

11. See Deyon, *Amiens*, pp. 273–74, and Couturier, *Recherches sur Châteaudun*, p. 155.

12. Mandrou, *Introduction à la France moderne*, p. 151. Altruistic devotion to family and group goals was not limited to France: in seventeenth-century Cambridgeshire, parents regularly established their children's careers as they came of age, and a father's gradual retirement began with the first marriage among his offspring; see Margaret Spufford, "Peasant Inheritance Customs and Land Distribution in Cam-

bridgeshire from the Sixteenth to the Eighteenth Centuries," in *Family and Inheritance: Rural Society in Western Europe, 1200–1800.*

13. Pierre Goubert, *Louis XIV et vingt millions de Français*, pp. 15–19; J. L. Flandrin, "La Cellule familiale et l'oeuvre de procréation dans l'ancienne société." Molière's own family was a good example of the reproductive imperative, since his father Jean had seven brothers and sisters, and Jean-Baptiste himself had five; see Jurgens and Maxfield-Miller, *Cent ans*, pp. 23–24.

14. Loysel, *Institutes coutumières*, 1:82; and Lebrun, *Le Vie conjugale*, pp. 25–30.

15. Marcel Gutwirth's remarkable essay "The Unity of Molière's *L'Avare*" stresses this point as a central link to the roles in the play; his argument is far more convincing than that of James Doolittle, "Bad Writing in *L'Avare*," who maintains that the play is both aesthetically and morally faulty; an interesting existentialist view that Harpagon's hoarded riches are a materialization of his identity, without which he refuses to exist, may be found in Georges-Arthur Goldschmidt, *Molière ou la liberté mise à nu*, pp. 130–45; and Ralph Albanese's "Argent et réification dans *L'Avare*" provides an interesting study of Harpagon in the light of Colbert's mercantilist policies.

16. In the Brissart and Sauvé engraving (*OC* La Grange, 4:94) Molière is shown, as Harpagon, dressed in a rather simple outfit of bourgeois cut, but with an archaic *fraise* and an upturned hat. This is confirmed by the inventory of Molière's goods, which lists the costume as "concistant en un manteau, chausse et pourpoint de satin noir, garny de dantelle ronde de soye noire, chappeau, peruque, soullier, prisé vingt livres" (*Cent Ans*, p. 568). To appreciate the social shock of Harpagon's overly frugal clothes, one need only turn to La Mothe Le Vayer's opuscule "Des habits et de leurs modes," where even kings and popes are reprehended for underdressing and sartorial conformity is lauded: "Il faut observer une certaine bienséance en nos habits, qui ait son rapport au temps, au lieu, et aux personnes. . . . ce serait être trop rigide de vouloir heurter toutes ces modes" (*Oeuvres*, 2:49–50).

17. Bluche, *La Vie quotidienne*, pp. 31–33; J. P. Labatut, "Situation sociale du Marais."

18. Antoine Adam stressed the importance of this scene in establishing Harpagon as a butt of ridicule rather than a sympathetic figure ("Molière," p. 374); W. G. Moore notes that the play is full of such concrete illustrations of moral qualities (*Molière, A New Criticism*, p. 22); Charles Dullin, in his memorable interpretation of Harpagon, emphasized that the miser's *idée fixe* demanded the sacrifice of everyone else in the play, through such sight gags as a candle that Maître Jacques continues to light and Harpagon to extinguish; see "On *L'Avare*," in , *Molière, A Collection of Critical Essays*, pp. 155–59.

19. Robert J. Nelson, "The Unreconstructed Heroes of Molière," in *Molière, A Collection of Critical Essays*, pp. 111–35.

20. Davis Bitton, *The French Nobility in Crisis, 1560–1640*, p. 72; Jean Domat, *Les Lois civiles*, p. 78; G. Zeller, "Une notion . . . la dérogeance," noted that usury was

listed in particular as a case of *dérogeance* for *élus* in 1627; Loyseau stated, "C'est proprement le gain vil et sordide qui déroge à la noblesse, de laquelle le propre est de vivre de ses rentes" (*Traité des ordres*, p. 62); see also G. A. de La Roque de la Lontière, *Traité de noblesse*, pp. 437–39.

21. The importance of Harpagon's madness to the comic structure of the play is discussed in David J. Wells, "The Structure of Laughter in Molière's *L'Avare*"; see also G. Chamaret, "Harpagon est-il un personnage comique?".

22. In fact, as Judd Hubert points out, Anselme's language reinforces the synthesis between aristocracy and bourgeoisie ("Theme and Structure in *L'Avare*").

23. David Hunt, *Parents and Children in History*, pp. 60–63.

24. Marivaux, *Théâtre complet*, 1:803. Legal precedent for Anselme's generous unilateral donations is found in Loysel, *Institutes coutumières*, 2:92; practical evidence in Couturier, *Recherches sur Châteaudun*, p. 147.

25. Riccoboni, *De la réformation du théâtre*, p. 294.

26. William O. Goode has shown, in "The Comic Recognition Scenes in *L'Avare*," that most of the recognition scenes in the play are of a perversely unhappy nature, but the final scene reverts to the classical pattern.

27. Chappuzeau, *Le Devoir général*, p. 134.

28. These figures are rounded to the nearest whole percentile and include Vadius's lines with those of the *salon*.

29. From Molière's postmortem inventory, in Jurgens and Maxfield-Miller, *Cent ans*, p. 568.

30. If, however, Chrysale is a merchant, he may possibly be in the cloth trade, since Goubert found that Amiens cloth merchants often had considerable sums outstanding in Lyon (Pierre Goubert, "Types de marchands amiénois au début du XVIIe siècle").

31. Furetière, *Le Roman bourgeois*, p. 920.

32. Roland Mousnier's *La Stratification sociale à Paris*, pp. 69, 94, confirms the association of Philaminte's dowry level with the officer class and notes that books, even at this high social level, were relatively rare and unevenly distributed.

33. Lebrun, *La Vie conjugale*, pp. 20–25.

34. Jacques Wilhelm, *La Vie quotidienne des Parisiens au temps du Roi-Soleil*, p. 45; see also, Mousnier, *Etat et société*, pp. 160–64.

35. Hunt, *Parents and Children in History*, pp. 57–67.

36. Domat, *Les Lois civiles*, 1:iv–vi.

37. Argou, *Institution au droit*, 1:23.

38. For a discussion of this sexual humor, see J. H. Périvier, "Equivoques moliéresques: le sonnet de Trissotin."

39. Lebrun points out, in *La Vie conjugale*, p. 22, that it was not permissible for a man to raise his status through marriage. Simon Jeune, in "Molière, le pédant et le

pouvoir," speculates that Molière's campaign against Trissotin, in reality the writer Gilles Ménage, entailed approval of the court power structure. More common is the identification of Trissotin as the abbé Cotin, a satirical portrait that may have been related to Molière's problems with some religious fanatics, as discussed in Jean Cazalbou and Denise Sevely, eds., *Les Femmes savantes*, pp. 20–36.

40. Audiger, *La Maison réglée*, p. 128. On the immobility and vulnerability of servants, see Roland Mousnier, *Paris*, pp. 232–33.

41. Molière, *Les Femmes savantes*, ed. H. Gaston Hall, p. 66. See Emmett Gossen, "*Les Femmes savantes*: métaphore et mouvement dramatique," for a study of Ariste's use of *biais* (obliqueness) to find truth.

Brisart d.

J. Sauvé f.

L'IMPOSTEUR

The end of the seduction scene in *Tartuffe*, showing the men's ecclesiastical collars and Elmire's fashionable attire. Brissart and Sauvé engraving for the 1682 Paris edition, republished in 1697. Reproduced by permission of the Houghton Library, Harvard University.

CHAPTER SIX

SOCIOECONOMIC INTEGRITY AND PARASITISM

The most far-reaching transgression of social codes to be treated in Molière's theater involves the imposition of external, parasitic processes on the carefully balanced systems of the *société d'états*. To appreciate the importance placed on socioeconomic integrity by the mid-seventeenth-century audience, it is essential to remember that to live in the world, *vivre dans le monde*, carried a connotation of unbroken contact with a network of human benefits and obligations. We have already seen in a variety of economic and social documents that Molière's contemporaries perceived themselves to be highly interdependent and subject to the unpredictable demands of a "permanent" power structure. Thus, there was always an emphasis on self-control, on the ability to subordinate the particular interest to the general well-being of the larger social body.

In society, where almost all considerations were relative, the introduction of absolute, nonsocial goals—especially those demanding total commitment from the head of the family— could disrupt the primary functions of exchange, drastically reorganize the structures of affiliation, and work to the detriment of family survival, consolidation of wealth, and the welfare of the state. It may seem incredible that such cancer-like distortions could take place in the conformist atmosphere of the ancien régime, but one must not forget the tremendous demands that this world made of its citizens: constant vigilance for indicators of rank, observance of specialized duties, and adherence to heterogenous standards of behavior must have placed a great burden on the burghers who were seeking at the same time to claim and defend the most advantageous positions in the changing order.[1] At times these overwhelming responsibilities must have forced some people to look for a simpler solution that would predetermine all questions of value and behavior, orienting priorities of kinship, finance, and status around a single transcendent end. A soul free of sin, a body impregnable to disease, or some other single goal is thus raised to an all-powerful position, and the person supposed to bring about the desired transformation is allowed by the gullible host to dictate disastrous terms to him.

The sort of parasitism that replaces mutual responsibility with personal imperatives was certainly what Jean Domat had in mind when he formulated his third general rule of law: "Ne faire rien en son particulier qui blesse l'ordre public."[2] The jurist's sweeping statement encompasses such a variety of misallocations of value that one is tempted to exclude apparently innocuous eccentricities, yet the two external goals on which *Le Tartuffe* and *Le Malade imaginaire* focus, the salvation of the soul and the body, belong to this same superficially harmless category. Molière's attention was drawn to these problems from a relatively early point in his career: the ill-defined movement of *préciosité* appears to exercise a pernicious influence over the family of Cathos, Magdalon, and Gorgibus in *Les Précieuses ridicules* (1659). A full-scale confrontation is only averted because the girls demonstrate a high degree of ineptitude and because their false noble suitors steal the show. No *précieux* parasite emerges to exploit the young ladies' absolute devotion to the language and lifestyle of *Le Grand Cyrus*.

It was in 1664, with the first production of *Le Tartuffe*, that the threat of an invasion of values first gained the complete attention of the dramatist. There is, of course, considerable disagreement among scholars as to what was contained in the 1664 version. Was it made up of approximately the first three acts of the eventual 1669 version, or was there, as John Cairncross has argued, a finished three-act play to which Molière later added acts two and five?[3] In either case, the radical realignment of Orgon's priorities under the influence of Tartuffe would have been clear, and there would have been some kind of unmasking of the hypocrite. The earliest version of the play already featured the conflict between the social interests of the household and the egotistical motives of Tartuffe. The hinge that joins these two elements is the comic *paterfamilias* Orgon. After all, Tartuffe's role, which was played by the character actor Du Croisy, is a vivid but relatively brief one in terms of stage time and proportion of lines. It is true that many critics have been preoccupied with the problem of identifying a real life prototype for the character, but his spiritual pronouncements (let us not make the mistake of calling them beliefs) represent a veritable fruit salad of religious doctrines, where Jansenist and Jesuit, Pascal and Bourdaloue, Bossuet and Fénelon, clergy and lay directors, Charpy de Sainte-Croix and the prince de Conti, Monsieur de Saci and Crétenet, all are combined into a single archetypal figure.[4]

It is the host Orgon who makes the arch-parasite possible. The character clearly was a delight for Molière, offering him an extraordinarily wide range of dramatic and comic techniques, from repetition and accumulation (the "pauvre homme" sequence), misdirected rage (unsuccessful attempts to strike the noisy Dorine), and extreme stupefaction (his delayed appearance from under the table), to ironic reversal of roles (his efforts to persuade Madame Pernelle that Tartuffe really is a cad). The audience cannot help but share Elmire's sentiment that Orgon is a dupe worthy of undivided attention: "A voir ce que je vois, je ne sais plus que dire, / Et votre aveuglement fait que je vous admire" (4. 3. 1313–14). Tartuffe can trick, amuse, and even surprise, as when he manages to turn the tables on Damis's accusations; but he is incapable of the depth of emotion, the exemplarity of error that has driven Orgon to admit a parasite into his house.[5]

The wealth of Orgon's family assures its members a high social standing and a maximum degree of worldly comfort — rare benefits in the 1660s. Orgon owns his own home, for it is included in the *donation* he signs over to Tartuffe between the third and fourth acts. His absence at the beginning of the play could well have been due to a visit to a property in the country, like the one from which Arnolphe returns in *L'Ecole des femmes*. Besides Mme Pernelle's maid, Flipote, the family has engaged the services of Dorine, an expensive *suivante*. Dorine alludes to her master's considerable wealth when she recommends that he use some of it to marry his daughter, Mariane, to a man of importance rather than to a penniless dévot: "A quel sujet aller, avec tout votre bien, / Choisir un gendre gueux?" (2. 2. 483–84). Luxury abounds, permitting the women of the household to wear the finest clothes, a state of ostentation that shocks Madame Pernelle. She tells her daughter-in-law: "Vous êtes dépensière; et cet *état* me blesse, / Que vous alliez vêtue ainsi qu'une princesse" (1. 1. 29–30; emphasis added). The word *état* points to a social significance. This petty jealousy over a showy gown for the radiant Elmire is a subtle indication of the uneasiness that accompanies success in the high bourgeois family. The existence of superfluous riches invites unusual patterns of consumption that sometimes inhibit Orgon's understanding of what is happening, as he describes in his account of his charitable gifts to Tartuffe: "Je lui faisais des dons; mais avec modestie / Il me voulait toujours en rendre une partie" (1. 5. 293–94). Con men through the ages have always known that a glut of money, even an imaginary one, will cause normally thrifty and prudent citizens to become disoriented and to fall victim to well-calculated schemes.

The abundance of money in Orgon's household affects the conduct of all its members. Mariane has an inheritance of her own, independent of the patrimony managed by her father, which she offers to surrender to him if he will refrain from ordering her to marry Tartuffe: "Vos tendresses pour lui ne me font point de peine; / Faites-les éclater, donnez-lui votre bien, / Et, si ce n'est assez, joignez-y tout le mien" (4. 3. 1294–96). Her suitor, Valère, has a carriage which he puts at the disposal of Orgon in order that he can flee Tartuffe's persecution in the fifth act. The ease that accompanies wealth is also perhaps at the root of Damis's hotheaded actions. After all, Orgon himself, even after donating the greater part of his possessions to Tartuffe, reveals that he still has at least 1,000 livres that he would trade for the frivolous purpose of taking a punch at Monsieur Loyal:

> Du meilleur de mon coeur je donnerais sur l'heure
> Les cent plus beaux louis de ce qui me demeure,
> Et pouvoir, à plaisir, sur ce mufle asséner
> Le plus grand coup de poing qui se puisse donner.
> [5. 4. 1797–1800]

Besides indications of the family fortune, there are also strong hints that Orgon is a royal officer. Dorine praises her master's valiant service to the crown during a time of troubles that calls to mind the revolts of the Fronde in 1648–52: "Nos troubles l'avaient mis sur le pied d'homme sage, / Et pour servir son prince il montra du courage" (1. 2. 181–82). Although it is possible that an ordinary bourgeois merchant or businessman might have rendered some service, it is far more likely that

Orgon is an *officier de longue robe*, either of the sovereign courts or the financial administration. This is further confirmed when Monsieur Loyal, himself an officer of the "short robe," explains that he has served Orgon's father during his forty-year tenure: "Toute votre maison m'a toujours été chère, / Et j'étais serviteur de Monsieur votre père" (5. 4. 1737–38). It would be quite natural that a counselor or other parliamentary officer would deal with a *sergent* or *huissier à verge*, and since the sovereign court offices were almost always hereditary, Orgon probably holds a rank at least equal to that of his prominent father, perhaps even *président à mortier*. A position of this level in the hierarchy would be worth hundreds of thousands of livres in itself, and its holder might even have acquired a personal title of comte or marquis.[6]

Molière thus selected as his parasite's victim an exemplary host, a man of wealth and power whose intimate knowledge of the hierarchy and its rules precluded such vulgar excuses as ignorance or want. The dramatist chose to portray an individual whose only vulnerable point was his susceptibility to absolute, asocial values. The dysfunctions of Orgon and his mother occur ironically at the moment of their manifest financial and political success. It would appear that, caught up in the dizzying spiral of social mobility, they became unsure of their places in the material world and were shaken by a profound *crise de conscience*.

Was this indecisive weakness caused by an attack of guilt over crossing so many social boundaries so rapidly?[7] Other comedies by Molière provide evidence of just such a tendency toward closure from below: Madame Jourdain, for instance, self-consciously mentions that great fortunes like that of her husband are not amassed by honorable means (*BG*, 3. 12). The idea that bourgeois people should be content to copy the behavior of their forebears and shun the ways of their superiors is echoed in *Le Tartuffe* by Madame Pernelle. When she says Elmire is attired like a princess, she is in fact accusing her daughter-in-law of dressing above her class in an ambitious manner. She compares the household to the court of *le roi Pêtaut*, injecting still another aristocratic element, however comic, into her reprisals (1. 1. 12). Her own expressions reflect clearly the vocabulary of an old-fashioned commoner: *mamie, forte en gueule, un sot en trois lettres, je ne mâche point ce que j'ai sur le coeur, Madame à jaser tient le dé.* Madame Pernelle, who may belong to the first generation of robe nobility, when membership in the second estate was considered personal but not familial, finds the presence of so many noble visitors in her son's house entirely disconcerting:

> Tout ce tracas qui suit les gens que vous hantez,
> Ces carrosses sans cesse à la porte plantés,
> Et de tant de laquais le bruyant assemblage
> Font un éclat fâcheux dans tout le voisinage.
>
> [1. 1. 87–90]

Thus, in Orgon's mother, and probably in the man himself, the mania of religious devotion seems to be linked to a guilty reluctance to assume the ostentatious way of life suitable to the clan of an important *noble de robe*, whose children, as third generation *parlementaires*, would acquire the legal distinction of *nobles de race*. The would-be pious citizens fall victim to an *horreur du monde*, and here the word *monde* assumes its triple significance of "nobility," "society," and "physical world."

Into the ideological void caused by this crisis of uncertainty steps the man with all the answers—Tartuffe. Orgon becomes so blinded by his simplistic, pious program that he loses all sight of family matters. The famous "pauvre homme" dialogue shows him to be more concerned about the hypocrite's appetite than about his wife's real ailments. When Cléante questions him about the crucial issue of Mariane's marriage, he gives only vague and evasive answers. Tartuffe's antics of ostentatious piety in the church and his subsequent teachings have led Orgon to accept an ideology of material dispossession and social irresponsibility, a delusion of poverty not uncommon among those suffering from guilty depression.

> Il m'enseigne à n'avoir affection pour rien,
> De toutes amitiés il détache mon âme;
> Et je verrais mourir frère, enfants, mère et femme,
> Que je m'en soucierais autant que de cela.
>
> [1. 5. 276–79]

According to Vladimir Jankélévitch's theory of the bad conscience, each pleasure is accompanied by a consciousness of its obverse pain and privation. Thus in Orgon's case, the enjoyment of his first fruitful marriage and his secure judicial office is marred by the death of his wife and the fall from power of his fellow magistrate Argas, apparently a victim of the post-Fronde purges. Physical diversion becomes virtually impossible—all the more so because of Orgon's double condemnation to wear the somber garments of mourning and the solemn robes of a judge. Jankélévitch's penetrating analysis of this mental condition is worth quoting:

> La conscience, acculée dans ses derniers retranchements, privée de ce "divertissement" qui, selon Pascal, la détourne de penser à soi, la conscience est directement aux prises avec elle-même; et comme elle ne peut ni se regarder en face, ni se détourner de cette vue, elle est tourmentée par la honte et les regrets. C'est l'un des éléments essentials de la mauvaise conscience que cette affreuse solitude d'une âme qui a dû renoncer à toute diversion et qui éprouve une sorte d'horreur panique ou d'agoraphobie morale à se sentir nue en présence du seul témoin auquel on ne puisse rien cacher puisque ce témoin, c'est moi-même.[8]

His second wife's vitality and social verve would only exacerbate Orgon's remorse and agoraphobia, especially since she immediately becomes a target for the reprimands of a natural rival, Mme Pernelle. Faced with the frightening duty of satisfying Elmire's appetite for pleasure, Orgon doubtlessly found it convenient to call pleasure itself into question and to retreat behind a shield to which all his legal training drove him: moral conscience. Of course, moral conscience systematizes guilt by encouraging an endless search for *cas de conscience* and by praising scruples that turn trivial and uninteresting details into occasions for sin. But moral conscience deprives its host of the important capacity to anticipate problems, and Orgon is particularly vulnerable because of his profession: "la conscience morale, elle, arrive toujours en retard, et elle est plutôt judiciaire que législative."[9] Tartuffe's secondhand doctrine of otherworldliness succeeds in anesthetizing the troubled *officier* to the emotional pains of his existence, without relieving the cause of his problems. Socially disaffected, Orgon lapses into a form of solipsism and hopes to avoid responsibility by closing his eyes, and to abolish the material evidence that (in his view, at least) incriminates him, by handing over all his goods to his *directeur de conscience*. Little does he dream that he has fallen into one of the traps outlined in the Sermon on the Mount: he has cast the pearls of his familial wealth and virtue before a swinish creature that will shortly turn on him and rend him.

For despite the protestations of critics who see Tartuffe's swindles as perfectly congruent with piety, this is not a case of holy divestiture but merely of transferred possession![10] The single aim of the scheme is to put the family wealth into the hands of the unscrupulous hypocrite, and the pennies Tartuffe doles out to the poor fulfill the same function as the token money used to deceive the "pigeon" in modern confidence games. Orgon is all the more attracted by the feigned indigence of his director. Dorine describes Tartuffe's first appearance as "un gueux qui, quand il vint, n'avait pas de souliers / Et dont l'habit entier valait bien six deniers" (1. 1. 63–64). When the lady's maid presents this objection to counter Orgon's plan of marrying his daughter to the upstart, the eminent Orgon claims that Tartuffe is really a gentleman who has let himself be cheated while preoccupied with pious charity:

> . . . Enfin de son bien il s'est laissé priver
> Par son trop peu de soin des choses temporelles,
> Et sa puissante attache aux choses éternelles.
> Mais mon secours pourra lui donner les moyens
> De sortir d'embarras et rentrer dans ses biens:
> Ce sont fiefs qu'à bon titre au pays on renomme;
> Et tel que l'on le voit, il est bien gentilhomme.
>
> [2. 2. 488–94]

What a treat for an *officier* to come to the rescue of a *noble de race* and what a temptation to fulfill his search for God by playing god himself! An existential psychologist might say that Orgon is attempting to compensate for his lack of identity and anxieties about the permanence of his status by transforming himself into an omnipotent hero of piety.[11] It is ironic that Orgon is utterly locked into the role of benefactor to the impoverished nobility. The Brissart and Sauvé engraving shows that he wears the same type of ecclesiastical collar as the hypocrite, but has also provided for the latter some of the trappings of a marquis: a foppish rhingrave, tiny pourpoint, and jabot.[12] He strives to be all-powerful by giving away power, to function by ceasing his normal functions.

The famous "pauvre homme" sequence (1. 4), where Orgon ignores Dorine's account of his wife's illness while repeating a sympathetic litany for his gluttonous guest, introduces the man as a mechanical, programmed individual. Obsessed with his spiritual *idée fixe*, he turns a deaf ear to his brother-in-law's warnings about the danger of succumbing to "dévots de la place" (1. 5. 361) and to his daughter's objections against marrying Tartuffe. Having eschewed all responsibilities as a bourgeois *père de famille*, Orgon is concerned only with providing for his *directeur*'s sexual and financial fulfillment by giving him his daughter and the family fortune. Any alternative to this artificial identity fills him with horror. Mariane tells her father that she has always followed the decisions of her elders with perfect obedience: "C'est où je mets aussi ma gloire la plus haute" (2. 1. 437). Yet, Orgon's frivolous plan to marry her to an upstart fanatic places her in an impossible position, unable to agree or refuse. When she learns that her father is capable of making a gross error that may cast shame on the whole family, she is stunned and never really recovers, despite the support of Dorine, Damis, and Cléante.

Mariane's predicament, which occupies the entire second act, elicits different responses from her three closest allies. Dorine makes every effort to awaken the girl to an active and personal sense of duty by coaxing and mocking her and by painting a vivid picture of the unpleasantness of marriage with the hypocrite. At the same time, her taunting repartee distracts her master by devaluing his speeches: "Chansons! . . . / Allez, ne croyez point à Monsieur votre père: / Il raille" (2. 2. 468–70). She also attacks Tartuffe at his most sensitive point; when he tries to hide her bosom beneath a handkerchief, she debunks both his prudery and his virility by declaring, "toute votre peau ne me tenterait pas" (2. 2. 868). But she herself admits that these gadfly tactics serve only to stall, rather than to alter the balance of power in the household.

Damis takes a bolder approach predicated by his own *condition*. Overproud of his position as the family's first *noble de race*, he impetuously takes it upon himself to expel the parasite

from the home through some dramatic confrontation that
would hopefully allow him to demonstrate his swordplay.
Though his awkward insistence on sincerity of expression,
regardless of the demands of social codes and amenities, recalls
the attitude of the haughty misanthrope Alceste (1. 1. 58–60),
Damis eventually proves that artistocratic *orgueil* has not
diluted his loyalty to the officer clan, for he returns from banishment intending to punish his father's persecutor: "C'est à
moi, tout d'un coup, de vous en affranchir" (5. 1. 1636). When
Damis surprises Tartuffe in the process of trying to seduce
Elmire, he assumes that he has achieved his mission of familial
liberation: "Mon âme est maintenant au comble de sa joie"
(3. 4. 1050). Nevertheless, he fails to reckon with his father's
patterned responses of sympathy for the false *dévot*, and his
accusations simply make Orgon more enraged: "Ah, traître,
oses-tu bien par cette fausseté / Vouloir de sa vertu ternir la
pureté?" (3. 6. 1087–88). In fact, the "fanfaron de la vertu," as
Cléante calls him, dominates Orgon so completely that it is
Damis who is sent packing, under threat of a beating, while
Tartuffe receives a gift of the entire patrimony. The thorough-
ness of the host's social dysfunction is embodied in his stubborn
intention not only to unite Mariane in a misalliance and to
impoverish himself and his son, but also to place his wife more
firmly in Tartuffe's clutches. A willing victim of parasitism,
Orgon has perversely taken as his motto "Faire enrager le monde
est ma plus grande joie" (3. 7. 1173).

More serious than Dorine and more lucid than Damis,
Cléante repeatedly tries to sway his brother-in-law with reason
and moderation. Early in the play, he explains to Orgon that
Tartuffe is among

> Ces gens qui, par une âme à l'intérêt soumise,
> Font de dévotion métier et marchandise,

Et veulent acheter crédit et dignités
A prix de faux clins d'yeux et d'élans affectés

[1. 5. 365–68]

Cléante's ingenious description of spiritual parasitism in simple
bourgeois terms of exchange such as *intérêt*, *crédit*, *marchan-
dise*, and *fausse monnaie* is good enough to enlighten the audience but has little effect on the dupe, for whom all systems of
exchange have become devalued. His subsequent conversations
with Tartuffe (4. 1) and with Orgon (5. 1) are equally fraught
with ethical humanism and dedicated to the viewpoint that
spiritual needs are compatible with rationality. This position
recalls that of Molière's old friend La Mothe Le Vayer: "Notre
religion n'est pas comme celle des Mahometans, où il n'est
jamais permis d'user de raisonnement. . . . En vérité, nous
serions plus modestes si nous étions aussi Chrétiens que nous en
faisons profession."[13] By comparing Tartuffe with real *dévots*
known in the community for their piety, Cléante illustrates that
Orgon is as inexperienced in religion as Monsieur Jourdain is in
aristocratic behavior. Unfortunately, the intellectual Cléante
operates on a totally different plane from that of his kinsman,
who has reduced himself to a burlesque caricature and remains
impervious to any but the most visceral stimuli.

By the end of the third act, Tartuffery has reached its apogee
of power. Mariane does not know where to turn, for when she
makes a final plea to her father, he merely intones in mock-
tragic style: "Allons, ferme, mon coeur, point de faiblesse
humaine" (4. 3. 1293). Damis has been sent away, Cléante's
speeches are unheeded, and Dorine has nearly run out of
maneuvers to avert the impending catastrophe. Neither the
gloire of the Old Nobility, nor the civil rationalism of the New,
nor the obedience of the officer group, nor the commoner's
badgering has caused Orgon's blind devotion to spiritual salva-

tion to lessen. It is left to Elmire, who has previously tried to remain apart from the struggle and to appeal, in vain, to Tartuffe's emotions, to sway her husband with empirical evidence that will stir a primitive possessive drive—fear of cuckoldry.

Orgon's wife is aware of the advantage of sexual influence over both her husband and the *directeur*. When Orgon returns from the country, she retires to her chambers to await him rather than greeting him downstairs with the rest of the family, which expects "moins d'amusement," as Cléante cleverly puts it. Skilled in the craft of extracting promises from those who visit her *ruelle*, Elmire shows no reluctance to blackmail Tartuffe with the threat of revealing his indiscretions: "N'appréhendez-vous point que je ne sois d'humeur / A dire à mon mari cette galante ardeur?" (3. 3. 1003–4). Nor does she flinch when it comes to proving Tartuffe's assault on her honor: "Mais que me répondrait votre incrédulité / Si je vous faisais voir qu'on vous dit vérité?" (4. 3. 1339–40).

Confident of her ability to play the *meneur du jeu*, Elmire arranges for a tête-à-tête with Tartuffe in the room where Orgon can be concealed conveniently to overhear the seduction, thus exposing herself a second time to the advances of her odious *soupirant*.[14] She hopes to force Orgon to reassume his responsibility by appealing to the fear of cuckoldry—a sense of sexual control that may have survived the parasite's onslaught on the values of earthly stewardship. Placing the whole weight of intervention on her husband, she stipulates that he must be the one to stop Tartuffe: "J'aurai lieu de cesser dès que vous vous rendrez, / Et les choses n'iront que jusqu'où vous voudrez. / C'est à vous d'arrêter son ardeur insensée" (4. 4. 1379–81). Ironically, the trap does not spring as easily as she had imagined; for Orgon's astonishing obduracy allows the lecherous parasite's efforts to proceed unhindered, and Elmire is nearly forced to accept Tartuffe's detestable licorice stick and much more, despite her desperate coughing signals to her husband. Crouched under the table, Orgon refuses to believe what is happening until Tartuffe's *ad hominem* remarks ("C'est un homme, entre nous, à mener par le nez" [4. 5. 1524]) rouse him from his stupor. Elmire's scheme ultimately works, but the re-awakening of Orgon's sexual urges and social identity is too little and too late to check the wily Tartuffe. The burgher's boastful, mendacious language proves that he needs a more powerful lesson before he can be reintegrated.

Even without the delicate matter of Orgon's having kept the rebel Argas's secret and incriminating papers, *Le Tartuffe* would have undergone a change of register, from the familial level to that of the state, at the end of the fourth act. After all, Orgon's *donation unilatérale*, having been already signed and sealed, would present a legal problem that would call for the intervention of formal authority in the shape of the courts. Molière's addition of an accusation of treason against Orgon is a legalistic expedient. It is evident that a donation involving dowry and patrimony is of questionable validity—a fact that would not have escaped the attention of the legacy-conscious audience. Yet, the possibility of treason on Orgon's part significantly increases Tartuffe's chance of retaining the property given him, for the goods of a traitor were sometimes confiscated and might well be redistributed to those who denounced him, especially if they had a religious motive or affiliation. In any case, treason is a matter that requires the attention of the monarch, thus putting the whole behavior of the Orgon family before the ultimate tribunal of appeal.

During the final act, the entire clan rallies around Orgon to support him; but the more vocal members, Cléante and Damis, advocate diplomatic deference or rash violence—solutions ill-suited to the threat of prosecution that hangs over the burgher's head. As for Madame Pernelle, her persistent disbelief in Tartuffe's treachery mirrors her son's stubbornness until, like him, she is given dramatic proof by the arrival of Monsieur Loyal, the *huissier à verge* sent to enforce Tartuffe's eviction notice. Even the most recalcitrant of the parasite's hosts is thus finally forced to admit that she had erred in allowing the behavior patterns of the family to be supplanted by extrinsic metaphysical concerns. It is this summit of reintegration that Dorine refers to as the "juste retour . . . des choses d'ici-bas" (5. 8. 1695)

Monsieur Loyal represents an extension of Tartuffe's perverse, self-centered materialism into the realm of civil law. As his ironic name indicates, superficial attributes alone cannot be trusted to furnish accurate impressions of social affiliation. Using the conventional formula of polite discourse, he proceeds to seize the property and to place its inhabitants under what amounts to house arrest. It now seems that the external element has gained a foothold in institutions of much wider range and power than the individual lineage. The monarch himself is named as a party to this antisocial conspiracy when Valère announces that Tartuffe has profited from a royal audience to obtain an arrest decree against his former host. All hope of escape appears to be lost when the hypocrite himself arrives with an *exempt* and a *lettre de cachet* presumably to carry out the arrest. The *exempt*'s white wand and the official writ were the incarnation of the king's sovereign power—one touch on the shoulder from the wand was all that was necessary to doom a man to the galleys, the Bastille, or the *place de Grève*. Thus, the question of parasitic influences is carried as far as logically possible: the monarch must ultimately either become the accomplice of the parasite, who preys on the society over which he stands in stewardship, or else he must eradicate the extrinsic concern. "Toute justice émane du roi," wrote Antoine Loysel, and it is now up to the king himself to arrange for a proper dénouement.[15]

Brossette relates that Boileau disapproved of the ending of *Le Tartuffe* and would have preferred to rewrite it so that it would conclude with a trial of the hypocrite within the family, after which all the relatives would participate in administering a hearty *bastonnade* to the interloper.[16] This alternative might appear to us now as being more "bourgeois," but it is certainly less "ancien régime" that the dénouement provided by Molière. Louis XIV had a moral and behavioral significance for his subjects that surpassed the level of politics, a fact that the author, who depended upon the king for the sponsorship of this very play, never forgot. Ralph Albanese has pointed out that the king could never really be separated from God himself, and that Louis, as the supreme *directeur de conscience*, owed it to himself to suppress irregular competition from the likes of Tartuffe.[17] He was widely admired as a *roi thaumaturge*, a royal healer who was supposed to be able to cure scrofula (*écrouelles*), the neck ailment now known to be caused by vitamin deficiency.[18] However, even though Louis's power was perceived to be an absolute (indeed, the only secular absolute), Molière's presentation of him in the fifth act of *Tartuffe* is not couched in terms of totalitarianism. In fact, the king appears as an incarnation of the golden mean, for Sa Majesté is eminently self-controlled.

> Chez Elle jamais rien ne surprend trop d'accès,
> Et sa ferme raison ne tombe en nul excès.
>
> [5. 7. 1911–12]

This hopeful picture of royalty, which doubtless would have been blurred by the subsequent revocation of the Edict of Nantes, shows sovereign power to coincide with reason, and reason to be the key to the *souverain bien*. In this light, his clemency toward Orgon surpasses the mere gift of a tyrant's preferment to a sometimes-obedient creature. The wrong done to Orgon, with or without his acquiescence, was exemplary—a family disaster that encompasses all families of the kingdom. Therefore, Orgon's importance as a social victim outweighs any personal (and evidently harmless) infraction he may have committed. Tartuffe, on the other hand, is revealed as a social criminal. Not only is he not the *gentilhomme* that the host thought him to be, but he is an incorrigible recidivist who has had many other shameful ventures. The king's justice embodies the concept of rational self-restraint, for unlike Orgon and his son, Damis, who were on the point of coming to blows with the hypocrite and his minions, Louis's *exempt* waits until the last possible minute before revealing his true mission, thus imparting to the peccant burgher the lesson that true authority rests first of all on a wise mastery of one's own hierarchical qualities. It is just the sort of epiphany that is required to restore Orgon to his social function as subject and *père de famille*. Effacing himself before the ultimate principle of good in society, Orgon hastens to acknowledge Sovereign and *souverain bien*, "ce premier devoir" (5. 7. 1959), before providing for the survival and prosperity of his lineage through the marriage of Mariane and Valère.

If the eventual production and success of *Le Tartuffe* in 1669 marked the most radiant stage in Molière's career, *Le Malade imaginaire* proved that in 1673, on the eve of his death, the dramatist's creative talent was intact and that his social interests continued to develop. As Robert Garapon has pointed out, the play is far more than a fleshed-out medical farce.[19] The key difference with earlier pieces such as *Le Médecin volant*, *L'Amour médecin*, and *Le Médecin malgré lui* is that the spotlight is on the patient. Here, for the first time, he sincerely believes himself to be afflicted and allows this condition to interfere with his role as the leader of the family unit.

Argan, the hypochondriac protagonist of *Le Malade imaginaire*, resembles Orgon not only in name but also in social station. Although the indicators in this play are somewhat less precise with regard to actual profession, it is clear that both men belong to the same upper segment of the bourgeoisie. Toinette first mentions the family's extensive wealth in terms that echo Dorine's advice: "Et avec tout le bien que vous avez, vous voudriez marier votre fille avec un médecin?" (1. 5). Later, Argan's brother, Béralde, voices the same sentiment, which reflects the general reputation of riches and eminence that the hypochondriac enjoys: "D'où vient, mon frère, qu'ayant le bien que vous avez, et n'ayant d'enfants qu'une fille, car je ne compte pas la petite . . . que vous parlez de la mettre dans un couvent?" (3. 3). These statements imply that Argan's wealth is enough to attract a very considerable match for his daughter. When making out a will of dubious legality in the first act, Argan reveals he has 20,000 livres in cash and two promissory notes totaling 10,000 livres:

> Je veux vous mettre entre les mains vingt mille francs en or, que j'ai dans le lambris de mon alcôve, et deux billets payables au porteur, qui me sont dus, l'un par Monsieur Damon, et l'autre par Monsieur Gérante . . . ils sont, mamie, l'un de quatre mille francs et l'autre de six. [1. 7]

Equal to the treasure in Harpagon's casket, this sum corroborates the testimony of Toinette and Béralde and places Argan on equal footing financially with officers of the *noblesse de robe*. The invalid's medical bills serve as a further indicator, for Argan adds up one month's figures in the first scene of the play: "Trois et deux font cinq, et cinq font dix, et dix font vingt. Soixante et trois livres, quatre sols, six deniers" (1. 1). Multiplying this by twelve, we arrive at a yearly total of about 760 livres for medicines and treatments alone—a great expense that represents more than the net worth of many *petits bourgeois*.

As for the hypochondriac's profession, we can infer from the notary scene that Argan is not an officer of the parlements. Monsieur Bonnefoy (seated on a *siège*, which indicates social inferiority to Argan) explains that in common law regions, such as Paris, the husband may not make his wife sole beneficiary of his estate:

> La Coutume y résiste. Si vous étiez en pays de droit écrit, cela se pourrait faire; mais à Paris, et dans les pays coutumiers, au moins dans la plupart, c'est ce qui ne se peut, et la disposition serait nulle. Tout l'avantage qu'homme et femme conjoints par mariage se peuvent faire l'un à l'autre, c'est un don mutuel entre vifs; encore faut-il qu'il n'y ait enfants, soit des deux conjoints, ou de l'un d'eux, lors du décès du premier mourant. [1. 7]

Surely a magistrate or parliamentarian could not be ignorant of such fundamental principles of the law of succession! No wonder Argan mentions that he has a lawyer to handle his ordinary legal affairs. Yet, even though he is not a judge, we should not underestimate Argan's wealth and power. Throughout the play, he is addressed by his fellow characters as *monsieur*, never as *seigneur* (term of address used for his inferior, the usurer Polichinelle). He remains seated in an armchair, thus manifesting authority through *préséance*.[20] He also provides a lady's maid for his wife and a music master for his elder child.

The first scene may furnish a clue to the source of Argan's money. In it we find him quickly and accurately figuring his apothecary bills, handling the *jetons*, making entries in the account book, taking discounts, and comparing totals against those of the previous months. Such skill in mathematics and bookkeeping was by no means commonplace in Molière's time, when these arts were perhaps even rarer than literacy itself. The task was rendered more difficult by the non-decimal monetary system of the ancien régime. It is possible that Argan's proficiency in mathematics and bookkeeping indicates a career in commerce or in the financial administration, both very respected fields during the ministry of Colbert.

The situation of Argan's family is one of the most interesting in Molière's theater. This *père de famille*, who enjoys wealth but apparently not nobility, has produced no sons, and his lineage seems doomed to extinction. In fact, there is in *Le Malade imaginaire*, as in *Tartuffe*, a definite atmosphere of transition, of both ending and beginning, that pervades the social framework of the play. Already, Argan's first wife has left him alone in the world with two daughters to rear. In a sense, his responsibilities are simplified, for the girls' dowries should be his primary concern, according to the codes of the socioeconomic system.

The hypochondriac's choices should be all the more straightforward because his daughter already has found a perfectly acceptable suitor in Cléante. Like other bourgeois daughters in Molière's theater, Angélique owes a life-debt to her young man: "Ne trouves-tu pas que cette action d'embrasser ma défense sans me connaître est tout à fait d'un honnête homme?" (1. 4). This confrontation, a gentlemanly defense of the helpless victim, undoubtedly involved some swordplay; it establishes Cléante not only as an *homme d'épée* but as an exemplary student of pastoral love, to boot.

> Un Berger était attentif aux beautés d'un spectacle, qui ne faisait que de commencer, lorsqu'il fut tiré de son attention par un bruit qu'il entendit à ses côtés. Il se retourne, et voit un brutal, qui de paroles insolentes maltraitait une Bergère. D'abord il prend les intérêts d'un sexe à qui tous les hommes doivent hommage; et après avoir donné au brutal le châtiment de son insolence, il vient à la Bergère, et voit une jeune personne qui, des deux plus beaux yeux qu'il eut jamais vus, versait des larmes. [2. 5]

Faced with simple decisions in fulfilling his duties prescribed by the social codes, Argan has overlooked, for reasons of self-indulgence, the well-being of his family. For him the entire socioeconomic system has become perverted by one exterior goal, the pursuit of physical health. This is a type of excellence analogous to Orgon's notion of spiritual salvation, and every bit as dangerous. The extent of Argan's social dysfunction is made evident by his abuse of the servant Toinette, the first human being he encounters in the play: "Drelin, drelin, drelin: carogne à tous les diables! Est-il possible qu'on laisse comme cela un pauvre malade tout seul?" (1. 1.).

Although the source of Argan's problem cannot be traced to a political event such as the Fronde, it is obvious that some powerful combination of events has so traumatized his personality that he has become obsessed to the point of paranoia with the fear of sickness, physical degeneration, and death. The audience knows that, like Orgon, Argan has lost a wife of many years, the mother of his two girls; but the imaginary invalid's response to that loss has caused him to overvalue his own physical survival, in contrast to the would-be *dévot*'s otherworldliness and dispossession. Orgon cannot wait to become an angel, whereas Argan rages so strongly against "the dying of the light" that he has attained the same state of unofficial civil death. If the loss of his wife placed Argan frighteningly face to face with death, the lack of a male heir constantly reminds him of his family's impending nominal extinction. Argan has failed to regenerate his male lineage, placing the genetic heritage along with the financial one at the ultimate disposal of other men. Though it is important to avoid the flights of sentimental fantasy that characterized Ariane Mnouchkine's recent quasi-biographical film, *Molière, ou l'histoire d'un honnête homme*, one must point out that Molière was in fact subjected to the same psychological privations as his characters, since he lost his mother at an impressionable age and produced no sons. Guilt, failure, sexual withdrawal, and alienation from relatives are perfectly natural reactions to such events, particularly when the subject, like Argan and Molière, lives in a house filled with women.

In contrast to Orgon, who had only one parasite, Argan has a collection of them who cater to his external preoccupation: the formidable Béline, her lover, and a pack of pernicious doctors. They all perform the same destructive service, since they assure the imaginary invalid that he is truly ill. Argan finds a ready-made identity as the physicians' patient and as Béline's helpless "child:"

> Hé bien! je vous crois, mon ami. Là, remettez-vous. . . . Çà, donnez-moi son manteau fourré et des oreillers, que je l'accommode dans sa chaise. Vous voilà je ne sais comment. Enfoncez bien votre bonnet jusque sur vos oreilles: il n'y a rien qui enrhume tant que de prendre l'air par les oreilles. [1. 6]

Béline and the doctors have been allowed to take over Argan's life on the premise that they alone can eliminate his sense of wrong and allow him to function. Both of the primary facts of Argan's life, the loss of his first wife and his inability to beget a male heir, stem from physical phenomena. Thus it is not odd that Argan has become fascinated with bodily functions rather than socioeconomic ones. He stockpiles medicines in his cabinets rather than capital in the patrimony, and is more concerned with the wording of prescriptions than marriage contracts. Purgation is more attractive to him than intercourse, and he measures his strength not by virile sperm and semen but by lifeless urine and feces. Eager to discuss his bowel movements with whoever will listen, he invites Toinette to peek into his chamber pot and inspect the contents; but the maid, who cares more for social decorum than does her master, vehemently declines: "Ma foi! je ne me mêle point de ces affaires-là: c'est à Monsieur Fleurant à y mettre le nez, puisqu'il en a le profit" (1. 2).[21]

The first scene of the play, which ranks with Harpagon's distress over the loss of his casket as one of Molière's truly great monologues, establishes beyond a shadow of a doubt that Argan's socioeconomic being has been perverted by his morbid search for health. Although he disagrees with the amounts that Fleurant charges for *clystères*, he seems to rejoice in enumerating the treatments. He even categorically states that the more he spends on doctors, the better he will feel: "Si bien donc que de ce mois j'ai pris . . . huit médecines . . . et douze lavements; et l'autre mois il y avait douze médecines, et vingt lavements. Je ne m'étonne pas si je ne me porte pas si bien ce mois-ci que l'autre" (1. 1). Health is perversely defined by the very treatments that supposedly indicate the presence of disease. Argan has hopelessly confused the medical and economic codes, and keeps parallel records of expenses and enemas! He is sure that he can buy health just as Orgon attempted to buy salvation by extending charity to Tartuffe. Moreover, a reconstruction of Argan's costume proves that he was a dapper patient who dressed for his illness as another might for a ball.[22] Perhaps, as some critics assert, the medical corps of this play is in part a travesty of the "untouchable" Faculty of Theology of Paris.[23] What is important, however, is that both elements are external and transcend individual identities through the seriousness of their challenge to the prevailing socioeconomic system.

The doctors are not the only beneficiaries of Argan's disorientation, for his second wife, Béline, also stands to receive remuneration for treating Argan as an invalid rather than a responsible burgher. He has foolishly agreed to reward her feigned devotion with his daughter's patrimony: "Pour tâcher de reconnaître l'amour que vous me portez, je veux, mon coeur . . . faire mon testament" (1. 6). Béline betrays her mercenary spirit at every turn. Angélique sarcastically alludes to her gold-digging schemes with the sharp wit of a wronged stepdaughter:

> Chacun a son but en se mariant. . . . Il y en a . . . qui font du mariage un commerce de pur intérêt, qui ne se marient que pour gagner des douaires, que pour s'enrichir par la mort de ceux qu'elles épousent, et courent sans scrupule de mari en mari, pour s'approprier leurs dépouilles. [2. 6]

The parasites threaten to disrupt not only the normal economic patterns of gaining and spending but also the exchange of women, for both the doctors and Béline covet Angélique's dowry money, and they have parallel plans for getting control of it. The doctors plan to marry the girl to Thomas Diafoirus, the imbecilic heir to a vast medical fortune:

> Monsieur Diafoirus n'a que ce fils-là pour tout héritier; et, de plus, Monsieur Purgon, qui n'a ni femme, ni enfants, lui donne tout son bien, en faveur de ce mariage; et Monsieur Purgon est un homme qui a huit mille bonnes livres de rente. [1. 5]

This sum, indicating a capital of perhaps 100,000 livres, at the *denier douze*, is less attractive to Argan, however, than the prospect of having a doctor in the family:

> Ma raison est que, me voyant infirme et malade comme je suis, je veux me faire un gendre et des alliés médecins, afin de m'appuyer de bons secours contre ma maladie, d'avoir dans ma famille les sources des remèdes qui me sont nécessaires, et d'être à même des consultations et des ordonnances. [1. 5]

The dowries of the economic system are utterly confused with the external element of dubious medical treatments. Thomas Diafoirus, a big oaf lacking in the social graces, symbolizes the gap between the demands of the social system and the goals of Argan. Confronted with his future family, the fool does not even know which rehearsed greeting to attempt first: "N'est-ce pas par le père qu'il convient commencer?" (2. 5) This antisocial quality is reinforced by an allusion to the doctors' disfavor at court: "A vous en parler franchement, notre métier auprès des grands ne m'a jamais paru agréable, et j'ai toujours trouvé qu'il valait mieux, pour nous autres, demeurer au public" (2. 5). Purgon and his cohorts shun the king because this monarch can expose their fraud and punish them for the harm they have brought to the entire nation by their insalubrious practices.

In fact, the doctors have gone so far as to usurp extensive authority in the system they seek to pervert. The medical prescription becomes a kind of *lettre de cachet* that cannot be disputed. When Béralde wisely dismisses Fleurant and insults the medical profession, Purgon, head of this "faculty," accuses Argan's brother of a heinous crime: "Un crime de *lèse-Faculté*, qui ne se peut assez punir" (3. 5).[24] Of course, *lèse-Majesté*, an offense against the person of the king and the most serious infraction of the age, had nothing to do with medicine. In likening themselves to the king, the doctors are escalating their dangerous ambitions in a manner reminiscent of Tartuffe, who also sought to speak with royal authority.

In addition to the doctors' plot, Béline has a scheme of her own; she wants both daughters sent away to a convent and disinherited. Her insistence on this point is mentioned by Argan very early in the play: "Ma femme, votre belle-mère, avait envie que je vous fisse religieuse, et votre petite soeur Louison aussi, et de tout temps elle a été aheurtée à cela" (1. 5). Later in the same scene, he threatens again to send Angélique to the nunnery, unless she marries Diafoirus. This is doubtlessly Béline's secondary plan, to have the girl sequestered for disputing her father's choice. While the doctors are bleeding her husband physically, Béline plans to bleed him financially by controlling all the cash in the household. She has manipulated Argan into a position directly opposed to the whole sense of the social order, for when the notary, Bonnefoy, explains the principles of common law, Argan replies, "Voilà une Coutume bien impertinente" (1. 7). One senses the *donation entre vifs* that she has been pressing her husband to make is strictly illegal.[25] In fact, it is probable that Béline supports the doctors so willingly because, as Béralde notes, they pose a definite threat to Argan's health:

> Une grande marque que vous vous portez bien et que vous avez un corps parfaitement bien composé, c'est qu'avec tous les soins que vous avez pris, vous n'avez pu parvenir encore à gâter la bonté de votre tempérament, et que vous n'êtes point crevé de toutes les médecines qu'on vous a fait prendre. [3. 3]

Béline is a kind of anti-Elmire, a stepmother who seeks to do away with the whole family, to sterilize the daughters by confining them behind the convent walls and to kill off the husband with excessive doctoring. She resembles the treacherous women of the *Affaire des poisons*, which was to surface within a few years.

Argan's dysfunction in the play is reinforced by two unusual dramatic devices that deserve some attention. The first is the comic interlude between the first two acts, where we meet the usurer, Polichinelle, a lesser bourgeois who has become dysfunctional because of infatuation:

> Pauvre Polichinelle, quelle diable de fantaisie t'es-tu allé mettre dans la cervelle? A quoi t'amuses-tu, misérable insensé que tu es? Tu quittes le soin de ton négoce, et tu laisses aller tes affaires à l'abandon. Tu ne manges plus, tu ne bois presque plus, tu perds le repos de la nuit. [1er Intermède]

In the midst of his Italian serenade, he is thrust into a conflict with a group of musicians and then fires a pistol at the town watch. The archers finally subdue him and threaten to toss him in prison, despite his appeal to his civil rights. As the price of his reentry into society, they charge him 60 livres in drinking money or a beating; he eventually opts for the former and retires. Polichinelle is a burlesque figure who is driven, like Argan, to become a degenerate and to oppose the laws of his society for the sake of a selfish goal. His goal is just as external as Argan's, for the representatives of the social order condemn his amorous escapades as much as they do Argan's gifts to Béline.

The second reinforcing device is the introduction of the younger sister, Louison, and her feigned death. Argan vows to whip the girl if she will not tell him the details of a visit by Cléante that she has overheard. Because she has promised to keep silent, Louison is faced with an impossible situation and resorts to imaginary disaster by pretending to be dead: "Ah! mon papa, vous m'avez blessée. Attendez: je suis morte" (2. 8).[26] Argan is genuinely distressed by this act, for he cannot tell truth from illusion at this point. Fortunately, the tender-hearted Louison quickly returns to life when she sees her father's tears. The incident serves to prefigure Toinette's ingenious solution to the problem of medical parasitism. It may also shake Argan from his blindness for a second, to show him the prospect of real death and to remind him of his own morbid acting.

Toinette's disguise as a doctor, a farce element that Molière had utilized in *Le Médecin volant*, also serves to attenuate Argan's faith in medicine. Her dizzying change of clothes, her obvious counterfeit of the "art," and her extravagant suggestions that her master pluck out his eye and lop off his arm leave Argan in need of proof. In this state, he readily agrees to the servant's suggestion that he play dead to demonstrate Béline's faith and love (3. 11). The greedy wife's response is very typical: "Il y a des papiers, il y a de l'argent dont je me veux saisir, et il n'est pas juste que j'aie passé sans fruit auprès de lui mes plus belles années. Viens, Toinette, prenons auparavent toutes ses clefs" (3. 12). The comic delight of the scene results from the fact that Argan's own pattern of hypochondriac exaggeration has prepared the way for this *pièce en abîme*.[27]

Of course, the resurrection of the "late" husband frightens the wife into flight and raises a number of interesting judicial questions. Does Argan have any legal basis for his understandable desire to divorce Béline? Can any further punishment be given her? Certainly she has robbed her husband, and in doing so she has forfeited any right to property held in the community or in usufruct by Argan; for the jurist Gabriel Argou specifies, "Quand la femme vole son mari les biens dotaux en sont responsables."[28] Furthermore, Charles Chappuzeau lists among the sufficient grounds for divorce adultery, maltreatment, and impotence (failure to consummate the marriage).[29] It is more than likely that Béline is guilty of all three . After all, what has she done but to sterilize Argan, pervert his natural drives, and turn him into a submissive "fils" rather than a responsible husband. Thus, the very socioeconomic system that Argan had spurned still offers him a possible means of reintegration.

Soon after testing Béline's true intentions, Argan tries the same experiment with Angélique and witnesses her sincere grief: "Ah! Cléante, ne parlons plus de rien. Laissons là toutes les pensées du mariage" (3. 14). After such clear proof of filial devotion, the hypochondriac is nearly prepared to allow his daughter to marry Cléante, except for one small item: "Qu'il se fasse médecin, je consens au mariage" (3. 14). Argan seems incapable of giving up entirely his extrasocial preoccupations, even after he has learned that his wife and her cohorts were exploiting him. He persists in his wish for a medico-marital alliance. The only alternative to further stagnation is his brother Béralde's scheme to make him believe that he can become his own doctor. The kindly Béralde will then serve as foster father to the young couple.

Béralde's burlesque medical ceremony resembles in some

ways the actual rites for initiation of doctors in the Faculty of Paris. It has less in common with the ending of *Le Tartuffe* than with that of *Le Bourgeois gentilhomme*. A common strategy of "accommodement à la fantaisie" runs through the two plays, and like Jourdain, Argan is only partially reclaimable to this society. The personal adjustment made by the "bachelierus" is far less costly and more convenient to the family than Argan's original wish to have his son-in-law become a doctor. After all, he can heal himself at least as well as the practioners in the play can heal him; his universal remedy of "Clysterium donare, postea seignare, ensuitta purgare" may be less harmful than those invented by the likes of Thomas Diafoirus. In a sense, Argan takes steps to exile himself from family affairs, since he declares during the ceremony that the Faculty now means more to him than his kin or his *condition*.

> Vobis, vobis debeo
> Bien plus qu'à naturae et qu'à patri meo:
> Natura et pater meus
> Hominem me habent factum;
> Mais vos me, ce qui est bien plus,
> Avetis factum medicum.
>
> [3ᵉ Intermède]

This distancing is linked to the more gruesome aspects of the medical burlesque, for along with wishes that he eat and drink well, Argan is given a license to kill: "Et occidendi / Impune per totam terram." It must, of course, be kept in mind that the only death that has taken place in play is a mock death, which proved quite salutory to the corpse in the long run! Thus, the repeated exhortations of "seignet et tuat" are mitigated in part by the context of illusion.[30] Also, one cannot disregard the effect of Stoic philosophy, which taught that the individual had to be constantly prepared for death, and that only by doing this could he hope to live a good life. This tradition was represented in Molière's circle of friends by the family of the learned La Mothe Le Vayer. Argan's hopes for happiness, and those of his clan, depend on his ability to confront successfully the possibility of death, rather than his trying to forestall the crisis through appeals to parasitic and extrasocial forces.

Argan and Orgon may differ in certain external details, but they do function as the alpha and omega of the disoriented upper bourgeois *père de famille*. Molière makes no attempt to present a thorough analysis of why the two men fell into a state of social dysfunction that allowed them to become the hosts of parasites like Tartuffe and Béline. He does, however, allude to vague past crises that swept through their families. Orgon had faced the Fronde and its polarization of political interests that caused the dissolution of time-honored alliances, such as that which existed between Orgon and Argas, and resulted in a dizzying climb to power for the victors. In *Le Malade imaginaire*, it is the loss of the beloved wife, combined with the impossibility, perceived if not real, of producing a male heir to carry on the financier lineage. Pious Tartuffery and Purgonian medicine can gain a foothold in those homes that have been shaken by guilt, doubt, and uncertainty, but they go on to threaten the state itself on a much wider scale.

Molière seems to suggest that the *société d'états* is only as strong as its weakest link, that what starts as an idiosyncrasy in one household may burgeon into a dangerous social perversion. Doctors and hypocrites reveal an insatiable desire for power and wealth, as they seek to monopolize all dowries, all inheritances, all women, eligible or not. Moreover, they try to withdraw their wealth and goods from the system of exchange, and to redirect sexual energy to their illicit gratification, at the expense of traditional imperatives like the consolidation of patrimony and the procreation of the lineage.[31] The parasites inevitably challenge the monarch himself, be it through the usurpation of royal prerogatives by a medical body or through the misuse of *lettres de cachet* and formal police authority. It is significant that the aims of socially responsible characters in the plays, such as Elmire, Dorine, Béralde, and Toinette, are not primarily to effect a psychological change in the host-protagonist or to stamp out the extrasocial influences for the sake of abstract morality, but to facilitate the uniting of life-giving couples, Mariane and Valère, Angélique and Cléante, who will pass by the huge obstacles that confront the generation of Argan and Orgon, ensuring the prospect of a bright future. Infinitely conscious of the formative influence and moral preponderance of the past, Molière nevertheless orients his plays toward a future that he associates with people better able to cope with the problems of a rapidly evolving world.

Le Tartuffe and *Le Malade imaginaire* function all the while within strictly worldly parameters. Identifying the major concern in *Le Tartuffe* as a question of *honnête* behavior, Francis Lawrence stresses, "It has nothing to do with instruction in the practice of religion."[32] An analogous observation could be made regarding *Le Malade imaginaire*: nowhere does the dramatist discuss anatomical truths or scientific method—there is no verdict on the circulation of blood or any other substantive issue, despite the fact that Molière's rumored work of translating Lucretius would have made him quite able to venture into biology if he desired. This lack of a detachable thesis is what distinguishes Molière's masterpiece from the "bourgeois dramas" of the following century, for Molière's art involves the construction of a network of structural relationships, rather than the replication of messages separate from the work itself. Instead of a collection of distinct but articulated thoughts, his ideology can only be described as a way of thinking, feeling, and seeing, all in one.

In Molière's theater, socioeconomic integrity is far more a material and temporal concern than a utopia. Like a living organism, the social body exists. It is not only mutable but also fragile, so that its energies must be directed toward regeneration and security. This is not to say that the individual units, Argan and Orgon, cease to exist. Indeed, they even have enough control over their existence to get themselves and their dependants into, and occasionally out of, trouble. They define themselves primarily through others, and their responsibilities proceed from their status as "mon mari" or "mon père" or "mon maître." A generic identity such as that of bourgeois can only provide a single point of reference in a fabric of *parentèles* without which identity itself was seen to be impossible.

1. The supreme example of the penalty for failure to observe these standards was the bitter fate of exile and imprisonment, experienced by one of Molière's former patrons, the finance minister Foucquet.

2. Domat, *Les Lois civiles*, p. vii.

3. John Cairncross, *New Light on Molière*.

4. Some of the more noteworthy attempts to discuss biographical keys to this work are: F. Baumal, *Tartuffe et ses avatars*; Henri d'Alméras, *Le Tartuffe de Molière*; P. Emard, *Tartuffe, sa vie, son milieu*; D. Mornet, "Un Prototype de Tartuffe," in *Mélanges de philologie et d'histoire littéraire offerts à Edmond Huguet*; and Mireille Girard, "Molière dans la correspondance de Madame de Sévigné." Historians have followed for the most part the same biographical approach in treating the play: Emmanuel Chill, "Tartuffe, Religion, and Courtly Culture"; and R. B. Landolt, "Molière and Louis XIV."

5. Two of the critics to set the focus squarely on Orgon were Ramon Fernandès, in his work of the 1930 recently reprinted as *Molière ou l'essence du génie comique*; and Will G. Moore, in "*Tartuffe* and the Comic Principle in Molière." Other works to follow in this scrupulous tradition are: Judd Hubert, *Molière and the Comedy of the Intellect*, pp. 255–64; Jacques Guicharnaud, *Molière, une aventure théâtrale*, pp. 1–162; Francis L. Lawrence, "The Raisonneur in Molière"; and Myrna Zwillenberg, "Dramatic Justice in Tartuffe."

6. Besides the definitive works of Mousnier and Bluche on the sovereign courts, mentioned earlier, useful books on the courts during the Fronde period are A. Lloyd Moote, *The Revolt of the Judges*, and Albert Hamscher, *The Parlement of Paris after the Fronde, 1653–1673*. Hamscher describes, on pp. 107–9, the judges' conflicts with Mazarin over special courts to prosecute Frondeurs such as Claude Vallée, who, like

Orgon's friend Argas, was banished; he warns, however, against drawing too close an association between the magistrates and the Jansenist movement—a caveat worth repeating in the case of *Tartuffe*.

7. Gustave Roupnel, in *La Ville et la campagne*, pp. 155–56, points out that the "esprit de caste" of the magistrates caused the downfall of urban autonomy, resulting in royal intervention in all of Dijon's internal matters by 1668. Certainly the royal government coerced the *noblesse de robe* into adopting a strict self-discipline, not unlike that advocated by Tartuffe, as Robert Mandrou explains in *L'Europe absolutiste*, p. 47: "Pour la noblesse de robe . . ., Louis XIV et Colbert se sont bornés à exiger d'elle . . . une obéissance absolue aux volontés royales, qui ne s'est pas démentie jusqu'aux dernières années 1712–1713, où l'affaire de la bulle *Unigenitus* marque le réveil de la magistrature."

8. Vladimir Jankélévitch, *La Mauvaise Conscience*, p. 37. On his notion of "la conscience douleureuse du plaisir," see pp. 18–31.

9. Ibid., pp. 46–55.

10. Two who deny the possibility of parasitic manipulation by a *dévot* are R. Picard, "*Tartuffe*, production impie?" in *Mélanges d'histoire littéraire (XVIe–XVIIe xiècle) offerts à Raymond Lebègue*; and J. Cairncross, "*Tartuffe* ou Molière hypocrite." On the other hand, Pierre Clarac's "La Morale de Molière d'après Le Tartuffe" presents a cogent summary of the evidence to the contrary (the comments following Clarac's paper are equally interesting).

11. See G. A Goldschmidt, *Molière ou la liberté mise à nu*, p. 63 ff.; Lionel Gossman, *Men and Masks: A Study of Molière*, pp. 100–144, contains an in-depth analysis of the power dimension in *Le Tartuffe*, including Orgon's megalomania.

12. *OC La Grange*, 5:24.

13. La Mothe Le Vayer, "De la dévotion," *Oeuvres*, 2:496–98.

14. Rousillon's 1980 production of *Tartuffe* portrayed Elmire as a veritable whore, unbuttoning her clothes to tempt a *beau ténébreux* Tartuffe; but though this version undoubtedly conveys a certain epidermal interest, it deviates radically from Elmire's structural and textual *honnêteté* and from the "beau museau" that Molière intended his *directeur* to be. See Philippe Sénart, review of *Tartuffe*.

15. A. Loysel, *Institutes coutumières*, p. 4.

16. Brossette, *Correspondance Boileau-Brossette*, pp. 516–17. Boileau was not the last to tamper with Molière's ending. Roger Planchon's production of *Le Tartuffe* made the Orgon household a kind of construction site for Classicism, complete with a veiled statue of Louis XIV that is uncovered as the imposter is arrested in a violent, CRS-style police raid; see Philippe Sénart's review.

17. Ralph Albanese, "Une lecture idéologique du dénouement de *Tartuffe*."

18. See Bloch, *Les Rois thaumaturges*, pp. 195–207, and Mousnier, *Paris*, p. 52.

19. Robert Garapon, *Le Dernier Molière*, p. 170.

20. The famous armchair on display at the Comédie-Française is supposed to have served Argan onstage. For an illustration, see Alfred Simon, *Molière* (Paris: Seuil, 1974), p. 39.

21. As Marcel Gutwirth has pointed out, in *Molière ou l'invention comique*, pp. 25–60, Toinette represents an important final stage in the feminization of the domestic staff, which coincides with the evolution from traditional comic types to more recognizable contemporary figures. J. T. Stoker notes, in "Toinette's Age and Temperament," that the maid's incessant sniping serves as a structural dramatic counterpoint to Béline's mollycoddling of Argan.

22. Stephen Varick Dock, "La Réconstitution du costume porté par Molière dans *Le Malade imaginaire*."

23. A. Adam, "Molière," p. 396; J. Cairncross, *Molière bourgeois et libertin*, p. 38. For a sensible assessment of these suggestions, see Garapon, *Le Dernier Molière*, pp. 155–58. Although the medical profession did maintain close ties with the church in seventeenth-century Paris, we cannot go so far as to agree with Carlo François, "Médecine et religion chez Molière, deux facettes d'une même absurdité," that the *droit coutumier* would have represented the Old Testament to Molière's audience, or that the Diafoirus clan is a satire on the Holy Trinity.

24. Such linguistic distortion by all three doctors in the play actually devalues language and threatens to destroy the codes of signification and identity on which society relies; see Will G. Moore, *Molière, A New Criticism*, pp. 63, 75–76.

25. Domat, *Les Lois civiles*, pp. 103–7.

26. Gustave Michaut's article, "Louison, du *Malade imaginaire*," in *Mélanges Ed. Huguet*, pp. 304–7, undertakes an analysis of this unusual father-daughter scene.

27. H. Gaston Hall, "Molière's Comic Images," in *Molière: Stage and Study*, pp. 43–60.

28. Argou, *Institution au droit français*, 2:91; see also A. Loysel, *Institutes coutumières*, pp. 161, 196.

29. Chappuzeau, *Le Devoir général*, p. 37.

30. In "*L'Impromptu de Versailles* Reconsidered," Robert J. Nelson disagrees with Gide's view that *Le Malade imaginaire* is a "farce tragique," and goes on to reflect that those who are triumphant in Molière's theater are "those who are willing to assume a mask." Though the theory is interesting, one wonders whether Argan is aware that he is masquerading.

31. The extrasocial forces are so much like deadly viruses in their effect that Marcel Gutwirth has called Tartuffe an "Andromeda strain"; see "Tartuffe and the Mysteries."

32. Francis Lawrence, "*Tartuffe*: A Question of Honnête Behavior."

P.Brisart d.   I.Sauué F.

IMPROMPTV DE VERSAILLE

L'Impromptu de Versailles, showing the ridiculous marquis's flaring *canons* and contrasting tasteful costume. Brissart and Sauvé engraving for the 1682 Paris edition, republished in 1697. Reproduced by permission of the Houghton Library, Harvard University.

CONCLUSION

MOLIERE AND IDEOLOGY

No study of the social structures in Molière's theater could be truly thorough without a discussion of their possible ideological ramifications. There is, after all, an appropriate progression from the analysis of status indicators, characters' identities, behavioral patterns, and configurations of values in the texts to an inquiry into the design, conscious or otherwise, that gave them form. Ideology is a controversial and sometimes deceptive term, long invested with a pejorative connotation, thanks to Marx's interpretation of it as "false consciousness."[1] Fortunately, Jorge Larrain's recent book on the problematics of ideology and Louis Althusser's reinvestigation of the topic have allowed for a more open and practical definition; in Althusser's terminology, it is "a representation of the imaginary relationship of individuals to their real conditions of existence."[2] In the case of Molière's comedies, this process of representation has more to do with a sensitivity to structural relationships than with actual social consciousness, a condition that, according to Althusser, is true of most ideological expression.[3] Since there do not exist any writings or personal papers in which Molière speaks abstractly or theoretically about society, the only way to gain an understanding of his ideology is through the inductive method of examining his dramatic works against the operative context of his environment. Thus, it is suitable to adopt an attitude that ideology is, in Larrain's words, positive ("the expression of a worldview"), objective ("impregnating the basic structure of society"), and coextensive ("with the whole cultural sphere usually called the ideological superstructure").[4]

Critics of early modern literature occasionally adopt a line of reasoning that may be summarized as follows: an author's work cannot have ideological content unless he is a philosopher; he cannot be a philosopher without a discrete and comprehensive philosophy; therefore, the lack of an acceptable system not only of ethics but also of ontology, epistemology, and so on, must signify a lack of ideological content. Surely this doubtful syllogism should not be applied to Molière. No one in the audience of the Palais-Royal would expect successful comic discourse to resemble that of Descartes or Gassendi. On the other hand, the public has always perceived to some extent the innate social and critical thrust of the comic. In the language of Keith Thomas, "Jokes are a pointer to joking situations, areas of structural ambiguity in society itself, and their subject matter can be a revealing guide to past tensions and anxieties."[5] Comic discourse can be far more penetrating in its ethical analysis than even the most rigorous formal philosophy, and one should never mistakenly assume, as did some of the positivist critics, that comedies need to be grafted onto other features of the ideological superstructure in order to be considered valid.

The representation that takes place in Molière's work surpasses simple reflection or refraction of "real life scenes" of Louis XIV's France.[6] Its function is less photographic and more similar to semiotic signification. Here lies the great difference between the Classical writer and the one who purports to express documentary truths, whether he be a pamphleteer in the service of Versailles or a more recent devotee of committed literature: the former always shuns the level of the referent, creating dramatic or dynamic relationships without pretending that his works actually participate in the organic experience of social living. Although a status indicator such as a sum of money or possession of property may help us classify characters like Harpagon or Arnolphe and evaluate their signified behavior, it is pointless to leap across the gap that separates the sign and the referent and to assume that Tartuffe is Charpy de Sainte-Croix, that Philaminte is a lady of the Hôtel de Rambouillet, or that Amphitryon is Monsieur de Montespan.[7]

The mode of indirection and signification in Molière's work coincides with the aesthetics of the Classical age, which condemned overt, partisan campaigning as a violation of the implicit artistic pact between writer and reader. The resultant absorption of ideology into technique is described by Jean Decottignies:

> Par vocation, c'est-à-dire en raison de son insertion historique, le texte classique tente de dérober son fonctionnement, d'occulter le *procès* qui le fait être. En lui, le dire — ou si l'on veut, la pratique — ne s'appréhende pas; sa perfection réside dans sa transparence, dans les ruses qu'il déploie pour évacuer de son espace l'activité investigatrice du lecteur, pour l'orienter vers les en-deça ou les au-delà. Le texte classique refuse en principe la lecture telle que nous l'entendons . . . C'est là que nous voyons l'idéologie à l'oeuvre, et c'est pour cette raison qu'elle nous préoccupe.[8]

Such a fusion is apparent in the work of the man some contemporaries called "The Painter." Like a visual artist using the techniques of *trompe l'oeil* composition (and his friendship with Mignard makes it highly likely that he was knowledgeable in this field), Molière invites us to consider the overview of the finished fresco while drawing attention away from the solid materials that support the system of signs.

Another effect of the oneness of technique and ideology is to blend inseparably Molière the artist-thinker and Molière the entertainer-craftsman. The advantages of such a position are readily revealed in *La Critique de l'Ecole des femmes* and in

L'Impromptu de Versailles, where the dramatist defuses the serious accusations of moral meddling leveled against him by resorting to a brand of meta-theatrical satire more subtle and more powerful than the crude, vitriolic discourse employed by his enemies in *Zélinde* or *Elomire hypocondre*. What more effective way for him to destroy his image as a social danger than to take up the mask of the clownish mimic and to flout the pompous declamation and gestures of his everyday rivals in the Hôtel de Bourgogne?

Perhaps one of the most important aspects of Molière's ideology is the fact that he exhibits a disdain for the dogmatic philosophical systems that prevailed in his day. The attitude did not stem from ignorance, for he numbered among his friends the skeptical savant La Mothe Le Vayer, is thought to have translated Lucretius's *De Rerum Natura*, and left numerous hints of his familiarity with philosophical literature; his antidogmatic stance results from his tendency to avoid reductive, *a priori* reasoning. In *Le Mariage forcé* the foolish old Sganarelle, like Rabelais's Panurge in the *Tiers Livre*, consults about his marriage prospects with diametrically opposed philosophers. Pancrace the Aristotelian is a prisoner of his own endlessly hairsplitting definitions:

> Je soutiens qu'il faut dire la figure d'un chapeau, et non pas la forme; d'autant qu'il y a cette différence entre la forme et la figure, que la forme est la disposition extérieure des corps que sont animés, et la figure, la disposition extérieure des corps qui sont inanimés; et puisque le chapeau est un corps inanimé, il faut dire la figure d'un chapeau et non pas la forme. . . . Ce sont les termes exprès d' Aristote dans le chapitre *de la Qualité*. [Scene 4]

Marphurius the Pyrrhonian, on the other hand, is immoblized by his system's denial of any certitude:

> Notre philosophie ordonne de ne point énoncer de proposition décisive, de parler de tout avec incertitude, de suspendre toujours son jugement, et, par cette raison, vous ne devez pas dire: "Je suis venu"; mais: "Il me semble que je suis venu". [Scene 5]

To the pragmatic Molière, such systems destroy their own erstwhile cohesiveness by relying too heavily on theories that conflict with observable fact. He is unwilling to allow himself to lose sight of human problems simply because of doctrinal disputes.

The reservations about erudition that are made in *Le Mariage forcé* remind one of Francis Bacon's *The Advancement of Learning*. Bacon attacks three "diseases of learning" that impede clear thinking, namely, excessively flowery language, contentiousness, and deceit. The second category, which Bacon explicitly links with Aristotelianism, applies equally well to Pancrace and to Marphurius:

> And such is their method, that rests not so much upon evidence of truth proved by arguments . . . as upon particular confutations and solutions of every scruple, cavillation, and objection; breeding for the most part one question as soon as it solveth another . . . so the generalities of the schoolmen are for a while good and proportionable; but when you descend into their distinctions and decisions, instead of a fruitful womb for the use and benefit of man's life, they end in monstrous altercations and barking questions.[9]

Since Molière presents a dramatic illustration of this disorder, he joins Bacon in anticipating the development of a modern scientific method based on induction, careful observation, and experimentation. However, he stops short of extolling progress, for the enthusiasm it sometimes engenders can dull and trick the senses, as it does when Bélise imagines she sees men in the moon through her telescope.

The ideology expressed in Molière's plays is best understood in a synchronic sense, rooted in the conditions of social awareness in mid-seventeenth-century France. Jorge Larrain states authoritatively, "Cultural phenomena are no longer understood as genetic products of a subject, but rather as subjectless, synchronic, underlying structures."[10] It is for this reason that Molière's characters are analyzed in relation to *états* rather than to Industrial Revolution classes or—what is worse—the feudal terminology so dear to some Marxist interpretations.[11]

Molière's insertion of his works into their historical context was quite deliberate. Instead of such timely characters as the salon hack, the director of conscience, and the aberrant officer, he could have used the jaded stereotypes that reappear with monotony in the works of other comic dramatists: the boastful captain, the pedant, the drunken servant, such as Jean Chevalier's Guillot, or the clever, seductive valet exemplified by Raymond Poisson's Crispin. Theater directors have learned through centuries of experience that one may remove Molière's figures from the seventeenth-century decor by placing them, for instance, in a twentieth-century living room instead of an antechamber, but that it is impossible to take the context out of the character: Alceste will always be a frustrated courtier who yearns for monarchial dominion, no matter what furniture he sits on or what clothes he wears. The dramatist was conscious of the need for synchronic homology, for he explained in *L'Impromptu de Versailles* that comic types were not static. Defending his recurrent use of the ridiculous marquis figure, he pointed out that this type of up-to-date fool had replaced the others and that the successful playwright must be watchful for such changes (scene 1). Furthermore, in concrete demonstration of this principle, he included in his comedy not only an "imaginary" marquis, portrayed by La Grange in the play-within-a-play, but also a "real" marquis, acted by La Thorillière, who annoys the troupe during

their rehearsal (scene 2). As a reader, Molière probably appreci-
ated the Roman-ness of the characters in Plautus's *Aulularia*;
but he inserted his own miser, Harpagon, into the midst of his
own age and its issues, with all the appropriate emphasis on *dot*
and *dignité*, on controlled lending and contractual procedure.
Thus, the ideological-technical synthesis in his theater is not
merely the effect of a certain intellectual background but a
deliberate step toward a more synchronic social representation
in the work of art.

In Molière's comedies, structures operate over a rather well-
defined field of social conditions, that of the urban ranks of the
officer-level middle bourgeoisie and the nobility of the court.
This field of influence is to a large degree identical with the
segments of the population that frequented the playhouses and
read published plays. Not surprisingly, Molière constructed the
comic situation in an environment with which he and his audience were intimately acquainted—the same layer of society that
was in so many countries the *sine qua non* of theater itself.
Other groups are not given a central position in his plays. Apart
from the second act of *Dom Juan*, peasants appear infrequently,
though village life had drawn the attention of such fellow dramatists as Brécourt, who wrote a comedy called *La Noce de village*
complete with sustained rural dialect. Nor did Molière depict
the world of the workers, artisans, and *petits bourgeois* other
than by a few sedan-chair porters and by the Sganarelles of *Le
Cocu imaginaire* and *Le Médecin malgré lui*, neither of which
devotes much space to behavior within the lower *roturier* household. Servants appear in the context of their domestic duties to
masters and mistresses and are assimilated into the concerns and
plans of their hierarchical superiors. The most radical example
of this is the snuff-taking Sganarelle of *Dom Juan*, who
becomes so wrapped up in his master's situation that he misses
his meals and forgets to hide away a few pistoles in case of hard

times. In general, the less-fortunate commoners are shown to be preoccupied with their immediate survival.

It may be argued that this concentration on the middle bourgeoisie and aristocracy constitutes neglect of the largest part of the French population, perhaps eighty to ninety percent of it. In fact, Ilutowicz, Roe, and Emelina have maintained in their studies on the lower portions of the populace in Molière's works that the author portrayed these groups negatively or sidestepped their social significance.[12] Neither accusation is really valid, however, since Molière was guided in his signifying of these social segments by technical as well as ideological requirements. There was an inherent contradiction in selecting Classical comic protagonists from groups subject to the misery of sporadic famine and ailing commerce. La Bruyère's well-known sketch of peasants as animals rooting in the earth grimly reflects the devastating *mortalités* that swept through the countryside. The urban poor — even the marginal groups of the *petite bourgeoisie* — were scarcely better off. In choosing the comic genre, Molière acquired the option of presenting non-noble figures; but he also accepted the paramount importance of pleasing the public, that is, of instilling in them delight and laughter. The predicament of lower *roturier* groups precluded this, and Molière was too truthful an artist to create a village full of "happy natives," as Brécourt had done, or to fabricate a Gallic version of *The Shoemaker's Holiday*.[13]

If it is unfair to brand Molière as an enemy of the masses simply because he does not incite the commoners to revolt, it is equally inaccurate to claim, as Stackelberg has done, that his sentiments reside with the oppressed rather than with their bourgeois or aristocratic overlords.[14] At times Dorine and other servants are certainly made to speak much more sensibly than their superiors, but it is on behalf of the interests of the masters themselves. Where the vulnerability of the servant condition is involved, as in Martine's dismissal in *Les Femmes savantes*, the customary paternalistic code is the only secure solution to the worker's helplessness to be offered by the text. Even Scapin, who commits a most outrageous action by beating his master, Géronte, in a sack, never attains the aggressive class consciousness of a Figaro. His boldness is attenuated by the exotic element in the play, as well as by the fact that he explains his *fourberies* to his timorous associate Silvestre in terms of whimsical adventurousness: "Je me plais à tenter des entreprises hasardeuses" (3. 1). His ultimate goal is merely to retain his status as a well-fed dependent, "au bout de la table, en attendant que je meure" (3. 13).

Central to the critical depiction of urban groups in Molière's theater is the bipolar nature of the social structures themselves. This phenomenon of contrast and antithesis has given rise to considerable discussion by Raymond Lebègue and more recently by Roger Ikor in *Molière double*.[15] Ikor sees the source of the polarity as a kind of benign moral schizophrenia in the author, but it is perhaps worthwhile to consider the question in a larger structural perspective. This study has concentrated on four areas of pronounced tension between widely recognized behavioral values and aberrant developments that threaten to subvert them. It is remarkable that Molière does not seem to envision the possibility of a mediation between the extremes, other than a purely illusory one on the model of Monsieur Jourdain's mamamouchization or Argan's "medical" transformation. Like Pascal, Molière reiterates the formula of *le tiers exclu*. The offender and his rationale, no matter how formidable, are ultimately overcome by means that range from benevolent deception through alienation and exclusion to outright execution, and the social fabric knits together again with no sign of lasting weakness. One might object that *Dom Juan* poses an exception to this pattern, and it is true that Molière's decision to adapt this

elaborate tradition, with its numerous set scenes already added
by Spanish, Italian, and French predecessors, imposed special
constraints with which the dramatist did not usually have to
deal. But one must ask oneself whether Dom Louis, Elvire, and
Sganarelle can possibly be in worse straits at the end of the play
than when the young rake was alive to degrade them. Is not the
life of Dom Carlos, who faced imminent death in one of Dom
Juan's duels, a triumph for social values and a hope that
noblesse will survive? Dom Juan himself rejects a series of con-
ciliatory efforts by other characters and eventually undermines
by his false piety in the fifth act any remaining possibility of
mediation between his former misbehavior and the demands of
society. Thus, even in the play that many critics have judged to
be the author's most ambiguous, the refusal of dialectical compromise is cleverly incorporated into the protagonist's own network of decisions. The Commander's statue, associated with the
punitive aspect of collective values, intervenes to enforce the
souverain bien when individual efforts by father, wife, creditor,
and fellow cavalier have failed to reclaim Dom Juan.

Although the polarities in Molière's works remain unmodi-
fied, an ideological mediation is achieved through the triumph
of the pluralistic *société d'états* over the forces of disintegration.
In order to appreciate this, it is important to understand that
the dramatist served as spokesman neither for an antiaristocratic
nor for an antibourgeois point of view. Let us first consider the
opinion that Molière was a bourgeois militant, as set forth in
typical, but by no means decisive, form by John Cairncross. He
claims that Molière incarnates "les premières années de Louis
XIV, période où l'alliance entre le roi et les éléments les plus
avancés de la bourgeoisie a favorisé l'éclosion du libertinage et
une campagne à fond contre les classes et les valeurs féodales."[16]
Cairncross goes on to offer as proof the statement that Molière
loved simplicity, naturalness, and frankness, virtues that were

supposedly reserved for the bourgeoisie alone! This intuitive approach is as rich in sociohistorical myth as it is lacking in scholarly rigor. If Molière were really expressing an antinoble ethos, why would he take such care to examine the codes of exemplarity that enshrine *noblesse* as the highest aspiration and reward of civil existence? Young men like Valère, Cléonte, and Clitandre derive their ability to defeat their aged or defective rivals from a solid adherence to the standards and values of the court. Furthermore, the character who is the great champion of the simple, the natural, and the frank, Alceste, is the least bourgeois figure in the entire Molière canon. Though Molière mocked the deviant behavior of foppish marquis, lawless *seigneurs*, bumbling usurpers, and power-hungry misanthropes, he never ridiculed the basic concepts of the noble code. Virtuous noblemen such as Dom Carlos and Philinte admit its contradictions and surmount them, winning grudging respect from their disbelieving counterparts.

The contrary viewpoint, that Molière is an antibourgeois ideologist, is also fraught with insufficiencies, even when it is advocated by a critic as eloquent and as profound as Paul Bénichou:

> Il suffit de parcourir le théâtre de Molière pour se rendre compte que le bourgeois y est presque toujours médiocre ou ridicule. Il n'est pas un seul des bourgeois de Molière qui présente, en tant que bourgeois, quelque élévation ou valeur morale; l'idée même de la vertu proprement bourgeoise se chercherait en vain à travers ses comédies. . . . Ce qui importe, c'est que l'infériorité sociale des bourgeois soit représentée avec tant de force.[17]

If this great comic body of literature lacks shopkeeper heroes, it is for the good reason that, apart from Monsieur Dimanche and Messieurs Josse and Guillaume of *L'Amour médecin*, it contains few shopkeepers of any kind, either positive or negative. However, there are a great number of officer clans and bourgeois families living nobly. It is not clear exactly what Bénichou would consider elevation or moral value, but it is evident that time and time again, these units emerge as very powerful forces in the comedies. The Arnolphes, Harpagons, and Orgons who attempt to subvert the behavioral codes generally fight a lonely struggle, and only in *Les Femmes savantes* is there something that briefly resembles an equality of numbers for and against bourgeois practices. To represent the positive forces of partial closure, reciprocity, and socioeconomic integrity, Molière creates not only a long line of "advisers" (Chrysalde, Géronimo, Cléante of *Tartuffe*, Ariste, Béralde) and concerned servants (Dorine, La Flèche, Nicole, Martine, Toinette) but also some of his most memorable family members, including Elmire, Cléante of *L'Avare*, Madame Jourdain, Henriette, and Angélique of *Le Malade imaginaire*. In the case of George Dandin, it is the transgressor himself who recalls the codes he is violating. Nor can one forget such officers as Cléonte, who demonstrates in *Le Bourgeois gentilhomme* that his good fortune has not obliterated his origins or given him a pretension to the rank of hereditary noble, but only imbued him with a sense of added dignity and civil behavior that is an extension, rather than a denial, of his status.

Proponents of Bénichou's thesis are likely to point particularly to the Greek plays (as they are designated in chapter two above) as proof of Molière's putative courtly ethic, and indeed those plays do deserve consideration. In them Molière created a fundamental structure of complete noble closure, but he chose to distance this closure from his audience through theatrical features (setting, costumes, decorations) and social elements (antique and mythological *conditions*) that were remote from everyday experience. Though perfectly conventional and acceptable in art, the characters in the Greek play certainly lacked the shock value of Tartuffe, dressed in contemporary *dévot* fashions, or Monsieur de Pourceaugnac, freshly arrived from Limoges in his gaudy clothes. Had the playwright chosen to make the princesse d'Elide a contemporary duchess or Amphitryon a general in Louis XIV's armies, or to make Tartuffe a Celtic priest or Pourceaugnac a citizen of Ephesus, our view of the Molière canon would be radically different, but in fact he did not. For example, *Amphitryon*, which is in almost every sense the most impressive of the Greek plays, has been cited innumerable times as unshakable evidence that Molière was an official symbolic spokesman for the throne, on the grounds that the comedy supposedly justified Louis's real-life affair with Madame de Montespan. However, it is, despite its beauties, among Molière's least original plays, being patterned very, very closely on a French source (Rotrou's *Les Sosies* [1636]) that was still fresh in the minds of many of his spectators. Unless one credits Rotrou with psychic powers, there can be no connection between his comedy and the king's love-life, for Louis was not born until 1638. Furthermore, Sosie and Mercure, the most important characters in both the Rotrou and Molière versions, have no identifiable historical counterparts. Obviously, any similarity between Alcmène and the lovely Mme de Montespan is an accidental case of life imitating art—Rotrou's art. Plays like *Amphitryon* and *Les Amants magnifiques* had an audience appeal in their day that qualifies as a form of escape literature, conjuring up a hazy Golden Age, a still-popular ideal of aristocracy that represents the theoretical end point of social mobility, when many spectators dreamed of emerging from their bourgeois coccoons into a more beautiful world. The closed noble society of the Greek plays thus has a distinct place in Molière's overall ideology, but it is not a preponderant or exclusive one and did not occupy the author's talents in the same magnificent way as noble unworthiness does in *Dom Juan* or bourgeois reciprocity in *Les Femmes savantes*.

It is hardly surprising that Molière chose not to heap ridicule on either the upwardly mobile bourgeoisie or the *noblesse*, since his creation of the comedy of manners was based on a new consensus. A study of the comedies offered by the Troupe du Roi during their visits to aristocratic and royal palaces reveals that they were accepted there with levels of enthusiasm roughly similar to those of the general public in the Parisian playhouse. The works that were first applauded at court, such as *Monsieur de Pourceaugnac* and *Le Bourgeois gentilhomme*, were greeted warmly by the crowds at the Palais-Royal, just as those that made their debut in Paris, including such farcical entertainments as *Sganarelle* and *L'Ecole des maris*, were heartily approved by elite audiences.[18] The fact that burghers and courtiers joined in giving their approbation to Molière was due in large part to his ability to achieve a sense of Classical comic plenitude unequaled by his rivals. His plays represent an imaginary network of social relationships that is remarkably homologous to the world view of the French literate public in the reign of Louis XIV. This ideology that seeks to defend the harmony of unlike elements against the challenges of revisionistic individuals can be described as polymorphous and polyvalent, for it encompasses a wide range of social conditions and assigns to each a distinct code of behavior.

The profundity of Molière's ideological differentiation finds few parallels in the theater, but it coincides with some of the leading intellectual trends of the seventeenth and eighteenth centuries. Perhaps the most interesting similarity involves Leibniz's theory of monads, which postulates a continuous chain of indivisible, inalterable units possessing distinct inherent qualities—much like the *états* of Molière's social continuum.[19] Despite Leibniz's German nationality, his development of monadology was closely associated with the mental climate of France, for its components were first discussed in his correspondence with the Jansenist Arnauld.[20] Leibniz was, moreover, quite aware of the social implications of his monads, for his *Théodicée* strongly affirms the principle of hierarchic gradation as the cornerstone of universal harmony; across the English Channel, Pope and Soame Jenyns expressed kindred outlooks.[21] Polymorphism spilled over from ethics and metaphysics into the area of the natural sciences, where *fixistes* such as Carl Linne, Buffon, and Bonnet professed a belief in the immutability of the species well into the era of the Enlightenment.[22]

In his theater of social differentiation, Molière accomplished a mediation for the highly diverse groups that made up the *société d'états*. His contemporaries could find in it an illustration, in praxis rather than in mere theory, of the great chain of social being. The comedies maintain the validity, but not the equality, of each *condition* and show that each must have a specific constellation of values adapted to its social environment. Molière, the consummate comic dramatist, exploited the virtually unlimited possibilities for combining the dissonances of humor—the joke, the trick, the humiliating situation—with the social dissonances of his time—unworthiness, usurpation, egotistical imbalance, and parasitism. And whenever he makes us perceive that the clown who fails to keep his equilibrium on the stage and the fool who fails to keep his equilibrium in the world are both victims of the same vertigo, we still laugh today.

1. Henri Lefebvre, *Sociologie de Marx*, pp. 49–74. See also L. G. Graham, "Ideology and the Sociological Understanding."

2. Louis Althusser, *Lenin and Philosophy and Other Essays*, p. 153. Jorge Larrain, in *The Concept of Ideology*, pp. 154–64, relates Althusser's opinions to those of John Mepham and Nicos Poulantzas, and cogently discusses the criticisms made by Jacques Rancière and Paul Q. Hirst. However, as the latter concern primarily the question of science supplanting ideology in the modern period, they do nothing to diminish the applicability of Althusser's apt definition to the early modern context.

3. Louis Althusser, *For Marx*, p. 233.

4. Larrain, *The Concept of Ideology*, p. 14. An excellent treatment of differing ideological techniques in *Tartuffe* and *Dom Juan* is Jean Jaffré's "Théâtre et idéologie: note sur la dramaturgie de Molière."

5. Keith Thomas, "The Idea of Laughter in Tudor and Stuart England."

6. Important contributions to reflection theory include: J. Duvignaud, *Sociologie du théâtre*; P. Machéry, *Pour une théorie de la production littéraire*; and C. Duchet, "Une écriture de la socialité."

7. One modern example of the tendency to see Molière as an author of *Schlüsselkomödie* is Paul Römer's *Molières Amphitryon und sein gesellschaftlicher Hintergrund.*

8. Jean Decottignies, "L'Inscription de l'idéologie dans la littérature. Propos théoriques."

9. Francis Bacon, *The Adventure of Learning and New Atlantis*, pp. 32–33. Bacon goes on to describe other "peccant humors" that afflict philosophy; these ideas are reorganized later in his *Novum Organum* into the "idols of the theatre." See Larrain, *The Concept of Ideology*, pp. 19–21.

10. Larrain, *The Concept of Ideology*, p. 15.

11. See the critique of Boris Porchnev's work in Roland Mousnier, "Quelques aspects de la fonction publique dans la société française du XVIIᵉ siècle," as well as Hubert Méthivier, *L'Ancien Régime*, pp. 75–78.

12. F. C. Roe, "Les Types sociaux dans la comédie de Molière: le valet et la servante"; Salomon Ilutowicz, *Le Peuple dans le théâtre de Molière*, pp. 111–17; and Emelina, *Les Valets et les servantes dans le théâtre de Molière*, p. 127 ff. Emelina's more recent book, *Les Valets et les servantes dans le théâtre comique* has, however, considerably modified his earlier findings.

13. Laughter is, of course, directed at *roturier* cowardice, particularly in Sganarelle (e.g., *Le Cocu imaginaire*, *Dom Juan*). However, the ridicule is prompted not by the survival function of cowardice but rather by characters who presume to be more than they are and then back down in times of crisis. Such behavior is ignoble, but then again so are the characters' pretensions (i.e., Sosie's attempt to claim a glorious part in the *récit* of Amphitryon's victory). More modest commoners are not always cowardly, as shown by the porters in *Les Précieuses ridicules* or Alain in *L'Ecole des femmes*. Unlike such rivals as Chevalier, Molière did not gratuitously mock the timorousness of the third estate.

14. Jurgen von Stackelberg, "Molière und die Gesellschaftsordnung seiner Zeit."

15. Lebègue, "La Bipolarité des personnages de Molière"; Roger Ikor, *Molière double*, pp. 110–38.

16. Cairncross, *Molière bourgeois et libertin*, pp. 7–8.

17. Bénichou, *Morales du Grand Siècle*, pp. 285–89.

18. Bray, *Molière, homme de théâtre*, pp. 132–39.

19. Gottfried Wilhelm Leibniz, *The Monadology of Leibniz*, pp. 36–43.

20. W. H. Barber, *Leibniz in France from Arnauld to Voltaire*, pp. 10–15. For the text of Leibniz's letters see *Lettres de Leibniz à Arnauld*. Marie Cariou, in *L'Atomisme: Gassendi, Leibniz, Bergson, et Lucrèce*, pp. 92–102, discusses Leibniz's refutations of Epicurean-Gassendian arithmetic mechanism (on the basis that their atomic theory cannot account for qualitative differences) and of Cartesian geometric mechanism (because mathematic points in space are purely representational and not real in a concrete sense). In *Le Système de Leibniz et ses modèles mathématiques*, Michel Serres discusses Leibniz's notion of biological multiplicity; see 1:326–31, and 2:573.

21. Besides these writers, Fontenelle also held that nature creates a continual differentiation of life forms. See Arthur O. Lovejoy, *The Great Chain of Being*, pp. 131, 200–207.

22. P. Flourens, *Histoire des travaux et des idées de Buffon*, pp. 96–101; and Jean Rostand, *Esquisse d'une histoire de la biologie*, pp. 34–40, 50, 79–80.

SELECTED BIBLIOGRAPHY

ABBREVIATIONS

OC Couton: Molière, *Oeuvres complètes*, ed. Georges Couton.

RHLF: *Revue d'Histoire Littéraire de la France*

RHT: *Revue d'Histoire du Théâtre*

XS: *XVIIe Siècle*

FR: *French Review*

PFSCL: *Papers on French Seventeenth Century Literature*

PART ONE: LITERATURE AND LITERARY CRITICISM

Adam, Antonie. "Molière." In *L'Apogée du siècle*. Vol. 3 of *L'Histoire de la littérature française au XVIIe siècle*. 2d ed. Paris: Del Duca, 1962. Pp. 181–408.

Albanese, Ralph, Jr. "Argent et réification dans *L'Avare*." *L'Esprit Créateur*, vol. 21, no. 3 (1981), pp. 35–50.

———. *Le Dynamisme de la peur chez Molière: une analyse socio-culturelle de Dom Juan, Tartuffe, et L'Ecole des femmes*. University, Miss.: Romance Monographs, 1976.

———. "Historical and Literary Perceptions on 17th Century French Criminality." *Stanford French Review* 4 (1980): 417–33.

———. "The Molière Myth in Nineteenth Century France." In *Pre-text, Text, Context: Essays on Nineteenth-Century French Literature*, ed. Robert L. Mitchell. Columbus: Ohio State University Press, 1980. pp. 238–54.

———. "Quelques héros criminels chez Molière." *French Forum* 1 (1976): 217–25.

———. "Solipsisme et parole dans *George Dandin*." *Kentucky Romance Quarterly* 27 (1980): 421–34.

———. "Théâtre et anomie: le cas du *Misanthrope*." *Cahiers Internationaux de Sociologie* 64 (1978): 113–26.

———. "Une lecture idéologique du dénouement de *Tartuffe*." *Romance Notes* 16 (1974–75): 623–35.

————. "Une sociocritique du mythe royal sous Louis XIV: *Tartuffe* et *Amphitryon.*" *French Literature Series* 3 (1976): 17–27.

Alter, Jean V. *Les Origines de la satire antibourgeoise en France.* Vol. 2: *L'Esprit antibourgeois sous l'Ancien Régime: littérature et tensions sociales aux XVIIe et XVIIIe siècles.* Geneva: Droz, 1970.

Arnavon, Jacques. *La Morale de Molière.* 1945: rpt. Geneva: Slatkine, 1970.

Aubignac, François Hédelin, abbé d'. *La Pratique du théâtre.* Ed. Pierre Martino. Paris: Champion, 1927.

Audiberti, Jacques. *Molière dramaturge.* Paris: L'Arche, 1954.

Auerbach, Eric. *Mimesis: The Representation of Reality in Western Literature.* Trans. Willard Trask. Princeton, N.J.: Princeton University Press, 1953.

Baillet, Adrien. *Jugements des savants sur les principaux ouvrages.* Paris: A. Dezallier, 1686.

Bar, Francis. *Le Genre burlesque en France au XVIIe siècle.* Paris: d'Artrey, 1960.

Barrault, Jean-Louis. "*Le Bourgeois* ou la poésie du rire." *Modern Drama* 16 (1973–74): 113–16.

Barthes, Roland. "Le Silence de Dom Juan." *Lettres nouvelles,* 1st ser. no. 12 (1954), pp. 264–67.

Baumal, Francis. *Tartuffe et ses avatars.* Paris: Nouvry, 1925.

Bayle, Pierre. *Dictionnaire historique et critique.* Ed. Chaufepié et al. Paris: Desoer, 1820–24. 12:252–64.

Beffara, Louis. *Dissertation sur J. B. Poquelin-Molière.* Paris: Vente, 1821.

Bénichou, Paul. *Morales du Grand Siècle.* Paris: Gallimard, 1963.

Boileau, Nicolas. *Oeuvres complètes.* Ed. Paul Chéron. Paris: Garnier, 1860.

Bossuet, Jacques-Bénigne. "Maximes et réflexions sur la comédie." In *L'Eglise et le théâtre.* Ed. Ch. Urbain and E. Levesque. Paris: Grasset, 1930.

Boulanger de Challuset. *Elomire hypocondre ou les médecins vengés.* In *OC* Couton 1:1143.

Bourdaloue, Louis. *Sermons choisis.* Ed. Louis Dimier. Paris: Garnier, n.d.

Bray, René. *Molière, homme de théâtre.* Paris: Mercure de France, 1954.

Brécourt, Guillaume Marcoureau, dit. *L'Ombre de Molière.* Ed. Paul Lacroix. Rpt. Geneva: Slatkine, 1969.

Brody, Jules. "*Dom Juan* and *Le Misanthrope,* or the Esthetics of Individualism in Molière." *PMLA* 84 (1969): 559–76.

————. "Esthétique et société chez Molière." In *Colloque des Sciences*

Humaines: Dramaturgie et Société au 17ᵉ siècle. Ed. Jean Jacquot. Paris: CNRS, 1968. 1:307–26.

Brunetière, Ferdinand. *Etudes critiques.* Paris: Hachette, 1898.

———. "Molière." In *Histoire de la littérature française classique.* Paris: Delagrave, 1904–31. 2:382–454.

Butler, Philip. "Orgon le dirigé." In *Gallica: Essays Presented to J. Haywood Thomas.* Cardiff: University of Wales, 1969. Pp. 103–19.

———. "Tartuffe et la direction spirituelle au XVIIᵉ siècle." In *Modern Miscellany Presented to Eugene Vinaver.* Ed. T. E. Lawrenson et al. New York: Barnes and Noble, 1969.

Cairncross, John. *Molière bourgeois et libertin.* Paris: Nizet, 1963.

———. *New Light on Molière.* Paris: Droz, 1956.

———. "*Tartuffe* ou Molière hypocrite." *RHLF* 72 (1972): 890–901.

Chamarat, G. "Harpagon est-il un personnage comique?" *Les Annales-Conferencia,* N. S., no. 157 (1963), pp. 20–32.

Chamfort, N. S. Roch de. "Eloge de Molière." In *Oeuvres complètes.* Ed. P. R. Auguis. Paris: Chaumerot Jeune, 1824. 1: 1–32.

Chevalley, Sylvie. *Molière en son temps 1622–1673.* Paris: Comédie-Française, 1970.

Chill, Emmanuel. "Tartuffe, Religion, and Courtly Culture." *French Historical Studies* 3 (1963): 151–83.

Clarac, Pierre. "La Morale de Molière d'après *Le Tartuffe.*" *RHT* 26 (1974): 15–26.

Coe, Richard N. "The Ambiguity of *Dom Juan.*" *Australian Journal of French Studies* 1 (1964): 23–35.

Collinet, Jean-Pierre. *Lectures de Molière.* Paris: A. Colin, 1974.

Conti, Armand de Bourbon, prince de. *Traité de la comédie et des spectacles selon la tradition de l'église.* Paris: Billaine, 1666.

Corcoran, Paul E. "The Bougeois and other Villains." *Journal of the History of Ideas* 38 (1977): 477–85.

Couton, Georges. "Tartuffe et le péché d'hypocrisie, cas réservé." *RHLF* 69 (1969): 404–13.

Davis, Millie Gerard. "Masters and Servants in the Plays of Moliere." In *Molière: Stage and Study; Essays in Honour of W. G. Moore,* ed. W. D. Howarth and Merlin Thomas. Oxford: Oxford University Press, 1973.

D'Alméras, Henri. *Le Tartuffe de Molière.* Amiens: E. Malpère, 1928.

D'Assouci, Charles Couppeau. "L'Ombre de Molière et son épitaphe." In *Recueil sur la mort de Molière*. Ed. Georges Monval. Rpt. Geneva: Slatkine, 1969. Pp. 59–85.

Decottignies, Jean. "L'Inscription de l'idéologie dans la littérature, propos théoriques." *Revue des Sciences Humaines* 38 (1973): 485–92.

Defaux, Gérard. "Alceste et les rieurs." *RHLF* 74 (1974): 579–99.

————. "Rêve et réalité dans le *Bourgeois gentilhomme*." *XS*, no. 117 (1977), pp. 19–33.

Deierkauf-Holsboer, S. Wilma. "La Famille de la mère de Molière." *XS*, no. 28 (1955), pp. 221–29.

Delon, M. "Lectures de Molière au XVIIIᵉ siècle." *Europe*, no. 523–24 (1972), pp. 92–101.

Dens, Jean-Pierre. "Dom Juan: Héroisme et désir." *FR* 50 (1977): 835–41.

Derche, R. "Encore un modèle possible de Tartuffe." *RHLF* 51 (1951): 129–153.

Descotes, Maurice. *Les grands rôles du théâtre de Molière*. Paris: PUF, 1960.

————. "Molière et le conflit des générations." *RHLF* 72 (1972): 786–99.

D'Estrée, Paul. "La Genèse de *George Dandin*." *RHLF* 10 (1903): 637–45.

Diderot, Denis. *Le Neveu de Rameau*. Ed. Jean Fabre. Geneva: Droz, 1963.

————. *Oeuvres complètes*. Ed. Roger Lewinter. Vols. 2 and 3. Paris: Club de Meilleur Livre, 1969.

Dock, Stephen Varick. "La Reconstitution du costume porté par Molière dans *Le Malade imaginaire*." *RHT* 30 (1978): 127–31.

Donneau de Visé, Jean. *Nouvelles nouvelles, 3ᵉ partie*. In *OC* Couton, 1:1018–19.

————. *Oraison funèbre de Molière*. Ed. Paul Lacroix. Rpt. Geneva: Slatkine, 1969.

Doolittle, James, "Bad Writing in *L'Avare*." *L'Esprit Créateur*, vol. 6, no. 3 (1966), pp. 197–206.

————. "The Humanity of Molière's *Dom Juan*." *PMLA* 68 (1953): 90–102.

Doubrovsky, Serge. "Arnolphe ou la chute du héros." *Mercure de France* 343 (1961): 111–18.

Dubu, Jean. "Dom Juan et la notion de l'honnêteté chez Molière." *Etudes sur Pézenas* 4 (1973): 31–34.

Duchêne, Roger. "Molière et la lettre." *Travaux de linguistique et littérature*, vol. 13, no. 2 (1975), pp. 261–73.

Duchet, C. "Une écriture de la socialité." *Poétique*, no. 16 (1973), pp. 446–54.

Duvignaud, Jean. *Sociologie du théâtre*. Pris: PUF, 1965.

Emard, Paul. *Tartuffe, sa vie, son milieu et la comédie de Molière* Paris: Droz, 1932.

Emelina, Jean. *Les Valets et les servantes dans le théâtre comique en France de 1610 à 1700*. Grenoble: Presse Universitaire de Grenoble, 1976.

———. *Les Valets et les servantes dans le théâtre de Molière*. Aix-en-Provence: Pensée Universitaire, 1958.

———. "Les Serviteurs du théâtre de Molière, ou la fête de l'inconvenance." *RHT* 26 (1974): 229–39.

Eustis, Alvin. *Molière as Ironic Contemplator*. The Hague: Mouton, 1973.

Fabre d'Eglantine, Philippe. *Le Philinte de Molière*. Amsterdam: G. Dufour, 1792.

Faguet, Emile. *En lisant Molière*. Paris: Hachette, 1914.

Fellows, Otis. *French Opinion of Molière 1800–1850*. Providence, R.I.: Brown University Press, 1937.

Fénelon, François de Salignac de la Mothe. *Oeuvres complètes*. Ed. M. Gosselin. 1851–52; rpt. Geneva: Slatkine, 1971. 6:637–38.

Fernandès, Ramon. *Molière ou l'essence du génie comique*. Paris: Grasset, 1980.

Fontenelle, Bernard Le Bouvier de. *Oeuvres*. Paris: Les Libraires Associés, 1766. 1:177–83.

Forkey, Leo. *The Role of Money in French Comedy during the Reign of Louis XIV*. Baltimore: Johns Hopkins University Press, 1947.

François, Carlo. "Médecine et religion chez Molière, deux facettes d'une même absurdité." *FR* 42 (1969): 665–72.

———. *La Notion de l'absurde dans la littérature française du XVIIᵉ siècle*. Paris: Klincksieck, 1973.

Furetière, Antoine. *Dictionnaire universel*. 3 vols. The Hague and Rotterdam: Leers, 1690.

———. *Le Roman bourgeois*. In *Romanciers du XVIIᵉ siècle*. Ed. A. Adam. Paris: Gallimard, 1958.

Gaines, James F. "The Burlesque *Récit* in Molière's Greek Plays." *FR* 52 (1979): 393–400.

———. "Usurpation, Dominance, and Social Closure in *L'Ecole des Femmes*." *PFSCL*, vol. 9, no. 17 (1982), pp. 607–26.

———. "Gambling in the Theatre of Molière's Contemporaries." *PFSCL*, vol. 15, no. 2 (1981), pp. 331–42.

———. "*Ménage* versus Salon in *Les Femmes savantes*." *L'Esprit Créateur*, vol. 21, no. 3 (1981), pp. 51–59.

———. "*Le Menteur* and *Dom Juan*: A Case of Theatrical and Literary Adaptation." Forthcoming in *Kentucky Romance Quarterly*.

———. "Social Structures in Molière's Major Plays." Ph.D. Diss., University of Pennsylvania, 1977.

Garapon, Robert. *Le Dernier Molière*. Paris: SEDES, 1977.

———. "La Langue et le style des différents personnages du *Bourgeois gentilhomme*." *Le Français Moderne* 26 (1958): 103–12.

Gendarme de Bévotte, G. *Le Festin de Pierre avant Molière*. Paris: Cornély, 1907.

Gérard, Mireille. "Molière dans la correspondance de Madame de Sévigné." *RHLF* 73 (1973): 608–25.

Girard, René. "Perilous Balance: A Comic Hypothesis." *Modern Language Notes* 87 (1972): 811–26.

Goldman, Lucien. *Le Dieu caché*. Paris: Gallimard, 1959.

———. *Sciences humaines et philosophie*. Paris: Gonthier, 1966.

Goldschmidt, Georges-Arthur. *Molière ou la liberté mise à nu*. Paris: Julliard, 1973.

Goode, William O. "The Comic Recognition Scenes in *L'Avare*." *Romance Notes* 14 (1972): 122–27.

———. "*Dom Juan* and Heaven's Spokesman." *FR* 45 (1972): 3–12.

Gossen, Emmett. "*Les Femmes savantes*: métaphore et mouvement dramatique." *FR* 45 (1972): 37–45.

Gossman, Lionel. *Men and Masks: A Study of Molière*. Baltimore: Johns Hopkins University Press, 1963.

Grimarest, J. L. de. *La Vie de Monsieur de Molière*. Ed. Georges Mongrédien. Paris: Brient, 1955.

Gross, Nathan. "Values in *Le Bourgeois gentilhomme*." *L'Esprit Créateur*, vol. 15, no. 1–2 (1975), pp. 105–18.

Guicharnaud, Jacques. *Molière, une aventure théâtrale*. Paris: Gallimard, 1963.

———, ed. *Molière: A Collection of Critical Essays*. Englewood Cliffs, N.J.: Prentice-Hall, 1964

Guitton, Edouard, "Molière juriste dans *Dom Juan.*" *RHLF* 72 (1972): 945–53.

Gutwirth, Marcel. "Le Comique du serviteur chez Molière." *Symposium* 4 (1950): 349–57.

———. "Dandin, ou les égarements de la pastorale." *Romance Notes*, vol. 15, suppl. 1 (1973), pp. 121–33.

———. *Molière ou l'invention comique.* Paris: Minard, 1966.

——— "Tartuffe and the Mysteries." *PMLA* 92 (1977): 33–40.

———. "The Unity of Molière's *L'Avare.*" *PMLA* 76 (1961): 359–66.

Herzel, Roger W. "The Décor of Molière's Stage: The Testimony of Brissart and Chauveau." *PMLA* 93 (1978): 934–37.

Hippeau, L. *Essai sur la morale de La Rochefoucauld.* Paris: Nizet, 1967.

Hope, Quentin. "Society in *Le Misanthrope.*" *FR* 32 (1959): 329–36.

Horville, Robert. "La Cohérence des dénouements de *Tartuffe*, de *Dom Juan*, et du *Misanthrope.*" *RHT* 26 (1974): 240–45.

Howarth, W. D. "Alceste, ou l'honnête homme imaginaire." *RHT* 26 (1974): 93–98.

———, and M. Thomas, eds. *Molière: Stage and Study; Essays in Honour of W. G. Moore.* Oxford: Oxford University Press, 1972.

Hubert, J. D. "From Corneille to Molière: The Metaphor of Value." In *French and English Drama of the Seventeenth Century.* Los Angeles: W. A. Clark Memorial Library, 1972.

———. *Molière and the Comedy of Intellect.* Berkeley: University of California Press, 1962.

———. "Theme and Structure in *L'Avare.*" *PMLA* 75 (1960): 31–36.

———. "Molière et les deux styles burlesques." *Cahiers de l'Association Internationale d'Etudes Françaises* 16 (1964): 235–48.

Hugo, Victor. *Les Contemplations.* Ed. L. Cellier. Paris: Garnier, 1969.

Ikor, Roger. *Molière double.* Paris: PUF, 1977.

Ilutowicz, Salomon. *Le Peuple dans le théâtre de Molière.* Toulouse: Lion et fils, 1932.

Jaffré, Jean. "Théâtre et idéologie: note sur la dramaturgie de Molière." *Littérature* 13 (1974): 58–75.

Jasinski, René. *Molière et Le Misanthrope.* Paris: A. Colin, 1951.

Jeannel, Charles. *La Morale de Molière.* Paris: E. Thorin, 1867.

Jeune, S. "Molière, le pédant et le pouvoir." *RHLF* 55 (1955): 145–54.

Jurgens, Madeleine, and Elizabeth Maxfield-Miller. *Cent ans de recherches sur Molière*. Paris: SEVPEN, 1963.

Knutson, Harold C. *Molière: An Archetypal Approach*. Toronto: University of Toronto Press, 1976.

―――. "Molière's *Raisonneur*: A Critical Assessment." *Oeuvre et critique*, vol. 1, no. 2 (1976): 129–31.

Krauss, J. *Le Dom Juan de Molière: une libération*. Paris: Nizet, 1970.

La Bruyère, Jean de. *Caractères*. Ed. Robert Garapon. Paris: Garnier, 1962.

La Croix, Paul, and Georges Monval, eds. *Collection moliéresque* and *Nouvelle collection moliéresque*. 37 vols. 1869–90; rpt. Geneva: Slatkine, 1969.

La Grange, Charles Varlet de. *Registre*. Ed. Burt and Grace Young. Paris: Droz, 1947.

Landolt, R. B. "Molière and Louis XIV." *History Today* 16 (1966): 756–64.

Larroumet, Gustave. *La Comédie de Molière: l'auteur et le milieu*. 4th ed. Paris: Hachette, 1893.

Laverdet, Auguste, ed. *Correspondence entre Boileau-Despréaux et Brossette*. Paris: Techener, 1858.

Lawrence, Francis. "*Dom Juan* and the Manifest God: Molière's Antitragic Hero." *PMLA* 93 (1978): 86–94.

―――. *Molière and the Comedy of Unreason*. New Orleans: Tulane Studies in Romance Languages and Literatures, 1968.

―――. "Our Alceste or Molière's?" *Revue des Langues Vivantes* 38 (1972): 477–87.

―――. "The Raisonneur in Molière." *L'Esprit Créateur*, vol. 6, no. 1 (1966), pp. 156–66.

―――. "*Tartuffe*: A Question of Honnête Behavior." *Romance Notes*, vol. 15, suppl. 1 (1973), pp. 135–44.

Lebègue, Raymond. "La Bipolarité des personnages de Molière." *RHT* 26 (1974): 53–57.

Leveaux, Alphonse. *L'Enseignement moral dans les comédies de Molière*. Compiègne: A. Mennecier, 1883.

Livet, Charles. *Lexique de la langue de Molière*. Paris: Imprimerie Nationale, 1895–97.

Machéry, P. *Pour une théorie de la production littéraire*. Paris: Maspero, 1967.

Magendie, Maurice. "Le véritable sens du *Misanthrope*." In *Mélanges de phi-*

lologie et d'histoire littéraire offerts à Edmond Huguet. Paris: Boivin, 1940. Pp. 281–86.

Magné, Bernard. "*L'Ecole des femmes* ou la conquête de la parole." *Revue des Sciences Humaines* 37 (1972): 125–43.

Marion, Jean. "Molière a-t-il songé à Colbert en composant le personnage de Jourdain?" *RHLF* 45 (1938): 145–80.

Marivaux, Pierre Carlet de. *Théâtre complet*. Ed. F. Deloffre. Paris: Garnier, 1968.

Marmontel, Jean-François. "Comédie." In *Encyclopédie ou dictionnaire raisonné des sciences, des arts, et des métiers*. Geneva: Pellet, 1778. 8:560–67.

Maxfield-Miller, Elizabeth. "La Famille de la mère de Molière." *XS*, no. 40 (1958), pp. 258–69.

––––––. "The Real Monsieur Jourdain of the *Bourgeois gentilhomme*," *Studies in Philology* 56 (1959): 62–73.

Mélanges de philologie et d'histoire littéraire offerts à Edmond Huguet. Paris: Boivin, 1940.

Méré, Antoine Gombaud, chevalier de. *Oeuvres complètes*. Ed. C. Boudhors. Paris: Roches, 1930.

Michaut, Gustave. *La Jeunesse de Molière, Les Débuts de Molière à Paris*, and *Les Luttes de Molière*. Paris: Hachette, 1922–25.

––––––. "Louison, du Malade imaginaire." In *Mélanges de philologie d'histoire littéraire offerts à Edmond Huguet*. Paris: Boivin, 1940. Pp. 304–7.

Molière, Jean-Baptiste Poquelin, dit. *L'Avare*. Ed. Léon Lejealle. Paris: Larousse, 1963.

––––––. *L'Ecole des femmes*. Paris: Guignard, 1663.

––––––. *Les Femmes savantes*. Ed. Jean Cazalbou and Denise Sevely. Paris: Editions Sociales, 1971.

––––––. *Les Femmes savantes*. Ed. H. Gaston Hall. Oxford: Oxford University Press, 1974.

––––––. *Le Misanthrope*. Ed. Lop and Sauvage. Paris: Editions Sociales, 1963.

––––––. *Oeuvres*. Ed. Charles Varlet de La Grange and Vivot. 8 vols. Paris: Thierry, Barbin, and Trabouillet, 1682.

––––––. *Oeuvres complètes*. Ed. E. Despois and P. Mesnard. 13 vols. Paris: Hachette, 1873–1900.

————. *Oeuvres complètes.* Ed. G. Couton. 2 vols. Paris: Gallimard, 1971.

Molière le critique et Mercure aux prises avec les philosophes. Holland: n.p., 1709.

Mongrédien, Georges, ed. *Recueil de textes et de documents du XVIIᵉ siècle relatifs à Molière.* 2 vols. Paris: CNRS, 1965.

————. *La Vie privée de Molière.* Paris: Hachette, 1950.

Moore, W. G. "*Dom Juan* Reconsidered." *Modern Language Review* 52 (1957): 510–17.

————. *Molière: A New Criticism.* Oxford: Clarendon, 1949.

————. "*Tartuffe* and the Comic Principle in Molière." *Modern Language Review* 43 (1948): 47–53.

Morel, Jacques. "A propos de la scène du pauvre dans *Dom Juan.*" *RHLF* 72 (1972): 939–44.

————. "Le Comique de Molière a-t-il un sens?" *RHT* 26 (1974): 111–17.

————. "Molière ou la dramaturgie de l'honnêteté." *Information Littéraire* 15 (1963): 185–91.

Mornet, Daniel. *Molière.* Paris: Boivin, 1943.

————. "Un prototype de Tartuffe." In *Mélanges de philologie et d'histoire littéraire offerts à Edmond Huguet.* Paris: Boivin, 1940. Pp. 308–12.

Musset, Alfred de. *Poésies complètes.* Ed. M. Allem. Paris: Gallimard, 1957.

Nelson, Robert J. "*L'Impromptu de Versailles* Reconsidered." *French Studies* 11 (1957): 305–14.

Nicolich, Robert N. "Classicism and Baroque in *Le Bourgeois gentilhomme.*" *FR* vol. 45, no. 4 (1972), pp. 21–30.

Peacock, W. A. "The Comic Ending of *George Dandin.*" *French Studies* 36 (1982): 144–53.

Pellisson, Maurice. *Les Comédies-ballets de Molière.* Paris: Hachette, 1914.

Pelous, Jean-Michel. "Les Métamorphoses de Sganarelle: la permanence d'un type comique." *RHLF* 72 (1972): 821–49.

Périvier, J. H. "Equivoques moliéresques: le sonnet de Trissotin." *Revue des Sciences Humaines* 38 (1974): 543–54.

Perrault, Charles. *Les Hommes illustres qui ont paru en France pendant ce siècle.* Paris: A. Dezallier, 1696.

Perry, Anne Amari. "*George Dandin*: Document social." *Chimères*, vol. 11, no. 2 (1978), pp. 41–52.

Picard, Raymond. "Molière comique ou tragique? Le cas d'Arnolphe." *RHLF* 72 (1972): 769–85.

_____. "*Tartuffe*, production impie?" In *Mélanges d'histoire littéraire (XVIᵉ-XVIIᵉ siècles) offerts à Raymond Lebègue*. Paris: Nizet, 1969. Pp. 227–40.

Pineau, Joseph. "Dom Juan 'mauvais élève.' " *Revue des Sciences Humaines* 37 (1973): 565–87.

Plantié, Jacqueline. "Molière et François de Sales." *RHLF* 72 (1972): 902–27.

Poisson, Raymond. *Les Faux Moscovites*. Paris: Quinet, 1669.

Portal, G. "Arnolphe Hitler." *Ecrits de Paris*, no. 327 (1973), pp. 124–27.

_____. "Le temps des profanateurs." *Ecrits de Paris*, no. 322 (1973), pp. 123–26.

Pruner, M. "La Notion de dette dans le *Dom Juan* de Molière." *RHT* 26 (1974): 254–71.

Purkis, Helen. "Les Intermèdes musicaux de *George Dandin*." *Baroque* 5 (1972): 63–69.

Riccoboni, Luigi. *De la réformation du théâtre*. 1767; rpt. Geneva: Slatkine, 1971.

_____. *Observations sur la comédie et sur le génie de Molière*. Paris: Pissot, 1736.

Rochemont, Barbier d'Aucour, sieur de. *Observations sur une comédie de Molière intitulé Le Festin de Pierre*. In *OC* Couton, 2:1199–1208.

Roe, F. C. "Les Types sociaux dans la comédie de Molière: le valet et la servante." *French Quarterly* 7 (1928): 170–78.

Römer, Paul. *Molières Amphitryon und sein gesellschaftlicher Hintergrund*. Bonn: Romanisches Seminar des Universität, 1967.

Romero, Laurence. *Molière: Traditions in Criticism, 1900–1970*. Chapel Hill: University of North Carolina Press, 1974.

Roullé, P. *Le Roi glorieux de ce monde*. In *OC* Couton, 1:1143 ff.

Rousseau, Jean-Jacques. *Lettre à M. D'Alembert sur les spectacles*. Ed. M. Fuchs. Geneva: Droz, 1948.

Sainte-Beuve, Charles-Augustin. "Molière." In *Les Grands Ecrivains français*. Ed. M. Allem. Paris: Garnier, 1927. 4:122–91.

Sauvage, Micheline. *Le Cas Don Juan*. Paris: Seuil, 1953.

Scherer, J. *La Dramaturgie classique en France*. Paris: Nizet, 1950.

———. *Structures de Tartuffe*. Paris: SEDES, 1966.

———. *Sur le Dom Juan de Molière*. Paris: SEDES, 1967.

Sénart, Philippe. Review of *Le Bourgeois gentilhomme* at the Comédie-Française. *Nouvelle Revue des Deux Mondes*, Jan.–Mar. 1973, pp. 431–33.

———. Review of *L'Ecole des femmes* at the Comédie-Française. *Nouvelle Revue des Deux Mondes*, Oct.–Dec. 1973, pp. 174–78.

———. Review of *Tartuffe* at the Théâtre de la Porte Saint-Martin. *Nouvelle Revue des Deux Mondes*, Jul.–Sept. 1974, pp. 690–93.

———. Review of *Tartuffe* at the Comédie-Française. *Nouvelle Revue des Deux Mondes*, Apr.–June 1980, pp. 440–45.

Shaw, David. "Egoism and Society: A Secular Interpretation of Molière's *Dom Juan*." *Modern Languages* 59 (1978): 121–30.

Simon, Alfred. *Molière par lui-même*. Paris: Seuil, 1957.

Sorel, Charles. *Histoire Comique de Francion*. In *Romanciers du XVIIᵉ siècle*. Ed. A. Adam. Paris: Gallimard, 1958.

———. "Les Lois de la galanterie." In *La Société française au XVIIᵉ siècle*. Ed. T. Crane. New York: Putnam, 1907.

Soulié, Eudore. *Recherches sur Molière et sur sa famille*. Paris: Hachette, 1863.

Stackelberg, J. Von. "Molière und die Gesellschaftsordnung seiner Zeit." *Germanisch-Romanische Monatsschrift* 56 (1975): 257–75.

Stoker, J. T. "Toinette's Age and Temperament." *Modern Languages* 37 (1955–56): 102–3.

Sweetser, Marie-Odile. "Structure et signification du *Misanthrope*." *FR* 49 (1976): 505–13.

Talamon, René. "La Marquise du *Bourgeois gentilhomme*." *Modern Language Notes* 50 (1935): 369–75.

Teyssier, J.-M. *Réflexions sur le Dom Juan de Molière*. Paris: Nizet, 1970.

Thomas, Keith. "The Idea of Laughter in Tudor and Stuart England." *Times Literary Supplement*, 21 January 1977, pp. 77–81.

Tzoneff, Stoyan. *L'Homme d'argent dans le théâtre français jusqu'à la Révolution*. Gap: Louis Jean, 1934.

Ubersfeld, Annie. "*Dom Juan* et le noble vieillard." *Europe*, no. 441–42 (Jan.–Feb. 1966), pp. 59–67.

Van Eerde, J. "The Historicity of the Valet Role in French Comedy during the Reign of Louis XIV." *Romanic Review* 48 (1957): 185–96.

Vedel, Valdemar. *Deux Classiques français vus par un critique étranger.* Paris: Champion, 1935.

Veuillot, Louis. *Molière et Bourdaloue.* Paris: Palme, 1877.

Voltaire. *Oeuvres complètes.* Ed. Beuchot. Paris: Garnier, 1878–80. Vols. 14, 21, 23, 33.

Walker, Hallam. "Action and Ending in *L'Avare.*" *FR* 34 (1960–61): 531–36.

———. "Strength and Style in *Le Bourgeois gentilhomme.*" *FR* 37 (1963–64): 282–87.

Waterson, Karolyn. *Molière et l'autorité.* Lexington, Ky.: French Forum, 1976.

Weinberg, Bernard. "Plot and Thesis in *L'Ecole des femmes.*" *Romance Notes*, vol. 15, suppl. 1 (1973–74), pp. 78–97.

Weinstein, Leo. *The Metamorphoses of Don Juan.* Palo Alto: Stanford University Press, 1959.

Wells, D. J. "The Structure of Laughter in Molière's *L'Avare.*" *South Central Bulletin* 32 (1972): 242–45.

Wood, Richard E. "The *Lingua Franca* in Molière's *Le Bourgeois gentilhomme.*" *University of South Florida Language Quarterly* 10 (1971): 2–6.

Yarrow, P. J. "A Reconsideration of Molière." *French Studies* 13 (1959): 314–31.

Zwillenberg, Myrna. "Arnolphe, Fate's Fool." *Modern Language Notes* 68 (1973): 202–8.

———. "Dramatic Justice in *Tartuffe.*" *Modern Language Notes* 90 (1975): 583–90.

PART TWO: HISTORICAL, SOCIOLOGICAL, AND IDEOLOGICAL WORKS

Albanese, Ralph, Jr. *Initiation aux problèmes socioculturels de la France au XVIIᵉ siècle.* Montpellier: Etudes Sociocritiques, 1977.

Althusser, Louis. *For Marx.* Trans. B. Brewster. London: Allen Lane, 1969.

———. *Lenin and Philosophy and Other Essays.* Trans. B. Brewster. London: New Left Books, 1971.

Ariès, Philippe. *L'Enfant et la vie familiale sous l'Ancien Régime.* Paris: Plon, 1960.

Argou, Gabriel. *Institution au droit français.* 2 vols. Paris: P. Aubouyn, P. Emery, and C. Clouzier, 1692.

Audiger. *La Maison réglée et l'art de diriger la maison.* Paris: N. Le Gras, 1692.

Bacon, Francis. *The Advancement of Learning and New Atlantis.* Ed. T. Case. London: Oxford University Press, 1906.

Bacquet, Jean. *Traicté . . . concernant les francs-fiefs.* Paris: S. Nivelle, 1582.

Baehrel, René. *Une Croissance: la Basse Provence rurale (fin du XVIe siècle-1789).* Paris: SEVPEN, 1961.

Baillard. *Discours du tabac.* Paris: M. Le Prest, 1668.

Barber, W. H. *Leibniz in France from Arnauld to Voltaire.* Oxford: Clarendon, 1955.

Barchilon, Jacques. "Charles Perrault à travers les documents . . . l'inventaire de ses meubles en 1672." *XS,* no. 65 (1964), pp. 3–13.

Barsis, Max. *The Common Man through the Centuries.* New York: Ungar, 1973.

Bercé, Yves-Marie. *Croquants et Nu-pieds: les soulèvements paysans en France.* Paris: Gallimard, 1974.

Bernard, L. L. "Molière and the Historian of French Society." *Review of Politics* 7 (1955): 530–44.

Billacois, François. "Le Parlement de Paris et les duels au XVIIe siècle." In *Crimes et criminalité en France sous l'Ancien Régime.* Paris: A. Colin, 1971. Pp. 33–48.

Bitton, Davis. *The French Nobility in Crisis 1560–1640.* Palo Alto: Stanford University Press, 1969.

Blanchet, A., and A. Dieudonné. *Manuel de numismatique française.* Paris: A. Picard, 1912. Vol. 2.

Bloch, Marc. *Les Rois thaumaturges.* Paris: Plon, 1961.

Bluche, François. *Les Magistrats au Parlement de Paris au XVIIIe siècle (1715–1771).* Paris: Belles Lettres, 1960.

———. *Les Magistrats de la Cour des Monnaires de Paris au XVIIIe siècle (1715–1790).* Paris: Belles Lettres, 1966.

———. *Les Magistrats du Grand Conseil au XVIIIe siècle (1690–1791).* Paris: Belles Lettres, 1966.

———. "L'Origine sociale des Secrétaires d'Etat de Louis XIV." *XS* no. 42–43 (1959), pp. 8–22.

————. *La Vie quotidienne de la noblesse française au XVIIIᵉ siècle*. Paris: Hachette, 1973.

Blum, André. *Histoire du costume: les modes aux XVIIᵉ et XVIIIᵉ siècles*. Paris: Hachette, 1928.

Braudel, Fernand. *Civilisation materielle et capitalisme, XVᵉ–XVIIIᵉ siècles*. Paris: A. Colin, 1976.

Briggs, Robin. *Early Modern France 1560–1715*. Oxford: Oxford University Press, 1977.

Campion, H. de *Mémoires*. Ed. M. C. Moreau. New ed. Paris: P. Jannet, 1857.

Cariou, Marie. *L'Atomisme: Gassendi, Leibniz, Bergson, et Lucrèce*. Paris: Aubier-Montaigne, 1978.

Carr, J. L. *Life in France under Louis XIV*. New York: Putnam, 1970.

Carrière, Charles. *Négociants marseillais au XVIIIᵉ siècle*. 2 vols. Marseille: Institut Historique de Provence, 1973.

Cassé, Charles. "Limoges et Quimper, terres d'éxil au XVIIᵉ siècle." *XS* no. 61 (1963), pp. 54–58.

Chagniot, Jean. "Mobilité sociale et armée (vers 1660–vers 1760)." *XS*, no. 122 (1979), pp. 37–49.

Chappuzeau, Charles. *Le Devoir général de l'homme en toutes conditions*. Paris: n.p., 1617.

Cheruel, P. A. *Dictionnaire historique des institutions, des moeurs, et des coutumes de la France*. 2 vols. 4th ed. Paris: Hachette, 1874.

Colle, Doriece. *Collars, Stocks, Cravats: 1655–1900*. Emmaus, Pa.: Rodale Press, 1972.

Constant, J.-M. "La Mobilité sociale dans une province de gentilshommes et de paysans: la Beauce." *XS*, no. 122 (1979), pp. 7–20.

Corvisier, André. "Les Généraux de Louis XIV et leur origine sociale." *XS*, no. 42–43 (1959), pp. 23–39.

Couturier, Marcel. *Recherches sur les structures sociales de Châteaudun 1525–1789*. Paris: SEVPEN, 1969.

Damase, Jacques. *Carriages*. Trans. W. Mitchell. New York: Putnam, 1968.

Degarne, M. "Etudes sur les soulèvements provinciaux en France avant la Fronde: la révolte du Rouerge." *XS*, no. 56 (1962), pp. 3–18.

Dessert, Daniel. "Le 'laquais-financier' au Grand Siècle: mythe ou réalité?" *XS*, no. 122 (1979), pp. 21–35.

De Vries, Jan. *The Economy of Europe in an Age of Crisis 1600–1750.* Cambridge: Cambridge University Press, 1976.

Deyon, Pierre. *Amiens capitale provinciale.* Paris: Mouton, 1967.

Domat, Jean. *Les Lois civiles dans leur ordre naturel.* Rev. ed. Paris: Compagnie des Libraires, 1767.

Drouot, Henri. *Mayenne et la Bourgogne: étude sur la Ligue (1587–1596).* Paris: A. Picard, 1937. Vol. 1.

Estienne, H., trans. *La Noblesse civile et chrestienne.* Paris: Quinet, 1645.

Flandrin, J. L. "La Cellule familiale et l'oeuvre de procréation dans l'ancienne société." *XS,* no. 102–3 (1974), pp. 3–14.

Flourens, P. *Histoire des travaux et des idées de Buffon.* 2d ed. 1850; rpt. Geneva: Slatkine, 1971.

Foisil, M. "Les Biens d'un receveur-général des finances à Paris." *XS,* no. 33 (1956), pp. 682–87.

Ford, Franklin. *Robe and Sword: The Regrouping of the French Aristocracy after Louis XIV.* Cambridge, Mass.: Harvard University Press, 1962.

Fracard, M. L. *Philippe de Montaut-Bénac, duc de Noailles et Maréchal de France (1619–1684).* Paris: Niort, 1920.

Frondeville, Odette and Henri. *Conseillers au parlement de Normandie de 1641 à 1715.* vol 4. Rouen: Lestrigent, 1970.

Gaillard, Françoise. "Au nom de la loi: Lacan, Althusser, et l'idéologie." In *Sociocritique.* Ed. Claude Duchet. Paris: Nathan, 1979. Pp. 11–24.

Gaudemet, J. "Législation canonique et attitudes séculières à l'égard du lien matrimonial au XVIIᵉ siècle." *XS,* no. 102–3 (1974), pp. 15–30.

Godard de Donville, Louise. *Signification de la mode sous Louis XIII.* Aix-en-Provence: Edisud, 1978.

Godefroy, Denis. *Abbrégé des trois états du clergé, de la noblesse, et du tiers état.* Paris: S. Cramoisy, 1682.

Goubert, Pierre. *L'Ancien Régime.* 2 vols. Paris: A. Colin, 1969.

———. *Beauvais et le Beauvaisis de 1600 à 1730.* 2 vols. Paris: SEVPEN, 1960. (Published as a single voulme in 1968 by Flammarion under the title *Cent mille provinciaux au XVIIᵉ siècle.*)

———. *Louis XIV et vingt millions de Français.* Paris: Fayard, 1966.

———. "Les Officiers royaux des présidiaux, baillages, et élections dans la société française au XVIIᵉ siècle." *XS,* no. 42–43 (1959), pp. 54–75.

_____. "Types de marchands amiénois au début du XVIIe siècle." *XS*, no. 33 (1956), pp. 648–70.

Gouesse, J. M. "La Formation du couple en Basse-Normandie." *XS*, no. 102–3 (1974), pp. 45–58.

Graham, L. G. "Ideology and the Sociological Understanding." In *Forms of Ideology*. Ed. D. J. Manning. London: George Allen and Unwin, 1980. Pp. 12–21.

Gueneau, L. *Les Conditions de la vie à Nevers (denrées, logements, salaires) à la fin de l'Ancien Régime*. Paris: Hachette, 1919.

Hamscher, Albert. *The Parlement of Paris after the Fronde 1653–1673*. Pittsburgh: Pittsburgh University Press, 1976.

Hauser, H. *Les Débuts de l'âge moderne*. 3d ed. Paris: PUF, 1946.

Heers, J. *Le Clan familial au Moyen Age*. Paris: PUF, 1974.

Hoffmann, H. *Les Monnaies royales en France depuis Hugues Capet jusqu'à Louis XVI*. Paris: Hoffmann, 1878.

Hunt, David. *Parents and Children in History*. 2d ed. New York: Harper Torchbooks, 1972.

Huppert, George. *Les Bourgeois gentilshommes*. Chicago: University of Chicago Press, 1977.

Imbert, Jean. *Histoire économique (des origines à 1789)*. Paris: PUF, 1965.

Jacquart, Jean. *La Crise rurale en l'Ile-de-France 1550–1670*. Paris: A. Colin, 1974.

Jankélévitch, Vladimir. *La Mauvaise Conscience*. Paris: Aubier-Montaigne, 1966.

Jougla de Morenas, H. *Noblesse 38*. Paris: Editions du Grand Armorial de France, 1938.

Labatut, Jean-Pierre. "Aspects de la fortune de Bullion." *XS*, no. 60 (1963), pp. 11–39.

_____. "Situation sociale du quartier du Marais pendant la Fronde parlementaire (1648–1649)." *XS*, no. 38 (1958), pp. 55–81.

La Mothe Le Vayer, François. *Oeuvres*. 2 vols. 3d Ed. Paris: Courbé, 1662.

Lapeyre, H. *Une famille de marchands: les Ruiz*. Paris: A. Colin, 1955.

La Roque, Louis de. *Armorial de la noblesse de Languedoc*. 1860; rpt. Marseille: Laffitte, 1972.

La Roque de la Lontière, G.-A. de. *Traité de noblesse*. Paris: E. Michallet, 1678.

Larrain, Jorge. *The Concept of Ideology*. Athens: University of Georgia Press, 1980.

Lavisse, E. *Histoire de France*. Vol 7. Paris: Hachette, 1911.

Lebigre, Arlette. *Les Grands Jours d'Auvergne: désordres et répression au XVIIe siècle*. Paris: Hachette, 1976.

Lebrun, François. *Histoire d'Angers*. Paris: Privat, 1975.

———. *Les Hommes et la mort en Anjou aux XVIIe et XVIIIe siècles*. Paris: Mouton, 1971.

———. *La Vie conjugale sous l'Ancien Régime*. Paris: A. Colin, 1975.

Lefebvre, Henri. *Sociologie de Marx*. Paris: PUF, 1966.

Leibniz, Wilhelm Gottfried von. *Lettres de Leibniz à Arnauld*. Ed. Geneviève Lewis. Paris: PUF, 1952.

———. *The Monadology of Leibniz*. Ed. H. W. Carr. Los Angeles: University of Southern California School of Philosophy, 1930.

Le Noble, Eustache. *L'Ecole du monde*. Paris: Jouvenel, 1695.

Lister, Martin D. *A Voyage to Paris in the Year 1698*. 2d ed. London: J. Tonson, 1699.

Lottin, A. "Vie et mort du couple — difficultés conjugales et divorce dans le Nord de la France aux XVIIe et XVIIIe siècles." *XS*, no. 102–3 (1974), pp. 59–78.

Lough, John. *Paris Theatre Audiences in the Seventeenth and Eighteenth Centuries*. London: Oxford University Press, 1957.

Lovejoy, Arthur O. *The Great Chain of Being*. Cambridge, Mass.: Harvard University Press, 1936.

Loyseau, Charles. *Traité des ordres et simples dignités*. Paris: A. L'Angelin, 1610.

Loysel, Antoine. *Institutes coutumières*. Ed. M. Dupin and E. Laboulaye. New ed. Paris: Durand and Videcoq, 1846.

Lublinskaya, A. D. *French Absolutism: The Crucial Period, 1620–1629*. Trans. B. Pierce. Cambridge: Cambridge University Press, 1968.

Mandrou, Robert. *Classes et luttes de classes en France au début du XVIIe siècle*. Florence: G. D'Anna, 1963.

———. *L'Europe absolutiste*. Paris: Fayard, 1977.

————. *Introduction à la France moderne, 1500–1640*. Paris: A. Michel, 1961.

————. *Louis XIV en son temps 1661–1715*. Paris: PUF, 1973.

Méthivier, Hubert. *L'Ancien Régime*. Paris: PUF, 1961.

Meuvret, Jean. *Etudes d'histoire économique*. Paris: Armand Colin, 1971.

Meyer, Jean. *Histoire de Rennes*. Paris: Privat, 1972.

————. *La Noblesse bretonne au XVIIIe siècle*. Paris: SEVPEN, 1966.

Michelet, Jules. *Louis XIV et la révocation de l'édit de Nantes*. 3d ed. Paris: Chamerot, 1863.

Mireaux, Emile. *Une province française au temps du Grand Roi: la Brie*. Paris: Hachette, 1958.

Mongrédien, Georges. *La Vie quotidienne sous Louis XIV*. Paris: Hachette, 1948.

Moote, A. L. *The Revolt of the Judges*. Princeton, N.J.: Princeton University Press, 1971.

Mousnier, Roland. *Etat et société en France aux XVIIe et XVIIIe siècles: I—le gouvernement du pays*. Paris: Centre de Documentation Universitaire, 1969.

————. *Fureurs paysannes: les paysans dans les révoltes du XVIIe siècle (France, Russie, Chine)*. Paris: Calmann-Lévy, 1967.

————. *Les Hiérarchies sociales de 1450 à nos jours*. Paris: PUF, 1969.

————. *Les Institutions de la France sous la monarchie absolue*. Vol. 1. Paris: PUF, 1974.

————. *Paris au XVIIe siècle*. Paris: Centre de Documentation Universitaire, n.d.

————. "Quelques aspects de la fonction publique dans la société française au XVIIe siècle." *XS*, no. 42–43 (1959), pp. 3–7.

————. "Recherches sur les soulèvements populaires avant la Fronde." *Revue d'Histoire Moderne et Contemporaine* 5 (1958): 81–113.

————. "Recherches sur les syndicats d'officiers pendant la Fronde: trésoriers généraux de France et élus dans la révolution." *XS*, no. 42–43 (1959), pp. 76–117.

————. *La Stratification sociale à Paris aux XVIIe et XVIIIe siècles: l'échantillon de 1634, 1635, 1636*. Paris: A. Pedone, 1975.

————. *La Vénalité des offices sous Henri IV et Louis XIII*. Rouen: Maugard, 1946.

Piton, Camille. *Le Costume civil en France du XIIIe au XIXe siècle*. Paris: Flammarion, 1926.

Poisson, J. P. "Introduction à l'étude du rôle socio-économique du notariat à la fin du XVIIᵉ siècle." *XS*, no. 100 (1973), pp. 3–18.

Porchnev, Boris. *Les Soulèvements populaires en France de 1623 à 1648*. New ed. Paris: SEVPEN, 1963.

Quicherat, J. *Histoire du costume en France*. Paris: Hachette, 1877.

Roncière, C. G. M. de la. *Histoire de la marine française*. Paris: Plon, 1910.

Rostand, Jean. *Esquisse d'une histoire de la biologie*. Paris: Gallimard, 1945.

Rothkrug, Lionel. *Opposition to Louis XIV*. Princeton, N.J.: Princeton University Press, 1965.

Roupnel, Gaston. *La Ville et la campagne au XVIIᵉ siècle*. Paris: E. Leroux, 1922.

Roy, Hippolyte. *La Vie, la mode, et le costume au XVIIᵉ siècle*. Paris: Champion, 1924.

Saint-Jacob, Pierre de. *Documents relatifs à la communauté villageoise en Bourgogne*. Paris: Belles Lettres, 1962.

Savary, Jacques. *Le Parfait Négociant*. Paris: Guignard, 1675.

Sedillot, René, and Franz Pick. *All the Monies of the World*. New York: Pick, 1971.

See, Henri. "Molière, peintre des conditions sociales." *Revue d'Histoire Économique et Sociale* 17 (1929): 205–12.

Serres, Michel. *Le Système de Leibniz et ses modèles mathématiques*. 2 vols. Paris: PUF, 1966–68.

Shennan, J. H. *Government and Society in France, 1461–1661*. London: George Allen and Unwin, 1972.

Spufford, Margaret. "Peasant Inheritance Customs and Land Distribution in Cambridgeshire from the Sixteenth to the Eighteenth Centuries." In *Family and Inheritance: Rural Society in Western Europe, 1200–1800*. Ed. Jack Goody et al. Cambridge: Cambridge University Press, 1976. Pp. 156–76.

Stockar, Jurg. *Kultur und Kleidung der Barockzeit*. Stuttgart: Warner Klassen, 1964.

Tapié, V.-L. "Les Officiers seigneuriaux dans la société provinciale du XVIIᵉ siècle." *XS*, no. 42–43 (1959), pp. 118–40.

Tarr, Laszlo. *The History of the Carriage*. Trans. E. Hoch. New York: Arco, 1969.

Tirat, Jean-Yves. "Les Voituriers par eau parisiens au milieu du XVIIᵉ siècle." *XS*, no. 57 (1962), pp. 43–65.

Toudouze, G. G. *Le Costume français*. Paris: Larousse, 1945.

Venard, Marc. *Bourgeois et paysans au XVIIᵉ siècle*. Paris: SEVPEN, 1957.

Voisin de la Noiraye, J.-B. *Mémoire sur la généralité de Rouen* (*1665*). Ed. E. Esmonin. Paris: Hachette, 1913.

Wilhelm, Jacques. *La Vie quotidienne des Parisiens au temps du Roi-Soleil 1660–1715*. Paris: Hachette, 1973.

Wolf, John B. *Louis XIV*. New York: Norton, 1968.

Wood, James B. "Endogamy and *Mésalliance*, the Marriage Patterns of the Nobility in the *Election* of Bayeux, 1430–1669." *French Historical Studies* 10 (1978): 375–92.

———. *The Nobility of the Election of Bayeux, 1463–1666: Continuity through Change*. Princeton, N.J.: Princeton University Press, 1980.

Zeller, Gaston. "Une Notion de caractère socio-historique: la dérogeance." *Cahiers internationaux de sociologie* 22 (1957): 40–74.

INDEX